Do you love magic that gathers within weathered stone walls? Are you fascinated by old houses where the weight of history presses down like a physical touch?

If so, you'll feel right at home at Draycott Abbey.

I'm frequently asked if my books have to be read in order. Definitely not! Each book is written to stand alone and all stories are self-contained. But many of you prefer to read a series in its order of writing, so this will guide you through the current Draycott collection.

The tale begins with the first novella, *Enchantment,* finally available after over a decade. This novella begins the Draycott Abbey series with the story of Nicholas Draycott—and the abbey's brooding ghost, Adrian. The second novella in the series continues Adrian's haunting story in *What Dreams May Come.* So many of you have asked for this poignant story, and I hope you have enjoyed meeting Adrian and Gray. Two people were never more bound in love.

Next come seven Draycott books, which may not all be in print when you read this. If you can't find a certain volume, drop me an e-mail. I'll steer you to the wonderful booksellers who stock signed copies of the Draycott books, new and used.

This is the order of the Draycott Abbey books, following the two novellas above:

*Hour of the Rose*
*Bridge of Dreams*
*Bride of the Mist*
*Key to Forever*
*Season of Wishes*
*Christmas Knight*
*The Perfect Gift*

Enjoy! Be sure to visit www.draycottabbey.com for new abbey videos, interviews, travelogues and details of new stories in the making. If you'd like a signed bookplate to go with your book, please drop me a note at bookplates@christinaskye.com. I'm always delighted to hear from readers! (If you have a reading group, let me know that, too. I'll send you special materials for your group.)

I'm thrilled that a brand-new Draycott Abbey book will go on sale in September of 2008. Watch for *To Catch a Thief,* which brings back the mesmerizing Dakota Smith from my Code Name books. This tough hero will be working with the strongest, most enigmatic woman he's ever met. Dakota is about to discover that there are many ways to fall, and all of them are deadly. Get ready to break the rules with *To Catch a Thief.*

And in case you're wondering, the answer is yes. I'm already at work on my next Draycott Abbey book. There are endless secrets waiting to unfold in this place of haunting beauty. Adrian and Gideon would have it no other way.

Finally, I know that Izzy's on your mind! You've made it clear you want this charming hunk to have his own book. I'm working on it, believe me, but the man is one tough customer. When he falls, he'll fall hard.

For a special look into Izzy's shadowy past and his secret case files describing past and future books, log on to www.christinaskye.com/izzyfiles. If you're among the first fifty readers to log in to Izzy's secret files, you'll win a limited edition T-shirt with Izzy's signature, along with code name access to an audio story that will not be available in stores or for sale. After all, Izzy's a techno kind of guy!

Meanwhile, enjoy the abbey's moonlight and the fragrance of its heirloom roses. Above all, savor its promise of beauty and unending love.

Until your next visit…happy reading.

Christina

# CHRISTINA
# SKYE

## DRAYCOTT ETERNAL

WHAT
DREAMS
MAY
COME
&
SEASON OF
WISHES

HQN™

ISBN-13: 978-0-373-77294-0
ISBN-10: 0-373-77294-7

DRAYCOTT ETERNAL: WHAT DREAMS MAY COME & SEASON OF WISHES

Copyright © 2008 by Harlequin Books S.A.

The publisher acknowledges the copyright holder of the individual works as follows:

WHAT DREAMS MAY COME
Copyright © 1992 by Roberta Helmer
First published by Avon Books in 1992

SEASON OF WISHES
Copyright © 1997 by Roberta Helmer
First published by Avon Books in 1997

## Acknowledgments

My deepest gratitude to all of you who have welcomed Adrian and Gideon into your hearts.

For fifteen years you have joined me on a poignant journey, sharing the abbey's haunting magic.

I couldn't have had better traveling companions than you have been.

And Adrian assures me that the *best* is yet to come....

# WHAT DREAMS MAY COME

# PROLOGUE

*Sussex, England*
*June, 1991*

RAGGED CLOUDS FLEW before a three-quarter moon.

Saturn was trine Uranus. Mars was in Scorpio.

Damn and blast, the black-clad figure thought, staring down into the darkness. No auspicious alignment here.

Idly, he swept a fall of lace from the braided cuffs of his frock coat, watching racing clouds shadow the stark, weathered parapets beneath his feet. Before him Draycott Abbey's one-story gatehouse lay silent, dappled with silver in the moonlight.

A man and yet not quite a man, the tall figure stood in brooding silence, while moonbeams played over his black damask waistcoat and elegant lace cravat.

In this world he was, yet somehow not quite *of* it.

Around him drifted the scent of roses, rich and fine now in the full flush of summer. 'Petite Lisette,' 'Gloire des Mousseux,' and 'Fantin Latour'—their names were as rich as the heritage that had bred them. Ornate and densely clustered, their velvet petals opened to the night, scenting the warm, still air with beauty.

Far away in the distance, past the rolling downs, past the silver river, past the sleeping village of Highgate, a bell chimed in the dead of night.

Twelve times it rang, and then once more.

High atop the granite parapets, Adrian Draycott turned and stared out at the lush park, the glossy waters of the spring-fed moat.

At the shimmering mullioned windows of this ancient house that he had always loved, not wisely but too well.

His lips twisted in a ghost of a smile.

He sensed more than heard the low rustle of fur against granite. He turned, looked down, his smile growing to a boyish grin. "Ah, Gideon, have you come to keep me company this night? If so, I'll thank you for it, old friend, for there is something about this night…something troubling." He looked up, his eyes ranging over the dark, wooded fields. "Something that summons up long-forgotten hopes and dreams that are better left buried." Slowly his smile faded and his expression hardened.

A cat glided over the parapet, long and starkly gray, paws tipped in black. Great amber eyes glowed against the darkness, keen and intelligent.

*Too* intelligent for a cat.

Frowning, the figure in starkest black stared out toward the Channel, watching a finger of lightning arc over the wooded hills. "Yes, there is something else out there tonight. You feel it, too, don't you, my friend? A gathering. A heaviness of spirit. And every second I sense that danger moving closer."

Sleek muscles flashing, the cat jumped to the top of the parapet and padded along the weathered stone face.

His companion's lips quirked. "Brazen as always, I see. You really must curb this impulse to recklessness, old friend. It will beget you much trouble otherwise, I fear."

The cat's eyes shone as he settled back on gray haunches. His ears twitched and then he looked down, initiating a delicate toilette in brazen disregard for the granite edge only inches away.

Beside him Adrian Draycott sighed. "So you think it's over, do you?" He leaned out across the wall and into the wind, the white ruffles at his neck tossing sharply as he studied the dark patchwork of fields and forest below. His long fingers smoothed his damask waistcoat thoughtfully. "Because my brother is wed and the men who chased him are dead?"

For a moment Adrian Draycott stiffened, tasting the bitter dregs of sadness. He had saved his brother from a pair of cold-blooded adventurers in search of a treasure buried far away in the mud of Thailand, where Nicholas Draycott had spent nearly a year in captivity.

Adrian had saved Nicholas from them, and in the process he had saved one other, a woman with golden hair and sparkling eyes. A woman to whom he'd lost his heart.

Two hundred years before.

Ever since, there had been a great emptiness in his life, which he'd tried hard to fill with his duties as guardian of this beloved abbey. Two centuries had passed since he'd slipped away from his dying body, and over the years, Adrian had found himself missing that physical form less and less.

*1790.* Yes, it had been a fine year—for wine, for women and for dying. But he still remembered what it felt like to walk in soft spring grass, to breathe the summer air and feel all the things that a physical body entitled one to feel.

And, of course, there had been those seven short years of boyhood, when he had been Nicholas's twin. But an accident had ended that life tragically.

Yes, those years counted hardly at all, Adrian thought.

But Nicholas and Kacey deserved their happiness, and Adrian was determined that they have it. His job now was simply to watch, to guard, to intervene in what small ways he could to protect this ancient place and all who resided within it.

Which meant that he was left alone once more, with no company but Gideon and the cold stone walls. With nothing but dark memories and the sad cry of the wind sweeping up from the sea.

But this duty was by Adrian Draycott's choice. He'd have it no other way.

So he'd always thought, at least.

Until tonight.

Until he began to remember things he shouldn't have remembered.

Things like the haunting scent of lavender on a summer breeze, the velvet texture of a woman's cheek. The slow, slanting smile that spoke of pleasures soon to come…

At the foot of the moat a small night creature rocketed from the darkness, screeching in pain as it crashed away through the underbrush.

With a sigh, the man on the parapet shook his head, his raven eyes hardening. "Aye, there is danger abroad tonight, Gideon. *Great* danger. I can almost feel it growing, somewhere out there in the darkness." He closed his eyes. "Dear God, not another test…"

At the edge of the parapet the great cat meowed.

"Indeed, I hope not, my friend. Long have I guarded these beloved walls, these fertile fields, and it has always been my joy, as well as my duty. But now—now I'm tired. Dear God, Gideon, I'm so…tired…"

In a dark rush the sadness returned, crushing him with thoughts of all the things he'd never have again.

His fingers, washed with moonlight, tightened abruptly.

Slowly Adrian Draycott turned, lace fluttering at his braided cuffs. He began to pace the abbey's lonely battlements.

Just as he had done every night for the last two hundred years.

And for six hundred before that.

Atop the sheer granite wall the great gray feline sat motionless, his body a slash of shadow against the rising moon. His amber eyes glowed keen and phosphorescent as the moon rose higher, wreathing him in a nimbus of silver. Purring softly, the cat watched his friend and liege keep a lonely vigil with dark memories and lost dreams.

Meanwhile the night slept on below them.

And with every passing second, the malevolence that had no name crept closer.

# CHAPTER ONE

*London*

THE ROSES WERE GLORIOUS.

Heavy-petaled, crimson peach and palest blush-pink, they glowed through the florist's window. Even through the glass Gray Mackenzie could almost smell their lush perfume.

Around her the honking horns and squealing brakes of Oxford Street faded away to nothing. As if in a dream, she watched herself turn and push open the door to the neat little florist shop.

She would buy a dozen of them.

For herself. Just because she wanted to.

It was a gesture totally unlike her, of course. Lingering jet lag, perhaps?

Gray worried her lower lip. She'd arrived only last night after a hellish flight from Philadelphia, and this morning her pale cheeks showed the strain.

"Yes, miss. 'Ow can I 'elp you?" The proprietor was short, red-cheeked and impatient to get on with his work, though he was trying hard not to show it.

Gray pointed. "Those roses in the window. They're— magnificent. No, not the modern hybrids. There, to the right— the old ones. The centifolia roses with the densely packed petals. 'Lisette,' aren't they?" She delighted in the cluster of rich fuchsia blooms tucked in an elegant crystal vase.

There was something sad about her, the bald-headed proprietor thought. Not like the usual Yanks who came in here, flashing their plastic, talking fast and loud. Only hybrids would do for their sort.

But this one was different. Careful and slow in her speech, she was. And she was a rare and proper beauty, what with that auburn hair spilling over her shoulders and skin that seemed almost too translucent to be real.

And those eyes! Purest sea-blue, they were. They put him in mind of a tropical beach at dawn.

The florist frowned, wondering why such a beauty went about dressed in a dark skirt and a nondescript gray jacket. Then he sniffed. None of his business, after all.

But the flowers were.

He nodded, approving her choice. "Quite right, miss. 'Petite Lisette.' 'Normandica' over 'ere. I've a few 'Fantin Latour,' as well. You know something of roses?"

"Not a great deal. It's just…a hobby." Gray knew the blooms must be terribly expensive. "I think—yes, I'll take them. All of them."

The florist's estimation of her soared several notches. She had good taste, this red-maned Yank. But perhaps she didn't understand exactly what she was looking at. "That will be ten pounds each," he murmured discreetly, just in case she wanted to back out.

Gray's eyes flickered. The figure was extortionate!

She did a quick calculation, counting nearly two dozen cut stems. In one sweep she saw most of her cash going.

But those roses would be worth every penny. Every shilling, she corrected herself, savoring the rich-veined damask of the petals, drinking in their heady scent. "I'll take them all," she said decisively.

Yes, it was time she put the past where it belonged and treated herself to something special.

The florist gave her an approving smile. "Very good, miss. I'll just fetch some paper to tie them up." A moment later, he disappeared into a curtained alcove.

Behind Gray the front door opened with the tinkle of a bell. Chill air swirled through the little shop. Crimson petals dipped in the swift currents and Gray brushed a curl from her cheek.

Behind her came the creak of a floorboard, and then the rasp of a dry voice.

A familiar voice, even after five years.

A voice straight out of her nightmares.

"Lovely, aren't they?"

She spun about, her heart pounding. *Dear God, don't let it be him. Anyone but him!*

But the man in the shadows by the door was broad-shouldered, his skin bronzed from long hours in the sun. Bleached nearly white, his long hair feathered low over his eyes.

Brown eyes, not green.

Not like her ex-husband's at all.

Gray squinted into the shadows. Appearances could be changed, after all. *She* of all people knew that.

The low, dry voice continued. "Such a pity that they die so soon after they're cut." The man's brow rose when Gray did not answer. A smile drifted over his lips. "Sadly, that is often the way with things of beauty. They never last, you know."

Suddenly all the old panic arose. Gray felt her hands begin to quiver. The cold eyes narrowed, studying her, frankly curious now.

"Ex-excuse me. I—I must go." She spun about and stumbled to the door, fear tightening her throat.

Behind her the curtain swished open.

"'Ere, miss, come back! You've forgotten your roses!"

But Gray was too busy stumbling through the impersonal crowds of Oxford Street to hear.

"JUST OVER THE HILL, it is. Take the first roundabout and then watch for the second turning. That road will take you direct to Draycott Abbey, miss."

Gray smiled her thanks to the healthy, red-faced village boy and put her rented Mini into gear, trying to forget the curiosity that had gleamed in the boy's eyes as she had asked directions to the abbey.

*When are you going to stop being so jumpy?* she asked herself angrily. *It's been five years, after all. Why can't you just let it go?*

But Gray knew why.

Because her ex-husband was free again. Because all the high-tech equipment in the world hadn't kept him behind bars.

Away from her.

And now it was just a matter of time until he tracked her down, just as he'd sworn to do.

Her fingers clenched against the steering wheel as she fought down dark memories. Memories of what he'd threatened to do if she revealed any part of the dirty little arrangements he excelled at.

But Gray *had* revealed what she'd heard. Every detail, every damning fact she had spilled to a packed courtroom and an army of eager reporters.

And the last thing Matt had screamed before he was jostled out of the courtroom was that he'd find her somehow. And when he did, he'd make her pay.

Biting down a jerky breath, Gray sailed through the roundabout and eased the gearshift to low. She tried to tell herself she was making too much of the situation. Matt had escaped, yes, but the security officers in Washington had assured Gray it would be just a matter of days until he was back behind bars.

Meanwhile, they had told her, a visit to England— especially to this quiet little backwater of Sussex—would be an excellent idea.

As Gray drove, she went over the conversation, looking for details she might have missed then. But no, the officer— Harrington, wasn't it?—had been calm, professional and totally unalarming.

There was absolutely nothing to worry about, he'd promised her. Not with all the levels of protection and security that had surrounded her case.

Yes, she was to go off to Sussex and work. Leave the heavy stuff to them, he'd ordered briskly.

The man was a professional. Of course he was right, Gray told herself as forested estates rushed past in a blur of green. She had to forget all this brouhaha about her ex-husband and concentrate on her work.

Especially now, when she had the assignment of a lifetime before her.

At that moment, a second lane came into view. Above the trees Gray caught a quick glimpse of weathered towers and stark stone walls.

Her heart began to pound.

How well she remembered her friend Kacey's letters describing the great moat-encircled structure with its picturesque stone gatehouse and climbing roses. Blond-haired Kacey, the new bride of the Twelfth Viscount Draycott, had been an unshakable friend to Gray at a time when she had desperately needed one.

And Gray was determined to do her best work for Kacey now.

She shoved the gearshift into Second and sent gravel flying up, savoring the feel of the Mini as it hummed down the narrow drive.

As she passed beneath a line of overhanging oaks, the years seemed to slip away. Suddenly she was young again, with all things possible.

Without warning a speckled brown deer darted across the road. She slammed her foot onto the brake and wrenched the wheel violently, barely managing to avoid the animal.

Gray's breath hissed free. Her fingers gripped the wheel. Abruptly, she remembered another time she'd driven down a quiet country lane, remembered how much she'd been enjoying the feel of speed and control when a dog had shot out onto the road.

Matt had cursed and wrenched the wheel away from her.

That night, they'd had their first disagreement. Their first full-blown quarrel. Their first—

White-faced, Gray clutched the wheel, struggling with fear and raw despair. Down, down, she pushed them, back into the dark cubicle she reserved for her past. For anything to do with the other woman she'd been before her name had been changed, and her features altered.

Before she'd become Gray Mackenzie.

Put everything to do with Matt out of your mind, the counselors had ordered. You're Gray Mackenzie now. Forget that Moira Jamieson ever existed.

With a ragged breath, Gray sat back.

She ought to be happy, after all. She was making a name for herself at last. Her work was found in architecture quarterlies and trade publications on three continents. She was almost established enough to pick and choose her assignments.

She was a success, by anyone's standards.

But inside, Gray knew differently. Inside she was still shy, gawky Moira Jamieson, an uncertain little nobody from a back-water town in central Maine.

Matt had known that, too. In fact, he'd never let her forget it.

Out of the corner of her eye Gray saw a dark shape separate from the thick woods.

Her heart lurched as a tall figure emerged from the dark tree line. Gray stiffened, half-expecting to see her ex-husband's sullen face swim into view before her.

But it didn't, of course. Matt would never find her here, not on this quiet estate tucked away in the middle of the English countryside. With any luck he might even be back behind bars already.

Keeping that thought firmly in mind, Gray turned to study the man walking toward the car. The moment she did, she regretted it.

Heat poured into her cheeks; her breath caught in her throat.

He was nothing at all like her former husband. Hard, keen eyes the color of wintry seas stared back at her from a rough, weather-hardened face. His nose was high and his lips were full. Dark and thick, his hair brushed the top of his broad shoulders.

It was a face capable of much pride, Gray thought. A face capable of much stubbornness. It was also a face dark with secrets, secrets that would not be easily revealed to anyone.

And it was indeed the face of a stranger, just as she'd known it must be.

Yet somehow not quite a stranger?

Something nagged at the back of Gray's mind. Something Kacey had told her in one of her short letters before she'd left on her honeymoon with Nicholas Draycott?

Gray frowned as she saw the man scowl, then move directly

in front of the car. Of all the colossal arrogance! The insolent fellow was blocking the road!

Reluctantly, Gray coasted to a halt, making no attempt to conceal her irritation. Muttering under his breath, the man stalked straight toward her.

A moment later, his black-clad legs banged full against the front fender, almost as if he were unaware that the car existed. Cursing roundly, he stared down at his knee, then looked back up at Gray.

Drinking, no doubt. Just her luck to run into an English lush! But sweet heaven, the man was tall—well over six feet.

Unconsciously Gray studied the hard muscles rippling beneath his soft dark shirt and the long thighs that braced and tensed as he moved around to stare at her through the open window.

And Gray stared back, pointedly and quite rudely.

Her interest was strictly professional, of course. Merely the impersonal concern of an artist assessing a possible subject.

But that explanation didn't stop strange tendrils of heat from licking at her cheeks and uncoiling through her stomach. And that knowledge only made Gray angrier.

She gulped down a deep breath, fighting for calm. *Get a hold on yourself, Mackenzie. The man's a stranger, remember? Just a stranger.*

"Where are *you* going, woman?"

His voice was low and richly accented. For some reason the sound of it made Gray flush, made the fine little hairs at the back of her neck prickle and rise.

"Straight up this drive—if you'd just move out of the way, that is." *Maybe even if you don't,* Gray thought irritably.

"What business have you here?"

Her hands tensed against the steering wheel. "I might ask the same of you!"

Gray glared, but even then the man did not move back from the window. Clearing her throat, she tried a more direct attack. "Do you mind? I've just had a long ride from London and I was hoping to—" She halted abruptly. "This *is* Draycott Abbey, isn't it? Don't tell me I missed the second turn."

With every word the man's black mood seemed to deepen. "Yes, of course this is the abbey, woman! And these are Draycott lands. But how in the name of all that's holy did I—" He stopped, then plunged long fingers through his thick black hair.

Gray barely noticed his tension, too relieved by the assurance that she was finally near her destination. Soon she would be ensconced in one of the lovely old chintz- and flower-filled rooms Kacey had described. There she would be safe from Matt, safe from any and all distractions while she completed the work she'd come here for.

But the man outside the window continued to frown, showing no sign of being finished with his interrogation. "What sort of game are you playing at, woman?"

Gray felt her cheeks redden. *Game?* Was the fellow mad or just terminally rude?

"I've come on an assignment—for Lord Draycott, not that it's any of *your* business." Suddenly she stiffened. "You can't be—good heavens, you aren't Lord Draycott, are you? That is, I expected someone—"

Shorter? Younger? Less imposing?

She didn't finish, held captive by the intensity of his slate-dark gaze.

"*I?* Nicholas Draycott?" The man's dark brows rose as he laughed bitterly. "By God, that's rich! The woman thinks—"

Suddenly a rustling at his feet called his attention to the ground, where a sleek gray cat pressed against his black-booted ankles.

He seemed to catch back his words, his eyes narrowing.

Gray didn't mean to give him time for any more questions. "Well, if you're not Lord Draycott, then I'm wasting my time here. So if you don't mind—" she gestured at the gravel drive "—I really would like to reach the abbey before the light goes."

The man's frown grew to a decided scowl. "Mind? Who am *I* to mind? When am *I* ever consulted about anything?" Suddenly he bent closer, his eyes scouring her face. "Ah! You must be the artist. American, I believe."

Gray merely glared. "Are you going to move or not?"

The slate eyes glittered. "I believe not—Miss Mackenzie."

Suddenly Gray felt cold—very cold. So what if he knew her name? Why did any of this matter?

But it did. For some reason it mattered intensely. Perhaps it was something about the man's face, something sad and bitter in the way he laughed…

*Enough, Mackenzie. Get out while you still can.*

One last question leaped to her lips. "Who are you? What gives *you* the right to cross-examine me?"

Did she merely imagine that he stiffened? "I? I am…Adrian. The caretaker, as you would call it."

Gray frowned. Caretaker? He was like no caretaker *she'd* ever met before. A tiny network of lines radiated from the corner of his eyes, and she had a sudden urge to touch them, smooth them.

"Have I ever—I mean, have we ever—"

Ridiculous! Of course they hadn't met before.

But how else was she to explain the familiarity of that lean face, her instinctive knowledge of the pain that haunted those wintry eyes? The heat hidden in that stern mouth?

With a gasp, Gray recovered herself. "N-never mind. Of course we haven't."

Outside the car the man smiled slightly. Draping his arm

along the metal roof, he bent closer, his eyes darkening. "If you mean by that obscure bit of gibberish have we met before, the answer is no. But I do have the advantage over you, Miss Mackenzie. Kacey told me you were coming."

It was a lie, of course. The viscount's bride had said nothing to Adrian Draycott about Gray Mackenzie. But a ghost had ways of hearing nearly everything that happened within his domain, particularly when he was a resident ghost of the guardian variety.

In that sense Adrian supposed his answer about his identity had not been a lie. In his role of guardian he had chanced to overhear Kacey and Nicholas speak about Gray Mackenzie several times before their departure.

But no amount of discussion could have prepared Adrian for the pure beauty of the woman who sat before him now.

Nothing could have captured the glow of her alabaster skin, the fiery sheen of her wild auburn hair.

The wariness that darkened her azure eyes.

And those things made Adrian want to sweep her against him and drive the fear from her eyes. To kiss her and tease her and coax a laugh from her soft lips.

And then carry her down to the ferns beside the moat and slide deep inside her, filling her with his hard heat until she shuddered and arched in breathless abandon beneath him.

Adrian stiffened. What in the name of heaven was wrong with him? He was a *ghost.* He hadn't had such raw impulses for years!

Two hundred years, to be exact.

He scowled, trying to fight down the heat that rose insidiously toward the seat of his manhood. Abstracted, he ran his finger down the rim of the roof, leaving a long trail in the dust atop the car.

But how was it possible? This woman *saw* him. She *heard*

him. And somehow he was beside her in physical form, with fingers that moved and felt and left a visible mark against dusty metal.

He had managed to materialize once or twice before, of course, in times of dire need. He had even appeared to Kacey once, desperate to warn her of the danger that she and Nicholas faced unless they found a way to trust each other.

But never had those appearances been more than temporary, and never had they involved a tangible flesh-and-blood body such as he now possessed. Certainly Adrian had never before felt the intensely physical things he was feeling now.

Yet here he stood, the wind ruffling his long black hair, the sun warming his neck, the metal of this clamorous four-wheeled conveyance cool and smooth against his all-too-real fingers.

In physical flesh-and-blood form, by God! Accomplished without conscious thought or effort of any sort. Damn, but it was unnerving.

Was this another test? Or was it simply a new twist to his ancient duties at the abbey?

He smothered a curse, trying to understand, knowing already that he would not succeed.

Meanwhile the look in the eyes of the woman beside him told Adrian that to her he was only *too* real, and that the sight made her vastly uncomfortable.

Somehow *that* hurt Adrian Draycott most of all.

For at that moment, he felt a stunning need to sweep the fear from those wary azure eyes forever. To see those petal-soft lips curve up in joy and wonder.

Shocked by the force of these unfamiliar emotions, he could only stare down at her pale face, fighting to understand this sudden and intense need to protect her.

Beside him, Gray swallowed. What was happening to her?

The man was handsome, there was no mistaking that. But the sun would soon be setting and, if she dawdled any longer, she would miss the best time for viewing the abbey. "I—I'd really better go."

She tried to look away, but the storm-black eyes continued to hold her. Motionless, the black-clad stranger merely stared back at her.

And the look was pure heat, a beam of summer sun poured through leaden clouds straight into her heart.

Frowning, Gray swept unsteady fingers over her forehead, then clutched the wheel. "I—I'm going to go now. If you don't want to lose a toe or two, I'd suggest you move back."

She tried to make her voice cool, but all she felt was utterly foolish as she looked down and fumbled with her keys. What in heaven's name was *wrong* with her?

In that second, a hard hand reached out to catch her fingers, pulling them from their trembling hold on the steering wheel. His eyes were tense, unreadable. "Don't go."

Gray's heart beat wildly. "I b-beg you pardon?"

"To the abbey. *Don't go.*" His voice was harsh. "Go back to London instead. And then go back home, Gray Mackenzie. Back to wherever you come from in America."

Gray nearly flinched. "*Don't go?* Just like that? After I've come ten hours by plane and another five by car?" She felt her cheeks burning. "Not on your life, mister!"

A vein pounded at Adrian's forehead. "Wretched female! There is danger here, don't you see? And somehow *you* are involved, though I cannot yet say how. But I bloody well won't permit my abbey—"

"*Your* abbey?" Gray laughed in disbelief. "Funny, I could have sworn that Nicholas Draycott was the abbey's owner!"

The caretaker's fingers tightened on hers. His calloused thumb inched across her cold palm, leaving an odd trail of warmth against her skin. His eyes flashed dangerously. "Of course he is. But Nicholas left me here to…to keep an eye on things, shall we say? In his absence, of course."

Muttering angrily, Gray tried to tug her fingers free but failed. "You take your duties very seriously, don't you? But then, I'm clearly a dangerous sort, just bristling with evil designs upon the abbey's treasures."

"You might be more dangerous than you know, Miss Mackenzie." For long seconds the frowning caretaker stared down at their entwined fingers. Abruptly he released her. "Mark me well. If you go farther, know that you do so on *my* land." His slate eyes narrowed. "And it will be *me* to whom you'll answer then."

Gray glared back at him. "No, I have a much better idea! You stay out of *my* way! My work will keep me quite busy enough as it is. Believe me, the very last thing I need is an ill-mannered, supercilious junior gardener with delusions of grandeur and an advanced case of paranoia poking around while I'm trying to concentrate!"

Without waiting for an answer, Gray wrenched at the gearshift and sent the car plunging forward. Gravel hissed and spun beneath the flying wheels and a moment later, the forest bled away in a blur of green.

But with every second, Gray felt her neck prickle, felt her cheeks flush. Somehow she knew the unblinking slate-gray eyes were following her still.

And she couldn't help but wonder at her nagging certainty that she'd seen those strange, implacable eyes somewhere before.

HE WATCHED, MOTIONLESS as her car sped down the drive and disappeared over the hill.

Damn and blast, he hadn't meant to frighten her! In fact, he hadn't meant to say most of the things he had. He'd only meant to warn her of the danger he felt and then try to find out if she could explain its source.

He *certainly* hadn't meant to touch the woman.

But he hadn't been thinking straight at the time.

After all, he hadn't expected to be knocked speechless by the vision of a wary beauty with a mane of auburn hair and azure eyes. He hadn't expected to see full crimson lips that trembled slightly at some private fear.

He certainly hadn't expected to feel this fierce compulsion to protect her. From everything and everyone.

*Even from yourself?*

Cursing roundly, Adrian turned away from the road. He raised one hand before him, then the other.

Slowly, almost hesitantly, he ran his fingers over his tense forearms, feeling soft wool and hard, bunching muscle beneath.

Frowning, he dragged his booted toe through the rich dark earth, then stared fixedly at the small furrow raised in its wake. "So I really am here. And I haven't the slightest memory, the slightest clue as to how it came about."

Grim-faced, he raised his head and stared at the spot where the noisy green car had just disappeared. "One minute I'm caught up in dreams and the next I'm thrust down without a hint of warning into dirt and noise and a body I can barely remember how to maneuver. The whole thing is bloody impossible!"

But there were the powerful forearms, the booted legs to prove him wrong. He scowled down at his outstretched palms. "Muscle. Blood. How strange it all feels. How…heavy. And how vast a responsibility…"

A butterfly with azure wings skimmed past, looped around his fingers, then settled onto his calloused palm.

For a moment Adrian Draycott's face darkened. He stood

unmoving, mesmerized by the sight of those frail wings fluttering upon his long, calloused fingers.

Just like her eyes, he thought.

Azure with flecks of gold. Like sunrise on a warm summer sea.

He shook his head abruptly, forcing away that particular memory, feeling a half-forgotten heat rush through his legs and move inexorably upward in a way that was distinctly disconcerting.

And all too human.

But Adrian Draycott was not about to be deterred from his ancient obligations. Not by anyone or anything.

And before the night was over, he was bloody well going to know just what in the blazes was going on here at his abbey!

## CHAPTER TWO

BY THE TIME GRAY LEFT the woods and circled up the drive to the gatehouse, her heart had stopped pounding. But her cheeks were still flushed.

Damn the man! Who did he think he was?

Then even he was swept from Gray's mind as Draycott Abbey's massive granite walls burst into view before her.

Her first thought as she looked upon the ancient structure was that she was glad she wasn't psychic. Within such a place there must be many ghosts. Even she, who'd never felt a hint of special intuition, sensed an off prickle at her spine as she stared up at the crenellated roof and mullioned windows.

The granite walls gleamed back at her, bathed with light in the slanting rays of the afternoon sun. Beneath the sheer stone faces, white swans skimmed across a lily-studded moat.

Gray's breath caught. There was a sense of timelessness to the place, a sense of utter peace that invaded one's very soul. It was almost as if past and present merged here, then formed a boundless, eternal present.

*Oh, right, Mackenzie! Next you'll be seeing mounted knights jousting for their ladies' honor!*

Somewhere over the hills came the sound of bells and the faint bleating of sheep. The engine died with a cough. Suddenly Gray was enveloped in a vast, luminous silence.

It was then that the house began to sing to her.

So long…so long since she had known such peace.

Her azure eyes rose to the granite parapets. For a moment, she thought she saw a hint of movement in a corner tower. But that was unlikely, of course, since Lord Draycott and his new bride were almost certainly in Paris by now, enjoying their honeymoon.

And Gray knew just how much Kacey and Nicholas deserved that happiness after escaping death at the hands of a pair of cold-blooded murderers searching for secrets Nicholas didn't possess.

Kacey had said little about the ordeal and Gray had known enough not to press her. In the meantime, Gray was delighted when Kacey had phoned with a commission to do a detailed rendering of the abbey. She was determined to give her friend the very best work she had ever done.

Already her practiced eye was at work, scanning the abbey for balance points, shadow values and angles of perspective. For these things were Gray's life now, the source of her few pleasures.

And in the last year, she had finally begun to make her mark. Offers poured in and she had actually had to turn down commissions. But a house had to sing to her, to give of itself freely before she agreed to take on an assignment, no matter how impressive the fee.

And Gray invariably left her clients delighted. As any one of them would have agreed, to own one of Gray Mackenzie's sketches was to own the heart of a house, its very soul.

But, oh, *this* house—this proud, magnificent abbey sang to Gray already and in many voices. Of heroic days, of bards and warriors girded in leather and mail. Of dark seasons when brother turned against brother and father against son.

As she sat silent, listening to a lark trill out a gay tune, Gray lost her heart. Somewhere behind her a fat trout jumped from the sparkling moat.

Already she knew that the sketches she did here would be her very finest work.

She was still sitting wide-eyed, fingers taut on the wheel, when the crunch of gravel roused her. She turned her head to see a man in a black jacket and incongruous red running shoes striding toward her, a careful smile on his ruddy face.

"Miss Mackenzie? Welcome to Draycott Abbey. I am Marston."

As Gray stepped from the car, she remembered Kacey's last, hasty note, which had reached her barely a week before.

> *Marston, Nicholas's butler, is a dear, but I'm sure the man will be overjoyed to see the last of us. He claims he can't concentrate on his work with the two of us forever mooning about. He swears it's making him dangerously matrimonial.*

Gray smiled to herself at the thought of this sober, correct gentleman's gentleman feeling "dangerously matrimonial."

The man looked about as emotional as a mackerel.

"Shall I take your bags up, Miss Mackenzie?"

Gray nodded, still enthralled by the massive walls hung with climbing roses. Quickly she dug into her satchel and tugged out a spiral sketchbook. Without another word, she settled herself against the hood of her rental car and began to work. Already her mind was humming with ways to capture the elegant angles of the ancient stone edifice.

Yes, the lovely centifolia roses would curl and climb just *so,* and the swans would glide just a little left of center…

Footfalls crunched softly over gravel. Gray heard them only dimly, already lost in balance points and texture sources.

In the only thing that had saved her life five years before.

THE SUN HUNG GOLDEN atop the trees when Gray finally looked up. Beside her lay her first three renderings of the abbey.

Slowly, she sat back and massaged her aching neck.

And then she saw the letter, cream vellum stock with an embossed coronet surrounded with double dragons. Vaguely Gray recalled Marston saying something about a letter—a letter from the viscountess, was it?

A smile flitted about the corners of her mouth. Gray wondered if she would ever get used to the idea of sweet, forthright Kacey Mallory being a viscountess.

Her smile grew as she tore open the envelope and read her friend's scrawled note, dated only two days earlier.

> *Sorry, Gray, not to be there to meet you, but our flight has been changed yet again. Marston will take care of anything you need though. The man is truly a wonder!*
>
> *Thanks again for coming on such short notice. I wanted the very best person for these renderings, and you were it. By the way, I'd like to keep these a secret from Nicholas until his birthday. Only Marston is to know about them for now.*
>
> *But I absolutely forbid you to bury yourself in your work the way you usually do. As your employer I hereby order you to borrow the car. Take a walk around the downs. The Sussex countryside is lovely in high summer. And you, my girl, were looking far too pale the last time I saw you.*

Gray's eyes crinkled as she recalled the last time they'd met. Their lunch had consisted of soft pretzels loaded with mustard, which they'd gulped down on a crowded Philadelphia street corner between jobs. Had it been only two months ago?

Gray's eyes returned to her friend's letter.

*By the way, if you should happen to hear thirteen bells, don't be upset. The locals say it has to do with an old abbey legend. You see, along with a moat and a priceless art collection, the abbey also has a resident ghost. And then the bells ring thirteen times—*

Here the letter ended in a jagged scrawl, then picked up a line lower, with the scrawl even more pronounced.

*Sorry, but Nicholas is growing impatient (as usual) and I really must go. I believe I have a way to put a smile back on his face, however. The limousine taking us to Heathrow has curtained windows and a smoked glass divider. The mind positively boggles at the possibilities...*
          *Love you.*
          *K.C.*

Gray found herself chuckling. No doubt Kacey would find a way to coax a smile from her husband. A certifiable beauty, she was also something even rarer: a kind and generous person. Only she seemed unaware of her beauty, and perhaps that was part of her charm.

Now *she* was a different matter entirely, Gray thought ruefully. Tall, auburn-haired, she had always been a little too tall, a little too shy, a little too bony. Most men felt uncomfortable just looking at her.

Or looking up at her, since she neared six feet without shoes.

For years, she had never seemed to fit into any mold and that had bothered her keenly. Then she had begun making her own mold.

That had worked well for a time. And then she'd met Matt...

Gray's fingers stiffened. Frowning, she brushed back a wild strand of wine-dark hair.

No, she refused to think about *him.* Her ex-husband belonged to that other life, to that dark time she was not supposed to think about anymore. The only way her change would be complete was if she made it *inside,* or so the counselors had warned her.

But it had been hard, far harder than she'd thought. She hadn't dreamed there would be so many cues, so many tiny details that bound a person to a specific place, a specific time, a specific identity.

*But your identity became a threat,* she reminded herself grimly. *Because of that it had to be changed, and the truth buried forever.*

Beyond the moat a curlew exploded from the woods and hurtled through the air, gray wings outlined as it cut through a cloudless turquoise sky.

*Do you really think that will stop him?* a cold voice whispered. *Do you think anything can stop a man like that?*

*And now he's free. The first thing he'll do is come looking for you. And when he finds you, he's going to—*

Gray bit her lip, feeling the old, familiar fear gnaw at her stomach. *But I'm safe here!* she told herself, watching the sun melt like warm honey over the forested hills above the moat.

*He can never trace me here.*

Yes, here at Draycott Abbey she would be safe.

*Wouldn't she?*


MARSTON WAS EVERY BIT as efficient as Kacey had promised. After an elegant dinner of marinated white asparagus, feather-light salmon mousse and an unforgettable crème brûlée, he'd led Gray out to the flower-hung gatehouse flanking the moat.

The taciturn butler had first offered her a room in the main house, but the gatehouse's floor-to-ceiling French doors overlooking the moat had instantly captured Gray's imagination.

And there she had stayed.

Now, after sketching for several hours, Gray still found herself no closer to sleep.

She glanced down at her watch. 3:00 a.m. Jet lag for sure.

Not that she could have slept anyway. There was something too rich about the air in this ancient, history-haunted place.

Yes, she could well believe that phantoms walked the parapets of Draycott Abbey. Hadn't Kacey mentioned something about a legendary family ghost?

A shiver played down her spine. She realized the night was growing cool. Pulling a wool throw over her shoulders, Gray curled up on an armchair before the opened doors, watching moonlight play over the shifting silver water.

Somewhere in the distance came the first faint peal of bells.

What was it Kacey had said about bells?

Gray frowned, unable to remember. She stifled a yawn as the scent of roses enveloped her, warm and inviting. Nice, she thought. More than nice…

Not that she'd be able to sleep, of course. She was far too keyed up. But at least she could rest and run through several possible compositions to try out in the morning.

Moments later, clutching an architecture manual in one hand and a Royal Geological Survey guide in the other, she sank onto the bed. Her eyes fluttered, then closed. Her head slid forward, auburn hair spilling over an embossed leather cover.

She never even heard the thirteenth chime.


THE ROSES SWAYED. A cloud ran before the three-quarter moon. *Mars in Scorpio. Saturn trine Uranus.*

The house seemed to catch its breath—to shudder. Quiet and yet not entirely quiet, the great walls slept on, caught in a restless silence.

Moonlight touched the edge of the opened French doors and a shadow that was not quite a shadow fell across the threshold.

Dear God, she was beautiful, he thought.

Her skin was like finest bisque, her lashes a dark curve against her cheeks.

And that glorious auburn hair...

The figure in the doorway moved closer, making no sound in these, the dead hours of night. Just as before, he sensed the danger enveloping her like a sullen black cloud.

Had she no idea at all?

At the window the curtains fluttered. A large cat crept through their swaying folds, gray tail all atwitch. Leaping to the white coverlet, he stretched out comfortably, his body curved like a dark comma against the apricot damask pillows.

Moonlight bounced off the moat, poured through the window and gleamed back from a small gilt mirror opposite the French doors. The room seemed to shimmer, ablaze with light, while the air filled with the dense summer scent of honeysuckle and roses.

On the bed, Gideon stirred. Flicking his tail, he gave a soft meow.

The man at the threshold frowned. She was nothing like Kacey, Adrian Draycott realized. She was nothing like any woman he'd ever known.

Or maybe she was...

A hint of memory pricked at his consciousness. A dim image of sad eyes in a pale and very noble face.

A flowing gown cut from silk that flashed like hammered gold.

The black-clad figure stiffened. Where in the blazes had *that* image come from?

A dream?

Or was it something more?

Faint, so faint, the phantom images danced before him, teasing and elusive, finally fading away into nothingness. Smothering a curse, Adrian Draycott slipped past the drifting curtains, then laughed bitterly at his unnecessary care.

For no one could hear his curses or his footfalls. Just as no one could see him when he walked his ancient parapets and gazed upon his beloved roses.

Not until *she* had come, that is.

The sense of uneasiness that had dogged Adrian grew sharper. Once more he was being pulled in, and he liked the prospect not at all. Aye, whether the obdurate female was a rare beauty or not!

After all, he'd succeeded once. After that precarious chase upon the cliffs, during which he'd saved Kacey and his brother from death, Adrian had bloody well earned the right to be left alone for a century or two!

The newly married couple was probably ensconced in a lovely old *auberge* outside Paris right now, resting and enjoying the fruits of Adrian's work at reconciling them.

The ghost of Draycott Abbey frowned, one brow rising.

Well, perhaps *resting* was not precisely the word for what the two would be doing in that great silk-hung bed...

Adrian tensed, feeling the old bitterness, the gnawing memories of regret and betrayal. Once, long ago, Kacey had been his, but in his arrogance, he had lost her.

Now it was Nicholas's chance to know the joy of her love.

Frowning, Adrian gazed down at the woman asleep on the bed, sensing the black wall around her grow ever more solid.

At her feet, Gideon stirred and raised his head.

"Yes, my friend, there is danger here—great danger. Perhaps even more than my brother faced from his old enemies."

Adrian sighed. He had a choice, of course. There was always

a choice. But he had never before shirked a duty to his abbey, and he didn't intend to do so now.

Yet something told him this time there would be other complications. Complications that included all the heated demands of this uncertain physical form he'd been given.

Lord, what was the use of it?

Gideon meowed softly from the bed.

"Yes, I know there are *some* things a body is useful for, old friend." As Adrian's eyes returned to the figure on the bed, he felt a sharp current of heat sweep down his spine.

His frown grew. Damn and blast! He hadn't felt such things for years. Even with Kacey it had been merely a remembered response. But with this woman…

The heat twisted, shimmered, coiled about him like a bright mist. Dim memories gathered, teased, took tangible form in the ashes of a desire he'd thought dead and long buried.

Buried, yes, but far from dead, as Adrian soon discovered.

It seemed desire had merely slept, century after century, awaiting this moment.

Time ground to a halt. Adrian stood rigid, staring at the auburn hair spread upon the pillow. His heart seemed to lurch, his hands to tremble. Who *was* she to affect him so?

Suddenly he was tasked with all the old dreams, all the thoughts of things that could never be his.

Because it was too late for him, far too late.

Outside in the moonlight a fish leaped from the moat and fell back in an explosion of light. Water scattered in a fury of silver, flashing ever outward beneath the moon.

Gideon blinked as the curtains danced, then drifted back to stillness. A moment later, the abbey's resident ghost disappeared into the night, trailing sadness behind him like a shimmering stream of silver.

*Sussex, England*
*February, 1191*

*Out beyond the moat, out beyond the old Roman track and the quiet rowan wood, blood-red fingers of light gathered across the darkening Western sky. Even now, the first beacon fires were being lit.*

*Dressed in a rough cloak and wimple, a woman moved past the unfinished stone tower and leaned over the crenellated wall. Tall and fair, she stared out into the gathering night while somewhere in the darkness a lone wolf howled. In the far hills above her others took up the wild, sad chant.*

Desolation. *It sat upon her like a shroud, inexorable as the coming of night.*

*Not even in her native Brittany, where the iron-gray seas heaved against the barren cliffs, had she known such dolor, such utter loneliness.*

*She shivered, clutching her homespun cloak closer about her shoulders. Gone the furs, gone the velvets in her liege's absence. And as so oft of late, she was gripped with ominous premonitions.*

*When would he return, the man she loved so well? Seven long months had passed, and yet she'd had no word, no news at all from the Holy Land where he marched at Richard's side.*

*She gripped the granite parapet with trembling fingers, in desperate need of the stone's reassuring strength.*

His *strength. Gleaned from* his *beloved stone walls.*

*Now they were among the few things she had left to remember her husband by. Even the brooch he had given her was gone, stolen in the night while she slept. Carefully worked in gold and jewel-like enamels, it was a clever piece, with two dragons intertwined about a golden coronet.*

His *device. And the Lady Anne of Draycotte knew she would never see the treasured brooch again.*

*She sighed. There was still so much to be done here. The south tower of the great house was only half-finished, its inner and outer faces truncated in a jagged shell. Only half the merlons rose above the high parapets. Even now, mounds of carefully made mortar lay discarded in heaps near the gaping wall.*

*But masons, quarrymen and smiths were gone, dismissed just as the rest of Draycotte's loyal servants had been. And now, the walls stood jagged and unfinished, a silent mockery of all that Draycotte's lord had sought to create here.*

*At least his beloved roses, gathered from far-flung Aquitaine and Castile, were now settled in fresh beds, the Lady Anne thought. This she had done with her own hands, trusting the job to no one else. Soon they would begin to put forth their first green shoots.*

*How sad her lord would be to miss their first budding against his granite walls.*

*Another beacon took flame, blazing in the black hills. The cottagers and villeins moved about it, keeping their silent vigil.*

*Just as Draycotte's lady did.*

Where are you, my love? *her heart cried out, as if it could cross the thousand lonely miles to his side.* Are you fallen before an infidel blade? Is your broad brow even now dry and baking beneath a cruel desert sun?

*The Lady Anne flinched and nearly cried aloud at the thought of it, her fingers pressed to fists.*

*No, he must be alive! He had sworn he would return to her. Had he been felled with mortal wound, she must know it, feel it in her very limbs!*

*No, he would return, her liege and lord. He would come back to Draycotte and this land he loved so well. She had to believe that. Even on this blackest of nights when her hope was nigh gone, she had to remember and be strong.*

*Crying shrilly, a kestrel winged home through the night. The manor's lady hoped that the bird found a safer roost than she had done, surrounded by sullen enemies who never let her from their sight.*

*But such was the lawlessness on the land. And now, by royal writ, her home was no longer her own.*

*She pushed back her wimple, feeling the coarse linen flow loose at her cheeks. Her fingers flexed, easing around her ripening stomach. At her gentle touch the babe within stirred and kicked.*

*Once she would have smiled at such a movement, but now it only made her catch her fingers tighter to protect the fragile life growing inside her. Feeling a moment of dizziness, she reached out to the granite parapet, pressing her fingers into the smooth, honed stone.*

*In two more months, the babe would come. She prayed that his father would be home in time to see his son's birth. And a son she knew the child would be. Yet somehow in her restless dreams she could never see more than a glimpse of the tiny face and keen, bright eyes.*

*And then naught but darkness...*

*To cheer herself, she tried to think of brighter things, recalling the image of their last meeting, out by the witch's pool.*

*There in the ferns he had loosed her kirtle and cloth-of-gold gown. Swiftly he had caught her to him, his fingers desperate, searching, his manhood hot and pulsing. All through the long hours of night he had held her and claimed her, ever more fierce, ever more urgent, almost as if he could drive away the morrow with the raw force of his desire.*

*Her eyes blurred with tears as she gazed out at the distant glitter of the pool. There they had loved and laughed seven months before.*

*It might have been a lifetime, in truth.*

*If only he would come to her again.*

*If only there were some way to drive these sullen wolves from her hearth.*

*But she knew it was impossible. Not even with a score of able men could such a thing be done.*

*And the Lady Anne had no more protectors. One by one they had sickened and died, or simply gone beyond the walls and never returned.*

*Now she was left alone, without waiting-maid or kin, a prisoner attended by those who wished her only ill.*

*Out in the darkness another beacon flamed white-hot to life. Watching the sparks shoot up, the Lady of Draycotte straightened her shoulders and shoved down her fear, knowing her lord would expect that of her. Aye, his pride was fierce; he would have demanded no less from her.*

*For those were his people out there in the darkness. Serf, villein, and cottager, they waited, with no other way than this to show their loyalty.*

*Now more than a score of fires glowed golden through the valley, turning night to day. The sight heartened her as nothing else could have. The Lord of Draycotte would have been proud, so proud of them.*

*Her hands curved protectively over her stomach. In the meantime, she must be strong, just as he would wish her to be. She must wait and pray for her own true love's return, even if it took ten years more, and a hundred after that!*

*Still, she would remember and still, she would be here waiting when he returned from his holy quest.*

By the witch's pool at midnight. 'Tis there I'll seek you. Forget it not.

*Even as the wrenching loneliness gripped her, the Lady Anne vowed to remember. And she would be there waiting for her lord and love when he came riding back to her over the lush green Draycotte hills.*

WITH A CHOKED MOAN, Gray shot upright in the soft bed, in the peaceful night, in the ancient gatehouse by the silver moat.

Her heart was hammering wildly. Her eyes were wide and haunted.

She peered into the shadows, frightened and disoriented. Her fingers dug into the damask coverlet as she tried to remember what had woken her.

A dream? If so, 'twas more real than her gray, cheerless reality.

She tried to catch back the shifting images, but her dreams poured through her fingers like white sand, leaving her with nothing but emptiness and an aching sense of loss.

And with fear, her old, familiar companion.

The room was wrapped in silence; moonlight glittered like frost before the half-open French doors.

Then Gray saw the perfect, densely petaled rose. It lay beside her on the bed, centered on an ivory pillow.

"Dear God…" she whispered.

But she was not the same person she had once been. No longer would she shove down her fear, shivering and waiting in silence and dread. This new person that she was exploded from the bed in an angry white storm of linen and damask.

Without a thought to the brevity of her satin nightshirt, she flung back the curtains, determined to find the person who dared invade the privacy of her room.

But there was no one.

Beyond the narrow flagstone terrace only a pair of swans

moved, necks arched and proud as they glided beneath the moon's opaque silver eye.

Nothing else stirred in this silent nightscape of black and glittering silver. Of soft mist and hard shadows.

Only the swans moved.

Only her dim, restless memories lingered.

Gray's fingers tensed against the chill metal of the terrace railing. She fought to hold back a racking sob.

Dear God, when would she learn how to forget? When would she ever be truly whole again?

A rustle of the curtains drew her eyes behind her, where a gray blur slipped through a beam of moonlight. A great cat, it drifted through the curtains out onto the little flagstone terrace.

It was the same cat she had seen this morning, curling about that insufferable caretaker's booted feet.

Amber eyes rose to study Gray, moon-bright, oddly keen.

They glittered at her, then narrowed as if in secret query.

Gray caught back a shiver. What new fancies were upon her now?

With the barest bunching of sleek muscles the cat jumped to the delicate wrought iron rail at the edge of the terrace and moved closer, stopping just short of Gray's right hand.

The hand that still clutched the rose.

A moist, black nose shoved at her closed fingers, tongue lapping, warm and faintly rough. A low, rich purr poured from the cat's throat.

Gray felt wild laughter build in her chest. Slowly, she slid her fingers over the soft pelt, delighting in the cat's silken warmth.

A hint of perfume drifted on the warm, still air. She turned, sniffing to trace its source. Abruptly she saw the dark outline of a climbing rose. Crimson petals spilled across the wall to her right, where the moat lapped against the side of the gate-house.

*Centifolia roses.* Just like the ones she had left behind in London.

Just like the rose clasped within her fingers.

A wild joy swept through Gray. It came unbidden, as if from some other place, some other time.

Without taking time to think, she swept over the railing and inched along the narrow strip of damp soil that ran between gatehouse and moat.

Twice her bare feet slipped, mud-slick, and twice, she caught herself.

And then she seized the vine itself. Struggling upright, she feasted on the wide-petaled beauty of the ancient roses covering the wall before her.

As if in a dream her fingers circled the satin petals. Perfume spilled around her, drowning the night in beauty, making her throat constrict with pain and a flood of exquisite, nearly forgotten memories.

In just such a place two lovers might have met to share whispered vows beneath the wind-tossed petals. Here, too, they might have shared lingering kisses, warm and gentle.

Then kisses not gentle at all…

"What in bloody hell are you doing to my roses?"

The words came at her without warning.

Gray started, let go of the vine and instantly lost her balance. Swaying wildly, she slipped down the muddy bank and realized that any second she was going to fall.

But strangely she did not.

Hard hands seized her shoulders, dragged her upright, spun her around.

And she gazed into eyes of slate, into eyes of pride and cunning.

She stared at an angular, weather-beaten face. *The care-taker?* But surely the man did not take his duties so seriously as this!

Her heart still thundering, Gray fought to recover her control. She frowned, shoving at his hands. "Just what do you think *you're* doing, Tarzan?"

"I believe I asked first, Miss Mackenzie. Your work here does not entitle you to decimate my gardens, after all."

Fury speared through Gray. And then she realized they were trapped on the narrow band of soil between rock and water, thigh to thigh, chest to chest.

Heart to pounding heart.

And it felt sinfully, *painfully* good.

Most of all, it felt oddly familiar somehow...

Red-faced with fury and embarrassment, she wrenched at his hands. "Let me go, you arrogant—" Her hand lashed out, driving against his chest.

His grip only tightened. "Who are you, woman, that you try me so sorely?"

*What was the madman talking about?* Painfully aware that she wore nothing but a satin nightshirt that barely skimmed her thighs, Gray tried to twist free.

And got nowhere. Her hands were captured securely between hard, calloused fingers.

In her struggling, Gray's hips brushed his taut thigh. Heat flared through her as she felt the powerful muscles bunch and flex at her touch.

Her captor flinched. His breath seemed to catch. "Who *are* you?" he repeated, his voice as raw as Gray's had been. "Is this some new sort of test?"

But when her eyes rose, Adrian Draycott read nothing but bewilderment in their azure depths. Sweet heaven, what was happening here? In truth, he was at least as confused as she!

A vein hammered at Adrian's temple as heat swept between their tense bodies. Around him the night swayed, and time slid to a halt. Had he been even halfway sane at that moment, he would have pulled away, stopped before it was too late...

But maybe it had been too late the first moment he'd seen this stubborn, exasperating creature. And sane was the very last thing Adrian Draycott was feeling right then. How could he be sane with her soft breasts caressing his chest, her slim thighs brushing his belly?

"By all the heavens above, woman, you task me beyond measure! But arrogant I always was. Damned, too, perhaps. If so, then it makes no difference if—"

It was reckless, of course. Worse yet, it was utterly dangerous. And yet...

And yet he cared not.

The next moment Gray was swept close, molded to his urgent body,

"S-stop this! What do you think you're doing—"

She got no further, her protests drowned beneath the hot silk of his probing lips, the velvet fury of his kiss.

*Kiss?* she thought dimly. *Kiss* was far too tame a word for this total possession, this storm of heat and hunger he unleashed.

And even as she struggled, cursing, Gray felt his need kindle an answering heat within her.

Impossible! Unthinkable!

And yet...

With a gasp, she wrenched at his iron grip, kicked at his legs, but all her efforts won her only a peal of dark laughter.

Mouth to mouth they strained, caught on the very edge of the moat, where the slightest misstep would send them both flying into the water.

Neither cared in the least. In furious silence they struggled, she to wrench free, he to drive closer. To claim and possess.

Infinitely. With a hunger that Adrian Draycott realized he had never known before, nor even dreamed of in a life spent pursuing every imaginable form of pleasure.

Somehow there was a fatedness to the moment, as if his roses had been left here over the long centuries, waiting for just such a meeting.

And in spite of all her fire and struggling, Adrian knew the woman in his arms felt it, too. Her breath was too ragged, her pulse too wild for it to be otherwise.

He knew he ought to let her go. He knew he should turn and melt back into the night where he belonged. But somehow he could not. Not tonight, not when he found such searing pleasure in her touch.

Just once, he told himself.

His mouth opened. He captured her velvet underlip in his teeth and savored the mystery of her mouth.

At that single exquisite movement, desire raged full-blown through Adrian's frame. His fingers sank into her hair as he slanted her face up to his, desperately afraid that if he released her, she would be torn from him forever.

Just a little longer, he promised himself...

Caught against his chest, Gray bit back a moan. What was *wrong* with her? "L-let me go, you—you snake, you—"

Too late, she found out her mistake. Her black-clad captor seized the moment and slid his tongue deep, caressing the inner textures of her mouth and searching out all its hot, forbidden secrets.

Suddenly the night was ashimmer, electric with danger. With a wild, reckless hunger that made Gray moan and strain against him.

She, who had never moaned, had never wanted, had never even *imagined* that such desire existed.

And now, in the span of an instant, she had discovered a thousand exquisite textures that she could no longer deny herself. Ablaze with wonder, she combed her fingers through the long hair that swept his shoulders, feeling it part like silk at her touch. She shivered as his breath surged ragged at her neck, raw and hot against her cheek.

His pulse hammered, echoing her own.

Blindly, Gray dug her fingers into his hard shoulders, glorying in his instant stiffening, in the groan that tore from his lips.

There beneath the moonlight, hunger flared between them like summer lightning, and Gray felt herself tossed like a leaf in the wind.

She moaned restlessly, sliding closer against his hard thighs, which clenched like forged steel in response.

Shivering, she felt the unmistakable thrust of his rock-hard arousal. Even then she could not pull away, could not forsake the heat she had discovered in his granite body.

For that, too, was somehow familiar.

"Damn and bloody blast!" Strangely enough, it was he who pulled free and stared down at her, scowling. "By the name of all the saints, woman—"

He never finished. His eyes glittered down into the flushed beauty of her cheeks, the dazed depths of her eyes, bright with passion still.

And as Adrian Draycott watched, a single tear squeezed free and inched slowly down Gray's cheek.

He cursed, his jaw clenching. Slowly his calloused finger rose to the salty bead.

As if in a dream, Gray felt his hard hands anchor her cheeks, saw his face slant down.

"I never meant…by God, I swear I never planned—"

And then, slow and infinitely gentle, his lips covered that single tear and eased it onto his tongue. Dazed, Gray felt his lips close, felt him draw the bead into his mouth.

In truth, she had no idea what had caused the tear. Not pain, of that there was no doubt. Nor did it stem from anger. Perhaps it was the sheer violence of the sensual discovery she'd just made.

And then Gray had no time left for thinking.

His lips tightened.

Slowly, exquisitely, he drew her delicate skin tight, molding every captive inch with his teeth. Heart pounding, Gray swayed, feeling the dark force of his possession. A low moan tore from her throat.

*Heat.*

*Need.*

*Dear God, the unimaginable power of touching and being touched in such a way, as if the whole world began and ended in texture and sensation.*

Sweet heaven, she'd never imagined the reckless wonder of it, the wild, sweet splendor of it.

She shivered, her nails digging into his neck.

An eternity passed. Around them the abbey slept and the night hung still, caught in timeless dreams while an ancient, primal drama raged on beneath its weathered walls.

Then, with one sleek tugging movement, Gray was free. Her intruder stood back, his eyes hooded, glittering.

"I'll not apologize, so don't expect it. For you puzzle me sorely, woman. You raise too many questions for which I have no answers. But I'll have my answers, every one. And until then, Gray Mackenzie, I leave you with something to remember me by. It has always been the punishment for stealing a Draycott rose." His fingers swept her flushed cheek. "Here. Here you will wear my mark."

Overhead, ragged clouds ran before the moon. Gray shivered, realizing she was standing half-naked in the reckless, heated embrace of an utter stranger.

"You arrogant, p-pigheaded—"

His smile was the merest curve of brightness in his dark face. "Completely, I'm afraid. And yet at this moment, I could almost wish that—"

Somewhere in the night a clock began to chime. Gray felt him stiffen.

And then, with a faint rustle of the ferns along the bank, he was gone, loping across the little terrace and skirting the bridge to disappear into the shadows beyond.

Even then, Gray did not move, shaken profoundly, feeling that a new person now occupied her body, a complete stranger.

Blood leaped to her cheeks. She shivered, feeling as if the man stood before her still, his breath ragged, his body tense with need.

*Just as your own is,* a mocking voice whispered.

Dazed, she raised trembling fingers to her cheek and traced the flushed skin where his mouth had lingered only seconds before.

Already, she could feel his mark rising.

# CHAPTER THREE

SUNLIGHT SPILLED THROUGH the opened French doors. Gray yawned and burrowed back beneath the satin pillows, smiling drowsily.

Roses. There had been roses.

Her lips curved as she remembered her rich, heady dreams of the night before.

Beacon fires burning in the darkness. A golden brooch with intertwined dragons.

A cat with eyes of unblinking amber.

And roses—roses everywhere, in every shape and color, their scent spilling out into the night.

But they were only dreams, she told herself, stifling another yawn. In one fluid motion she stretched, then tossed back the covers and came to her feet.

And there she went absolutely still, reeling as the full truth of the night returned. The hard truth of a man, brooding and reckless, driven by implacable need.

The raw truth of her own wanton response.

She, who had seemed fated to feel nothing. She, who was always distant, cool, detached.

*Grieving.* For what, Gray was never quite sure.

Her hands cupped her flaming cheeks. What in the name of heaven was happening to her? How could she possibly have—

A faint movement shifted the coverlet. Looking down, Gray saw a sleek figure curled at the foot of her bed.

It was the cat she'd seen last night, gray-furred with paws of black. The same cat who had trod so delicately across the terrace railing.

*His* cat.

Anger shot through her. Who was this infuriating man to invade her privacy, to thrust his pet upon her even while she slept, defenseless?

Angrily, she jerked the pillow from the bed, sending her two architecture books crashing to the floor.

The cat did not move.

"Go! Shoo!"

But the creature only inched down onto his paws and curled his tail around his haunches, his keen eyes never leaving Gray's face.

"*Go,* I said!" Gray waved her hands wildly.

Still, the cat remained, content, unmoving, silkily alert.

So he meant to be stubborn, did he?

Grimly, Gray began to tug at the coverlet, wishing that it were the cat's master she was dumping onto the floor instead.

At that moment, she caught a glimpse of herself in the gilt-edged Regency mirror across the room. Her cheeks were flushed, her hair a wild cascade of auburn at her shoulders. During her restless sleep, the top buttons of her nightshirt had come free, revealing the shadowed softness of her breasts.

She looked, in short, like a woman who'd just come from her lover's bed, flushed with memories of sensual excess.

Like a woman who'd enjoyed every wanton second of it.

With a low cry, Gray stumbled backward, unable to tear her eyes from the image in the mirror.

What in the name of heaven was happening to her? She was never so reckless, never so emotional.

*And what about the rest?* a dark voice asked. *What of the other thing he promised you?*

She inched forward, her pulse like thunder in her ears.

The mark was just where she had known it would be, a faint pattern of raised skin where her captor had pressed a love-mark onto her cream cheek.

*His* mark, given in wild, reckless passion.

And oddly it looked like a perfect, dense-leaved rose.

Gray stood, frozen, her gaze fixed upon the mirror. Behind her on the bed the great cat began to purr.

"MORE EGGS, MISS? Or kippers, perhaps?"

Marston was as cool as ever, dressed in a crisp navy blazer that fairly screamed Burberry. This morning, however, his formality was muted by neon-green running shoes that peeked out beneath sober gray flannels.

Gray shook her head absently, not really listening. She had barely slept the night before and all through breakfast she'd toyed with her food. All she could do was stare out blindly at the roses climbing in riotous color across the abbey's granite walls.

The night had shaken her profoundly.

Even now, a thousand questions pressed at her, each one screaming for answers.

But she had work to do, sketches to finish. She had absolutely no time for or interest in an arrogant, insufferable Englishman with more libido than sense!

Gray set down her Limoges cup too forcefully, trying to shake off her distraction. She realized belatedly that Marston had asked her a question. "I beg your pardon?"

"You slept well, I trust?"

Gray frowned, twisting the fragile cup between her fingers. "Passably, but this deafening silence of yours is going to take some getting used to. In Philadelphia it's never really quiet—not *this* quiet, anyway. There's something…unsettling about so much silence."

Marston bent to refill her teacup, his sharp eyes flickering over her face.

Had he noticed her distraction, the dark circles beneath her eyes? Gray wondered. And what of the other marks left from the night?

Her fingers rose, tracing the bandage she had shoved over the telltale mark at her cheek. At the thought of that wild, savage kiss, fire swept across her face.

Damn the man anyway!

Suddenly her eyes narrowed on Marston's back. "Are you—the only one here? That is—" Blast it, how was she to phrase this? "I mean, the abbey must require a large staff, but I've seen no others about."

The butler straightened, staring out over the moat. "Oh, at one time there must have been well over a hundred working here. In more recent years, Edward, the last viscount, employed a staff of thirty or so. But now, what with government regulations and the crippling inheritance taxes…" Marston sighed. "Ah, well, now there's only myself, miss, though Lord Draycott has others in when the need arises."

Gray swirled the tea idly in her cup. "But the grounds are so extensive. There are the formal gardens, the maze, the moat and all those lovely roses. Surely you can't manage all that."

Marston unbent so far as to smile slightly. "Indeed not. Not that his lordship wouldn't set me at it if I showed the slightest aptitude. You see, a rose sees me coming and immediately withers—which suits me just fine, for I've no patience with greenery, no patience at all. No, his lordship has a professional in to care for the grounds. A nice enough chap, although he seems a bit on the quiet side. Brewer, his name is."

Gray's fingers tightened on the fine porcelain saucer. "He—he lives nearby?"

"Brewer? Down by the main road, as a matter of fact. There's an old cottage there, and I understand he's done wonders with repairing the thatched roof and flower beds." A crease appeared between Marston's brows. "I heard he's taken his daughter and gone abroad for a holiday. He has relatives in the south of France, I think."

Gray stared out at the rose-covered wall, trying to make sense of this new information. "Well, he's back now." She flushed faintly. "I passed him yesterday on the way in."

For a moment, Gray considered telling Marston the rest of the night's happenings, but in the end she decided not to. Some things were better left unmentioned. No, she would just push the whole wretched business from her mind. Besides, she could handle the insufferable caretaker on her own if she had to.

"Ah, well." Marston shrugged. "He must have returned, in that case. Jolly well time, too, what with the roses in high bloom and the weirs to be tended."

Gray swallowed. "His daughter—and his wife—live there, too?"

"Oh, he's no wife, not now. Widower, he is. No, there's just the two of them."

"What about the cat?"

Marston stiffened. "Cat?"

"The great gray thing that follows him about."

"You—you *saw* it?" Marston looked shocked.

Whatever was wrong with the man? "I more than saw him—I touched him, too. He was prowling about the terrace last night. The impudent creature even snuck into my room and spent the night curled up on my bed."

Marston made a strangled sound that might have been a cough or a gasp. "Did it—were the cat's paws black?"

"That's the one," Gray said, starting to grow impatient. "But why—"

"The ghost." Marston's voice was low and very soft. "The ghost and that infernal cat of his."

"Ghost?" Gray felt tendrils of fear brush her neck. Abruptly, she remembered Kacey's letter. *Along with a moat and a priceless art collection, the abbey also has a resident ghost.*

But that was impossible, of course. There had to be a simple explanation. "The cat was every bit as real as I am, Marston. And as for this ghost Kacey mentioned, don't you find that a little bit hard to swallow in this day and age? I mean, we've put men on the moon, after all. We've split the atom. We've…we've invented panty hose. Nonsmudge mascara!" she concluded triumphantly, setting down her cup with a decisive click. "No, the cat was simply a stray, looking for a warm meal and a soft berth for the night."

Marston nodded slowly, folding and unfolding a napkin. "Yes…of course, you're right. These cats do come nosing about occasionally. The moat's full of fish, after all." He dropped the napkin, nodding resolutely. "Yes, a stray, that's what it was." A moment later, he looked up at Gray, his lips pursed. "Just the same, if the cat bothers you, keep the French doors closed. Which might be a good idea anyway, considering…" His gaze wandered off to the moat.

"Considering what?" Gray prompted impatiently.

"What? Oh, yes, well, old places such as this seem…seem unpredictable somehow. They have hidden corners, extra shadows that appear when you least expect them. They…play tricks on you." The butler looked grave for a moment, then shrugged.

Gray found herself wondering just what sort of tricks Marston was talking about. But the butler was already busying himself with the tea things, and his somber expression did not invite further questioning. "Will you be requiring anything else, Ms. Mackenzie?"

"Gray."

"I beg you pardon?"

"Gray. Call me Gray, please. Whenever you say 'Ms. Mackenzie,' I look around expecting to see my mother."

Marston's eyes crinkled. "Very well, miss—er, Gray. It was just the same with the viscountess, as I recall." The butler's veneer of formality slipped away for a moment. When he bent back to his work, his lips were curved in a secret smile.

*Ghosts!* Gray thought angrily. No doubt it suited that insufferable gardener to see such a story circulated. All to protect his precious roses, no doubt! Lazy, that's what the man was. Probably hadn't done a decent day's work in his life! And that cat of his was most likely purchased to enhance the effect.

*Well, I'm not about to be cowed so easily,* Gray swore. *And this is one handyman who will soon have a few lessons coming!*

TWENTY MINUTES LATER, sketch pad in hand, Gray edged along the far side of the moat, searching for the best angle to capture the abbey's massive walls.

The problem, she soon decided, was not which wall or which angle but how she was going to choose from the wealth of magnificent possibilities.

She tried angle after angle, composition after composition, until the ground at her feet was littered with crumpled paper. Again and again she attacked the rough, textured sheets she favored, only to cast down another effort in disgust.

Wrong and wrong again! Something was still eluding her.

Squinting, Gray looked across the moat at the south tower. Yes, that area was particularly bothersome. No matter how she varied contour lines and tone values, she couldn't seem to capture the effect of those sheer, curving walls.

Muttering beneath her breath, she flung down another aborted effort and held up her charcoal pencil, sighting the crenellated roof of the tower. Yes, the proportions at the top *were* inconsistent, as if the tower had been built in stages, to different plans.

But Gray meant to stay right where she was until she got the elusive tower down on paper at last.

SUNSHINE SHIMMERED off the moat, bouncing from the high, mullioned gallery windows. Seconds trickled into minutes and then hours.

Hunching her shoulders, Gray studied the weathered battlements, trying to concentrate. Passing bees droned noisily in the climbing roses and the moat murmured from some hidden, spring-fed corner. With every passing second, she found it harder and harder to focus on her work.

Even now, the scene fought her, always slightly out of kilter, the perspective wrong.

She squinted up at the corner tower, half-expecting to see an ominous, ghostly figure loom out from behind a merlon.

But nothing moved in the hazy midday heat. The tower was empty.

*Of course it's empty, Mackenzie! Were you expecting to see the abbey's so-called ghost?*

Muttering angrily, Gray snapped her pad open to a fresh sheet and sent charcoal slashing against fiber.

But with every stroke the abbey's surfaces seemed to shift infinitesimally, as if to deny Gray the solidity she sought.

And somehow, between the droning of the bees and the whisper of the wind, Gray found herself nodding, slipping back to an earlier age.

An age of dreams.

An age when armor flashed and destriers pawed the ground into raw furrows.

"Heat stroke," she muttered, jerking upright and ripping off another half-finished sheet. A second later, a misshapen ball of paper struck the wall. "Jet lag! Maybe even incipient senility!"

Frowning, Gray sat back against the sun-warmed wall. Her charcoal pencil hissed as it sped back and forth over the vellum sketch sheet. Against the paper weathered stone walls took shape, followed by a bank of mullioned windows, and finally the haze of the moat and the dark home wood beyond.

This one was good. Gray could feel the surging emotion, the intensity of vision that went far beyond mortar, stone and plaster.

All great buildings had an inner intensity, of course. And it was Gray's singular skill to be able to unveil that central essence and render it on paper in grays and black.

At that moment, peace descended upon Gray, a peace such as she hadn't known for years. For five years, to be exact. The day she'd discovered about Matt.

*Matt.*

Fear pricked at her neck, but she shoved it away, refusing to allow anything to disturb the peace that Draycott Abbey seemed to impart so well.

In the sunlight the far bank of the moat seemed to shimmer and blur. Gray rubbed her eyes, which had begun to ache from hours of steady work in the sun.

And as she watched, the haze twisted, then resolved into glittering images. Sunlight flashed off steel breastplates as a row of ghostly war-horses pounded along the far side of the moat. Banners twitched in a phantom wind, red silk swirling with intertwined dragons.

Far away Gray seemed to hear the stamp of great hooves, the harsh call of a leader to his men. Over the green land the spectral army stamped, armor ablaze, pennants snapping.

Moving a foot and more above the ground.

And as they thundered past in blazing splendor, the rose shrubs beside the moat seemed to straighten, to raise their branches and climb up into walls of blue-gray and green, their foliage twisted like some wild, living thing.

The leader raised a sword of steel and crystal, then cried a single word of command—low and rich, the remnant of some old, forgotten tongue.

Gray shivered and drew her hands across her watering eyes, even then unable to tear her gaze away.

As she watched, speechless, the foliage formed a living arch above the riders' heads. Every stem burst into wild bloom—crimson, fuchsia and white scattered against a vivid sea of green.

She caught back a moan. Dropping her sketch pad, she stumbled to her feet and spun around, putting her back to the moat.

*A dream. A mirage. Merely a trick of light and shadow, just as Marston had warned her...*

Behind her came a wild, excited shout as the phantom company thundered onward, ever closer to the steps of the gatehouse, where the great oak door creaked open in welcome.

And then there was a new sound, a high female cry.

Shivering, Gray opened her eyes.

A woman ran from the opened gate, her long gown gleaming golden in the sunlight. The man at the front of the line let out a shout and shot forward, bending low and swinging her up before him on the saddle.

Suddenly Gray felt a savage pain tear at her heart, a raw anguish such as she had never known before.

Tears began to flood down her face. Her breath came sharp and ragged as she swayed beneath a flood of churning emotions beyond logic or comprehension.

"N-no! It—it's a dream, all of it!"

Fingers trembling, Gray rubbed her eyes willing the madness to pass.

Overhead she heard the shrill cry of a kestrel. An errant gust of wind played through her long hair.

Slowly she opened her eyes.

The parade was gone, the bank empty. Only the roses moved now, their dense petals nodding sleepily on the far shore.

Gray fought back a sob, wrenched by a raw, ineffable longing. For what, she could not say.

Clenching her fingers, she stared at the sunny ground. "Way too much sun and fresh air for you, Gray Mackenzie, to say nothing of Marston's excellent cooking! But now the hocus-pocus is over. It's time to get back to work."

With a sigh, she looked down at the sketchbook dangling from her fingers. At least this one was passable. But the sketch still lacked something.

She yawned, brushing a glistening strand of hair from her eyes.

Pondering the problem, she sank down against a sun-washed boulder and braced her back.

She stifled another yawn and smoothed the half-finished sheet. Yes, there was something decidedly troubling about that south tower jutting out over the moat. The proportions were all wrong…

And that was Gray's last clear thought.

A moment later, her eyes blinked, then fluttered shut.

Her head eased back against the sun-warmed stone. Unnoticed, the charcoal pencil slipped from her fingers.

HE SLID OUT OF THE shimmering noonday heat, his face angular, brooding.

In taut silence he stood, an imposing figure in dark clothes that seemed ill-suited to his powerful frame. His face was bronzed, carved with deep lines. Smaller lines of laughter, care and concentration radiated out from the corners of his glittering eyes.

It was his eyes that moved now, hooded yet keen, blazing from slate-gray depths. They flowed over the woman before him, anger and resentment warring with even more primitive emotions.

*Why are you here?* It was a silent shout of frustration. Of confusion. Of something that bordered on pain.

And Adrian Draycott was not used to being confused about anything.

Another test? he asked himself, as the wind tossed silky auburn strands about her shoulders.

Damn and blast, he had not known it could be so troubling, so personal, so intensely *physical* to return this way!

Frowning, Adrian stared down at his arms and legs, slanting a look of particular disgust at his dusty shoes.

By heaven, there was no dignity in such clothes! No beauty. No grace whatsoever.

*But your velvets and lace were put down centuries ago. Right now they lie hidden in dusty, forgotten chests, fallen to threads and fragments.*

Slowly Adrian dragged a hand through his long black hair. Yes, this new age, this garish, clamorous age, called for different clothes and he must adopt them or withdraw.

Suddenly a sleek shadow loomed at his feet, long tail atwitch.

"What of the danger, old friend?" he asked of the animal beside him.

The cat meowed softly, his amber eyes never leaving Adrian's face.

"So bad as that?" For a moment, rage coursed through the abbey's dark-clad guardian. If only he could see more clearly! In the past, he had always been able to summon up at least some intuition of the dangers that threatened his beloved home.

But not now. Not with *her* on Draycott lands.

With her before him, Adrian found he couldn't think normally at all. All he could do was *feel*. All he could do was drown in the sweet scent of her, in the silver heat that spiraled through him as he watched the soft rise and fall of her breasts.

Her hair was really quite extraordinary, he thought, fighting an urge to run his hand along its silken length. In the sunlight the auburn strands flashed in a thousand shades of red and bronze.

The wind caught a thick curl and tossed it playfully about her cheek. Adrian felt a sharp prick of jealousy that he could not do the same, burying his fingers in those gleaming depths.

His hands curled into fists as he was rocked by a knifelike desire. Bone by bone, it slammed down his spine, from his head to his feet.

He stumbled backward, breathless, fighting for control.

Who *was* this woman? Why did she affect him so? And what, in the name of heaven, was he doing here beside her, with a physical ache that threatened to burst his tenuous control any second?

Only inches away, the subject of these ruminations shifted. Sighing, she turned her head. Her fingers brushed the sun-warmed stone.

As he stared down at her, Adrian felt a need too long suppressed explode to life.

Dear God, he had never expected, never imagined—

He caught his hand just as it rose to comb through her hair. To skim the perfect curve of her cheek.

*Stay clear!* he warned himself grimly, even while his fingers trembled at the effort. *Look, advise—assist, even. But she is not for you to touch. For, like the rose, she bears fierce thorns.*

*Even for a between-worlds creature like yourself.*

But still, he stared—and still, he dreamed, pondering the sleeping face before him, luminous in all its innocence and peace.

For a moment, regret clung to him, as raw as a winter wind. His eyes narrowed, dark with regret and a thousand shattered dreams. He shivered, feeling images that were too faint to be called memories press at his head.

But when he tried to seize them, they vanished like thistle-down on the wind.

At that moment Adrian's eyes fell to the sketch pad balanced precariously on Gray's knees. An odd, sad smile twisted his hard lips.

"So you love my abbey, don't you, Gray Mackenzie?" His voice was carried in the whisper of the wind, in the drone of the passing bees and the murmur of the moat.

Already he was fading. He could feel the telltale lightening, the not quite painful tingle at wrist and ankle.

Surely not so soon?

He lifted his head to the sun, closed his eyes and centered his thoughts.

Slowly the tingling faded. With a faint sigh, he knelt to study Gray's sketch more intently.

*You've come close, woman. Perhaps too close.*

Something about the sketch left him distinctly uncomfortable—naked and vulnerable. Perhaps it was because no one had ever before come so close to capturing the abbey's heart as she had just done.

And in a very real sense, Adrian Draycott knew that the abbey's heart was *his* heart.

*Yes, you're good, Gray Mackenzie. You're more than good.*

*Nearly as skillful as you are innocent and beautiful, in fact. But that stunning innocence of yours is deadly. Already, it captures me, entraps me, until I can think of nothing else but you.*

*Is that what you've come here for? To threaten every bloody thing I've ever loved and valued and fought to protect?*

Adrian expected no answer, of course. But as he studied the hot blaze of the sun in her hair, he had the raw certainty that the next hours would bring danger—and a testing such as he had never known before.

Yet even with that knowledge, he could not seem to pull his eyes away.

Catching himself with a muffled curse, Adrian forced himself to look away. As he did so, he saw Gray's rendering of the south tower. It was slightly off, he realized. The tower's curve should have been broader and the crenels deeper. The moat, too, was off, twisting to the right where it should have veered slightly toward the left...

A wrenching pain exploded up his spine. The day flashed like lightning before his eyes. He felt reality heave and twist, then slowly begin to fade.

Or perhaps to return.

It was all a question of perspective, after all.

Slowly he bent down, his face lined with pain as he struggled to finish one last task before his vision faded and the darkness reclaimed him.

Grimacing, he shoved the charcoal pencil into Gray's fingers, circled her hand and began to draw.

THE SUN POURED like warm honey onto Gray's closed eyelids. She swept a hair from her eyes and stretched dreamily.

Her eyes finally opened. She frowned, looking down and searching for her pencil. Everything was blurred, her head throbbing.

Too much sun, she thought, rubbing her stiff neck, feeling as if she'd been asleep for a hundred years.

Eight hundred years, more like.

Now where had *that* thought come from? she wondered. And then she froze, recalling the strange images she had seen across the moat. Wide-eyed, she studied the far bank, recalling her dream of the night before.

Chill darkness lit by a score of beacon fires.

Danger on every side.

She gasped. Could the two things be somehow related?

Her fingers tensed and a moment later, the charcoal pencil in her hand snapped cleanly in two.

Dear Lord, what was happening to her here? What was it about this beautiful, crazy place that affected her so?

A gust of wind eddied up from the moat and tugged at the corner of her sketch pad. Slowly the paper rose. Whispering softly, it fell open to her last sketch.

At least it *had* been her sketch. But no longer. Now it showed the mark of a stranger's powerful hand.

A shiver worked through Gray as she stared down into a landscape of dreams, captured in exquisite, inspired strokes such as she had never seen before in all her years of work and study.

At that moment, Gray realized she was looking down into a distant age and a world long gone. Into a valiant time, when the world rang to the cries of heroes and magic was commonplace. Each stroke captured the power of that distant era, suggesting but never quite revealing whence the magic sprung.

More dreams?

She shivered, studying the proud walls sketched upon the

paper. Wrought with strength, they were yet insubstantial, their edges softened and blurred. Like poured emotion, like feeling made tangible, they stood with all their textures dreamlike and hazy.

And at the same time stunningly real.

The sketch was utterly different from her own work, which was almost superrealistic. In fact, the sketch was totally unlike any work Gray had ever seen before.

And it was absolutely beautiful, almost alive somehow, a dream spun of charcoal, patience, and love. A love so strong that Gray could almost touch it.

Dazed, she studied the sketch, understanding none of it. And something told her the longer she stayed in this ancient place, the less she would understand it.

Then Gray saw the other sheet. A mere scrap, it had been torn from her sketch pad and tucked into the pocket of her flowered skirt. The charcoal lettering was as bold and restless as the sketch of the abbey.

She shivered as she read the two scrawled lines.

*Tonight at midnight. By the witch's pool.*

*If you dare.*

## CHAPTER FOUR

GRAY'S BREATH CAUGHT. Raw indignation swept over her.

But in its wake came a fierce, forbidden curiosity.

She wouldn't dream of going, of course. There could be no question of that. She had far too many other things on her mind to worry about an insolent caretaker with an attitude problem and a dislike for women who didn't know their place.

Which for him probably meant the kitchen or the bedroom.

At that thought her cheeks flared with furious color.

Muttering angrily, she slapped open a new page, determined to complete her quota of sketches before the best of the sunlight was gone.

Yet her fingers, as she smoothed down that last, odd sketch, were surprisingly gentle.

"WHERE IS THE WITCH'S POOL?"

To Gray's utter horror, the words burst from her lips the instant Marston finished pouring tea after dinner. Cursing silently, she glared down at her rose-strewn porcelain cup.

Horrified.

Infuriated.

But most of all gripped by curiosity as she waited for Marston's answer.

Abruptly, she shook her head, her cheeks aflame. "Never

mind. I can't imagine why—" Her fingers tensed on the base of her teacup. "It—it doesn't matter."

*Of course it didn't matter! She wasn't about to go anywhere tonight!*

"The witch's pool." Marston straightened slowly, his brow creased. "Ah, now there's a term I've not heard in years. Let me think." His expression grew distant. "Down on the far side of the moat, it is, Miss Gray. Spring-fed and surrounded by thick reeds. A strange place, sure enough. Water bubbles up crystal-clear there, warm all year round. The problem is that sometimes a swan gets caught beyond the reeds and can't get back out. I hear them crying there sometimes, in the silence of the night. Several times I've gone down to carry them back to the moat, but they never seem to want to go. The crazy things just struggle back as if they're searching for something."

The butler folded and refolded a damask napkin, his eyes fixed on the twilight shadows beyond the dining-room window. "Aye, it's a strange place, sure enough. Some say it's a haunted place. Legend has it that long ago a thane's wife, distraught and despondent after her husband's long absence, was found drowned there."

Gray swallowed. Suddenly she was finding it difficult to breathe.

Somewhere in the house a clock chimed seven o'clock. Marston studied her curiously. "But why were you asking, miss? You're not going to work down there, are you? I can't say as I'd advise that, for it's an odd sort of place. And what with the mist always drifting about, you could find yourself lost before you knew it."

*Lost?* Gray felt as if she were hopelessly lost already!

Somehow she managed a lopsided smile. "No, I won't be working down there, Marston. I was just…curious. Kacey must have mentioned the pool in one of her letters."

"I see. Will you have more tea?"

Gray shook her head. Speech was entirely beyond her. Dear God, what was happening to her in this strange place?

She started, realizing Marston was speaking to her again.

"…mousse. Or maybe some chocolate soufflé, if you'd prefer."

She shook her head, feeling panic wash over her. Dear God, she could feel all the old vulnerability, all the raw, choking helplessness creep over her again. Only now it was worse, because now she wondered if her very sanity was in question.

"…quite all right? Shall I call a doctor?"

Around her the air seemed to hum and shiver, light and sound swirling together in odd, churning waves. And with it came the fear, like cold fingers inching down her spine.

"No!" In a sharp burst of movement, Gray tossed down her napkin and jerked to her feet, her hands clenched to keep them from trembling. "No, everything was lovely, Marston. Thank you s-so much. I'm—I'm afraid I had a bit too much sun this afternoon, though. I'd better make an early night of it."

Once again the keen sideways glance, the slightly pursed lips. "Of course…" The kind voice drifted in and out of her hearing. "…hotter than you think, no doubt…better in the morning…good night's sleep."

But as Gray walked through the quiet courtyard and over the narrow stone bridge to the gatehouse, she had a sharp sense of purple shadows pressing close, menacing somehow.

And with them came an inexplicable sense of loneliness, of bitter regret and utter fatedness.

Almost as if the ancient abbey had been merely sleeping, merely waiting, guarding its dark secrets until the day she returned.


SHE WOULDN'T GO, of course.

Gray squared her shoulders.

She wasn't about to be goaded and manipulated. Not again. She had learned that lesson too well with Matt.

And the first thing she would do to prove it would be to rip up the note. Then, after a long hot bath, she'd go straight to sleep.

Ten minutes later, steam twisted around Gray's head. Lulled by the warm water, she shifted idly, stirring the crystal waters and watching mist rise in frothy white plumes.

For some reason the drifting shapes made her think of the moat, shimmering with heat beneath the noonday sun.

Glowing silver beneath the rising moon.

*At midnight.*

Jerking up with a start, Gray seized a bar of hand-milled lavender soap and scrubbed her arms with a ferocity that bordered on pain.

And still, the words lingered, haunting her.

*At midnight. By the witch's pool...*

"I won't go, do you hear?" Scowling, she rinsed off the white suds, wishing she could brush away the nagging voice with equal ease.

*If you dare.*

Muttering, Gray slid low in the heated water. Yes, let the bloody man wait in vain! She would just sit here and soak in sweet contented peace.

She stifled a yawn. Plumes of steam drifted up, twisted, enveloped her.

ONCE MORE THE BEACON FIRES *were lit.*

*The Lady of Draycotte watched numbly, clutching her shawl closer about her shoulders while the wind keened across the half-finished south tower.*

*Far below, dim laughter echoed up from the great hall, where her jailers sat to their ale, busy with belching and toasting.*

*If only Draycotte's lord would return! If only she could be wrapped in his strong arms once more, safe and secure.*

*But he did not come. And here she remained, a prisoner surrounded by vengeful, cold-eyed spies.*

*Without warning, the first pain came. Sudden and racking, it bent her over double, made her clutch blindly at her swollen belly.*

*No, it could not be! Not so soon.*

*But nature had different plans, it seemed. Another spasm ripped through her and she slid down along the granite wall, her lips locked against the pain.*

*Something was wrong, very wrong. The child was not due for almost a month yet!*

*Too late she remembered the broth they'd forced on her at dinner. It had tasted odd, heavy with herbs and something else that left a faint, metallic taste.*

Poison?

*Slowly she slid to her knees. A terrible roaring filled her head. Wildly she clutched at her middle, where already the first terrible convulsions had begun.*

*She had promised him she would wait! She* must *be waiting for him when he returned.*

*There by the silver-black glade when he came riding across the lush green Draycotte fields.*

*Tears wet her cheeks as she struggled to rise. Blindly, she felt for the wall's reassuring bulk, even as her head throbbed with the malignant fury of a thousand war drums.*

*And then, as if from a vast distance, she saw a blurring shadow detach from the ragged edge of the south tower.*

*"Dear God, is that you, my love? Are you c-come back to me at last?"*

*But the torchlight danced lower, playing over flat, sullen eyes. Over thin, cruel lips.*

*Not the man she wished to see at all.*

*"No!" she cried, inching back along the cold stone.*

*The sullen eyes tightened; hard lips curved to an ugly smile. And the man in the darkness was still smiling as the Lady Anne fell senseless to the parapet's cold granite floor.*

*Except that Anne was* not *her real name, not to those who knew her best.*

*Back in her native Brittany, where she'd spent twenty summers before being summoned to Draycotte, she was called Griza. Griza for the iron tones of the wintry seas she loved. Griza for her velvet eyes the color of a cooing dove.*

*Griza.*

*Gray.*

A BELL WAS CHIMING over the hills when Gray awoke.

She shook her head, fighting her way up through angry dreams, feeling the clutch of terror and something else she ought to remember but could not.

Wind rushed into the room playing through her unbound hair, sending steam up in ragged eddies. Goose bumps broke out on her chest, across her shoulders, along her neck, where it rose above the warm water.

*If you dare, Gray Mackenzie.* The words echoed through her head.

"Forget it! Just *forget* it!"

Scowling, she sloshed from the tub and wrenched a towel embroidered with intertwined dragons around her trembling body.

The room beyond was silent, just as it should have been. Yet when Gray looked at the great gilt mirror on the wall, she saw it wore a light haze of steam.

And there in the mist hung a faint mark.

The lush, perfect outline of a densely petaled rose.

And beneath it hung three words, traced by the same phantom hand.

*If you dare.*

# CHAPTER FIVE

FURY CRACKLED THROUGH HER.

In its raw showering force Gray felt the long years of denial and regret burn away. Never again would she hide or give way to her fear. She would go or not go, but it would be by *her* choice and no one else's!

"Oh, yes, I dare! I *dare,* do you hear?"

Damp towel clutched to her chest, she turned, searching for her robe, only to find it was no longer on the chair where she'd left it.

Muttering furiously, she stalked to the mahogany dresser across from the bed and flung open the top drawer.

Her eyes widened in disbelief.

She opened drawer after drawer, all with the same result.

Empty, absolutely empty. She hadn't a stitch of clothing left! "You loathsome, despicable—"

Only then did Gray notice that the French doors were open, their silken curtains fluttering in the breeze.

And the door of the heavy oaken armoire was also ajar. Grabbing a chair and holding it before her, Gray stalked closer.

"Come out, you miserable—"

The door creaked open.

But it was only a cat, slipping like a gray shadow across the polished floor.

White with rage, Gray pounded to the armoire and flung open its doors.

Inside hung a film of white lace.

Film was the only word to describe the gown's white froth, as thin and fine as thistledown.

Low-necked and long-sleeved it hung, cut of alençon lace so sheer it might have been worked of faery webs. And at the bodice, caught between lacings of silk ribbon, hung a perfect centifolia rose.

Without quite knowing why she did it, Gray ran her hands across the cloud-soft fabric, delighting in its exquisite textures. As she did, she had a sudden impression of a similar dress from an age long gone. A dress such as a great lady might have worn in the privacy of her chamber.

To entrance and delight the man she loved.

With a sigh, Gray closed her eyes, enveloped in a fantasy which quickly progressed to something more. Suddenly she was flooded with images so real that they verged on being memories.

Memories of hard hands that loosed a filigree girdle and slipped a line of lacing free. Memories of calloused fingers that eased a froth of white lace over restless, heated skin.

And then a woman's breath hissing out in a sigh while she ran her fingers over taut male flesh.

Gray froze.

Dear God, it was *her* breath she heard. *Her* fingers she felt!

White-faced, she stood before the armoire, her heart pounding at the savage force of the images exploding through her. And as Gray stared at the exquisite gown, she had a shattering vision of lovers from a distant age who met at midnight beneath a climbing rose.

Lace parted over flushed skin. There in the quiet of midnight two dreamers strained close, twining urgent limbs and restless fingers as they pledged a love that could not die or ever be forgotten.

A love to light the coldest night.

A love that would last beyond the bounds of time or space or hope itself.

With a choked cry Gray stumbled back from the armoire, staring at the white gown in shock and bewilderment. Her breath came wild and ragged as a thousand questions churned up inside her.

But there was only one way she would have any answers. That was at the witch's pool.

At midnight.

As THE MOON ROSE over the dark, wooded hills a car glided from the highway and slipped along the narrow graveled drive that led to Draycott Abbey.

It was a nondescript car, of no striking color or make. A car that moved slowly, careful not to invite attention or comment.

Just like its driver.

At the first turning the headlights dimmed. Carefully the car inched onto the grass and came to rest behind a copse of beech and oak.

Abruptly the twin beams disappeared. Darkness closed over the landscape once more.

Only now it was a restless, fitful thing.

A BOAT WAS WAITING for Gray at the edge of the moat.

The bloody man thought of everything, didn't he?

Frowning, she tugged her shawl about her shoulders, trying to cover the elegant wisp of lace that had been her only choice of clothing. But with every movement the sheer fabric clung and teased her skin, as light as a lover's fingers, making it impossible to forget the sensual images that had flooded over her earlier that night.

Images? Or were they memories?

Memories of herself and a man with slate-gray eyes? A man she barely knew and certainly did not like?

With fingers oddly unsteady, Gray untied the frayed rope and cast off in silence, feeling the night press wary and watchful around her.

Almost as if it were waiting.

Through the steam the boat glided, parting the strange shifting shapes that eddied upward as she passed.

It was like entering another world, Gray thought, a world resembling the normal world but not quite the same.

A world where magic lived and dreams were real.

In silence she glided on, the only sound the faint *splosh* of her pole. And then the far bank was before her, and with it the narrow reeded channel that led to the pool.

The witch's pool.

*At midnight. If you dare.*

Gray's lips tensed. Oh, yes, she dared! She only wished it hadn't taken her this long in her life to realize it.

As her foot touched the fern-soft shore, a bell began to chime, far away across the forested hills.

Twelve times it rang, and then once more.

Beyond a thick screen of reeds, Gray glimpsed the little glade that Marston had spoken of. And at its center, circled by yew, rowan and beech, heated water shone silver in the moonlight.

But glade and pool were empty.

Gray wasn't sure whether to be relieved or irritated by that fact. What was she *doing* here, anyway? Especially dressed in this wretched, ridiculous, *beautiful* dress!

She heard the step only an instant before he loomed up

beside her, dressed all in black with a soft shirt that clung to his broad shoulders.

For long, tense moments he did not move, his eyes probing her flushed face. "You came." And then, simply, "I'm…glad."

"Of c-course I came!" Gray snapped. "How could I ignore such diabolical messages?"

The next moment she bit back a cry. Looking down, she saw blood pool up on her fingers, where she clutched her forgotten rose.

*His* rose.

At her cry the wind seemed to swirl around her, shaking the rowan boughs and roiling the silver surface of the pool.

She heard him smother an oath. "You've hurt yourself." His voice was low, rough.

Pure heat. Just like the hands that circled her wrist a second later.

Before she could draw a ragged breath in protest, his lips covered her finger, tugging gently.

Gray shivered, fighting his sensory onslaught. But even as she struggled, she had a vision of his lips sliding higher, foraging hungrily over a thousand aching pleasure points.

"D-don't!" she cried, jerking free and stumbling away from him.

He did not seem to hear. His eyes glittered, lit with inner fires. Slowly his hand rose.

Gray flinched as she watched the rock-hard arm ascend.

Memories flooded over her, memories of Matt and all his twisted games, memories of the fear that she could never quite escape, even now.

With a shriek, wind gusted through the glade, sending dead leaves and fallen twigs skittering up in a dark circle. With the whirling wind came a chill so fierce that it caught at Gray's breath.

And in its wake came a raw, inchoate anger. A black regret. A savage, wordless longing.

Suddenly Gray saw that Adrian's hand was stayed, his fingers rigid. Her eyes widened as she realized they were trembling slightly.

"Don't move, Gray Mackenzie." His eyes narrowed, smoky with desire. Dark with unnameable secrets.

Very gently, he reached past her and plucked a great white moth from her hair. The pale wings fluttered against his long fingers, open and closed, open and closed. Then the insect sailed back into the darkness.

Adrian's face hardened. "Next time you might not be so lucky. Did my warning mean nothing to you?"

"I can take care of myself!"

"Can you?" One black brow rose to a commanding point. "Are you so sure of that, Gray Mackenzie?"

"Of course I am!" Gray glared up at his shadowed features.

"I only wish I could say the same." His voice was low, raw. "But when I'm near you as I am now, thinking is the very last thing on my mind."

Gray could only stare, her breath coming fast and jerky. A vein began to pulse at his forehead, and somehow she could not drag her eyes away from it.

She wondered what it would feel like to touch that tiny throbbing inch of skin, to ease her lips close and touch his ragged pulse. To tease a moan from his hard, chiseled lips.

Gasping, she forced down her unruly imagination and summoned up her anger instead. She pulled her shawl tighter across her lace-clad chest. "You broke into my room! You drew in my sketchbook!"

"How do you know it was I?"

For a moment, Gray faltered before his unblinking gaze. She

had no proof, of course. But outside of Marston who else was at the abbey?

"Did you view me at these infamies perhaps?"

"Of course I didn't. You're far too clever for that."

"Ah, if you thought that, you'd be right, Gray Mackenzie. But come, name me my other sins. On your lips…" Adrian's dark gaze fell to her trembling mouth. "On your lips, my sweet, they sound almost like virtues."

"I'm not your sweet!" Shoving her hands onto her hips, Gray called up her fury as armor against his caressing look. "And you—you took my clothes, you arrogant snake!"

Adrian's lips curved faintly. "They are merely hidden, I assure you. And that gown looks utterly ravishing, if I may say so."

"No, you may *not* say so! Who are you to leave me notes, to interrogate me? To meddle in my affairs?"

The dark eyes glittered. "Affairs? Now there's an interesting word."

Gray ignored his innuendo, ignored his mocking smile. Angrily, she seized a gossamer bit of lace at her hem. "And then you left me nothing to wear but this—this *thing!*"

"Beautiful, isn't it?" His voice was dark and smooth as the night. "Especially with you filling it, my love."

As he spoke, a breeze tugged softly at Gray's hair and brushed the fine lace until it clung to the aching swell of her breast and thigh.

So sweet. So soft. Like a lover's touch.

Would his hands feel just as good?

She shivered, fury forgotten as a new heat began to build inside her. A rich, insidious heat such as she hadn't known for years.

*For centuries?*

"I'm not your love! I'm not *your* anything!"

"Then why did you come?"

Gray's heart pounded wildly. "Because I had no choice. Not after all those sneaking messages you left me! And because I had something to tell you." With trembling fingers, she clutched at her shawl, trying to quell the creeping heat that grew stronger every second. "S-stay out of my room, do you hear? Stay out of my sketchbook! Most of all, stay out of my life!"

"What about your heart, Gray Mackenzie?"

Gray's breath caught at his dark, rough words. "What has my *heart* got to do with anything?"

The black-clad figure before her did not move. His eyes were all smoke and heat. Dark with an infinity of need, they roamed her face, missing nothing of her trembling response. "Everything, I should imagine. Because I want you, Gray Mackenzie. I want you very badly."

His voice dropped to a husky, intimate whisper. "And tonight, stubborn one, tonight I'm going to have you."

## CHAPTER SIX

GRAY BLINKED, SUDDENLY DIZZY. Suddenly hungry.

For things she could not even name.

She stumbled backward, her hands tensed atop her heaving chest. "You're—you're crazy, do you know that?"

"I've little doubt of it." Adrian took a step closer.

"Stay away from me."

His eyes glittered. He moved again.

"Stop it! You don't—you can't possibly be serious about this!"

"No? Why not, Gray Mackenzie?" His voice was dark, compelling. Utterly ruthless.

Gray tugged desperately at her shawl. "Because you—you just can't!"

"Why not?" he repeated, softly this time.

"Because—because you don't know me. Not the slightest thing about me."

He was close enough to touch her now, but he did not. He only stared down at her, his eyes dark with the hunger of hundreds of wasted years.

Thousands of lonely nights.

"I know you've a temper to match that glorious auburn hair of yours. I know you snore quite impudently when you sleep." He gave her the ghost of a smile. "Marriages have been built on less familiarity than that."

*Mine certainly was,* Gray thought bitterly.

"So enlighten me, if you will. Why can't I want you? Tell me all the reasons. Tell me that my pulse isn't racing painfully right now. And that yours isn't racing just the same," he added huskily.

Gray swallowed, fighting for control. "Because you—you just can't!"

His eyes never left her face, harsh with need and something else Gray couldn't quite make out. "Why? The truth, remember?"

Her face turned a shade paler, and the sight made Adrian curse silently. Had he any other choice, he would have left off then and there. But now, in this place and this time, he could not.

For time was the one thing Adrian Draycott did not have.

"Well?" His eyes were mocking. "Not turning faint-hearted on me, are you?"

Instantly her chin rose.

Ah, that had done it. Somehow he'd thought it would.

He arched a jet-black brow and waited.

His patience was soon rewarded.

"All right, damn you, I'll tell you why! I'll tell you *all* the ugly little reasons." With trembling fingers Gray flung the shawl from her shoulders, baring her slim, lace-clad form to his hungry gaze. "B-because I'm t-too tall. Because I'm all bones and sharp angles. Not soft. Not de-desirable at all. B-because touching me is the next best thing to t-taking an ice bath!"

With a wild cry she spun about, her arms locked rigid about her chest.

Adrian could only stare at her back, wordless, uncomprehending. Even then heat licked at his loins, made his gut tense and churn.

Bony? Ugly? Undesirable? What in the name of heaven was the crazed female talking about?

Abruptly his eyes narrowed. Sweet saints above, could she really believe—

His fingers clenched to fists. "Who told you such things? Who made you believe such lies?"

He heard her smother a soft sob.

"Does it matter?" Gray countered bitterly. "All that matters is it's true, every last word of it."

Adrian went perfectly still. He ached to seize her, ached to press her trembling body against his. Damn and blast, a minute or two would do it. One hot slide of lips and tongue, one slow foray over her unbound, pouting breasts and she'd be his!

But even as the realization hit him, Adrian fought it down.

He didn't want it that way, didn't want *her* that way.

For some unnameable reason he'd been called here, called back through space and time to find her. And he bloody well wasn't about to settle for anything less than knowing why— all the reasons why. And for every sweet inch of her, given to him willingly.

"Oh, it matters. Far more than you can imagine. And whoever told you such things was either an utter fool or a patent liar. Probably both."

Gray's fingers shook. "It's not business of yours! Why do you care about any of this?"

"Because you affect me, Gray Mackenzie. In ways I've never been affected before. And I intend to find out why."

"Oh, why don't you just go! It's—it's better this way, don't you see? *Safer.*" Gray brushed a furtive hand across her cheeks. Only then did Adrian see the glint of tears in her eyes.

The sight made him stiffen, made his innards twist to furious knots.

But he hid his anger well, knowing she would mistake its

cause. He took another step closer. "Better off *this* way? With you dead inside? Oh, well said, woman, except you've no notion of what you're talking about." His voice hardened. "You've no notion of—death, and you can thank God for it. For you, Gray Mackenzie, were meant to hum with life. To burn with passion."

"I *can't,* don't you see? Maybe I never could. Matt told me often enough that it was all my fault he—"

Adrian cut her off with a hoarse curse. "Enough! I'll hear no more of the bastard's name, nor of his lies. For lies are all they were, Gray!"

Gray's face was a mask of alabaster in the filtered moonlight. "I—I've tried to believe that. Dear God, don't you think I've tried?"

Adrian reached out slowly. "Then give me your hand, Gray Mackenzie. Give me your hand, and I'll give you answers in return."

She studied him warily, her chest rising and falling jerkily.

In the moonlight he could see the shadowed areolae strain against the fine lace at her chest.

Instantly he was on fire. Sweet Lord, he couldn't bear another aching second!

Somehow he managed to keep his face impassive. "If you truly want answers, that is. If you truly want to leave the past behind. The choice is yours."

Gray took a ragged breath. Her shoulders straightened. Without a word she raised her hand and put it in his.

White fingers fitted to hard bronze.

Perfect, Adrian thought, feeling that one light touch rock him all the way to his suddenly shaky knees.

Unimaginably perfect. Just as if they'd been made for each other.

He wondered if the rest of them would fit together so well.

But at that thought, a storm of erotic images rushed over him, shaking his resolve. He drowned in dreams of rose-tipped breasts, of restless, naked limbs, of dew-slick skin that eased apart to sheath him.

Endlessly.

He cleared his throat loudly. "Good. There, we've made a beginning." His thumb trailed slowly over her pounding pulse. He would have liked to think that pulse leaped with the same passion he felt. But Adrian knew her too well now, knew it was a darker emotion than desire that made her tremble. That thought helped him combat the angry need that roared and screamed and threatened to overrun its banks.

Impulsively, he raised her hand to his lips, permitting himself the luxury of a slow, hot slide across her palm, along her fragile wrist.

He carried her fingers to the open collar of his shirt, then lower until her hand rested over the warm skin where his heart hammered madly.

"There's a first answer for you." He stared at her, letting her see the heat in his eyes, the hard need that gripped him. "Does that feel like a man who's repulsed? A man who's had a—what did you call it?—a bloody ice bath?"

Her fingers flinched slightly, but did not draw back.

And what she did next stole Adrian's breath away.

Her fingers curved and slid gently through the crisp black hair at his chest.

At the simple gesture his eyes turned to smoke. His breath slid hoarse between his taut lips.

He didn't even try to hide the force of it. He wanted her to see, to know every single blessed thing she was doing to him.

He watched her eyes widen, watched a hundred different emotions war in her face.

"There it is, woman. Plain enough for even your doubting eyes, I should think."

Her surprise was all too obvious. Surprise, and then disbelief. But she was brave, this woman. Watching her lips clench, her eyes darken with determination, Adrian began to think she was the bravest person he knew.

And she didn't even know it.

He framed a silent prayer, knowing he was going to need every shred of patience and strength tonight. And Adrian Draycott had never been noted for his patience.

A second later, she inched closer, ran her hands gently over his rigid shoulders and cupped his face.

And then she drew him down to her.

He exploded like a Roman candle, halfway between heaven and hell by the time her lips settled as light as cobwebs against his own.

Sweet. Dear God, so unbelievably sweet. He was going to die grandly from that sweetness any second!

But when his hands rose to caress her neck, they were gentle, as tentative as her kiss.

Even at that, she shivered, pulled away. Her wide eyes locked upon his face. "Did you—did that—"

"I did and it was," he said hoarsely.

Her face flushed crimson.

"Ah, God, don't blush, woman. Every time you do it sets me off, and I'm near to dead already. Sweet Lord, have mercy on a poor, defenseless male!"

Instantly Gray's face flamed brighter, but Adrian hadn't missed the faint smile that tugged at her lips.

He groaned softly, burying his fingers in her hair.

"Did you really? Like it, that is? Just—a little?" Her voice was as soft as the night breeze. But Adrian wanted to shout with triumph when he heard it, to crush her close.

Instead he merely crooked one sable brow. "No." And then as her beautiful forehead furrowed, "Not just a little, stubborn one. Endlessly, unimaginably more than *just a little*. In fact, the way I want you right now is causing me mortal, racking pain!"

Gray's eyes narrowed thoughtfully. She caught her lip between straight white teeth.

Dear God, what torture had the woman in mind for him next?

It had been two hundred years, after all, since he'd last felt such things! But of course, she couldn't know that, Adrian reminded himself wryly.

Absently, she slid the tip of her tongue across her lip. Adrian smothered a raw curse at the sight.

"Did—did you say something?"

"Who, me?"

Reassured, she turned back to her contemplation of his mouth.

At her slow scrutiny Adrian felt his manhood throb painfully. Closing his eyes he began a rather desperate cataloging of some of the finer paintings in the abbey's collection.

Two Turners.

The Whistler, of course.

A few middling sketches by da Vinci.

An indifferent Constable.

A rather masterful portrait of the Tenth Viscount by Sargent.

And of course, he mustn't overlook that one thoroughly forgettable canvas by—

Adrian was jerked back to agonizing reality as her lips slid wetly down his neck and caressed his suddenly bared chest. "What in the name of all the saints—"

He got no further. His breath exploded and his pulse went wild as her lips circled, then closed softly over his nipple.

A groan tore from his lips. His hands went utterly still against her neck. The pleasure was unbearable, unspeakable.

And all that he'd ever expected heaven to be.

In a fraction of a second, he was gone, six feet under, toes cocked, drowning in sensation. He shuddered, feeling her soft fingers at his shoulders, her sweet breath playing over his chest.

Most of all, he felt the wild, erotic slide of her lips, gentle and tentative with discovery.

He started to speak, and found to his fury that he had to clear his throat. "I think—yes, I really think that that's enough, my dear."

His fingers tensed in her silky hair. He was perilously close to the edge, Adrian realized.

But she did not cease. Her tongue slid back and forth across his taut skin.

"Gray—stop." He grimaced as her teeth brushed the aching nub of his sensation. *"Now."*

Something in his voice penetrated her haze. She pulled back, eyes dazed, breath ragged. "Did I—is something wrong?"

Adrian managed a raw laugh. *"Wrong?* On the contrary, my heart. Something's far too right—and that's what is wrong."

"Well, then—why can't I—"

"Because, my sweet, dim-witted, splendid little fool, there are *two* of us here, in case you've forgotten. And if you keep doing such wildly abandoned things to me, *one* of that pair is going to lose his head and bury himself inside you until we both go over the edge."

Adrian tensed as soon as he'd said the words, certain she would flinch and retreat from him.

But wondrously, miraculously, she did not. Instead her eyes narrowed thoughtfully. "It's…really true then." Her glorious lips curved gently.

The sight was like pure sunlight poured into all the dark corners of Adrian's ancient, embittered heart. If he had nothing else, it would still be worth all the pain, all the frustration just to know the sight of that one soft, sweet smile.

"But now, I really think it's time you had a taste of your own medicine, temptress." His eyes glittered with a hint of wickedness.

Gray pursed her lips. "Oh, no, I don't think—I never planned—"

Adrian groaned inwardly. He had his work cut out for him, that was certain.

He took a measured step forward—and watched her take one back. "Fair is fair, woman. You must realize that." He took another step.

She retreated in turn.

"Afraid, my stormy one? I can hardly believe it." He moved again.

She countered with another step of retreat.

"There's nothing to fear, I assure you."

She retreated once more, but the movement was slower this time, indecisive.

Adrian's smile grew to a wolfish grin as he watched her back right into the gnarled trunk of a rowan tree.

He didn't give her time to think, time to run. He lodged his hands beside her head and eased his hard body close, his lips pressed against her trembling mouth.

Heaven fell. The sky sang. Light, time and matter dissolved into dreams.

But no dream could taste as good as she did.

And then her lips opened and Adrian groaned, catapulted into a whole new universe of sensation.

"Gray," he murmured. "Can you feel it now? Can you feel how much I want you?"

He felt her lips curve beneath him in answer.

Emboldened by that gesture, he drove his tongue deeper, seeking out the secrets of her mouth.

When he felt her fingers clutch at his shoulders, felt her tongue slide softly against his, Adrian thought he would howl from utter pain and perfect pleasure.

And then—only joy. Only wanton, breathless discovery.

Only Gray.

He knew it would be enough to last him forever.

But it wasn't, Adrian soon discovered, enough for her.

Her fingers curved, insistent at his shoulders. Her hips moved gently against his rigid thighs.

And her tongue, dear God, her tongue was doing *carnal* things, forbidden things, indescribable things.

Things that Adrian Draycott, profligate though he'd always been, hedonist and confirmed cynic, had never even dreamed existed.

And had certainly never expected to feel. Not two hundred years dead as he was.

A moment later, his lips closed around her restless tongue. Somehow his fingers were unlacing her bodice, exploring the exquisite curve of her breasts, his nails grazing the pebbled nipples that strained upward beneath the flimsy lace.

"Gray…sweeting…you're heaven itself…" Heat raced through him white-hot, blinding.

Unimaginable.

It left Adrian stunned, breathless, shaking.

Maybe that was why he didn't hear her moan, didn't feel her tense against him until it was too late.

But her soft, breathless cries were unmistakable in the ragged silence, as was the tension that suddenly gripped her slender frame.

Her eyes widened. She cried out against him, passion cresting through her.

Adrian caught her close, smiling as he felt the first velvet tremor rip through her. Her suddenly locked fingers and shuddering body told him everything he needed to know.

And he gloried in every tremor, in every soft gasp. Sweet Lord, the woman was nothing short of magnificent!

Shifting slightly, he captured her between his braced thighs. With a delicate movement he triggered her sensory storm anew, sending her arching wildly against him.

And he caught each moan, each breathless, shuddering sigh against his lips, cherishing every one.

Without warning, her fingers tensed. With a wild cry Gray stumbled sideways, a trembling hand locked to her mouth, her eyes hazy with unshed tears. "N-no! I don't want—I never wanted—"

And then she was gone, her gown a spiral of moonlight against the soft, dark grass.

## CHAPTER SEVEN

She turned and ran, her heart hammering painfully.

What had she done? How had this man broken down all her defenses? It was inconceivable. Sheer madness!

Branches ripped at her hem, vines caught at her feet, but still, Gray stumbled forward, blind to everything but her pain and shame.

*How?* How could she have let such a thing happen?

She stumbled, her foot catching on an unseen vine. With a wild cry she pitched forward. Her head struck stone with a dull, sickening thud.

But Gray barely noticed the pain. Not the pain in her head, at least. For at that moment, Gray Mackenzie, *née* Moira Jamieson, was beyond feeling little things like contusions or fractures. It was the pain in her heart that tore her apart and sent hot tears spilling down her cheeks.

Dear God, how *could* she have?

She shuddered, still reeling from the sensual explosion she'd just experienced, from the unforgivable bliss she'd just discovered in the arms of a stranger.

When his strong hands circled her shoulders, she flinched and wildly shoved them away. "G-go away!"

Adrian ducked to avoid her flailing arms. "Contain yourself, woman. It's hardly worth such a fuss."

"It is! I h-hate you!"

"Very well, but must you—ah—struggle so while you do it?" Sharp nails whipped past Adrian's cheek, and he growled a graphic oath.

Gray was beyond hearing, nearly beyond reason. "You see—how soon it begins? But I don't want it, do you hear? Not this cursed thing you call love. This raw, bleeding wound that never heals. I don't want to *feel* again, not ever. There's just too damned much pain in it!"

Adrian ducked again. "Sometimes, just sometimes, it's the pain that lets you know you're alive."

Gray wiggled furiously. "Never! You'll never set a hand—not the slightest finger—on me again, do you hear?"

He caught her grimly, hauled her up struggling into his arms. "Stop fighting me! You head needs tending, you intractable harridan. And—by God, you're bleeding!"

"What are you— Where in the—"

"Enough arguing, woman!" He strode over the dark, soft grass until he came to the far side of the pool. There Adrian settled her gently in the ferns, then dipped his fingers into the water and caught up a palmful of moonlight, which he trickled carefully over her bleeding forehead.

It was not a deep gash, but it would pain her when the shock wore off. Grimly, he tugged at a handful of fragrant grass, then brushed away the last traces of blood.

"Better?"

Gray shivered, catching the fragrance of verbena and mint leaves crushed in his fingers.

"W-why?" she stammered. "Why do you care? Just let me go. I—I don't know how much more I can take." It was an admission given shudderingly, at great cost.

Adrian heard how much the admission pained her, and the knowledge filled him with fury for the man who had left her so vulnerable. But he gave no sign of his inner rage. His hands simply continued to move, gentle at their task. "I don't know why, sweeting. But I do know this. I could no more let you go than I could cease to breathe. For you're in my blood now, Gray Mackenzie, part of my very soul. And you're not leaving here until you accept that."

She shoved unsteadily at his fingers. "I don't want this, do you hear? I never wanted it!"

"It's too late for that. Too late for running. Too late for wishing things were different. What's done is done. And the sight of your sweet, shocked passion was the most beautiful thing I ever hope to see." His voice hardened, as fierce and angry as Gray had ever heard it. "So don't bloody try to twist it into something dirty and contemptible—for that it never could be."

Gray wanted to scream, wanted to shout that he was wrong. But the barely leashed hunger in his eyes held her silent, made her dream it might be so, just for a second or two.

And damn him, he noticed—noticed the exact instant she hesitated. At that very second his patient nursing turned to raw, premeditated seduction.

His fingers slid into her hair. His thigh wedged against her hip.

"No, damn you! I won't…" But her voice was husky.

"You want it, Gray. Let me give it to you. Dear God, this one thing at least I can give you."

She fought it. Oh, God, how hard she fought it. But he was part of the night, part of her dreams, part of the soft scent of mint and verbena.

Part of *her.*

And it had all begun with that damned, beautiful dress he'd left entwined with a perfect blood-red rose.

It was unfair, totally unfair! Everything conspired against her, even her own traitorous body.

"Don't touch me."

His hands curved gently, anchoring her neck.

"Don't bloody touch me."

He eased closer, his need an unbearable seduction.

"I'm going back now. Don't try to stop me."

He didn't believe her bluff for a second. "Why can't you admit it, sweeting? Admit you're already half in love with this place. I saw it in that sketch you did today. And if you love my abbey, then you're halfway to loving me."

"Do you have answers for *everything?*" A reckless instinct drove Gray to attack. Anything to avoid facing the truth of what he said.

And the pain of decision.

"And you, sweet harridan, do *you* have nothing but questions?"

A distant peal drifted over the hills, faint and crystalline. The sound was ethereal, otherworldly.

Achingly sad.

Adrian sighed. "I've one answer, at least." Before she could pull away, his head slanted down. His lips skimmed over hers. Slowly his hands moved lower, molding her rigid shoulders. "Gray. Gray…" His mouth played over her, hot and light. "Sweet Gray. Soft Gray. Beautiful, stubborn Gray."

The first touch sent sparks shooting through her. Suddenly she was finding it hard to breathe.

Adrian raised his head, his expression unreadable. "You wear my rose. It dims before your beauty." His hands tightened. Gray could have sworn they were trembling.

And that slight sign of vulnerability shook her as nothing else had. She felt the hard walls around her heart heave, shudder and finally crack.

*Heat.* She had never felt, never imagined such heat.

Such yearning, blind and sweet…

Without knowing quite how or why, she was lifting her face to his, flowing into the wine-dark beauty of his kiss.

"Dear God, Gray—" He caught her close, his breath ragged at her cheek. "Let me touch you. It's…you can't understand, but this is the only bloody thing I have left to give you."

At his words, at the slow glide of his hands across her chest, Gray shuddered. Dark images spiraled through her, images that she sensed were something more. *Memories,* they were, welling up from some long-forgotten part of her.

Just as the parade of ghostly figures she'd seen by the moat had been memories, not daydreams.

Suddenly Gray knew she wanted this man in any way she could have him. She wanted him fast and mindless, reckless and blinding.

She wanted him slow and hard and endlessly patient…

She even wanted him angry and unrepentant. Slaking the heat of a body too long denied. For that, too, was part of him, just as it was part of her. A part of her she'd tried too long to ignore.

Like her drawing, the only question was where she was going to start.

Her eyes began to glisten, to shimmer in the moonlight. It was madness. It was rankest folly. But somehow Gray didn't care. She cast logic to the farthest winds.

Her lips met the hard angle of his jaw, and she felt him shudder, heard him groan.

Danger. Bliss. Endless wanting…

"See what you do to me. Do I act like a man repelled, uninterested? Dear God, were I any *more* attracted, I'd…"

Gray smiled softly, staring at the moonbeams dancing over his face and neck.

And then she touched him. His chest was hot beneath her

fingers. She could feel the racing pulse at his neck, as wild as her own.

And in that instant Gray knew for certain that nothing else mattered, not the fear, not the regret.

He gave her a crooked and utterly devastating smile. "Well? So bad as that? It's been a while for me, but—"

"Rather—too right, I think." Her fingers slid to his shirt. The last two buttons sprang free.

Adrian's breath caught. "Gray. Sweeting. You really don't have to—"

Thoughtfully Gray continued. She spread the soft dark fabric and eased it from his shoulders, while moonlight spilled across them.

Her eyes darkened, locked on the broad, muscled torso revealed beneath his shirt. A wild churning invaded her blood and sent her pulse tripping double-time.

Her hands went absolutely still, poised just above his waist.

Not a sound, not the slightest motion came from Adrian's rigid body.

Slowly Gray looked up. In his dark eyes, she saw something she'd never expected to see.

Honor. Perfect candor.

The look said he wouldn't push her, even now. It was all up to her.

And suddenly, as Gray stared into his eyes, she saw other images, felt a bewildering flood of sound and color and emotion.

Of *memory*.

Memories of a steel-clad warrior who sat a pawing charger, pennants flying as he raced against the wind into battle. Memories of a wheeling falcon that screamed, then shot low to perch on a mail-covered arm.

And then Gray herself, long hair unbound as she waited and

watched for a warrior long from home, fighting at Richard's side for ideals as inchoate and shifting as the desert sands where he watched his comrades fall, one by one.

Week after week she had waited, month after month. Until seasons changed and months stretched into years.

And still, he had not come.

True, she thought blindly, her eyes blurred with tears. All of it true. The sensations were too tangible, too intensely *real* to be an illusion.

And somehow in his raw, sensitized state Adrian read the same images, images he had never seen before.

Images that were memories for him, as well.

He went utterly still. "Good, sweet God Almighty. It—it cannot be." The realization left him reeling. "You—you were there. We—" A groan rocked through him.

Gray touched his chest gently, understanding exactly what he was feeling. "All that sadness…now I think I understand. All those long years…" She brushed furtively at her cheeks, looking back down dark, twisting corridors of time to another woman who'd lain against the soft green grass, shedding tears for the man who was beside her now.

"Eight hundred years…" Adrian's voice was raw. "It's too long, far too long to grieve, sweeting." He touched her cheek, cursing when he felt the telltale moisture touch his fingers. "What a fool I was. And all from pride, I can see that now. It's always been my damnable pride that's led me astray. But you, my sweet—how could I have let *you* bear the price of it?"

Adrian caught her cheeks and raised her face to him. "When I came back—they said you'd drowned by the pool." His gaze was fierce, as if he were awaiting a killing blow. "It was a lie, wasn't it?"

Gray shivered in his arms as bleak memories poured over

her. And suddenly she was powerless to hold back the tears, to hold back the years.

She could only nod silently, while tears ran silver down her cheeks.

Adrian's fingers dug into her shoulders. With a groan he crushed her close, so close that Gray could feel the anger rack him.

"Lies…all lies. Dear God, what was it? They didn't—sweet Lord, I couldn't bear it if they hurt you—"

Gray swallowed. "No, not that. It—it was poison, I think. I remember the first pains, the convulsions. And after that, nothing, just darkness. They must have made up that other story about the drowning to protect themselves."

Adrian's head slanted down until his forehead rested against the top of her head. "I always wondered…it never made sense to me…"

Gray felt the shudder that rocked him then, felt the hot salty rain of tears that fell against her hair and slid onto her neck. "Don't, Adrian," she whispered. "Please—don't."

"*Don't?* Dear God, you *died* because of me! I might just as well have signed the death warrant myself! I should have known what would happen if I left you here, unprotected."

Her hands sank into his hair, holding him close. "It…it doesn't matter. Not now. All that matters is that we're here again. That we're together."

"It *does* matter! I betrayed you! And when I finally did return, I was stupid enough to believe you'd forgotten. I even began to think it might have happened just as they'd told me. That you'd lost your reason, snapped—"

"Hush." Gray silenced him with a fierce kiss. She felt him tense, felt him strain against her. "It's—it's over, Adrian. Done and gone for eight centuries now. Just…just love me. Give me your joy and…yes, your pride. The way it should have been all those years ago."

She moved her open lips over his, hungry, searching.

*Remembering…*

Dear God, she remembered all of it now. All the pain and joy of those few sweet months they'd had together.

And the force of those memories nearly snapped her heart in two.

"Love me, Adrian," she whispered. "*Now.* Let me feel what it should have been then. I've waited so long…"

He cut her off with a raw groan, arching her back against him as his mouth spread hers to receive his hot invasion.

Suddenly pain and sadness were gone. All that was left was the joy and the hot sweetness of homecoming.

Now neither minded that it had come eight centuries too late.

Gray slowly combed her fingers through the long black hair at Adrian's shoulder. "It's—it's all still here, isn't it? You and I…all we felt. Dear God, it never ends, does it? It only changes. Only grows…"

Adrian's eyes glittered. "And trust? What of that, my heart? Have the ages dimmed your trust? Have my pride and stupidity lost me the only thing I truly need?" His voice fell to a hoarse whisper. "I can see how very much I hurt you then."

Gray touched his cheek gently. "Whatever you did, I've long since forgiven you for."

Adrian's breath slid free in a hiss. "Gray—sweeting, how long I've waited, wanted…" His voice caught, low and raw. "I swear, it will be magic. One night full of sweet, silver magic."

Her head fell back as his lips worked dizzying patterns along her neck, her shoulder, her collarbone. She shivered, opening to his touch, flowering like the perfect petals of the centifolia rose he swept against her skin.

Like the love-mark she carried on her cheek.

"A-Adrian?" She shifted restlessly as heat swirled through her. Until her heart was full enough to break.

"Soon," he whispered, coaxing a moan from her as his lips worshipped the pale swell of her breast, eased from beneath her lacy gown.

Gray shuddered as she felt his lips close around the velvet bud of her nipple. Her fingers tensed, buried deep in his dark hair, holding him close while pleasure unfolded inside her, petal by exquisite petal.

On and on the pleasure grew. On and on his mouth coaxed, circled, never giving her time to think, to prepare for the next drugging onslaught of ecstasy. She felt the mist cling to her face, felt the air shimmer, supercharged with the raw fury of their primal need.

Slowly, powerfully, he laid her back against the grass and eased the wisp of lace from her skin. And then for long moments, Adrian did nothing but look at her. He memorized the pale supple beauty of her body, the dusky seduction of her pebbled nipples and the auburn curls at her thighs.

The wind sighed. The damp ferns whispered.

Then with a harsh groan he found her silken heat and brought their long years of separation to a breathless end.

"A-Adrian—"

"Hush, woman. I've years—*centuries* to make up for."

"But I—"

Gray gasped as he tongued a path of fire across her belly and teased the auburn triangle just below. "Adrian, I don't— You can't—"

And then only raw pleasure, only burning silver joy as he bared her and gave her all the sweetness of his soul. She arched mindlessly, drowning in unimaginable pleasure.

He caught her close, whispering hot love words on her hungry skin. "Open to me, my love. Open to me while I touch you, taste you. Ah, God, I've heat enough to sweep away all the fear, all the darkness."

And then no more words. Only the sweet, sleek parting of skin. Only the restless, velvet probing.

And with each movement, Gray opened farther, fell deeper. Light drifted around them, cast off the gleaming currents, little flashes and pinpoints of energy that danced over their hot, urgent skin.

And always the roses, filling the air with sweetness, with rich, ineffable memories of all the other times they'd strained and yearned and loved this way.

Like a circle never broken. A circle ever widening, forged of joy and tears.

A circle that never died, only grew brighter and expanded.

Gray felt herself bud, felt her heart open in splendor as she reached to catch every perfect, silver ray. "Adrian!"

The night flashed before her, light poured in radiant columns before her eyes. And then she was falling, down through heaven, down through time, down through dark, forgotten centuries until she once again rested on the damp soil, with his hard, beloved body there to protect her.

Fierce and hungry, his eyes searched her face. "God, how I love you, woman. When I think of all those years…all those bloody wasted years—"

Gray pressed upward and cut him off. Her hips shifted, searching for his heat, yearning to feel him drive deep inside her.

An odd glimmer rose from their heated skin and hung like a veil of bright mist across the glade. Fury raged between them, an equal thing now, a wild flow of male might and pliant velvet strength as Gray moved to meet him, sheathe him, welcome him.

With his first hot thrust she gasped, feeling the sheer size and force of him.

Swiftly, he drove home, filling her in one fierce, perfect slide. Then slowly he drew back, prolonging her exquisite pleasure until she cried out in breathless abandon.

Adrian threw back his head, shuddering. His eyes closed as passion swirled between them. "Dear God, *again,* Gray. Flower for me once more. Flower around me—give me all your sweetness, for it's my only home, the only home I'll ever know!"

Gray's heart lurched and took flight.

And when it did, she found his waiting.

Dimly, she felt his thighs lock, felt tension grip his powerful, braced forearms.

And realized, even now, he denied himself for fear of hurting her.

She slid her feet over his clenched calves, smiling when she felt him shudder.

"No, by all the saints! I'll not be gainsaid, woman. Our first time will be *my* way—"

But Adrian Draycott, lord of ten thousand men, sovereign power of Draycott Abbey and all its lands, had not counted on the willfulness of a single, stubborn, twentieth-century female.

His eyes blazed as he fought her pull, fought her knowing movements. Velvet muscles rippled and then closed around the part of him buried deep inside her.

He gasped and was lost. "Gray! Sweet God, Gray, don't! I can't—"

"Then *don't.* Oh, God, don't wait!"

At the first savage, unbridled thrust, Gray realized just how much he'd been holding back. Even then, she welcomed his hot, crushing possession, her thighs locked to his as she rose and caught his shoulder, planting a love-mark of her own against his skin.

With a roar Adrian dragged her close, then twisted them together until she sprawled atop his chest.

His eyes shone black as he caught her straining hips and guided her down to meet each silken thrust. Gray shuddered, feeling his fingers shift, driving her to blindness, to frenzy.

To heaven.

"Again, love." His voice was dark, raw, a seduction in itself. *"Again."*

She shattered against him, blood thundering, breath flown, mind and body aflame in the dark, lush night.

His laughter broke over her in soft waves amid the violence of her release. Amid the breathless churning storm where he carried her.

Just as her tremors reached their peak and began to fade, he raised her high and pulled her down once more, groaning when he felt her clutch his hot, aching flesh anew.

In joyous abandon he filled her, again and again, while her soul leaped free and his own joined hers, two comets flaming through the star-flung sky.

"A-Adrian! Oh, I can't—it's too—"

"Here, love. I'm right here. Ah, God, so sweet you are— Take me with you, Gray. Take me now!"

He gripped her tensely, head thrown back as pleasure found its stunning climax, as the softness of moss and ferns cushioned their wild, driving movements.

Together they spun and tumbled through boundless space, watching stars flash past, hearing the darkness sing around them.

Home again at last. Together. Just where they were always meant to be.

And neither time nor fate, Adrian swore, would ever separate them again.

# CHAPTER EIGHT

SOFT AND DARK, HIS LAUGHTER welcomed her back, cushioned her fall into flesh and weight and earthbound gravity. Gray opened her eyes.

"Adrian, I—"

But before the first doubts could intrude, before the first fears could rear their ugly heads, he pulled her beneath him and loosed the joy anew.

Silver ripples of pleasure lapped and surged and broke over Gray's exquisitely sensitized body.

"A-again?" She shivered, her eyes smoky, dazed, luminous with love and inquiry. "You—you can't!"

Smiling darkly, he brushed the crown of one upswept, silken breast, delighting in her instant tremor of response. "Eight hundred years is a long time to wait, sweeting. I'm afraid you'll have to forgive my intemperance…"

Fire burst from the dusky crest where his clever lips foraged and suckled. "Forgive?" Gray shuddered, arching mindlessly as the wild pleasure grew. "Sweet heaven, for *th-this?*"

His laughter rumbled over the glade and suddenly it was as if night had fled and light gleamed silver over vine and bough and wave. It was the same world, the same night, Gray thought dimly, and yet both were entirely different now.

Somewhere in the dark woods beyond the glade, distant bells began to peal, low and faint.

Adrian stiffened, flinging back his head, feeling the first raw pangs of despair.

*No! Not so soon!*

"Not yet," Adrian breathed hoarsely, struggling to hold back the transformation. "Not bloody yet…"

But already he felt it. Even without looking, he knew his body had the faint glow that signaled the coming change.

*No, not yet! By heaven and all the saints, it was too soon!*

He shuddered, clenching his hands and holding her close, letting the sweet tide of her passion wash over him. He watched her gasp, felt her long legs wrap around him as she rode down into ecstasy.

"Ah, Gray, so good…" He caught a strand of hair and eased it from her cheek, drinking in the beauty of her wild response.

And then Adrian saw his fingers begin to gleam where bone and tendon shifted and strained.

*More time. Please—just a little more time.*

But words would change nothing. The high clear music was in his ears, resonating through his shifting body.

Calling him home.

*No!* he screamed in desperate silence. *This is home. Where she is will always be my home!*

The tones sharpened, vibration turning to a low thunder.

And as Adrian stared down at Gray's beautiful features, he saw his hand begin to glow, saw right through his skin to the rapidly fading outline of his bone.

Sweat dripped from his brow. He caught her fiercely, drinking in her last, breathless cries, memorizing the rhythm of her wild tremors.

Desperately, he fought the call, strained to hold his slipping atoms tight-packed, dense, earthbound.

But it was impossible. The ringing grew, plunging into his blood, turning liquid into shimmering networks of light.

"Gray—" His voice was raw. "Gray, I—must go."

She only shivered, tightening her grip on his shoulders.

Gritting his teeth, Adrian pulled from her sweet heat, struggling against the transformation that threatened to come any second. "You—you, too, must go, sweeting. There is danger growing, and I want you safe until it's over."

At that, her eyes finally opened, dark with sated passion.

And then those azure eyes widened. Gray tensed, seeing the light that gleamed over Adrian's face and chest and shoulders. Wildly, she reached out for him, only to stare disbelievingly as her fingers slid right through the shimmering mass that only seconds before had been his arm and chest.

*"N-no!"* It was a ragged cry of shock.

Grim-faced, Adrian fell to his knees beside her. By a savage force of will, he drove the blinding radiance back to a dim phosphorescence. "I—love you, Gray Mackenzie. Never—never doubt that. And by all the heavens above, I'll—come back to you. This…I swear."

Gray stifled a sob, pressing her fingers to her mouth as she watched him sway and waver before her. "You can't be—dear God, this can't be real!"

But it was. Even the brightness of his body was fading. She could see a glowing outline at his shoulders and head.

"The…the boat's moored by the far bank." His voice was barely a whisper now. "Gideon…waiting…"

"Adrian! No, don't go!" Gray's trembling hands locked across her chest as she watched him shimmer, then swirl apart into waves of purest light.

For a moment, his eyes darkened, fixed on her terrified face. "Wait for me," he whispered. "I'll—*find*—you…"

And then he simply blinked out, like a candle caught in a wayward gust of wind. Where bone and flesh had once stood, haloed in light, there were now only leaden shadows.

Gray stumbled to her feet, staring blindly at the dark, empty ground where moments before Adrian had stood. "It's just a trick! You—you're just trying to frighten me! Aren't you, Adrian? Tell me, damn you!"

But no voice rose in answer. The glade was silent, chill, all light fled.

And somewhere, far away in the distance, Gray heard the faint peal of bells.

BLINDLY, SHE STUMBLED to her feet and crossed the moss-covered bank, her shawl clutched to her chest. Through a blur of tears she made out Gideon's dark form, waiting for her beside the little boat.

For a moment, hysteria surged up through her. *It was all a dream, wasn't it? Or some great, elaborate joke?*

But the faint soreness at her thighs told her that the night had been far more than a heated fantasy. She would have to begin to face that—along with all the rest of the night's discoveries.

*Including the fact that the man you love is the ghost of Draycott Abbey?* Gray bit back a hysterical laugh.

Where had it gone, all the magic and splendor? Now the night was cold and all her dreams had fled.

Glittering amber eyes stared up as Gray tugged at the pole and stumbled into the shallow boat. Scrubbing at her tears, she glared at the regal gray form on the bank. "Well, are you coming or not? If I can t-talk to ghosts, I suppose I can talk to a cat!"

The long gray tail arched and twitched. Gideon's sleek head turned, staring off into the restless, rustling woods beyond the glade, where Adrian had vanished moments before.

The cat gave a long, low cry.

Only silence met him, along with the faint hiss of the wind.

A moment later Gideon turned and jumped into the boat, his black paws clearing the wooden side effortlessly.

Shivering, Gray turned and shoved off.

"There's something about you, my friend. Something that's less—and a great deal more—than I've ever seen in any other cat."

Gray shook her head and turned to focus on the lapping waters. Mist dragged at the boat in spiraling fingers, denser now that the night air had grown colder. At the center of the moat Gray slowed her movements, barely able to see through the swirling bank of mist.

At her feet, Gideon meowed, gliding up to a perch on the wooden seat as he stared out into the drifting whiteness.

And then they were through the worst of it, only yards from shore."

"There, that wasn't so bad. I only wish I could feel the same about all the other bizarre things I've seen tonight," Gray muttered, clutching her shawl closer about her shoulders.

Slowly she poled to the bank, studying the French doors beyond the terrace.

They were open.

Fear worked up her neck. She would have sworn she'd left them closed.

Her hands clenched on the worn wooden pole as the boat hissed to a halt in the mud and sand at the bank. Gray stared up at the gleaming glass panes, feeling panic well up inside her.

And the fear was with her again, as blind and wrenching as it had been *then*, when she first realized Matt was trying to kill her. Because she knew too much.

A dark shape glided up the bank, and Gray realized that Gideon was making for the open door.

"Gideon, come back!"

She heard the faint *whoosh* of a curtain, then nothing but

silence. She tried to move, and felt the fear seize her, hold her helpless, paralyzed.

But because she had to prove that she was not the same woman she had been, that she had learned to conquer her fear, Gray flung down her pole, jumped to the bank and plunged up to the gatehouse.

The chill darkness hit her like a fist. Nothing moved in the shadows. "Gideon?"

She moved forward blindly, hands outstretched.

Her knee grazed the leg of a chair. Frowning, she turned toward the wall. There was a mustiness to the room that hadn't been there before, along with a faint, acrid sweetness.

Her neck prickled with fear.

Her hand met the silk-covered wall. She found the welcome outline of the light switch and flipped it down.

The first thing she saw was Gideon, tense as an Egyptian marble statue, hissing softly as he stared at the door of the bathroom. His head cocked; his tail arched.

Slowly, as if in as dream, Gray moved forward.

And then she froze, seized by horror that drove the breath from her lungs.

The dead bird lay on the floor of the bathroom, its dark feathers matted with blood. And on the wall above was scrawled a warning, traced in blood.

*Silly, stupid bitch. Did you really think you could escape me?*

OUT IN THE DARKNESS, the man waited and watched, fury a poison in his mind and blood.

She could not be allowed to escape him, not again! The beautiful bitch had betrayed him once, but for that, too, she would pay. And for all the rest of her perfidy, he thought furiously, watching her slim shadow cross through the gatehouse.

The bitch had always valued her silly little scrawls more

than she valued him, right from the very beginning. He swore foully, madness seizing him.

But not much longer, he thought. First he would strip away her pride, and then he'd seize her very sanity.

Just the way they'd seized his, during those hellish months in prison. He laughed softly.

*Soon you'll be begging again, Moira. On your knees the way you're supposed to be.*

*Crying. Pleading for me to touch you. Just the way you used to plead.*

*And if you don't, I'll do to you the same thing I'm going to do to that damned cat of yours.*

# CHAPTER NINE

GRAY STUMBLED BACKWARD, her hands to her nerveless lips. With a wild cry, she caught up her trailing hem and plunged toward the outer door.

Only inches from the frame she froze, watching the knob turn silently.

All her worst nightmares came to life.

"Adrian—dear God, *Adrian!*"

Gray spun about, one hand crushed to her mouth. She called his name without knowing it, then saw a tall shadow fall across the terrace. Relief exploded through her. "Adrian, I—"

But the cry was cut off stillborn.

Gray saw that it was a different face outside the opened doors. A stranger's face.

A man with darkly tanned skin and sun-bleached hair low on his brow. The man from the florist shop in London?

And then Gray's throat twisted in a knot of fear as she recognized the furtive movements, the hardened sneer—so familiar, even after five years.

No, not a stranger at all.

Just her ex-husband.

Come to kill her, as he'd promised when they'd pulled him cursing from the crowded courtroom.

Gray turned and ran for the front door, stumbling against a mahogany side table.

*Adrian! Dear God, come to me now, if you can hear me!*

There was a rustling in the air around her, a tingling at her neck.

The next moment the glass doors from the terrace gave way with an explosive crash. "Moira? Where are you, dammit? Where are you, my sweet, lying wife?"

White-faced, Gray inched backward into the darkness of the front alcove, praying that he wouldn't hear her.

Behind her, thick shoes crunched over shattered glass. "Clever, weren't you? Changing your face, your eye color. Taking a new name and a new identity. But I was even more clever, because I did the same—changed my hair, darkened my skin. You see, the thought of finding you was the only thing that kept me alive in that stinking cell."

Closer the steps came, even closer. Any second now he would see her!

"And you can forget about running, my sweet. There's no one here to help you now, no one here but the two of us. Now it will be just the way it always used to be. And we're going to do things the same way we did then. You remember, don't you? How it felt?"

Gray shoved her fist to her lips to keep from gagging, to keep from screaming. Dear God, the door had to be close now!

Behind her the flat voice droned on. "I saw the butler drive off hours ago. Even that damned gray cat's gone. I would have killed him first, but the big devil was too smart, I'll say that much for him."

Her ex-husband's eyes narrowed, hazed with madness. "*You'll* be much easier to kill, my sweet."

And then Gray found the cold metal knob. Her heart pounding, she wrenched open the door and plunged into the darkness as an angry growl erupted behind her.

*Where, Adrian? Where are you?*

*Steady, sweeting.* The words were a mere murmur in her head, a faint warmth at her shoulders.

But they were there, a lifeline to sanity. Where—where are you? Gray cried raggedly.

*I can't—be with you, sweeting. Not yet. But circle around to the glade and cross to the south tower. There's a door there, a very old door. I'll show you how to find it.*

She obeyed without question or hesitation, trying to shut out the angry curses that followed her as she ran through the moon-lit night.

She made her way past the stables, past the maze and around to the far side of the little glade, guided by Adrian's silent directions every step of the way. The man behind her crashed on more slowly, having no such guidance.

And with every step his rage grew. Gray knew the pattern all too well.

She forced back a sob, stopping at the bank of the moat to listen to the soft night wind, waiting for Adrian's silent prompting.

But none came.

And then on the far bank where the abbey walls rose up straight and sheer from the moat, she saw a sleek gray shadow detach from the night.

Burning amber eyes rose to greet her.

"Gideon!"

Plunging into the water, she swam toward the cat who waited on the bank like a marble sentinel. At that moment a shot rang out, shrieking past her ear and slamming into the water only inches from her head.

Wildly, Gray churned on, hearing more shots hiss past. Half-blind with fear, she struggled from the water to find Gideon pacing before the tower's weathered stone base.

In her terror, Gray had no time to wonder how the great cat

came to be there or why she should find the sight of him so comforting.

Behind her came the splash of a large body hitting water. Gray gritted her teeth against the terror that threatened to shatter her reason. "He—he said there was a door. But *where,* Gideon?"

She ran tense fingers over the rough stone, finding no sign of an opening. Abruptly, Gideon darted past her feet.

"Where is it, Adrian? I—I can't find it!"

The voice came from the lapping of the waves, the sigh of the wind. *Close your eyes, sweeting. Look with your heart, not your eyes. See my abbey the way it was then, in my picture.*

Desperately Gray scanned the stone base, calling up the image of Adrian's sketch. And then she remembered that the tower had been slightly off, more rounded than its mate to the north. She ran to the center of the curve, fingers pressed to the rough granite.

And as she did, she stumbled on a half-hidden vine and pitched to her knees. She cried out as her arm struck the wall with a dull, ringing echo.

The next moment stone grated against stone. Gray felt the bank beneath her begin to heave.

And then she was sliding down into a black hole that gaped where once the foundation had stood.

Warm fur brushed her face as she clawed through the loose, damp earth and stumbled to her feet. "Gideon?" she rasped.

A faint meow rose in answer.

Shivering, Gray studied the tunnel that stretched before her, dark and damp. She saw glowing amber pinpoints drift through the shadows at her side and move upward.

Gray followed blindly, feeling loose dirt give way to hard-packed clay and finally to rough stone steps.

Up Gray went, her gaze riveted on the amber eyes that

gleamed beside her. Ten steps, twenty…until she began to lose count.

Behind her, an angry cruse exploded up the tunnel. "Dammit, Moira, you can't hope to get away! Not *this* time. And this time, by God, you're going to pay! You're going to beg and beg!"

Shuddering, Gray blocked off the sound of that hated voice, the threats she knew too well. Her hands to the cool stone, she circled round and round, climbing ever higher with Gideon right beside her.

Abruptly the steps came to an end. Her hands met stone, nothing but cold stone on three sides. "—Sweet heaven, what now?"

The cat meowed softly, sliding past her ankles, while angry curses filtered up the narrow stairway.

And then Gray felt the familiar tingling at her spine, the soft kiss of an unseen wind.

*Lower, my heart. Down by Gideon…*

Awkwardly, Gray bent down and searched the wall, crying out in triumph when she felt a narrow gap in the stone. But could she manage to fit?

*Ah, we were all a bit smaller then, my heart. But you'll fit, never fear. And when you're through, I'll be there waiting.*

Wildly Gray pushed through the narrow opening, clawing her way across a layer of rough, damp stones. Something dug into her wrist and she flinched as a small, sharp object pricked her skin. As she crawled forward, she felt it snag in the folds of her lace gown.

But she paid it no thought, all too aware of the curses that were growing closer every second. Before her she could make out a faint gleam, and she realized it was the star-flung sky.

"I'm…coming…Adrian!"

And then she was through, out into the chill night. Before

her on the abbey's high parapet stars gleamed like cold diamonds flung across a lapis sky.

Best of all, a tall shadow paced the windswept battlements.

His arms opened. Gray flung herself inside.

"Well done. Oh, well done, my heart."

Joy welled up as Gray felt the hard muscles flex, tense, crush her close.

Real again. As real in bone and muscle as she ever needed a man to be. And no matter who—or *what*—he was, being held like this was all Gray wanted or needed from life.

Adrian's lips brushed her hair, soft as the sweep of filtered moonlight. Warm as the kiss of the summer wind.

The shot rang out before she knew it, cracking off the stone walls. Cursing, Adrian shoved her behind him and lunged toward the narrow opening that led from the stairs.

Suddenly moonlight glinted off cold steel and the night exploded into sound. White-faced, Gray saw Adrian sway.

Again and again the gun coughed. This time Adrian stumbled back against the wall.

"Run," he ordered. "Door to the house—beyond the far tower—"

"Dear God, no!" Frozen, Gray watched Adrian's tall form sway. His eyes were wide, raw with desperation and pain.

"Go…now…sweeting. So d-damned s-sorry—"

Oblivious to the stocky figure crawling out from the inner stairway, oblivious to everything but Adrian's growing pallor, Gray plunged forward to catch him.

But it was too late. Her hands slid through warm blood.

For a moment his fingers dug into her wrists. "R-run!" he cried.

Then, with a gasp, he stiffened and fell back onto the cold stone roof.

Gray barely heard the muffled snarl, the squish of soft soles on stone. Even Gideon's angry hiss seemed far, far away.

"You're next, Moira my sweet. After we finish our business, of course."

Wild-eyed, Gray stared down at the cold slabs where Adrian's body lay unmoving, blood pooling in a dark ring about his chest.

Harsh laughter hammered over the parapets, but even then, she did not move, unable to stop crying, unable to tear her eyes from Adrian's pale features.

*How young he looks,* she thought. His features were calm, perfectly chiseled, almost as if he were sleeping.

Instead of dead.

Dead a second time.

Behind Gray came low cursing. "Did you really think you could escape me?"

Suddenly a gun clinked against stone. "Now, Moira, turn around. I want to see your face when I pull the trigger. By God, I want to hear you beg."

Gray hugged her chest, biting down a sob as she watched the wind riffle Adrian's long hair. *Someday, my love. Maybe… someday…*

And then she turned to face her nightmare, knowing this was what Adrian would have wanted most.

He was smaller than she remembered, his face unre-markable, his eyes flat and unintelligent. He was altogether forgettable—not the great menacing figure she had imagined.

He was just a man, Gray realized, just a sick twisted man who needed a victim. She shook her head, feeling the fear and hatred slide away until she was free of her past at last.

"But I'm not begging, Matt. And I'm not afraid of you at all. It's over. You've come too late."

He bellowed a curse and raised a shaking arm to strike her,

but the next moment a hissing gray cloud of fur exploded through the darkness and landed on his shoulders.

His gun flashed, erupting in a pinpoint of flame. Gray felt something whine past her cheek. A second shot followed, searing along her wrist.

She barely flinched. "You're too late, Matt. I'll never run again. And that was all you wanted anyway, wasn't it? To see me run."

Every word stoked her pursuer's fury. Cursing, he started toward her. "No, you'll never be free of me! *Never,* do you hear?"

Gray inched back, sickened by his hatred, wanting only to be done with him and all that reminded her of him. But she was not going to give him the pleasure of seeing her run—not when she had no hope of succeeding.

Her fingers dug into the granite wall. She looked away, out over the sleeping countryside, over the wooded hills and shimmering moat.

A low singing rose through her head. Far away there came a distant peal of bells.

Something about the sound made Gray think of home, the home she'd never known.

Once again the gun blazed in the darkness. Dimly she realized she must be in shock, because she barely registered the impact of the third bullet.

She swayed, catching at the stone wall for support. She felt a brief burning, then the hot, thick rush of blood at her breast.

But the pain was far away, blurred, as if it belonged to someone else.

Behind her Matt cursed, then stumbled about in furious surprise. "What in the devil—"

He never finished. A low, harsh voice cut him off.

A voice Gray found achingly familiar.

Her breath caught. She spun around.

Faint spirals of light glinted off the windswept walls, growing brighter every second. And at the center of the strange, swirling radiance stood a man, broad-shouldered and long-limbed, his form growing brighter and more solid every second.

"You! But—you're *dead!* I—I saw you die!" Gray's ex-husband stumbled backward, his face locked in a grimace of fear and disbelief.

His ghostly pursuer threw back his head and laughed, filling the stone walls with a dark rumble of sound. And then he started forward, his face as hard as marble, his eyes glowing like blood-red coals.

"Get—get away, damn you! It's all a t-trick. You don't frighten m-me, do you hear?" But the man before Adrian trembled, his breath coming jerky and fast. He staggered backward in a desperate effort to escape.

"No? Then perhaps *this* will frighten you." With an unearthly laugh, Adrian Draycott leveled gleaming, outstretched fingers.

And dragged them right through his terrified killer's body.

"But—you c-can't—dammit! I won't—"

With a shrill cry, the man turned and shoved wildly through the gap into the stairway, his gun clattering, forgotten behind him. Dark laughter and wild, dancing light followed him every step of the way as he crashed down the stairwell and threw himself desperately into the moat.

Adrian laughed softly. "Gideon? I believe it's your turn."

Hissing angrily, the big gray cat flicked his tail, then turned and glided off into the night.

Only then did Adrian turn, a smile on his face. Slowly the fury faded from his eyes and was replaced with a look of crushing pain. "Dear God, if only I'd known—if only I could have spared you this."

Gray swayed, suddenly weak. She reached out for Adrian as the parapet seemed to sway and the stars to dance a dizzy jig overhead.

Far away she heard the first low moan of approaching sirens.

"Adrian, I don't feel—"

"Here, love. Right here." Hard hands caught her close, pressed her to his chest.

And then Gray saw the faint silver glow that trickled from her own hands, lapping about her arms and chest.

She stared down, speechless, as the glow grew to dancing sparks, and the sparks to solid swirls of light.

Her eyes sought Adrian's, hazy with pain and shock.

His hands tightened convulsively. Protectively. Infinitely gentle. "I love you, Gray Mackenzie. Will that love be enough for you? Enough for you to trust me? Now and forever?"

She caught a ragged breath, feeling the dizziness grow. Around her the ancient stone walls gleamed, bathed in shimmering columns of light.

She managed a nod and let her eyes finish the answer, shining with a love she'd never hoped to find again.

He caught her up, secure in his arms, his long fingers buried in her silken hair. His smile then was just for her, full of love, full of light, full of joy and promise.

Beneath her ear Gray heard his heart race and felt the heat of his love surround her, part of the same shimmering glow that lit the night.

Adrian's fingers twined tenderly through hers. "Then…then let's go home, my heart. These old stone walls have missed you far too long."

A whirring filled Gray's ears, echoed inside her head. Light and sound swirled up, cascading together into exquisite, luminous melodies. Her fingers tightened.

Into the music they went.

Into the light.

Gray was still smiling when the music spilled out and the abbey walls shimmered away to nothing behind her.

## *EPILOGUE*

THE MIDDAY SUN POURED DOWN from a cloudless sky onto a green lawn full of mail-clad knights and giggling, wimple-clad maidens.

High above, in one of Draycott Abbey's mullioned windows, Kacey Mallory Draycott, the wife of the twelfth Viscount, watched the festivities of the abbey's first "Medieval Faire," a faint frown tightening her beautiful brow.

"It doesn't seem right, Nicholas. So much gaiety and life when…"

Behind her Nicholas Draycott frowned. She was still too pale, still too quiet. And he'd so bloody hoped this idea of hers would cheer her up, help her forget.

Long, gentle fingers circled Kacey's shoulders and swept aside her silky blond hair. Warm lips skimmed her neck. "It was *your* idea, remember? You've put Draycott Abbey back on the map." He slanted an ironic glance at the laughing figures below. "Although I'm not sure I'm entirely thrilled at the idea." His hands tightened. "But it's what Gray would have wanted, I think. Certainly that's what matters most."

Kacey sighed, staring out at the billowing tents and colorful stalls. Slowly she nodded: "You're right, of course. You're always right, you insufferable man." Her hands reached up to clasp her husband close. "It *is* what Gray would have wanted. But do you know, sometimes I almost feel as if she's still here, that I hear her soft laughter drifting over the moat. It's crazy, I know, but—"

Abruptly she stopped, staring down at the milling figures.

"Look, Nicholas!"

"At what, my love? The dancing bear or the monk who's rapidly losing his sandals?"

"No, *there,* just beyond the moat. The woman with the auburn hair. It's—I could swear it's Gray!"

Nicholas's lips tightened. His hands locked about Kacey's shoulders.

"Oh, I know it can't be. I know it's crazy and impossible. But just the same I—"

This time it was Nicholas who gasped, seeing a tall figure in armor and black velvet stride across the green lawns. "It *can't* be!"

"Can't be what, Nicholas?"

"Adrian!" He shook his head soundly. "No, of course, it isn't." Slowly his mouth curved in a dark smile as he watched the two figures fall laughing into each other's arms, watched the tall, bearded man lift the woman with auburn hair up and spin her around in circles.

A long sleek cat inched from one of the nearby stalls and stood studying the laughing pair.

"By God! Yes, he just might…" Nicholas's smile grew to a wolfish grin.

"Nicholas?" Kacey turned to stare at her grinning husband. "What are you muttering about? *Who* can't it be—"

And then she sputtered as her husband cut her off with a fierce kiss planted fiercely against her still-parted lips.

With a soft sigh Kacey slid closer, twining her hands about her husband's neck. Abruptly, she pulled back, her eyes wide with worry. "Nicholas, you can't. *We* can't! The mayor and his wife will be here any minute to judge the costume parade. And then there will be a joust and fortune-telling and—"

His hands eased over her silk-clad chest. "I don't need my fortune told, sweet one. I'm doomed to a life of utter bliss in the arms of my beautiful wife." He angled her a besotted smile. "And Marston will manage all of those things splendidly. He always does. Sometimes I even wonder why I bother to appear at all." His fingers slid the fragile silk straps from his wife's shoulders. "And Marston will certainly see to it that the mayor and his wife are kept suitably entertained for another hour or so while we—"

"But Nicholas, I—"

His hands eased the wisp of apricot satin lower. "You're impossibly beautiful, do you know that?"

Kacey's eyes darkened as his fingers slid over the warm skin he had just bared. "But those two—they were—"

Nicholas tongued the pebbled crest that spilled into his fingers. "Come, love, can't you leave a pair of lovers to enjoy a moment's rest?"

"But they weren't resting, they were—" Her eyes closed as her husband's lips slid over her aching skin. "Oh, Nicholas."

In the soft, erotic rustle of silk and heated skin that followed, the laughing pair below were entirely forgotten.

OUT IN THE HOME WOOD, where the green leaves whispered and the pool bubbled up crystal from the little glade, two shadows drifted, then shimmered to luminous reality.

Sunlight glinted off auburn hair, spilling forward onto gleaming black.

"Adrian! They saw us, I'm sure of it!"

"Of course they saw us, woman. As guardian spirits, we *must* make ourselves visible to the owners of the abbey now and again. Just to keep them on their toes, of course. There, I think I've finally mastered the business. First you fix your gaze. Then you draw a slow, steady breath and count backward from twenty." His body swirled, then took on solid form, sunlight gleaming off polished armor.

"Wonderfully done! Twenty, you say?" Gray's eyes narrowed as she began to count.

A moment later, she, too, shimmered into full form, her long golden gown gleaming about her ankles. "I *did* it!"

She looked down and studied the brooch pinned to her dress. "I'm so glad I found your brooch. It must have fallen there in the tunnel all those years go."

Warm fingers slid beneath her long hair. She sighed, easing back against the hard body behind her. "But, Adrian, surely not—not *here?* Anyone might come across us!"

"Ah, that's the beauty of it, love. Only Kacey and Nicholas can see us. And they, I assure you, are far too busy to go out searching for ghosts right now, guardian or any other sort."

His fingers slid lovingly over the sweet curves barely covered by Gray's tissue silk gown. "Ah, God, Gray, you task me sorely! From morning to night you set me working with no reward. Had I known our partnership would be like this—"

"You had a kiss at dawn and rather more than a kiss at noon, stubborn man."

Adrian's lips slid hungrily over her neck. "Bloody less than I wanted," he grumbled.

"Well, there was that kitten to be rescued from the moat. And those wretched men from London were going to chop down that ancient oak beside the road. You couldn't allow that, could you?"

The man beside her gave a long-suffering sigh and mumbled something about letting the whole damned home woods be hewn down to twigs.

Gray turned and twined her arms about Adrian's neck,

nibbling a path across his hard jaw. "And there were the roses. Only you seem to be able to work such magic with them." Her tongue teased his ear.

"Stop that! Damn and blast, woman, that's unfair! Not when I can't—"

Adrian's breath caught as he watched her silken gown skim to the ground in an erotic *whoosh*. "Sweet God almighty! Gray—"

"Now who's too busy to—"

Laughter rang out over the glade, a soft sound formed of birdsong and the sighing of the wind.

And the soft moans that only lovers know.

There beneath the shadows of a giant rowan, one might have sworn two lovers pressed close, eyes like smoke, hands urgent and hungry.

And there in the quiet glade, while the moat bubbled happily and lazy bees droned from rose to rose, the two shadows met and became one.

And the long years of sadness were banished from Draycott Abbey forever.

\* \* \* \* \*

# SEASON OF WISHES

# PROLOGUE

*Mid-October*
*The Marshes*
*Essex, England*

FOR A BIG MAN, Ian McCall's hands were amazingly gentle as he eased the dial of the shortwave radio. Inside the crowded van greenish diodes left trails of cold light across his face. "Any answer yet?"

The man beside him shook his head. "They're still counting the money."

Ian McCall fought his exhaustion. As Security International's most seasoned kidnap negotiator, he knew the next decision was his. "They've had fifteen minutes to count the money. It's time to push them. Otherwise, they'll run—and they'll put a bullet in that little girl first," he said harshly.

His boss, Sir George Rolland, rubbed his neck impatiently. "It's your call, Ian. You've been mediating with them for three months now. If anyone knows what these animals will do, it's you."

"They aren't professionals. They're unpredictable and probably shot high on drugs. If we don't act now, we lose our edge. Then there's no telling what they'll do to their hostage."

The director nodded grimly. "Take over."

Ian drew a hard breath and flipped on the broadcast switch

near his left palm. His voice was precise, but carried the hint of soft Highland cadences. "Largo, are you there?"

There was no answer.

"Largo, this is Baker." The code name rolled smoothly from Ian's tongue. Field personnel in hostage situations knew better than to use their real names. If they didn't know that, they didn't survive for long. "What the hell is taking so long in there? We want the girl out now. Get her in front of the cottage where we can see her."

Static rose in a sharp wave, followed by a voice rough with exhaustion and raw excitement. "We're still checking the money, Baker. Three stacks to go. Your people had better not have left anything out."

"Listen to me, Largo. Get the girl out now, or a team will be in with dogs and infrared tracers. If that happens, there won't be enough of you left to enjoy a single bloody pound."

"Threats, Baker? I thought smooth negotiating was your style."

"My style just changed. Something tells me you've lost control over your comrades in there. If you're not careful, you're going to end up a splotch on a wall." Ian lowered his voice. "You might be interested to know that the Italian has done this before. Both times, he pulled the trigger on his victim minutes after the ransom was paid. Then he vanished with the money. Do you catch my drift, Largo?"

The kidnapper made a low, crude sound. "How do you know that?"

"We're in touch with Interpol, of course. The Italian's M.O. was clear from week one. The only one who didn't know his style was you. Obviously, he's setting you up for the same trick."

A string of curses filled the wire.

Ian flipped off the transmit button and sat back. Sweat glistened green over his brow in the light of the shifting diodes.

"What happens now?" Rolland asked anxiously.

"Now we pray. The next move is up to Largo." Ian studied a video screen to his left. "Still no movement at the site, dammit."

"You did everything you could, McCall. It looks like you were right on target about that bloody fellow Alberto. Let's hope Largo gets to the girl first."

Ian swung off his headset and motioned to the officer at his left, who immediately took his place. "It's finished, Rolland. I can feel it. They've got most of their damned money and now they'll start tidying up." Suddenly he bent over the video screen. "Wait a minute…"

A moment later, the air crackled with the urgent voice of one of Security International's support team. "Baker, are you there? The door is opening. Someone's coming out. Hold fire until my order, understood? Baker, do you read me?"

Ian shoved his headphones back in place, responding to his code name. "I'm here, Able. We can see the field. Any ID on who's coming out?"

"It looks like the girl. It's— She's out! Baker, do you copy? *She's out!*"

Ian's hands were not quite steady as he adjusted the grainy video image. "I read you, Able. Any sign of the Italian?"

"Our people in the rear just picked up a body falling from the porch. Looks like he took a round in the head."

Ian murmured something soft in Gaelic. "What about the girl? Any sign of pursuit?"

"Not yet. She's almost to the front steps. You can see her red hat."

Ian frowned. "Red hat?"

"That's it. As soon as she's beyond the porch, we can rush

her. My men will run cover while they get her to safety. Two teams are standing by to close in as soon as she is clear."

Ian's fingers moved restlessly over the console. He studied each window and door of the dilapidated cottage on the edge of the lonely Essex marshes. "Not yet, Able, do you copy? Don't panic these people. They're jittery and tired, running on pure adrenaline. Largo has followed through so far, so let's give him a little more time."

A taut silence followed. "Rover, are you in agreement?"

Sir George Rolland spoke into his handheld receiver. "Agent Baker is right. He knows these people. I suggest you do what he says and give them some space."

"But—"

"Now," Rolland said curtly.

"Very well, Rover. They have one more minute."

Time crawled by. The four men in the cramped communications van watched the eight-year-old heiress to a chain of grocery stores wander dazedly across the yard, a toy bear clutched to her chest.

"God, she's so bloody young," Rolland said softly.

"She's almost to the gate," McCall whispered. "Two more feet. Come on, Terri. Get clear."

As she skirted a row of withered cornstalks, black figures exploded out of nowhere, surrounding the freed victim and covering her with their Kevlar-protected bodies. Up the hill two mobile assault teams crept toward the isolated farmhouse.

Rolland gripped his receiver anxiously. "Konrad's men have her."

McCall's breath rasped free. He sank back against the padded chair, his eyes closed. His part of the operation was over. The ransom had been negotiated and the victim was free and unharmed.

"Good work." Rolland pressed his shoulder. "Now you can take some time off and—"

"Baker?" The field officer's voice broke in urgently.

"Right here."

"Terri wants to see you. She's—she's pretty broken up, and she keeps asking to see the man on the radio who told her about the teddy bear's picnic." The officer's usually unemotional voice was unsteady.

"Where are her parents?"

"In a car down the hill. But she wants to see you first, Baker. She's…bloody insistent. A real fighter, that one."

"That's what kept her alive," Ian said flatly. He pushed out of his chair and rubbed the fatigue from his eyes. "Tell Terri I'm on my way."

THEY MADE AN ODD PAIR, the man with the hard face and the little girl clutching his callused hand. Though the uniformed troops were too far away to pick up the discussion, they saw the girl rub her eyes and sway. A moment later Ian crouched beside her and smoothed her tangled braids. The bear dangled perilously when she gripped his neck.

Two dozen pairs of eyes softened at the sight of a child's bravery and the tenderness of a man whose ruthless determination had kept her safe. Ian took the threadbare toy of antique chenille and shook hands with exaggerated formality. When the little girl curtsied with equal formality, her uncertain laugh drifted on the wind, and more than one brawny military officer cleared a suddenly raw throat.

Ian McCall pulled the girl into his arms and walked slowly over the field, the wind ruffling his dark hair. At his back, a trail of smoke rose from the burning farmhouse. Four kidnappers stumbled out onto the front porch swarming with military snipers.

But Terri St. James didn't notice. Her small hands clutched Ian McCall's neck and her beloved bear at the same time. Snowflakes danced down from the sky, dusting the battered old toy and glistening on the little girl's cheeks and eyelashes.

She was smiling tentatively as her parents broke from their waiting car, with the first soft snowfall of the year eddying around them.

# CHAPTER ONE

*November*
*Draycott Abbey*
*Southeastern England*

THE ROOM WAS WARM and the sherry excellent. Ian McCall, tenth laird of Glenlyle, savored both as he bent over the crackling flames in Draycott Abbey's massive stone fireplace. He did not look up when the door opened behind him.

"Brooding again, Ian?"

"It's what we Scots do best, don't you know that, Nicholas?" Pushing to his feet, Ian studied the abbey's owner, the twelfth viscount Draycott. He saw flecks of gray that had not been in his friend's dark hair the last time they had met. Ian supposed his own hair looked much the same. Fast friends since they were six, the two men had met every year thereafter, and Nicholas had visited Scotland as often as he could manage.

Ian studied Nicholas's face intently and read the tension his old friend was at pains to conceal. The years had made him familiar enough to be blunt. "Why the urgent summons, Nicholas? You must have had something in mind besides my sampling the abbey's vintage sherry."

Nicholas shook his hand firmly, then poured a generous glass of the sherry for himself. "You're right as usual, Ian. I called you because I have someone I want you to meet."

Ian smiled crookedly. "Not another marriage-minded female, I hope. The last time I was here, you introduced me to a French actress and a German tennis star."

Nicholas shrugged sympathetically. "My wife's doing, I'm afraid. She can't stand to see any man she likes remain single. Matrimony is in her genetic makeup. And you, my friend, are definitely on Kacey's marriage list."

"And then there was the music reviewer with purple hair who assured me she was the very latest thing on MTV." Ian rubbed his neck ruefully. "What's MTV, by the way?"

"It would take too long to explain, old man. She wasn't your type anyway."

Ian studied his sherry. "The black lipstick was a bit extreme, as I recall." His eyes narrowed. "I trust you and Kacey don't plan on any more matchmaking. I'm seriously not in the mood."

Nicholas emptied his glass and frowned. "No matchmaking. Not this time."

"So it's business."

"I'm afraid so. Of course, you are free to say no."

Ian chuckled dryly. "No one ever says no to you, Nicholas. It's all those centuries of English arrogance and impeccable bloodlines. You're far too well-bred to be heavy-handed, of course." Ian sank into a comfortably worn chintz wing chair angled toward the fire and waited for the offer that would follow.

The offer he was already steeling himself to refuse.

Nicholas held out a package. "I just got back from London. I saw Terri St. James and her parents. They're old friends, Ian, and I can't thank you enough for what you did."

"I only did my job, Nicholas."

"And then some. I know something's been distracting you lately."

Ian didn't answer.

"Terri sent you this. She said it would help you remember her."

"As if I could forget. That child has more courage than most adults." He tugged open the cardboard box and pulled out a worn chenille bear with a crimson ribbon around its neck.

Ian swallowed, feeling pressure build in his throat. "Rupert, she called him. This little fellow helped her get through hell in Essex, Nicholas. She shouldn't part with him."

"It was her choice. She said the ribbon was because you got your colors mixed up."

Ian frowned at the worn toy.

"May I ask you a question, Ian?"

"You will anyway," Ian muttered.

"Too true. So why are you really leaving Security International? You've got at least ten good years left in the business."

Ian's gaze moved restlessly to the fire. He squinted, watching the shifting flames. "Personal reasons."

"Care to be more specific?"

The laird of Glenlyle shook his head.

Nicholas Draycott sighed. "Then I'll get right to the point. A young woman with a great deal of wealth has been targeted for kidnapping. As you always point out, preventing a kidnapping is a hell of a lot easier than trying to negotiate a release later. This is your chance."

"Friend of yours? Or is she family?"

"Both. She's an acquaintance of Kacey's and a distant relative of my uncle."

Ian sighed. "I'm sorry to hear it, Nicholas. But the fact is, I'm no good in the field. My reflexes aren't what they were."

Nicholas Draycott made a hard, impatient sound. "You're still class-A rated in marksmanship and your evasive driving skills are second to none. You've handled six kidnappings in the last year, and every one of them resulted in a clean victim turnover."

Ian swirled his sherry. "Luck."

"Rubbish. You're the best, Ian. You know how these people think. You know when to calm them down and when to shake them up. That makes you better than any muscle boy."

"The answer's still no, Nicky," Ian said, shaking his head. "For you I wish it could be otherwise. But…no." His soft Scottish accent grew more pronounced. "There comes a time when every man has to step down, and my time has come."

"Hear me out, please." Nicholas produced a pair of small, half-moon reading glasses. "Bloody things. If it weren't for Kacey, I'd toss them in the nearest waste bin." He sifted through a pile of papers on his desk and retrieved a thick file. A photo was clipped to the outside cover. He studied the photo, then tossed it onto the table next to Ian. "That's your client. She's American, twenty-four, very smart and very independent. She's also a well-known textile designer. You may have seen some of her pieces at the National Gallery."

Ian raised one dark brow. "Not a place I've visited lately."

"Nor have I. I'll sum up by saying the lady is very, very good. According to Kacey, her designs fetch enormous prices when they become available, which isn't often. Jamee—as she's known to her friends—has been traveling through Asia for the past month. While she's been gone, inquiries have been made into her personal assets. Nothing obtrusive, all very smooth and very professional." Nicholas pulled out a page from the file and his eyes narrowed. "If her brother hadn't had a corporate security team keeping permanent tabs on Jamee the whole matter might have been overlooked. But someone is interested in her, all right. One of her friends even received a call from a company claiming to be validating a credit application for her. They wanted to know the names and ages of her friends, her business associates, what her usual workday consisted of. Hardly routine questions. Especially since Jamee Night had never made an application to that or any other company."

Ian made an impatient gesture with his hand. Nicholas Draycott could be relentless when an idea took hold of him. Ian hated to disappoint him, but this time he had no choice. "Security International has a dozen other men experienced in close protection. Your friend Dominic Montserrat could recommend even more. Why do you want me?"

Nicholas paced back and forth before the fire. "Because Jamee's family asked for the best man, and that's you. They're offering quite a bit of money for this job, by the way."

Ian laughed darkly. "Money isn't the answer most people think it is, Nicholas. This involves nasty work, weeks of running on adrenaline and raw nerves until you begin to suspect everyone. Even yourself by the end." He set his glass down firmly. "The answer is no. I'm sorry to bow out on you, but I'd be no help."

"You won't be operating alone."

"The answer's still no."

"If you sense any threat at all, a backup team will be sent in immediately," Nicholas continued relentlessly.

"Out in the field 'immediately' is one second too late," Ian said dryly. "You should know that."

Nicholas braced one hand on the heavily carved sill of a window overlooking the abbey's sunlit moat. "Everything is prepared. You'll have complete autonomy in all decisions. No one will second-guess you, and there will be no expense spared to see this thing through. Jamee's brother has already set up a team of investigators and equipped them with the very latest information-gathering systems."

"He'll need more than computer analysts and surveillance reports if he wants to keep his sister safe."

"That's exactly what I told him. You're the missing piece he needs."

"He'll have to find someone else."

Nicholas stared at Ian. "While Adam Night's people are doing computer searches on probable suspects and running down the source of those questionable inquiries, Security International has handpicked a backup team to protect Jamee until she returns from Asia. Adam felt his own team might not be up to this new threat. You see, you have absolutely nothing to worry about."

"Except that whenever I hear that particular phrase, things generally start going downhill fast."

Nicholas pulled off his reading glasses and shoved them into his pocket. "You're truly set on refusing this job?"

Ian nodded, his eyes hard.

"I see." Nicholas sighed. "I'm sorry to hear it. The Night family has been through too much pain already."

"Night?" A frown worked along Ian's forehead. "You mean, Gareth and Alice Night? The founders of Nightingale Electronics?"

"That's right. You knew them?"

"Not well. I met Gareth only once. He was doing feasibility tests on a new shortwave communications system I was training with. He was a brilliant man." Ian smiled faintly. "Almost as brilliant as his wife, I gathered from what he told me about her."

Nicholas nodded. "They were very much in love."

"So I guessed. We were huddled on an oil rig in the North Sea during a nasty midwinter gale. I remember he told me how much his family had sacrificed while he built Nightingale Electronics. All the traveling and long hours at work took a toll. He said he'd missed most of the important events in his children's lives, but he was planning to slow down and spend more time with them. Then he and his wife died in that car crash in Nova Scotia." Ian frowned down at his empty glass. "How long has it been?"

"Six years next month."

Ian made a flat, angry sound. "And his daughter is the target you mentioned?"

"Jamesina. Her friends call her Jamee."

Ian looked down at the photo on the desk. Four men and a laughing young woman with long red hair were tangled in a frantic game of touch football. Water glinted in the distance beyond a hill covered with wildflowers. "Jamee Night?"

Nicholas nodded. "They love to play touch football—even her brother, Bennett. Though he plays with a cane and ten pounds of steel pins and surgical plastic in his leg. Amazing family," he said softly.

Ian tapped a figure whose high cheekbones were eloquent testimony to a Native-American heritage. "Another brother?"

"Adam is adopted, just like Jamee's other brother." Nicholas pointed to a crouched figure whose Eurasian features were creased in a broad grin. "William was found at the age of six begging for food in a back alley in Hong Kong's Wanchai district. Mother—Chinese. Father could be any number of things. Today William Wu Night is probably one of the most brilliant software designers in the world."

"And then there's Jamee," Ian said tightly. "Kidnapped when she was seventeen and locked in a closet for five days. It was a bloody business, bungled at every stage. After the ransom was paid, the kidnappers nearly escaped. It took the police two days to corner the men after they went to ground in an isolated cabin in northern Idaho."

"You've got a good memory for a crime that happened seven years ago," Nicholas murmured.

"The details were drummed into us during our military

training. It was the perfect case study: all the reasons why expert negotiators should be used in kidnap cases rather than amateurs or even seasoned military personnel. Mishaps like what happened to Jamee Night can *always* be avoided," Ian said savagely. "The money should never have been paid without adequate guarantees of her safety and location."

"Not everyone is as good as you are, Ian."

"Then they shouldn't be in the business," he said coldly.

Nicholas stared out at the moat. Three swans cut a perfect path through silver waters, ruffling the reflection of Draycott Abbey's granite walls. "What you might not know is that Jamee Night is personally worth somewhere in the area of twenty million dollars, thanks to her wedge of Nightingale Electronics stock. Her parents started out in a makeshift workshop in their basement and last year, annual revenues exceeded two hundred million dollars. For that kind of money a lot of people would kidnap their own mothers."

Afternoon light shimmered off a row of precious Murano glass paperweights, casting sparks of light over the face of the woman in the photograph. Ian picked up another photo. Here Jamee Night laughed as she shoved her brother Adam down beneath a great oak tree. Nearby, her other brothers cheered her on, one leaning on a cane while the other aimed a gun holding huge sponge arrows. The third sat on the branch of an oak tree, looking very proud of his family. Their love for one another was a tangible part of the photo, as marked as their exuberance.

Maybe nearly losing a sister to kidnappers made you appreciate the basic joys of life, Ian thought grimly. "What's her itinerary when she reaches London?" he asked, curious in spite of himself.

"She's set to arrive in Scotland two weeks from today. I thought you could pick up her trail in Edinburgh and keep her secure after that."

Light danced over the four smiling faces, drawing Ian into their laughter. He thought about his own boyhood, regimented and lonely, without the company of any siblings. Beautiful or not, a fifteenth-century castle in the Inner Hebrides was a solitary place for a boy to grow up. There had been little laughter at Glenlyle Castle, especially after…

*Forget it,* Ian told himself flatly. The curtain was definitely down on his professional career. Taking this job would be irresponsible—not only to himself, but to the vital, laughing woman who tantalized him from the photo.

"There's more, I'm afraid," Nicholas said. He tapped the lanky figure astride the tree branch. "Two years ago, Jamee's older brother, Terence, was run down when he pulled a pregnant woman out of the way of a drunk driver. Mother and child were fine, but Terence didn't make it. It was a nasty blow for all of them."

Ian made an angry sound and dropped the sheet back on the desk. "The answer is still *no,* Nicholas." His fingers tightened on the polished arm of the wing chair. "I can't. Not this time."

"Can't. Or won't?"

"Sometimes the two are the same," Ian muttered, staring into the fire.

"For other men, but not for you. I know that damned Glenlyle stubbornness of yours. I followed you up a mountain in the blinding snow when you were seven, remember?"

Ian gave a low laugh. "Exhilarating, wasn't it? When we weren't worrying that we would die of frostbite."

"Or fall off a cliff," Nicholas added.

"Or be skinned alive by our parents when they found out what we'd done." Ian's smile slowly faded. "But the answer's still *no.*"

"I see," Nicholas said slowly.

He didn't see, of course. No one did. Ian meant it to stay that way. Pride demanded nothing less.

He frowned as he heard Nicholas crossing to the door. "I meant it, Nicholas."

"Fine. In that case, you won't mind telling Jamee's brother the same thing."

Ian slammed to his feet. "Dammit, Nicky, I—"

The door opened on a man with high, chiseled cheekbones and relentless eyes, his features immediately recognizable from the photo. Adam Lonetree Night cleared six feet and his wiry frame was all muscle. He moved in utter silence through the room, wearing a suit Ian recognized as the product of Savile Row's finest tailor. Oddly, the beaded band circling his forehead did nothing to mar the effect of cool, understated elegance. Every step he took made Ian think of a sleek wild creature restrained beneath a thin veneer of civilization.

The American held out one hand. "A hell of a request, isn't it?"

Ian couldn't help grinning, surprised by Adam Night's frankness. "You could say that." He shook Adam's hand, then stepped back. "At any other time I might consider it, but now—" He shrugged. "Unfortunately, it's out of the question."

"You come very well recommended. I'd hoped…" Something bleak swept across Adam Night's face before he looked away.

"Have you established a motive yet? Is it a terrorist, an ideologue or someone with a straight financial motive? An estranged employee, perhaps. The motive will be key to choosing your tactics."

Adam pulled a file from his briefcase. "Here's what we have so far. It isn't much, I'm afraid. We've kept up long-range surveillance of our sister in Asia and found nothing unusual. But someone has shown undue interest in our family banking records and three attempts have been made to access private financial files kept on our corporate computers."

"Any idea who?"

"Not yet. Only that they're smart and they seem very well equipped."

"Never a good combination." Ian glanced through the half-dozen sheets in the file. "You're using Ryan Nicholson's team for the surveillance of your sister in Asia?"

"That's right. He came highly recommended by Lord Draycott."

Ian nodded. "You can trust his findings. He used to work at Security International. A good man. He doesn't embroider and he doesn't make guesses." Ian pulled out another photograph. Jamee Night smiled up at him, this time standing beside a waterfall and wearing two orchid leis. Her vitality fairly jumped out at him from the photo. No mistake about it, Jamesina Night was beautiful, her eyes snapping and her smile electric. "Taken on vacation in the islands?"

"On business. Her designs fill two of the largest hotels in Hawaii. My sister has a design cooperative on Maui employing thirty people."

Ian tapped the file. "What about her itinerary in Scotland? Have you checked for possible target points?"

"We're trying." Looking uncomfortable, Adam Night rubbed his neck. "Her final destination is a place called Dunraven."

Ian's brow rose. "Duncan MacKinnon's estate?"

Adam nodded. "She has personal business on the way. Then she planned a visit with Duncan's wife, who has commissioned several textiles for Dunraven Castle."

"I see. And you want someone who can blend in with the locale, is that it? Someone who can get close and stay close."

Adam nodded eagerly. "Exactly. I've been told you're the

best, Mr. McCall. Since Jamee is dead-set on this visit to Scotland—"

"Why don't you just tell her what you've found?" Ian asked abruptly. "Surely that would convince her to postpone her trip."

"I can't do that. She's spent too long learning how to forget, how to trust and be independent. Until we have something solid, I don't want her confidence shaken."

"Security International has dozens of people who know the Highlands as well as I do. There's Nicholson and his team—"

"They'd stick out after Asia. She'd recognize them in a second. We sent them in undercover as a team of petrochemical engineers. Though they haven't yet gotten very close, I'm sure she would remember them. White men tend to stand out in the Asian hill country."

Nicholas cleared his throat. "Jamee is wary of bodyguards, Ian. She doesn't like to be…crowded."

Adam gazed out the window at the dark line of the distant hills. "She's worked hard to put the memories behind her. She's careful, she checks in with us every week, but she wants to have some semblance of a normal life."

"Maybe she doesn't have that luxury anymore."

"You know about the kidnapping, I take it?"

Ian nodded.

"After that, I suppose we all spoiled Jamee. Maybe we smothered her, too. My sister doesn't care much for security people, Mr. McCall. As for surveillance—well, she isn't thrilled with that, either. It makes her feel claustrophobic."

"Feeling claustrophobic is a hell of a lot better than being kidnapped."

"You're wrong," Adam said grimly. "To my sister they're the same. After she was seized, she was held in a locked closet in total darkness. She lived on food and water shoved in through a hole. But she is a fighter. She refuses to become a prisoner to her past. I intend to do everything in my power to see that she doesn't have to."

Ian ran a finger along the edge of Jamee's photograph, captivated by the frank joy in her face. What must it have cost her to keep that joy in the face of her painful memories. Then losing her parents and her brother…

There was a knock at the door. Nicholas Draycott's butler entered, garbed in meticulous black set off by a pair of blinding orange running shoes. "Your call to Bali should be coming through at any moment, Mr. Night. Shall I transfer it in here?"

"Thank you, Marston." Adam glanced at Nicholas. "Can we put it on speaker?"

"Of course," Nicholas said. "But why—"

"Blackmail," Adam said bluntly. "I'm hoping it will help change Mr. McCall's mind."

In spite of his irritation, Ian felt a gleam of respect for Adam Night's honesty and persistence. Not that they would do the least bit of good. "It won't work."

"I hope you're wrong, Mr. McCall." Adam smiled at Marston. "Maybe you should bring my brother in, too. He must be pacing like a demented gorilla by now."

Marston chuckled. "An apt description. I shall fetch the gentleman." The butler's lips twitched. "Assuming that I can pull him away from his electronic gaming device."

William Wu Night strode through the door ten seconds later. His tawny eyes and Eurasian features were arresting, and he moved with relentless energy. Ian decided that William Night probably had the kind of exotic good looks that fascinated women—and irritated their husbands.

"Dammit, Adam, what's going on?" William scowled at his adoptive brother, ignoring the sleek electronic game module that winked in his hands.

"I'm speaking to Mr. McCall," Adam said patiently.

"McCall, eh?" William studied Ian, then stuck out his free hand. "Are you as good as they say?"

Adam sighed. "William, please."

"What?" William Night's features tensed in a frown. "I'm just asking the basic questions here."

"If he wasn't good, do you think he would tell you?" Adam asked.

William crossed his arms defiantly. "I still want to hear it from him."

Ian was saved from answering when William's wristwatch began to chime softly. "Dammit, why haven't they reached her yet? Maybe there was another coup over there. Maybe she was caught in a mudslide. I *knew* we should have kept her from going off to Java or whatever blasted place she went to this time."

"She's in Bali now," Adam said calmly. "And stop worrying, William."

His brother paced impatiently. "I can't stop worrying. I don't want Jamee wandering around some powder-keg country in the middle of Asia."

"Bali is stable, William. They haven't had any government coups in the last few years."

"That doesn't make me feel any better." William Wu Night glared at the small electronic module in his hands. He expertly demolished two attacking extraterrestrial fighter craft, nuked an alien mother ship, hit the hyperdrive, then shoved the portable game prototype into his pocket. "Not one damned bit. And the call has taken twenty-eight minutes, forty-two seconds already. Something's wrong."

"Nothing's wrong," Adam insisted.

"Blast it, Adam, they should have found her by now. Maybe she's had some kind of accident. Maybe she's been…" His voice was anguished as he held his brother's gaze.

"Jamee has *not* been kidnapped," Adam said fiercely. "Do you think I'd let her wander through Asia without protection?" Adam sighed. "I've had someone assigned to keep tabs on her since before she left San Francisco last month."

William's eyes lit with interest. "Someone from that company in London?"

Adam nodded. "Security International also happens to be Mr. McCall's company." He frowned at Ian. "But perhaps I should be calling you Lord Glenlyle. That is your title, I believe."

"Ian will be fine."

William fidgeted with one cuff. "If Jamee would stop wandering from one side of the globe to the other, things would be a whole lot easier."

"For us. Not for her," Adam corrected.

"That's exactly what Terence would have said," William muttered irritably.

"And he would have been right." Adam glanced at Nicholas and Ian. "Terence, our brother…he died two years ago." Adam's jaw hardened. "Forgive us for our bickering. It's become something of a habit, I'm afraid."

At that moment, the phone rang. All four men looked expectantly at the desk.

After a nod from Nicholas, Adam crossed the room and pushed a button on the speaker phone. "Jamee, is that you?"

A breathless voice cut through a cloud of static. "It's me, Adam."

Ian felt the small hairs rise at the back of his neck. His hands tightened on the arm of the chair as he listened to what sounded like drums and chanting.

"What's going on, Jamee?" Adam demanded.

"Sorry, Adam. They're having some sort of ceremony here."

"No more walking on coals, I hope," William called.

"Is that you, William?" His sister laughed delightedly. "No, the firewalk was in India. By the way, William, how many alien droids have you demolished today?"

Williams eyes gleamed. "Sixty-one."

"So the boy genius is losing his touch, is he? Last month it was over two hundred."

As Jamee Night's throaty laughter filled the room, touching every corner with sunlight, Ian felt his body tighten. He wanted to stand up and walk out, away from temptation.

Away from the sound of that vibrant, unforgettable laughter.

William leaned toward the phone. "No way. This is a new program I designed. The old one was too easy."

"Show-off. So send me a sample and I'll test-rate it for you. You know I always beat you in the hard levels, where flexible thinking is required." Her voice rose against the constant drumming. "Adam, are you still there?"

"Right here."

"Is Bennett there?"

Adam slanted a glance at William. "No, Bennett ducked out of this business trip. He's minding the store in San Francisco."

"I've got good news for him. I've found a place here in Bali that will manufacture those voice-synthesizer units he wanted. A long-term contract will give the village some economic stability. After the weather they've had, they desperately need any help they can get. They'll need a turnkey operation and close initial guidance, but they're skilled in general circuitry already. Send over the specs, will you?"

Ian frowned. The woman was smart, as well as having an amazing voice.

Not that either would influence him in the slightest.

Adam chuckled. "Can we skip the finder's fee since it's all in the family?"

"Dream on, big brother," Jamee said. "How else am I going

to finance all this traveling in search of new fibers for my weaving?" Abruptly, the drumming rose in a roar, drowning out Jamee's voice.

Against every inclination, Ian found himself sitting forward, straining for her next words.

There was only the sound of drums.

"Jamee, are you still there?" Adam demanded.

"I'm afraid I have to go, Adam. The chief is offering some kind of boar's head."

"When will you be back?" Adam asked tightly.

"I'll finish up next week. Did I tell you I found a county where they can make up silk cocoons to my special design? They were burning the broken cocoons in the fields to keep away the birds. Burning silkworm cocoons, can you imagine that? Now I've really got to go. The chief's son is about to model one of my ikat sarongs. He's got great teeth, did I tell you? And he has this amazing tattoo that runs across his back and all the way down to his—"

Adam shot a glance at Ian and hid a smile. "I can guess exactly where it runs. Just you be careful over there."

"Be careful of men with tattoos," William called out urgently. "You can't trust them for a second."

"You have a tattoo, William," his sister answered.

"Yeah, that's why I'm so worried."

"I love you idiots. Go find Bennett and play a game of touch football. While you do, think of me carving up a boar's head. Heavens, now they're bringing some kind of roasted insect that looks like an overgrown cockroach. I think I'm going to have to look honored with the gift. Talk to you next week."

"From where?" William bent closer, frowning.

"Java."

"But you said—"

The line clicked off in a burst of static. Ian sat back slowly, aware of a strange letdown in the wake of Jamee Night's call. *No, McCall. Out of the bloody question.*

"So she's headed to Java." Scowling, Adam rubbed his jaw. "As I recall, that's an island southeast of Sumatra. Population roughly sixty million with the major language group being—"

"Dammit, Adam, doesn't it *bother* you?" William exploded. "She's wandering around the world, taking risks we can't even imagine and all *you* can do is quote language groups and population figures!"

Adam's sculpted features turned fierce. Ian realized this was a man he would not care to meet as an enemy.

"Yes, William, it bothers me deeply. As my friend Nicholas knows, I would cut off my right hand to have Jamee back, just as you would. But she must come back because *she* chooses to—not because we want her to."

William sighed and ran his hands through his long hair. "You're right, of course. You usually are. Okay, so why don't we make her want to come back? Tell her you're getting *married* or something."

"Married?" Adam's brow rose. "Me?"

"Okay, so make it something that's believable."

"And lie to Jamee?" Adam shook his head. "She'd hate it and she'd hate us when she found out. We'll just have to find someone to shadow her, someone who will see that she's protected at all times in Scotland. Nicholson's team is with her in Asia, but we'll need someone different when she gets over here. I'm hoping that person is you, Mr. McCall. Sir George Rolland told me you're the best man he has and I believe him."

Ian studied the woman smiling in the photo. "How long?" he asked, thinking he should have his sanity checked.

"Four weeks. No more than five," Adam said promptly. "She is expected back home in San Francisco by Christmas, and she'd never miss that."

"And during this time, your sister is not to know who I am and what I'm really doing?"

Adam nodded.

"How much?" Ian said flatly, using practicality to justify a totally irrational inclination based on nothing more than a pair of vibrant eyes and a laugh that could warm a subzero freezer.

"A quarter of a million pounds for four weeks. Extra for any time beyond that."

"Terence would have liked you. I'll double that amount," William added calmly.

Ian gave a silent whistle. "A man could make a lot of plans with money like that." Abruptly, he stood up. "But it makes no difference. I can't take this job."

Nicholas cursed softly. "Ian, is there something you want to tell me? Nothing you say will leave this room."

The hiss and pop of the fire suddenly seemed very loud.

Ian stiffened. Then he slowly shook his head.

Adam Night pulled a rectangular box from his briefcase. His gaze flickered to Nicholas as he moved to the television.

"Adam, no," William snapped. "Not that."

"Yes. I told you I'd do whatever was necessary to keep Jamee safe." Ignoring William's outstretched hand, Adam pulled a videocassette from the box and pushed it into the VCR.

Ian closed his eyes, knowing he didn't want to see the tape. He was *not* getting involved. These people needed a man who was sharp and confident.

A man at the peak of his form.

"This will change nothing," Ian muttered.

"Maybe. Maybe not." Adam pressed a button and the tape gears began to spin.

"I refuse to watch. I refuse to be a part of *any* of this," William hissed. He strode angrily from the room, slamming the door behind him.

Ian frowned as black-and-white images flickered across the screen. His eyes narrowed when he heard a faint feminine whimper coming from what appeared to be a hospital room with a bed and two chairs.

"If this doesn't convince you, nothing can, Mr. McCall," Adam said bleakly.

The video zoomed in on the bed, where a figure lay motionless beneath white sheets.

"I meant what I said, Night. I cannot possibly…" Ian's voice trailed off as he saw the face resting upon the pillow, the long hair that slid over one shoulder.

*Jamee Night.*

Something hard and cold clawed at Ian's chest. Feeling like the worst kind of voyeur, he swung around toward Adam. "I'm beginning to agree with your brother. I'm leaving."

Adam's eyes were pleading. "Stay. Just for a few moments. If you can forget what you see, so be it."

The woman in the picture began to move, slowly at first, then more urgently. One hand gripped the edge of the bed, her fingers raking the white sheets.

Sweat broke out on Ian's forehead. *It doesn't matter,* he told himself. He couldn't allow himself to care.

The sleeping woman moaned softly and shoved away the top cover. The camera panned over the scene, leaving the dark circles under her eyes clearly visible.

"Where is she?" Ian asked.

"In the sleep-disorder clinic of a major New York hospital," Adam said quietly. "My sister wanted to be cured, Mr. McCall.

She wanted to forget. So she checked in, hoping to get some answers. This is the tape of her first night there."

Ian watched Jamee Night grip the neck of her hospital pajamas. Her eyes squeezed shut in terror as she dug her fingers beneath the stiff cotton. With a ragged sob she twisted sideways, tore away the top button, and tried desperately to claw free of the garment.

"She's smothering, Mr. McCall," Adam explained grimly. "She relives being locked in a closet. And she'll have to confront worse things than these nightmares if this threat turns out to be real."

Ian cursed, unable to look away. His hands tightened on the arm of his chair. "Turn if off."

"Not yet. I want you to see how they left her. Then tell me no, Mr. McCall."

Jamee continued to tear at her pajama top. Wrenching her arms free, she tossed the garment onto the floor. Ian saw her strain against invisible walls.

"Dammit, Night, that's enough. Turn the damn thing off."

"Jamee has these dreams at least once a month," Adam said, ignoring Ian's protest. "More, if she's under stress."

"I don't care," Ian growled as Jamee pushed to her knees, huddled against the head of the bed. For the first time, her eyes opened, wide and dilated, staring at a point just above the camera.

Ian realized she saw nothing but her dreams. He watched her struggle free of her pajama bottoms and throw them away. Her slender body was covered by a white cotton bodysuit. Ian felt a sick sense of fury as she struggled mechanically to stand, then tottered to the floor. She moved awkwardly, straining against invisible barriers like a mime in a horror show.

Ian strode to the VCR, slammed the tape to a halt, and ejected the cartridge. "What if I tell her you showed this to me?"

Adam flinched, but did not look away. "I'll bear the consequences. You're the best, McCall. That's why I want you to protect my sister."

"I told you it was impossible."

"But you didn't say why."

"The reason is irrelevant." But though he'd stopped the tape, Ian continued to see Jamee's pale face and jerky movements. He called himself a bloody fool as he fingered the file Adam had given him. "This file says that she was once engaged to be married. What happened?"

Adam shrugged. "Apparently they decided to stay friends instead. I got the impression that Jamee wasn't ready for anything more…intense."

"Did her fiancé feel the same way? Maybe he took the news a little harder."

"As in considering retaliation? No way. Noel Shipton-Jones is too busy with his limited partnerships and wholly owned subsidiaries to be bothered by a minor thing like being cut adrift by his fiancée."

"Where's he now?"

"In France, pitching a huge contract for computerized maintenance services on the Channel tunnel. There's no way he could be a suspect. Noel's a junior partner with one of the biggest computer firms in the world."

"Have you checked for criminal background or drug use? Possible debts from an expensive mistress or a hidden gambling problem? Any of those might make him consider a quick fix for his problems. Given his prior contacts with Jamee, he'd have the opportunity. When you add motive to opportunity, generally you've got your man."

Adam frowned. "They still talk occasionally. I'll look into it, but—"

"No buts. In a kidnapping, everyone's a suspect. Even family." Ian laughed mirthlessly. "*Especially* family."

"Not in this case," Nicholas interrupted. "I know Noel."

"You'll have to let me be the judge of that. The imprisonment of a human being for money is a damnable thing. The kind of mind that plans a kidnapping can be either very sick or very clever. Usually both." Ian shoved the file under his arm and tossed the cassette to Adam. "From now on, I'll make the decisions, Night. If you have a problem with that, tell me now. It will save a hell of a lot of trouble later."

"You don't make things easy, do you, Mr. McCall?"

"That's the general idea." Ian crossed his arms, waiting.

After a moment, Adam smiled faintly. "You're right, of course. Very well, you have a deal. Would you like your fee now? I have found that cash often facilitates things." Adam opened a compartment in his briefcase and calmly began counting stacks of bills. At any moment, Ian expected to wake up and find out this was a very bad dream.

When the crisp pound notes hit his fingers, he knew he wasn't going to wake up. "I hope you won't regret this."

Adam made a sharp movement with his hand. "Just see that you keep her safe, Mr. McCall. Any way you can. We'll take care of hunting down whoever is making the inquiries into Jamee's finances and personal life. Our in-house investigators are pretty damned good." He handed Ian the last stack of notes. "One more thing."

"What's that?"

"My brother William will pay you another quarter of a million when you return Jamee safely to San Francisco on Christmas Eve."

Over the rolling downs a sound rang out, almost like the clang of distant bells.

If he was dreaming, Ian decided now would be a bloody good time to wake up.

# *CHAPTER TWO*

MIST CURLED OVER the weathered stone and clung to the dark network of vines that grew over Draycott Abbey's granite walls. White lace gleamed against black satin as a figure emerged from the darkness of the high, crenelated walls.

"I *hate* Christmas." Adrian Draycott's hard features were tense with irritation as he strode through the night without parting the mist or disturbing it in any way. "Yes, I *know* Christmas is Nicholas's favorite time of year. I also know that the abbey looks its very best when strung with holly and agleam with candles. And I still don't care," he muttered. "All this merrymaking makes me feel old."

Through the drifting fog a gray cat moved with imperious grace. In one powerful bound he sprang up to the parapet and perched on the granite edge, ears alert.

The guardian ghost of Draycott Abbey scowled down at his longtime companion and friend. "Well, of course, I *am* old. Nine hundred seventy-one years, by a rough estimate and depending on your definition of time." Adrian frowned at the cat. "No, I will *not* be drawn into another discussion of the theoretical anomalies unanswered by current time-space theories." His eyes were brooding as he flicked a ruffle of lace from one cuff with expert skill. "The only problem is Christmas. I have always hated Christmas."

The cat's tail arched.

"No, I am *not* going to change my mind just because a lot of loathsome strangers are descending on my abbey. In fact, I think I shall teach them a lesson about the dangers of invading someone's private domain with their despicable laughter and relentless good cheer." Adrian's gray eyes glinted. "A good manifestation will soon clear them out. Or perhaps I should try something more dramatic this time." He raised his hands and hovered like a shadow against the fog. "Something like this, I think…"

The cat gave a low meow, then curled up in a smooth gray ball.

"Don't you dare go to sleep on me, Gideon. I can summon a better manifestation than that." The abbey's resident ghost frowned as he smoothed the white lace jabot at his neck. Abruptly, he gave a diabolical laugh. His head shimmered and grew indistinct and then his stern features vanished entirely.

Headless, gruesome in black with fluttering lace cuffs, he paced the misty roof. A creature of flesh and blood would have found the sight terrifying, but the great cat did not so much as blink.

"What do you think of *that?*" Adrian demanded, summoning up a ghastly aura of green light around his headless shoulders. "They won't soon forget this sight," he crowed triumphantly.

The cat showed an utter lack of interest.

"Damnation, what do you mean, you've seen better at Windsor? When were you there last?"

The cat's tail swished.

In a blur of phosphorescence Adrian's head popped back through the frilled lace at his collar. "*That* weekend? Of course I remember. Yes, the viscount did an adequate job of representing Draycott Abbey on the occasion of the announcement of the royal wedding. But I saw no headless figures lumbering about the royal corridors."

The cat's eyes burned purest amber.

"I was *not* too busy seducing the lush creature who welcomed us. Miranda was simply being companionable. She was cut down in her prime by a very nasty riding accident, and I thought it rather decent of me to comfort her."

The cat stretched, meowing softly.

"We did no such thing!" Adrian's hard features burned through the drifting mist. "At least, we didn't do it in public." He strode to the notched granite edge of the roof. "But that was ages ago, and today I am a changed man. Reformed and absolutely incorruptible." He studied the patterns of fog skimming the dark earth. "By the way, where is Gray? She was supposed to have been here hours ago."

The cat's paws rustled on the cold stone.

"She's doing what?" Adrian stopped, an arrested look on his face. "A present for me. Truly?"

The cat eased onto coal-black paws, his eyes unblinking.

"She is making it herself? What can I possibly find for her, Gideon? I haven't a single thing good enough."

The cat meowed softly.

"She told you that? The very same thing about me?" This plunged the abbey ghost further into gloom. "You see how unworthy I am?" Hands clasped at his back, he disappeared across the roof. Only his voice rang out, melancholy in the mist. "You must help me, Gideon. Watch her like a hawk and discover what she wants. No matter how precious or rare, I will find a way to obtain it for her. She lost so much when she came to the abbey—everything, all swept away for me. How can I ever hope to repay her?"

Somewhere a bird cried from the darkness. The cat eased forward, suddenly alert.

"You are right, Gideon. Our guests approach. Maybe I shall find what I need among their baggage. The people of this noisy century seem to travel with mounds of possessions, even those outlandish objects they use for exercise. In my age, we would have called them instruments of torture." His voice rose, suddenly decisive. "Come, Gideon. The game is afoot, to quote that unpleasant doctor named—" He frowned. "What was that fellow's name?"

The cat purred.

"Yes, of course that's who I mean. That Arthur fellow. Conan something. That's right, Doyle. A most officious kind of pest. The blasted man actually caught my impression on that ectoplasm device he insisted on trying out during his last visit here." Adrian Draycott stopped in midstride. "Do you suppose a photograph would please Gray? That infernal device of Doyle's is still somewhere about the abbey, perhaps up in the north attic. The fellow was so frightened when I materialized in his bedroom that he bolted in the middle of a snowstorm. All talk and no action, if you ask me." He tapped his jaw thoughtfully. "Yes, a spectral portrait would do the trick. What do you say, Gideon?"

The cat peered intently at the drive.

"Someone there, you say?"

The cat eased to his feet, his body rigid.

"I do feel something," Adrian murmured, his jaw hard. "Faint but intrusive. And moving toward us." He spun about, staring into the darkness beside a twelve-foot chimney. "I believe we are about to have a visitor," he said coldly.

At his booted feet the great cat swayed, his eyes locked on the darkness at the edge of the vast roof. Something flashed in the silence, more sound than image. To Adrian the sound seemed a mix of birdsong, rain and laughter. "Do you hear it, Gideon?"

At his feet the cat stiffened, listening to a sound like the sigh of a swift creek or the rustle of small, pungent grasses.

Sound became form, slowly, awkwardly. In the space of five seconds, a man walked from the chimney, frowning and looking very lost. "Am I here yet?" he demanded, running one hand through his blond hair.

"Where, my fellow, is *here?*" Adrian drew himself to his full height.

The man scratched his jaw. "Some sort of abbey, I think."

Adrian's features grew even more hash. "Some sort of abbey? Draycott Abbey perhaps? *My* abbey?"

The man looked impressed. "Yours, is it? Good, then I've got the hang of it. Moving from place to place still takes some doing for me." He eased his long legs over the roof with the grace of a long-distance runner, which is exactly what he had been.

Until he died crossing the street to save a pregnant woman from a drunken driver.

He put out one hand, smiling apologetically. "I'm Terence. Sorry to intrude."

Adrian looked him up and down slowly, then sniffed. "Is that name supposed to stir some recognition?"

"Terence Night. Jamee's brother." He smiled crookedly, his hair picking up sunlight where none existed. "At least I used to be. Before…"

"Yes, before you died. It's clear enough to see that you've moved into spirit. But by the good and powerful Queen Bess, what gives you the right to intrude here?"

"I can't say." Terence shrugged, and the movement sent light dancing over his worn blue jeans and white T-shirt. There was a glow of muted gold about his face and hands. "I was simply told to come."

"And you can just as simply leave." Adrian moved closer, his face threatening. "Right now."

"I'm afraid I can't do that," Terence said, his smile sweet and infinitely apologetic.

Adrian simmered. He fumed. Smoke coiled and billowed about his body. "Then I guarantee you will be very sorry, Mr. Terence Night, who is brother to Jamee Night, who is someone I have never met nor care to meet. Hear me well: Draycott Abbey is *my* territory. Go find your own humans to guard."

The new arrival's eyes widened. "Are you one, too? Who would have thought it, to see you dressed that way."

"Dressed," Adrian said coldly, "in *what* way?"

"All satin and lace. Very impressive, especially the boots. But it's just not…helpful. I mean, anyone would think you were some kind of hallucination rather than a spirit sent to assist them."

The smoke positively boiled around Adrian's head. "So I am a hallucination, am I?" He seemed to expand, his shadow growing longer. "Let us see how it feels when a hallucination pitches you to the ground."

Gideon meowed once, low and sharp.

Adrian looked down, frowning. "You know this…this creature, Gideon?"

Terence smiled as he crossed the roof. "Oh, we've met before." He bent and stroked the cat's smooth fur, and with each movement, light flickered from his hands. "Your friend helped me out when I was in the process of making a complete mess of my last assignment."

"Somehow *that* doesn't surprise me," Adrian said crossly. Then he froze. "Wait one minute. Him? You helped *him*, Gideon? I refuse to believe it."

The cat blinked, purring beneath Terence Night's stroking fingers.

"Traitor."

Terence glanced up. "Helps you, too, does he? You must be very lucky, for this fellow is special. Gideon, is that your name?"

The cat blinked. His amber eyes burned with pure, restless light.

"It's a pleasure to meet you, too." When Terence Night laughed, the sound was also image, pinks and greens and perfect blues shimmering over the old granite. "I could use your help again," he said ruefully. "This one is important. I'm frightened because it's someone I love, and I couldn't bear to bungle things. I left so much undone when I died. So much unsaid, especially to Jamee." He sighed. After giving the cat a final stroke, he stood up. "Now I've been sent, and I don't know why. I only know that she needs me."

Adrian's brow rose. "Your sister?"

"Jamee. She always knew how to cut through our worries and find a way to make us laugh, all of us."

"How many of you *are* there?" Adrian asked warily.

"I have three brothers. All still alive," he explained quickly, seeing Adrian's frown. "They won't be around to bother you. At least I don't think they will."

Adrian studied the great cat purring by Terence's leg. "So I have no choice, is that it?" He toyed with the lace at his cuff, his eyes narrowed. "There was something about those men who came to visit Nicholas today. I'm beginning to wish I had listened more carefully. But then Gray and I had to visit Lyon's Leap after the rabbits were caught in the weir."

When Adrian turned, he saw Terence Night begin to shimmer and fade. "What are you doing now, you incompetent? Hasn't anyone taught you how to hold your shape?"

"Something…wrong," Terence said unsteadily. "Got to find Jamee."

"Wait," Adrian commanded. "You're not ready to help anyone yet. In fact, your inexperience is utterly appalling. Since Gideon insists, I suppose I might be able to give you some assistance."

"…Appreciate…advice. Later." With a last burst of color, Terence Night's image blinked away into darkness.

"Damned fool. He should have let me help him."

Gideon's tail flicked from side to side.

"He'll be back, you say?" Adrian turned, sniffing the air. "What is that peculiar smell? Something sweet—like chocolate." He shrugged and smoothed his elegant black waistcoat as lights swept over the abbey's winding drive. "I hear them, too, Gideon. Let us be gone." White lace fluttered. "Ritual demands that we be on hand for the arrival of our guests."

Behind him, the great cat uncoiled. His amber eyes fixed unblinkingly on the road twisting over the dark landscape, while Adrian's tall form shimmered, then vanished in the mist.

"Gideon, where the devil are you?"

The cat's tail ached as laughter spilled into the silence. Purring softly, he flicked one ear, then followed Adrian, melting away into a beautiful chimney of solid, four-hundred-year-old granite.

THE SEA WIND ROSE in salty gusts, brushing Jamee Night's long braid onto her shoulder. She stood at the end of the small jetty and drew a long breath of air sharp with salt and sea and the fish loaded onto nearby boats. She shivered, cold yet more than cold. Hungry for the wildness that rang from the brooding hills and sang from the restless sea. She could see now why her father had loved this place, why his heart had never found deep roots anywhere else but in his native Scotland.

*It's real, yet none of it looks real,* Jamee thought. She drank in the green, girding mountains while blue water flashed on three sides of the great bay. Mist coiled idly, paling the colors, drawing shadows on a landscape that looked too perfect to be real.

A little drunk with the beauty around her, she approached a man testing a line at the end of the pier. "Excuse me…"

The man looked at her but he did not speak.

"I'm looking for this place." Feeling foolish, Jamee held out a photograph. "Cliffs above the ocean."

If the old Scotsman thought this a strange request, he did not show it. He fingered the bamboo pole gently, lost in thought.

"Do you know how to get there?" Jamee prodded.

"Aye." The cool eyes swept her face before returning to the sea.

"Then—can you tell me where it is?"

"I can that, miss."

Jamee tottered between irritation and amusement. She had come four thousand miles in the last three days, the last hundred in ceaseless rain over very bad roads. She wasn't ready for the Zen treatment, especially not in Scotland. "Will you tell me?"

He looked at her again, his teeth working the worn old pipe clamped between his lips. "I might, that."

Jamee waited. She was learning that a different sense of time set the pace of life here in the shadow of dark and timeless mountains by the sea.

"Not an easy drive to get to those cliffs." The fisherman stared off where squall lines darkened the west. "Rain soon. Mist first." He sniffed the air. "A bad day for driving."

"I'll manage."

"Will you now?" The question was as impersonal as the sea that frothed and sucked at the uneven boards of the jetty beneath them.

Jamee shrugged. "I always have before."

That, too, the fisherman digested in silence as he gently trolled his line. "West, it is. Along the Dunraven road." Gray arms of mist rose up, clinging to his chest and drifting over his weathered face. "Take the first fork beyond Treshnish, then watch for the rocks of Fionn. Shaped like bread loaves, they are. That will find you on the right road." His keen eyes narrowed. "If you still wish to go, that is."

"I do. Most certainly."

He seemed to hesitate before adding, "You won't wish to drive that way in the darkness, miss. Not with the road being what it is."

Jamee carefully eased the worn photo back into her pocket. "I'll manage. I'm driving on to Dunraven Castle afterward. It's not far, I think."

"Not far. Aye, on some days." The man's keen gaze ranged over the restless water. "On others it might take forever."

Jamee shoved the heavy braid back over her shoulder. "In that case, I'd better be going," she said briskly.

The Scotsman turned his back to the biting wind. "Dunraven Castle is a very fine place. Listen for the piper in the mist."

"Piper?"

"Some do say as his ghostly tune welcomes any fair lass to the castle." His lips pulled at his smokeless pipe. "If maid she be." He might have hidden a smile.

"I thank you for your directions. And for the record, I do not believe in ghosts."

"Do you not?"

"No," Jamee said flatly. "There's only death, nothing after. We believe in ghosts to make ourselves feel better." Pain filled her chest as she remembered the howl of sirens, the flare of lights and the flat stare of curious strangers. Then the officer, sad and trying not to show it. *I'm afraid...there's been an accident, Jamesina.*

First her parents. Then Terence.

"Something troubles you?"

Jamee's memories were cold, as clinging as the mist. "I'd better be going."

"Watch for Treshnish and the dark stones beyond."

It could have been a soft warning that came on the music of his voice. But Jamee didn't believe in ghosts or in warnings. That was why she was always moving, always drifting, always running away from what she couldn't bear to remember.

As the salty wind ruffled her hair, she wondered if maybe she had forgotten how to stay.

THREE PHONES RANG simultaneously as a box of lace gloves flew through the air. A wheeled frame with a dozen organza gowns rumbled over Dunraven Castle's polished marble floor.

"Fax for you, Kara! And don't forget you have two calls from New York on hold."

"Ah'll be wiff you aff foon aff I can," the editor of *New Bride* magazine mumbled, her mouth full of pins. Auburn curls spilled riotously over her shoulders as she bent over an exquisite brocade gown with a draped train of douppioni silk. A cut-velvet rose tumbled from the pleated waist, dragging a trail of lace along with it.

Kara Fitzgerald MacKinnon, wife of the sixth laird of Dunraven, said a very unladylike phrase and pulled out the last pin, stabbing her finger in the process. "On second thought, Megan, maybe you'd better take that last call for me."

An American with a frank smile and a million freckles, Kara's assistant answered the phone calmly, as if she were well-used to this sort of chaos. "Dunraven Castle. May I help you?"

Another box flew past and Megan ducked easily. "Of course. One moment, please." She covered the phone. "It's for Duncan. Is he still in the study?"

Kara frowned at the chaos of silk and lace around her. "I think he's taken refuge as far away as possible, which might be in the middle of the ocean. I can't say I blame him. The poor man had no idea what he was getting into when he married me."

A tall figure in the bright shades of the MacKinnon tartan strode into the ballroom, his kilt swirling about his powerful legs. "Aye, a terrrrrible great surprise it was to yer puir husband," the laird of Dunraven said in a booming brogue. "But dinna hope ye'll escape from him now, lassie." He caught his wife about the waist and whirled her up into the air, delighting in the way her face flamed.

Her bare feet flapped like small, quick fish. "Duncan, please!"

"Please what, lass? Dinna tell me you're wishing to take another break already. That makes three today," he said in mock dismay.

The flush in Kara's cheeks deepened and the laird's dark eyes twinkled as he lowered her to the ground. Frowning, he touched her face. "You're working too hard, Kara Fitzgerald. I will not have it."

"Only three more days, Duncan. Four at the outside, I promise."

"Until then, you'll rest. I will not have a word of protest." He raised his voice. "Do you hear that, Megan? You, too, Hidoshi?"

"Aye, aye, Captain," Kara's hardworking assistant and her staff photographer said in unison.

Megan held out the phone. "I believe this call is for you."

The MacKinnon's black brows rose sharply. "Someone is calling for me? I thought the world had forgotten that anyone besides the famous American bridal consultant lived here at Dunraven."

Megan chuckled. "As if anyone could forget Dunraven's magnificent laird." She slanted him a provocative look as she handed him the phone. "Especially when he's wearing such a cute little skirt."

"That's kilt to you, Megan O'Hara." Ignoring her cheeky smile, he raised the phone to his ear. "This is the laird of Dunraven," Duncan thundered. He ducked as another box sailed through the air, barely missing his broad shoulder.

"Duncan, I'm glad I caught you in."

"Ian?" Duncan's lips curved. "Where are you, man? It sounds like Tibet with all that static."

"I'm calling from the car. I'm about to get on the ferry. I've a favor to ask."

"Whatever it is, the answer is yes, you know that."

"I thought I might come and spend several days at Dunraven. Nice and quiet up there, is it?"

Duncan looked about him at the chaos of lace gloves, open jewelry boxes and photographic equipment. Electric wires crisscrossed the floor and four female models huddled in the corner before a rack of bridal gowns, listening to the enthusiastic directions of a Japanese-American photographer whose hair was currently streaked green and bright purple. "Quiet, you say?" He smiled cockily. "Not exactly. But you're still welcome."

"Thank you, Duncan. We should be there before dusk."

"Be careful on the coast road. It looks like fog is setting in." Suddenly Duncan frowned. "We? Are you traveling with someone?" He barely noticed as one of the reed-thin models calmly peeled off her silk camisole.

"I'm planning to pick someone up on the way, but I'll explain later. It's…rather complicated."

"It's business, you mean." Another layer of silk sailed

through the air. Duncan beat a hasty retreat, cordless telephone in hand. "Kara and I will be delighted to see you. The truth is, I'd be glad of some more male company up here."

JAMEE SHIVERED, eyeing her flimsy T-shirt in disgust and shoving the rental car's heater another notch higher. She had come straight from Java via Edinburgh, and her wardrobe was not exactly adequate for the damp Highland wind. Her father had told her long bedtime stories of the wild seas and lonely moors of his native Scotland, but no story could have prepared her for the changing light and the wind that gusted up without warning.

She still wasn't quite sure what she was doing here, driving on a narrow, winding road at the very edge of the British Isles where an unbroken expanse of water shimmered a dozen shades of blue. In fact, Jamee wasn't entirely certain what she was doing anywhere. For the last two years since her brother's death, she had more or less existed, hurrying from one day to the next, one job to the next and one country to the next. She had made a habit of not knowing where the next month would find her.

Maybe because she was afraid of losing another person she loved. Losing her parents had been devastating. Losing her beloved eccentric brother had been almost more than she could bear.

She stopped the car. Her head sank down against the steering wheel and she blinked back tears.

It was then that Jamee saw the sharply notched coast stretching before her. A silver cove beckoned to her left, its heather-clad cliffs remarkably similar to those in the photograph on the seat beside her. She glanced down at the mass of roses, a memorial to her lost parents, who had loved these wild shores. Jamee had come today to say her final goodbyes.

Clouds draped the hills and streaked the road as she stepped on the accelerator. The fisherman had been right, she realized. The drive would be treacherous at the best of times. It didn't help that she still hadn't caught the hang of driving on the left.

High in the distance the sun broke through the clouds. Bars of light glistened on the slate roofs and round towers of a castle of fairy-tale beauty. Dunraven, Jamee knew. Recognizing the turrets from her parents' description.

Seeing a turnoff, she pulled over along the coast. The sea stretched before her, dotted with green islands and seabirds rocking like tiny boats.

This curving shoreline was the spot her parents had described so lovingly, a quiet cliff found during their second honeymoon, which they had spent at Dunraven Castle. Her father had said this spot felt like the end of the world, a place to face your very soul.

Jamee hoped she would do the same here. It was time to let go of the shadows that had haunted her since her parents' sudden death on a lonely road in Nova Scotia. Maybe it was time to start thinking about cutting back her travel and staying home for a while.

"You were right, Da," she whispered. "It's like the very end of the world here." A plover cut through the sky and sailed toward the open sea. Then there was only mist again, only water and ever-changing light. Nothing but cliffs and sand wherever she looked. "I can see why you two never forgot this place."

Jamee knew her parents couldn't hear her, of course. The belief in ghosts was something to soothe the living, not placate the dead. But they had made her promise to visit Dunraven one day. They had assured her the visit would be unforgettable.

They were right.

Roses in hand, Jamee made her way toward the row of boulders at the spine of the cliff. "I know you will like the roses. These are *Souvenir de Malmaison,* the largest I could find this time of year. It took a bit of doing." Jamee didn't feel odd talking to herself. The silent cliffs seemed to invite quiet monologue.

She brushed away a tear. "Lord, how I miss you two. Terence, too. Probably every hour of every day. Adam, Will and Bennett have been wonderful, of course. Too wonderful, I sometimes think. They're trying to help, but they won't let me make my own mistakes."

She frowned at a long-stemmed bloom. Cold mist clung to her cinnamon-colored hair as she tossed the first flower out to sea. End over end it sailed, a flash of red against the mist before it hit the churning waves. "Tell them I need to make my own mistakes. Tell them I need to breathe. Tell them not to worry about me so much," she whispered as the wind ruffled her cheeks like the brush of spectral fingers.

A fishing boat steamed away to the north as the roses fell one by one, rocking on the sea. With each one, Jamee felt another layer of sadness fade, releasing the dark grief that had gripped her since she had learned of her parents' death. "I know Terence is with you now. I'm glad about that. Tell him…I love him. I wish I could have said goodbye."

Jamee had a sudden vision of her parents, their eyes shining, their arms looped at each other's waists. Their love had been unshakable. Jamee doubted she would ever know a pale imitation of such emotion.

Out went her last rose. Crimson petals tore free in the wind and whirled in a mad circle, then scattered at her feet.

"I only wish there had been more time," Jamee whispered, brushing tears from her cheek. Suddenly, she was aware of the silence that seemed to follow the mist. The little hairs lifted along her neck and she had the sharp feeling she was no longer alone.

She looked around.

The heather shivered between the gray boulders.

"Is…someone there?"

Only a bird soared high above, breaking the chill silence. Jamee turned away from the sea, where the last red bloom had slid from sight. The wind tore at her cheeks, as if to scrub away the tears her parents would neither want, nor expect. They would want her to be happy.

If only she could discover how.

Sighing, Jamee turned back toward the road, then abruptly froze.

A man stood on the cliff, his black hair ruffled by the breeze. He looked out of place with his polished leather satchel and well-cut Harris tweeds among the silence and the empty rocks. Sensing that he did not wish to be disturbed, Jamee moved back behind a lichen-covered boulder, then started up the slope to her car, respecting his privacy. But something made her stop.

What was he doing out here?

He moved to the rim of the cliff and studied the water shimmering far below, then dropped his bag. His gaze stayed locked on the sea.

Jamee told herself it was none of her business. She should leave him alone to savor his thoughts, which were clearly as dark as her own.

But she couldn't turn away, held by the sadness in his face. Or maybe it was the way he stared far to the west, ignoring the jagged cliff edge so near his feet.

His face was hard. The wind tore at his hair as he moved closer to the deadly emptiness. He frowned, studying the rough line of the coast.

One step. Two. He bent to one knee.

Jamee stiffened in a sudden jolt of realization.

He was going to *jump*.

## CHAPTER THREE

JAMEE LUNGED FORWARD against his chest. "You can't," she cried. Pain jolted through her ankle as she collided with a boulder and toppled them both onto the damp moss. "Doing this won't solve anything."

A dark strand of hair fell over his brow as he tried to raise his head. "Doing what?"

Jamee caught his arms and held him to the ground, ignoring the pain at her ankle. "Jumping."

He raised his eyebrows. "I beg your pardon."

"I know you were going to jump. Suicide is no answer, believe me." When he tried to move, she pressed her body down against him. "Stop fighting me."

"Fighting?"

"It won't work. I won't let you jump."

He stared at her as if she were mad. "I assure you, I was not—"

"It's no good," Jamee rushed on breathlessly. "You'd only hurt the people who love you. Besides, it's cowardly." Her lips pursed. "Somehow you don't strike me as a coward."

Something flickered in his eyes, sharp eyes that held shadows of an old pain. His face was deeply lined below a broad brow, more tanned than she had expected. As she stared down, Jamee felt drawn into his face, mesmerized by the play of emotions he fought to keep hidden. He was a man who kept secrets well, she thought.

She blinked and shook her head. "Promise you'll give it up."

He dislodged her arm and pushed onto one elbow in one smooth motion. "And you think you can stop me?" His voice held the soft, rolling cadences of the native Highlander.

He was stronger than she'd thought, Jamee realized. She pressed down harder, all too aware that her strength would never match his. "I just did."

"Sweet God above."

"You obviously didn't expect anyone to see you out here, but I'm not about to let you end your life like this."

"Why not?" he growled. "You don't know anything about me."

"What does *that* matter?" Jamee tried to gauge his next move. The man was far too controlled, far too good at hiding his feelings.

Jamee had never been very good at either.

She dug her feet into the fine dirt, tightening her hold on his arm. "It's never that bad," she said gravely. "You think it is. You feel there's no way you can go on another second. But somehow you do, and then the pain begins to fade. One day you find yourself smiling at something small and stupid, and you know it's going to be okay. And it will," she insisted. "You've got to believe me."

He eased her leg to one side, scowling. "That sounds like firsthand experience."

Jamee liked the Gaelic in his voice. "It is."

His smile was slightly cynical. "You're very obliging, considering I'm a complete stranger."

"I don't walk away from problems, if that's what you mean."

He moved restlessly beneath her. "I'm afraid you've got this all wrong."

"No, you've got it wrong," Jamee said flatly, trying to hold him still. "If it's some kind of sickness, there's bound to be hope. All sorts of medicines are discovered every day. Doctors can work miracles now."

His jaw hardened. "It's not a question of sickness or of miracles."

She didn't move. She wasn't about to let him rush her and push free now. The cliff was far too close. "If it's money…"

"Not money, either."

"No?" She gnawed at her lip, then gave him a slow, knowing nod. "Woman trouble. Did she dump you for someone younger? That happened to me once. Rotten feeling, isn't it?"

There seemed to be something wrong with his jaw. It just kept quivering. "Wrong again."

"Yeah, that only happens to the woman." Jamee shoved his arm back to the ground, frowning. "So what was it, incompatibility? Some sort of sexual problem?"

"If you'll move your thigh off my hip," the Scotsman said dryly, "I'll tell you."

Jamee didn't budge. "What's your name?"

His deep-green eyes flickered, the color of summer moss. "Ian."

"Promise you won't try anything, Ian? Nothing desperate, I mean."

"I swear."

Jamee eased away, but kept one hand on his arm. She knew that depressed people could behave unpredictably. "Things can look very bad," she said gravely. "But there are always options, always opportunities. You'll find another woman." Jamee studied him seriously, then nodded. "You're very attractive. Good bone structure. In spite of that sexual problem you mentioned…"

His brow rose sharply. "My dear woman—you are American, I believe."

"Yes."

"I am sorry to disappoint you, but I do *not* have any sexual problems. A fair number of women will vouch for that fact. Nor was I about to jump off that cliff when you tackled me like a demented linebacker."

Jamee blinked. "You weren't?"

He glanced down at her fingers wrapped around his arm and her thigh straddling his hip. "No. And unless you move, you're going to have very explicit evidence of my lack of sexual problems."

Jamee felt her face flame. "You mean—" She struggled bacward and slid to one knee. "So that was all an act? Of all the treacherous, unspeakably despicable—" Furious, she scrambled to her feet. "Just what kind of *creep* are you?"

Ian muttered a curse. "Stop."

"Stop?" she repeated raggedly, stumbling on a loose bit of granite. "So you can laugh at the poor, dumb American who thought she was helping someone in distress?"

"Stop *now*." He scowled at her as he pushed to his feet.

Jamee paid no attention, furious at herself, furious at the impulsive nature she could never quite control. What had made her think she was a Good Samaritan?

He lunged with sudden grace, clutching her waist, and Jamee struggled wildly, desperate to escape his keen, knowing eyes.

He drove her to her knees, palms to the ground. His arms locked around her chest. "Stop fighting, dammit. Otherwise, we'll both go plunging over those rocks."

She twisted sideways and aimed a perfect right hook at his chest. "Fool me once, buster."

Cursing, he worked one leg between hers and shoved her to the ground. "*Listen* to me, dammit."

The tweed of the man's jacket made Jamee's nose itch. She sneezed. "Why should I?"

"That's why." He stretched out his hand and Jamee blinked. The ragged cliff edge yawned only inches away. One more step and they both would have fallen onto the rocks.

Jamee swallowed, staring at the deadly emptiness.

"Now do you understand?"

She nodded jerkily.

"You won't move, will you? We're still too close. The edge could give way any second."

She nodded again, shuddering this time.

"Good. Move along with me. We're getting to our feet now. While we do, you can tell me your name."

She pushed upright slowly, barely aware of his hand at her waist. "J-Jamee."

"Very good. Now, listen to me, Jamee. The fog is closing in again. Stay right beside me, understand?"

His lips were very close to her ear, but Jamee barely heard him as she stared at the foam slamming against the dark rocks far below. The sea seemed to call to her, restless and urgent, pulling her forward in some elemental way.

Suddenly her chest ached and she couldn't breathe. She felt herself swaying forward, out toward nothingness—and the deadly rocks.

*"Don't look down."* His fingers dug into her waist. "Do you hear me, Jamee?"

Her legs began to shake. She managed a nod.

"Jamee what?" he asked tightly.

"N-Night."

He caught her forearm. "Listen to me, Jamee Night. We're going back in now, one step at a time."

A distant flash of movement drew her gaze to the horizon.

"No, don't look down. Look at me. Listen to my voice. Forget everything else."

As the mist closed in, Jamee grew disoriented. "I—I can't see."

"Just listen. You'll hear the wind in a moment, then the birds. Now, stay with me, because we're heading in now."

The cloud wall stretched without end, cutting off all color, dampening every sound. Unconsciously, Jamee pressed closer to the stranger's chest as he took a first, slow step. "Are you sure we're going the right way?"

"Absolutely." His hand cupped her back. "Now we're going to take five steps to my left. Stay with me."

"Like lint. You couldn't scrape me off," she rasped. "H-how much farther is it?"

"Almost there. Just keep moving."

She took a ragged breath and tried to relax. "You're Scottish?"

"I was born to the north."

Jamee forced her whole being to focus on the slow cadence of his voice, low and smooth at her ear. Anything but the emptiness that yawned somewhere to the left, hidden by deadly fog. She had just begun to relax when her heel caught. As she lurched forward, hard hands reached out to catch her.

"Careful."

"Who said Scotland was a place for peace and quiet?"

"Oh, the Highlands can be quiet, all right." He inched backward, his hands holding her waist tightly. "But only when they're not being wild and treacherous." A quick step, then another. Mist swirled past in shapeless streams. "But you've got to take the land as you find it, for it holds its own surprises."

"I think I've had enough surprises for one day," she muttered.

"Almost there. That boulder you just tripped over was at the edge of the cliff." His hand slid into the small of her back, guiding her to safety.

Jamee felt her shoulder brush the solid line of a granite overhang. She reached out dizzily, her chin jammed against his neck. "Are we safe yet?"

"We're safe. How are you doing, Jamee Night?"

She realized she was shivering. She laughed wildly as she clutched the soft wool lapels of his jacket. "Good. So good I think I might be sick any second." She held on tight, savoring his warmth and the scratch of the weathered tweed.

Something touched her hair. "Better?"

"I might actually be able to breathe again." Her head tilted back. "You never told me your whole name."

"Ian McCall.'

Jamee smiled crookedly. "Hello, Ian McCall," she whispered.

"Hello, to you, Jamee Night."

She wondered why being wrapped in his arms felt so comfortable.

Jamee felt an odd lurch in her chest. There was only the heat and weight of their bodies, the scrape of his tweed at her cool cheek.

"You're crying," he said gruffly, his palm covering her cheek.

"I am *not.*"

His hand opened, finding dampness. "Then what's this?"

"Mist."

"Mist, is it?" Ian asked gravely. His fingers slid down her braid, knot by heavy knot. "You've got wonderful hair, Jamee Night."

"You can't see it in this fog."

"But I can feel it," he whispered as his hands caught the weight of her hair.

Jamee tensed, expecting to panic at the caress. How long had it been since a man had touched her like this? Six months? A year?

Abruptly, his hands slid away. He muttered a phrase she didn't understand. "That was damn stupid of you. You could have been killed diving at me that way."

"It seemed the thing to do at the time. I couldn't walk away when you were in danger."

"You're brave. Maybe too brave."

"Tell that to my knocking knees," Jamee said weakly. "You really weren't going to jump?"

"No, I was not."

She frowned. "Then what were you doing out there on the cliff edge?"

He made an irritated sound. "I was looking for something."

"And did you find it?"

He eased back against a granite boulder, taking her with him, curled against his chest. "You ask too many questions."

"That's not an answer." Jamee made out his smile, slow and grave. She realized it was heartbreakingly beautiful as it lit every corner of his face.

"I don't believe I did. But I think maybe I found something else."

His lips brushed her nose, then swept over her open mouth. She forgot everything but the weight of his hands at her back and the warm touch of his mouth as something stirred inside her.

The ache grew into a feeling Jamee hadn't known for months.

Desire, slow and sweet.

The shock of it made her hand tremble at his neck. "I don't think this is such a good idea."

"You're right, it isn't," he said, frowning.

Jamee closed her eyes and shivered.

"Jamee?"

She swallowed, unable to speak. The cold fear returned, overwhelming her with harsh memories. After all these years, she still tasted the terror of being betrayed and held against her will.

"Jamee, we're safe."

She shook her head blindly. Why did the panic always sweep up out of her memory? Why couldn't the past stay finished and forgotten?

She pushed away from him. "I'd better go. My car is over there by the road." She turned, frowning at the blank wall of clouds. Her car was totally hidden now.

A black shape shot past her head. "What was that?"

"A seagull. The fog's getting worse."

"I've got to get away. Out of here. N-now." She fought to keep the anxiety from her voice.

"You're not going anywhere near the road. This fog could last for hours—or even days. We've got to get to shelter while we can still see."

"No. I'm heading to my car and then I'm driving back to the village of Dunraven. I have business there," she said desperately.

Ian cupped her shoulder. "Look around you, Jamee. You can't possibly drive in this."

"I can't stay," she said raggedly, trying to pull free of his grip.

"Dammit, will you stop and listen? Keep going that way and you'll walk right off the cliff."

"You're wrong." Her voice faltered. "Aren't you?"

"Go ahead and find out. Just don't expect me to follow you this time."

She stood uncertainly, shifting from foot to foot while the fog pushed past in wet streaks. He was right, she couldn't see even a foot away. Her hands clenched. "Where would we go?"

"There's an old crofter's cottage about a quarter of a mile up the hill. With luck, I should be able to guide us there, but not if we stand here talking. It will be dark in a few minutes."

"But it's barely two!"

Ian shrugged. "Welcome to the Highlands, Ms. Night."

"Why can't we go to Dunraven Castle? I'm expected later today with a set of textiles for the laird and his wife. Everything was planned."

"Dunraven Castle is at least ten kilometers from here," Ian said impatiently. "I have no intention of trying to drive there or anywhere else in this fog. One miscalculation and we'd be flotsam on the beach."

Jamee made a low, angry sound. "All right," she said warily. "But first I need to call Dunraven Castle and tell them what's happened."

"There's a telephone in my car." Sighing, Ian gripped her hand and tugged her across the gravel toward a battered Jeep. Without a word he pushed her into the passenger seat, then leaned down to pull a mobile phone from the floor. "Make your call, then let's go."

"Thank you," Jamee said tightly.

Ian strode toward the front of the car, scowling. He had been following her since dawn, careful to stay well out of sight. The deception irritated him. Keeping a distance generally misfired, just as it had this morning when Jamee had turned off the cliff road several kilometers back. He had missed her turn and had had to double back until he'd caught sight of her parked car. He had been looking for *her* when he'd been caught off guard and knocked squarely to the ground by the very person he was supposed to protect.

Adam Night was wrong, Ian thought grimly. This was *not* going to work. But before he could find a replacement, he'd have to get Jamee to safety, out of this fog and off these bloody cliffs.

"Kara?" Ian heard Jamee's breathless voice behind him. "Is this Dunraven Castle? What— Hello? Hello?"

Moments passed. Ian turned as the door creaked open. "Something wrong?"

"I lost the connection. The static was terrible."

"You can try again later." Ian closed the phone and slid it beneath the seat. "We have to go. Unless maybe you'd rather spend the night here, freezing in the car."

"I need my bag. It's across the road." Before he could stop her, Jamee followed the gravel edge of the road to a row of boulders.

Through the mist Ian saw her reach for a white canvas bag and pull it over her shoulder. The fabric strained, every inch crammed full. "You need to carry all of that?"

"Yes, I do." Jamee winced, shifting the bag over her shoulder.

Ian started up the slope, the wet turf slippery beneath his feet. "This climb may turn rough. In a few minutes it's going to be black as peat out here." He shoved his leather knapsack over his shoulder and tugged a compass from his pocket. One misjudged step would take them both plunging off one of the small, rocky spurs that surrounded the trail. Muttering, he grasped Jamee's arm and pulled her up the slope.

"You really *are* worried, aren't you?" she said softly.

"Of course I'm worried. The weather can change in an instant. There's a reason a dozen or so hikers are lost in these mountains every year."

To Ian's surprise, Jamee didn't complain as they struggled over low rocks and wet peat. In fact, he could almost have sworn he heard her reflexive gasp turn into a chuckle as they plunged into an icy burn.

"I don't suppose you could manage to find the dry route."

"I'll be lucky to find any route at all." How could the woman be so calm? That bag had to be hurting her shoulder, and they both might as well have been blind in this weather. "Are you all right with that satchel?"

"Fine," she said breathlessly. "It's kind of exciting. The smell is wonderful, all saltwater and pine trees." Abruptly, the wind changed, bringing a musky scent. Jamee laughed softly. "Even I know what that is. Your famous Scottish sheep."

"Some would call them infamous." Ian pulled the compass out again and squinted at the face, nearly invisible in the thick gray pall of unnatural dusk. "There should be three flat boulders somewhere to our left."

"What about to the right?"

"A marsh that I'd greatly prefer to avoid." A deadly cliff dropped off to the right of the marsh, but Ian didn't tell Jamee that. Once they were safe and dry, it would make an exciting story rather than a gruesome possibility.

"Does that mean we're close?"

"Less than twenty yards, assuming I haven't lost all sense of direction in this bloody fog." Abruptly, Ian pulled Jamee to a halt. "Listen." An ominous whisper rose around them.

"What is it?"

"A waterfall. Not where it should be, either." Ian frowned. "Where did you smell those sheep?"

"To my right. About three o'clock, I'd say."

The sheep would know how to avoid the swollen stream, and with it the deadly crags just beyond. "We'll go where the sheep go."

"Why?"

"Because they have a path, and their way is the shortest way up."

"Are you sure?" Jamee said dubiously.

"Of course I'm sure." As sure as he could be of anything in this fog. "Let's go." The air was darker, gray instead of the dirty white it had been when they'd crossed the burn. Ian pulled the heavy bag from Jamee's shoulder as she swayed under its weight, then took her arm, helping her over the wet turf.

"Wait. I felt something by my foot." Jamee bent down, running her hands over the ground. "How many stones did you say there were supposed to be?"

"Three. Flat and about as high as your knee."

"Here they are," she announced.

"Follow the angle of the stones upward." Ian cursed soundlessly. Moisture slid past his collar, chilling his neck and back. He prayed there would be dry peat and kindling in the cottage.

"Ian?"

"What?"

"I felt something else." Jamee's teeth were chattering. "Down by my foot. This was no rock."

"Don't move," he said harshly.

A shape lumbered out of the fog, brushing against their legs. Low bleating rose in a sad protest.

Jamee burst into startled laughter. "We've found those mountain-climbing sheep of yours. Now, if we can only find that cottage. It's getting cold out here."

Five steps more, Ian calculated, tugging Jamee beside him. As his hand brushed weathered wood, a wave of relief hit him. He didn't like the way this scenario was developing, and he wanted Jamee inside where she would be safe.

He felt his way to the heavy metal door latch. "One fire coming up," he announced, sweeping open the cottage door.

THE COTTAGE WASN'T sumptuous, but a quick glance told Ian it held the basic necessities. He shrugged out of his wet jacket and handed Jamee a candle on a tin holder. "Use this until I can make a fire."

Within minutes, he found two oil lanterns and a box of homemade candles. Soon warm golden light filled the room, outlining the thick stone fireplace and rows of copper pans, which hung on the adjoining walls. Baskets were suspended from the low rafters, full of drying flowers and bunches of herbs. Hand-woven tartan blankets were piled on a long sofa that had seen better days. Two spindly chairs flanked the far door leading to a back scullery room.

Ian deftly swung two pieces of dried peat into the smoke-stained fireplace and angled them into a wedge above a mound of kindling. Flame spiraled upward, lighting his face and streaking his dark hair with lines of gold.

"Worrying?"

Jamee blinked and met his gaze. "About what?"

"If you'll be safe here alone with me."

She took a few seconds to answer. "Should I be worried?"

"You don't know the slightest thing about me," Ian said. "I could be an ax murderer, for all you know."

"Funny, I don't see any axes sticking out of your pocket."

"I'm serious," he said, angry at her for being flippant. Angrier at himself for letting them get caught in such a mess. He should have been monitoring the weather more closely. He also should have noticed her turn from the road sooner. Now the fog might strand them here for days.

"So am I. Like it or not, you have an honest face, Ian McCall."

"Criminals don't always look like Boris Karloff," he said grimly, watching flames lick at the peat. A second after he said it, Ian could have kicked himself.

But Jamee hardly seemed to notice, fascinated by the dance of the fire as she shrugged out of her damp coat and began unbraiding her hair. Ian sat back on his heels, watching her work a brush through the long, thick strands. Each coil gleamed red-gold in the firelight, every wave alive with shadows and vibrant color. He wondered how her hair would feel wrapped around his fingers.

He pushed to his feet, all too aware of Jamee Night as a woman, rather than a client. Frowning, he strode to the far wall.

"Can I help?"

"I saw a kettle in that chest." Ian's search revealed a black iron kettle, two chipped mugs and a canister each of sugar and flour. "Not exactly Cordon Bleu, but they'll do." He turned and found Jamee looking up at him while she continued to brush her hair.

"I have some tea in my bag."

Ian realized he was staring at her hair. "Good. I'll go fetch some water," he said abruptly.

"You're not going all the way back to that stream, are you?"

Ian pulled open the back door. As he'd hoped, there was a rain barrel just outside. "No farther than this," he called over his shoulder. "Rainwater makes the finest tea in the world."

When he returned, Jamee had shrugged out of her sodden sweater and jeans and wrapped herself in a tartan blanket. She searched in her canvas bag.

"Cherry-oatmeal granola bars or—" She looked up and smiled faintly. "Cherry-oatmeal granola bars?"

Ian thought longingly of the pine-grilled salmon that was Dunraven's specialty. He could almost taste the steaming baby potatoes and shiitake mushrooms. "Granola bars," he repeated. "What kind of tea?"

"Chamomile. Very soothing."

Ian had been dreaming of something, single malt with a definite kick. "The chamomile will be fine." He examined the bags gingerly, then dropped them into the mugs. When the kettle began to hiss, Ian filled both to the brim.

Jamee eyed him curiously. "You look comfortable in a kitchen."

"I get by," he muttered, handing her a steaming mug.

"Tell me what you think."

He'd hoped she wouldn't ask. The granola bars tasted like cardboard and the tea didn't smell much better. Ian swallowed and managed a smile. "Wonderful."

Jamee settled back, took a sip, then set her mug on the floor and watched him expectantly. "Now you can get on the telephone and check the weather."

Ian took another bite of dried oatmeal and forced himself to swallow. "Sorry, but there's no phone up here. You already know what the weather has done to reception on the car phone—even if we could get back there."

She tapped restlessly on the floor. "Then try the radio."

"No radio, either, I'm afraid."

"You *can't* be serious."

Ian wondered if he could stash the rest of the granola bar, but decided she was too sharp. Unable to swallow, he merely nodded in reply.

"I don't believe it." Jamee twisted, searching the room.

Ian took the opportunity to toss the thick wad neatly into the fire.

"There's really nothing here?" she demanded. "No radio? No telephone?"

"No electricity, either."

Jamee's blanket slipped forgotten from her shoulders. "Then how are you going to tell anyone we're here? How are we going to get *help?*"

Ian set his mug down by the hearth. "We're not."

He didn't like the situation any more than she did, but at least he hadn't detected any sign that she was being followed—by anyone other than himself.

Jamee stumbled to her feet and clutched the blanket tighter over her damp camisole. The movement made her hair spill wildly about her shoulders. "I only agreed to come up here because I assumed there would be some contact with the outside world—if not a phone, then at least some way of tracking this blasted fog and knowing when we'll get out of here. I—I can't stay," she said unsteadily. "Not here. People are expecting me at Dunraven."

She was fighting her fear with anger, Ian realized. He wondered yet again why she had been out on the cliffs above the sea. "We'll get out when we get out, Ms. Night," he said coolly, refusing to lie to her. She had been told enough lies.

"And just when will *that* be?"

"When the fog lifts and not a second before."

Jamee kicked the blanket out of her way and struggled into her wet jeans, presenting Ian with a view of smooth, slender thighs. "That's it, I'm out of here. You probably are an ax murderer after all." She shoved her canvas bag over her shoulder, then yanked open the door.

Mist blanketed the hillside, swirling like steam as it coiled over the floor. Beyond the doorway nothing was visible but a wall of gray.

"I'm *still* going." Damp white strands feathered over Jamee's neck and made her shiver. "Right now." She glared at the ground and cursed softly.

Ian slanted one broad shoulder against the smoke-stained fireplace and waited. She was impetuous, but he knew she wasn't stupid.

Her hands moved restlessly. "I have to go," she whispered. Without a word Ian crossed the room, reached for her bag and turned her around. "Sit down and relax. No one could go anywhere in that fog. I promise I'll tell you as soon as there's a break in the weather."

Jamee paced stiffly before the fire, her eyes dark with worry.

"What's wrong? Is there a boyfriend somewhere who'll be impatient when you don't phone?"

"No."

"No boyfriend, or no, he won't be impatient?"

"No boyfriend." Shivering, she picked up the blanket and wrapped it around her shoulders as she sank to the floor. "That fog will have to lift sometime. What's another hour or two?"

Ian didn't have the heart to tell her it was going to be a lot longer than a few hours before the weather changed. Instinct told him they were in for a long stay.

Outside the window, the fog frothed. Clinging to the old hills, it blotted out sky and earth, thicker than night.

Colder than memories.

"HE'S WHAT?" Darkness wrapped the weathered walls of Draycott Abbey as Nicholas Draycott gripped the phone tensely, staring at the moat.

"Disappeared. He called me earlier today from the ferry on the way to Dunraven. Then nothing." Duncan MacKinnon's voice boomed over the line. "He should have been here hours ago, Nicholas. Of course we didn't count on the bloody fog."

Nicholas remembered the vagaries of the Highland climate all too well. "How bad is it?"

"Bad enough for me to consider taking a nice investment property in the Caymans," Duncan said irritably.

"Ian's no fool. He probably pulled over to wait things out."

"There aren't many places to pull over on the cliff road," the Scotsman said. "He also mentioned that he wouldn't be coming alone."

"Damn." Nicholas sank into the worn leather chair behind his desk. "I just hope he found her in time."

"Found who?"

Nicholas hesitated, but Duncan would have to know sooner or later. "Jamee Night."

"Jamee Night, the textile designer? She was coming up here to discuss the hangings we've commissioned for Dunraven. I didn't realize she and Ian were friends."

"They weren't." Nicholas's voice was hard. "This is business."

Silence stretched out.

"The bloody monsters," Duncan said savagely. "Wasn't once enough?"

Nicholas glared out at the night sky, cold and chill with only a sprinkling of stars. "Kidnappers don't stop trying. If they do, there are always more to take their place. Especially with the kind of money that Nightingale Electronics stock commands. Jamee's family believes another attempt will be made. They've hired Ian to protect her."

"And now they've both disappeared. I don't like it, Nicholas, but it could be simple enough. You know how this fog can be." Duncan made a flat, angry sound. "I'd take the coast road down and look for them, but it would be suicidal until visibility improves."

"Unfortunately, I have to agree, which leaves us right where we started. Meanwhile, Jamee's brothers have been ringing me every ten minutes, demanding news. They're threatening to send in the cavalry."

"They won't find any cavalry up here," Duncan said. "Ian is the closest thing they'll find. If anyone can get her to safety, it will be him."

Nicholas didn't answer.

"What are you telling me?" Duncan demanded.

"You always did have a habit of reading people's minds. Damned uncanny of you, MacKinnon. Must be too much time with Kara."

"You're begging the question, my friend. If there's trouble, I want to know."

"It seems Jamee's old kidnapper has been bragging to his cellmate that he's about to come into a great deal of money. The prison psychiatrist mentioned that the man also went into a rage during a recent session and made threats against Jamee. He swore, she would have the punishment she deserved for escaping before. Apparently he was convincing enough that the psychiatrist felt he had to violate confidentiality and report the threats."

Duncan muttered a long string of Gaelic curses. "What can I do to help at this end?"

"Adam Night is wild with worry, but until this weather clears, there is very little any of us can do."

"I'll check the area via phone and see if any strangers were seen on the coast road. Maybe we can pinpoint their location."

"Just be discreet," Nicholas said tightly. "We can't be sure who else might be listening in."

"You think that—"

Nicholas picked up a Murano glass paperweight. The cold crystal rolled back and forth in his hands. "I don't know what to think, Duncan. Only that we'd better not make any mistakes. If we do, Jamee Night will be the one who pays." His voice hardened. "Again."

# CHAPTER FOUR

SHE COULDN'T STAY.

Jamee shivered and snuggled closer into the blanket. She hadn't slept well in years, not since she was kidnapped. All too often, she fell asleep, only to awake naked on the floor, cold and shaking, tangled in a mound of covers. The experts she had seen after the kidnapping had called it the residual effect of her trauma. In her sleep, she relived the hours of captivity, stripping off her clothes and fighting memories that wouldn't fade.

The last thing she wanted was to wake up stark-naked next to a total stranger. Even in her most far-flung travels, Jamee had always managed to find a room for herself and bolt the door to ward off any humiliating late-night encounters.

But not tonight.

Fine, Jamee decided. She simply wouldn't go to sleep. She would watch the fire and work on her new designs for Lord Dunraven and his wife. Heaven knew, she had enough yet to do. She sighed, thinking how wonderful a double mocha latte would taste.

Ian was bent over the fire, nursing more heat out of the glowing peat, his face unreadable. As Jamee watched, his features began to waver and blur. He had very nice eyes, the fresh green of summer moss. Though his hands were big, they were strangely graceful as he nudged the embers with a poker.

Jamee blinked and straightened. She didn't dare go to sleep.

When he had finished with the fire, Ian braced one arm on the mantel and murmured something in soft, rolling Gaelic.

"What did you just say?"

"An old Gaelic phrase."

Jamee sat up straighter as her eyelids began to grow heavy.

"Why don't you get some rest?"

"I'll be fine," she said firmly. "Was that some kind of prayer?"

Firelight glinted on Ian's face, shadowing his chin and cheek. "You might call it that, though it was composed long before kirk or cloister came to these hills," he said gravely.

"What does it mean?"

His voice softened and drifted toward her in a lyrical cadence. "Blaze of sun, flare of moon, glow of fire and burn of lightning. Be you today my strengths."

"It's lovely," Jamee breathed.

"There's power in the words, so my mother always said." He pushed away from the mantel. "You'd better rest. I'm hopeful we'll have better winds with morning. Meanwhile, we'll be fine in here."

The soft vowels lulled Jamee while she snuggled back into her blanket and tucked a corner of the lumpy sofa cushion beneath her arm. She wasn't actually going to sleep, of course. She would daydream a little and think about Scottish sheep while she watched the glowing peat. Just for a moment or two...

A moment later, her eyes fluttered shut.

DARKNESS PRESSED BLACK and cold at the windows as Ian stirred the fire. Though several hours had passed, the fog had still not lifted. Nor had his mood.

Jamee's hair tumbled over the blanket as she tossed and turned in her sleep, one hand outstretched. At any moment, Ian expected her to gasp and push to her feet, clawing at her clothes in fear. What would he do then?

He never should have accepted Adam Night's offer. No amount of money would make up for a careless mistake that harmed a life. Why had he let the man persuade him, especially now?

He squinted at the fire, studying the shifting shades of red and gold. There was no more blurring of his vision, thank God. His color perception seemed true enough. But how long would it stay that way?

Quietly, he turned Jamee's sweater and his trousers, then stretched them across a pole by the fire to dry. One of the tartan blankets was caught about his waist, pleated with a belt in a creditable imitation of the very first tartans worn by his Highland ancestors. Mel Gibson would have howled. Then again, Mel Gibson would never have gotten himself into such a ludicrous situation, Ian thought grimly.

As the fog grew thicker, Ian slid his portable telephone from its case, but he was answered with static, not an uncommon occurrence in these remote areas. He replaced the wallet-size unit, then turned as Jamee mumbled sharply.

"Ian?" She sat bolt upright. "Ian, are you there?" Her voice rose, edged with panic. She glanced down, then clutched the sheet to her chest with a sigh.

Ian knew what that sigh meant and what had put the fear in her voice. "Right here," he said calmly. "Sleep well?"

She shoved back her hair, light winking and gleaming across the amber strands. "Not really. What time is it?"

"Nearly ten."

"I slept that long?" She shifted, trying to peer out the window. "Has the fog lifted yet?"

"I'm afraid not." Ian looked away, ignoring how the light played over her bare shoulders. Trying to, at least.

"I like the skirt." She pointed at his makeshift kilt.

"It's called a tartan, woman."

"Very *Braveheart*. Mel Gibson would be jealous." Jamee's smile faded. "How do you know the fog is getting worse?"

"Because I just checked."

"Maybe something has changed," she said hopefully.

"In two minutes? I doubt it. Why don't you go back to sleep?"

"No." Her voice fell. "I don't usually sleep well."

Ian heard the unmistakable edge of tension in her voice, but knew he couldn't betray his knowledge of the source. "Is something wrong?"

She tugged the blanket about her shoulders and propped one elbow on her knee. "Nothing I can't handle."

Ian heard her determination and wondered exactly what it cost her. Her memories couldn't be pleasant ones.

Not that his interest was personal. Jamee Night was his business now. Anything that affected her also affected his ability to protect her, and that included any problems she might be having.

But he wasn't thinking about problems or business as firelight gilded her expressive mouth and unbound hair. Muttering, he pulled a notepad onto his lap and began to write.

"What are you doing?"

"Writing."

"What kind of writing?"

Ian flipped a page. "Nothing important."

Jamee's blanket rustled. She hitched it back over one shoulder. "You can tell me." She spoke quickly, as if searching for distraction. Any distraction. "Is it a novel? Poetry? A Ph.D. thesis on the evolution of Scottish sheep?"

Ian hid a smile. "Go back to sleep, Jamee."

"I told you, I wasn't really sleeping."

"Then go back to whatever it was you were doing."

"I was thinking." Jamee's blanket rustled again. "I thought I saw a strange light back there on the cliff. At first I thought it was another car. But now I think it was them."

"Them?" Was she aware she might be followed? Had Adam let something slip about the possibility of another kidnap attempt? "You mean, someone you saw on the cliffs?"

"No, I mean, aliens." She spoke very deliberately, watching for his reaction.

Ian blinked. "I beg your pardon."

"They're here, you know." She hunched forward conspiratorially. "All around us."

"Illegal aliens? You mean people from Albania and Argentina?"

"I mean, people from a whole lot farther than that." Jamee studied the fire, her face grave.

"Like Australia?"

"No, like the Horsehead Nebula."

Ian frowned, his writing forgotten. She couldn't be serious. "Fascinating theory," he muttered.

"Oh, it's no theory." Jamee wiggled closer. "There's all sorts of concrete proof, from records of thousands of alien abductions to implants of strange technology. Even crop circles. They've been here for decades, maybe for centuries, but our governments don't want us to know." She gave a disgusted sigh. "Sheesh, where have you been for the last decade, McCall?"

Ian slapped down his pen and met her gaze. "Living a nice, logical life, Ms. Night."

"With your head buried in the sand? I can see I'm going to have to take you on a vacation to Area Fifty-one," she said firmly.

Ian blinked again. "I don't know what you're talking about."

"Unbelievable. The biggest government cover-up of the

century and the man's never even heard of it." She shook her head. "Wait until I tell you about the cow mutilations," she said, turning so quickly that her blanket gaped.

Ian forced his gaze away from the long arch of her creamy neck. "Now, just a minute—"

Abruptly her hair spilled forward, distracting him. She yanked the pad from his lap. "Got it!" Jamee danced to the other side of the room, scanning his lines of handwritten text. "Scottish castle, fifteenth century. Grade One listed, in a peaceful setting with full views of the Outer Isles. Remnants of moat intact." She looked up, frowning. "What does *that* mean?"

"Give me those papers." Ian spoke with soft menace as he pushed to his feet.

Jamee pulled the pages out of reach and picked up where she had left off. "One thousand acres, including salmon stream and grouse hunting. Sweep netting rights. Grouse shooting, deer stalking and loch fishing." She lowered the pad and stared at him. "This sounds like a real-estate description."

Ian made another grab for his papers. Jamee twisted away, ignoring him. "Working hatchery, deer larder. Separate stone-built farmhouse and five estate cottages. One thousand forty-one ewes and fifty-six cows." She tilted her head. "Do you write travel guides?"

"No, I do *not*," he growled.

Jamee stayed carefully out of range. "Then what is this?"

"Something that is none of your business." He was coldly precise in his fury, watching for his moment to strike.

"Touchy, aren't we?"

Ian lunged. He pinned her to the wall with one arm across her waist while he grabbed for his papers. The contact brought them flush, shoulder to shoulder, thigh to thigh.

The peat in the fireplace whispered. Jamee's body stilled,

her eyes filled with amber light. She flushed as his thigh wedged between hers. "One thousand forty-one eyes?"

He didn't move, didn't smile.

She swallowed. "That was supposed to be a joke, McCall," she said unsteadily. "A joke—as in laughter. Because if we don't laugh," she said softly, "in a few seconds we're going to do something very...stupid."

*Stupid* was far too polite for the thoughts Ian was having. He made a rough sound, staring at his hands buried in her hair and his thigh braced between hers. Her blanket had slipped again, revealing too much creamy skin.

"I know that you saved my life on the way up here," Jamee said huskily. "And all I did was act angry." She glanced down at the pad locked between their bodies, but Ian thought she was seeing something else entirely. Something that wasn't pleasant. "I'm sorry for that. Being angry was easier than..." She shook her head, shivering. "What I mean is, I should have been thanking you."

"There was no need," Ian said hoarsely. "I was in the right place at the right time. Simple luck, that's all."

She tilted her head and studied his face. The force of her gaze made Ian wish they weren't nearly so close.

"I've never been a believer in simple luck."

Ian took a sharp breath and pulled the papers out of her suddenly unresisting fingers, trying not to notice her pallor. Shadows played through her indigo eyes and suddenly the memory of Adam Night's video unreeled in Ian's mind.

What was he doing? This woman was plagued by nightmares, haunted by memories of men who had torn away her freedom and her dignity. He had no right to touch her or crowd her in any way.

Unfortunately, his body did not quite agree.

"Ian," she whispered.

He felt the words as her breath feathered his neck. He was fascinated by the sound of his name sliding off her lips. He wanted to hear her say it again.

Slowly. Huskily.

Paper tore beneath his fingers. "Jamee, I—"

A scratching sound came from the rear of the cottage. Jamee stiffened, pulling the blanket around her shoulders. "What was that?"

Ian frowned. "It could have been the wind."

The sound came again, low and hollow, like large nails dragged across metal.

"That was *not* the wind."

"No, it damned well wasn't." Ian reached for his jacket pocket and felt the comforting outline of his pistol. He had no intention of drawing it in front of Jamee, of course. Not unless absolutely necessary.

Silently he picked up the heavy iron poker. Something soft bumped his shoulder as he moved toward the door. He turned to find Jamee only inches behind him. "What are you doing?"

"I'm coming with you," she whispered.

Ian scowled. He didn't have time to argue with her, not at a time like this. "You're staying," he ordered.

"I'm coming. You might need help."

Muttering a string of Gaelic that would have made his mother wash out his mouth with charcoal, Ian anchored the poker in his right hand and yanked open the door.

Darkness seemed to swallow the faint light of the peat fire.

Something rustled close to the ground.

"Come out where I can see you, before I shoot." He itched to cradle his handgun, but experience had taught him that firearms limited one's choices. He would protect Jamee any way it took, but no bullets would fly until he knew exactly what he was facing.

The rustling ceased, sucked up by the damp mist. Jamee inched closer. "What now?" she whispered.

"Will you be quiet?" Ian raised the poker and inched forward into the mist. "This is the last time I'm going to ask. Who's there?"

Silence stretched around them.

Ian took another step, and Jamee was right behind him. "They're not coming out."

Ian glared at the darkness. "On the count of ten I start firing randomly." He pulled out his penknife and scraped the metal of the door handle. It wouldn't fool a ballistics expert, but to anyone else it would sound as if he were reloading. "One. Two."

Jamee was pressed against his back. "Ian…"

"Four. Five…"

Silence, long and heavy.

"Eight. Nine." Ian's hand slid into his pocket and cradled the cold barrel of his pistol. Frowning, he eased the safety free. What kind of professional would make a move in this kind of fog? It made no sense. "Ten. My patience is done. I'm coming after you."

Something rustled in the darkness and Ian heard a faint scrape of metal. A pistol being readied? "Go back inside," he ordered, shielding Jamee with his body.

"Please," she whispered. "Not alone."

Ian heard the break in her voice and for a moment his decision wavered. "I can't let you go. It's too dangerous."

Her eyes darkened. "I won't get in your way. Besides," she said uncertainly, "you can't really be expecting trouble. Not out here in the middle of nowhere."

"I'm *always* expecting trouble," Ian muttered, striding into the mist, careful to keep his body squarely in front of Jamee's.

## CHAPTER FIVE

IAN VANISHED after taking two steps. There was no sound, no shape, only a clinging veil of clouds, which swallowed him up instantly.

"Ian, wait!" Jamee surged after him, her heart pounding.

A hand circled her wrist. "I told you to stay inside."

"No." She stood rigid against his back. The clouds were suffocating, pressing down on her. Dammit, she *wouldn't* shiver. She wouldn't let herself remember. It was fog, water vapor, and nothing more. Not like then, when she was locked inside a closet with no room to move. "Ian," she said tightly, "I want to go with you. I *need* to go."

"Bloody hell. Come on then." Holding her wrist, Ian strode forward.

"Wasn't that a light?" Jamee asked warily, pointing past his shoulder.

"Where?"

"To the right." Her voice fell. "Ian, I think someone's out there."

"Stay close, dammit. And be quiet."

The ground angled up sharply, crossing a patch of bare rock. Jamee realized Ian was heading straight toward the light.

Why a light out here? she wondered. Was someone else lost in the fog? If so, why were Ian's hands so tense? Wouldn't a lost traveler be shouting for assistance?

As they moved beyond the light from the cottage into un-relenting darkness, Jamee finally acknowledged what she had suspected for long minutes now. Ian was acting as if he ex-pected danger. He was also acting like someone fully prepared to deal with that danger.

She didn't like the conclusion she was reaching. "Ian, I—"

"Shh."

Something rustled in the darkness. Suddenly Jamee was very glad of his hand on her wrist.

He took another cautious step. His boots scraped against a ridge of stone.

Something damp brushed past Jamee's legs and she yelped.

The fog parted to reveal a sheep, which bleated in fright and charged into Ian, who stumbled forward with a curse. A bell clattered as the bleating animal lurched off into the fog.

"Ian, it was just a sheep." Jamee's only answer was the sud-den splash of water. "Ian, where *are* you?"

He caught her outstretched hand. "Right here."

"You're soaked!"

"I took a wrong turn and landed in the creek." Ian's teeth were chattering as he stared into the fog, his jaw taut. There had been a light out there, on a slope where no light should be. He had seen its flicker again just before he'd tripped over that wretched sheep. Fortunately, Jamee seemed to have missed the second occurrence. "Let's get back." If there was one person outside, there could be others, and he wanted Jamee under cover where he could protect her.

He pushed Jamee through the door and bolted it, then took their trousers down from the pole before the fire. "These are dry." He tossed over her clothes.

Jamee stood stiffly. "You were worried by that light, weren't you?"

Ian avoided her gaze.

"And you knew what you were doing out there."

Ian shrugged.

"Answer my question."

"Would you mind turning around first?"

"Why?"

Ian's hands slid to his belt. "Because I want to change."

Jamee glanced lower and saw his hand on his belt. "Oh." Blushing, she turned her back to him, then yanked on her sweater and stepped into her well-worn jeans. "There was something out there. I saw it."

Ian pulled on his dry pants, cursing silently. He wasn't about to reveal his suspicions without a lot more evidence. "A sheep," he said tightly.

"No, before that. I saw a flash of light back toward the cliffs."

Ian found a dry sweater, and the heavy, oiled wool warmed him immediately, taking some of the tension from his shoulders. "Just a sheep."

"I didn't realize sheep carried lights," she snapped.

"Jamee, you could have imagined the light."

When she spun around, her face was pale. "But I didn't imagine the look on your face. You were worried, Ian. I want to know why."

She deserved more than lies, he thought angrily. But her brother had made the rules, and Ian had foolishly agreed to them. "I have a suspicious nature. Too much time spent living in cities, I suppose."

Her eyes narrowed. "What exactly do you do in those cities?"

Ian shrugged. "This and that."

"I think you're a police officer," Jamee said accusingly. "I want a straight answer. Are you with the police or aren't you?"

Ian slid on his belt. "No."

Not a lie. Not quite. Most of his work was with the government or private security groups.

Jamee glared at him. "Then why do you keep looking at the windows every few minutes? Why have you gotten up to check the door twice since we came in?"

She was too damned observant, Ian thought. He'd have to be more careful in the future. "I noticed that the bolt was stuck. I wanted to make sure the door doesn't blow open."

"I *hate* being lied to."

"I'll be sure to remember that." Ian stretched out on the floor, his back against a lumpy sofa cushion as he studied the fire.

"Did Adam put you up to this?"

"Who's Adam?" Ian said coolly.

"You're not going to tell me anything, are you?"

He worked a blanket beneath his head. "There's nothing to tell. Now, why don't you get some rest?"

"I told you I don't sleep very well." Muttering, Jamee sat on the floor and turned her bag over, dumping a dozen mounds of bright yarn into her lap. After fingering several balls, she picked up a skein of mohair the soft orange shade of a Highland sunset.

"Colorful." Ian wondered how long he had left to appreciate that particular shade of orange.

"What's wrong? Why are you staring like that?"

"No reason." Ian propped his head on one hand. She was too smart, and he was not going to give her any reason for alarm. "What are you making?"

"A sweater, probably." Jamee's hands moved with the ease of a practiced knitter. Beneath her needles the thick yarn fell into even rows. "Knitting helps me think."

Ian wasn't sure he wanted her to think right now. Not until he had some clear answers. He didn't like the thought of being followed, even though the backup team from London wouldn't be far behind him.

"Since you refuse to discuss what you saw in the fog, tell me about that description in your notebook."

This was a safer topic of conversation, Ian decided. "My castle, you mean?"

The needles went still. "Are you serious? A fifteenth-century castle, fifty-six cows and four outbuildings? Yours?"

"Every brick and shed."

Jamee looked stunned. "Does this castle happen to have a name?"

"Glenlyle. That happens to be my name, too."

"A title?" Jamee shook her head in shock. "A real, live lord? I saved a real live lord from jumping."

"I was *not* about to jump."

"Don't bother me with fine points." Her eyes gleamed. "Glenlyle Castle. And it's really fifteenth-century?"

"Some of it is even older. There are carved stones in the courtyard that probably predate the Vikings."

"Haunted, no doubt?"

Ian shook his head. "Not that I've ever seen." He'd heard, of course. Over the breakfast table every visitor to Glenlyle reported at least one strange encounter from the night before. And then there was the story of Glenlyle's cursed lovers.

Another row of orange knots formed beneath Jamee's expert fingers. "So why did you need the description?"

Ian thought of Glenlyle's windswept towers facing the restless sea. A weight settled over his chest. "It isn't important. Go to sleep." He rose abruptly and strode to the window. In the fireplace the peat hissed softly, while fog pressed outside at the glass. Despite his tension, he was suddenly conscious of their solitude and the intimacy of the scene. "You could have been hurt coming after me in the dark, you know. Did you stop to think of that?"

"No."

"You should have," he said tightly.

"If I stop to think about things, I get frightened or embarrassed and then I'm afraid to finish. Now I try not to plan things too much." She shrugged. "Adam gives me hell for it."

"And who," Ian asked, "is Adam? Boyfriend or lover?"

"Brother," she said.

"No lovers? No boyfriends of any sort?"

"Is that odd?" she asked, utterly guileless. Her eyes were filled with firelight, and her skin glowed the color of Botticelli's Madonna that hung in the library at Glenlyle. For another woman it would be odd, but not for Jamee.

Not after what she'd been through.

*Don't let it get personal,* Ian told himself. She was beautiful and vulnerable, despite her determined front. And he couldn't let any of that touch him.

But light danced in her hair, outlining the full curve of her mouth as she watched him, unblinking. Ian wondered if her eyes would change if he pulled her into his arms. He wondered how she would taste if he kissed her slowly, feeling her come alive beneath his touch.

He bit back a Gaelic curse, blocking the heated images.

"Was that another prayer?"

"I wish it were." He stirred the fire. "Stop looking at me like that."

"Like what?"

"As if you trusted me."

"I do trust you," she said calmly.

"What if I were some kind of criminal? Maybe I even have a gun."

"You don't. I checked your bag when you went out to get water."

Ian was stunned. He was also glad he had been wearing his jacket when he went out. Another thing to remember in the future.

"Tell me what you were doing out on that cliff," Ian said, changing the subject. "Before you decided to rescue me, of course."

Jamee shrugged. "Oh, this and that."

"That doesn't tell me much."

"No, I don't suppose it does."

"Are you always this secretive?" Ian asked.

"Are you always this inquisitive?" Her needles clicked back and forth. "Is there a wife at that castle of yours?"

"Does it matter?"

Her hands slowed. "I'm not sure. You have a beautiful mouth, you know."

This time Ian's Gaelic curse was longer and more inventive than the last. Ian Fraser Douglass McCall did *not* have a beautiful mouth. A laird of Glenlyle did *not have a beautiful mouth*.

He was all set to tell her that when he heard her yawn. She was two feet away, snuggled against the cushions, telling him he had a beautiful mouth. Then she yawned while he entertained fantasies that were fast becoming uncomfortably graphic.

"Dammit, I do not have a beautiful—" Ian stopped. "Jamee?"

She was sound asleep, yarn dropped at her side, knitting needles forgotten at her chest.

Ian took a long, slow breath, feeling her beauty eat into his very soul.

He covered her gently, trying to ignore the warmth of her

hair, cascading red and golden over his fingers. Only then did he realize his hands were trembling.

A fine protector *he* made.

"A beautiful mouth indeed," he said roughly. He found a spot as far away from her as the walls of the cottage would allow.

It wasn't nearly far enough, he discovered, watching Jamee sleep.

*HEAT RISES IN SLOW WAVES, each breath coming harder. There is no running, no crying out. The silence knows where to follow and it always finds her. Chokes her.*

*She shakes, so terrified she can only whimper, her lips dry and broken.*

*There is no time in the Dream. No past, no future. Only the sick, shattering now.*

*"You can't get away," the Dream people whisper, tying her hands and shoving her over the mud.*

*"N-no." She fights as she had then. Useless.*

*"Get in."*

*She screams. He hits her, not enough to knock her out. Just enough to make sure she obeys.*

*"Get in and be quiet."*

*The closet is small and black and hot. She can't close her eyes.*

*Not again. Not down there in the darkness and the heat.*

*"Why?" As always, she tries to understand something for which there is no understanding.*

*"Because you're here and we're hungry. You're the meal ticket. Mommy and Daddy will pay. Nice Mommy and Daddy."*

*The laughter rises, cold and loud.*

*"Not in the closet. Please…"*

*Outside in the night the moon burns in the summer sky.*

*Hard hands press at her back. She whimpers in the darkness when the heavy door slams shut behind her. So alone.*

*There is no time in the Dream. No past, no future. Only the sick, shattering now.*

THE SCRAPE OF METAL woke Ian. He lurched upright, instantly alert. Something cold brushed his face.

The door was open. Fog frothed over the threshold, ghostly in the light of the dying fire.

"Jamee?"

Nothing moved. Her blanket was on the table. Her sweater was tossed on the floor, her jeans slung crazily on a chair across the room.

But the woman who had worn them was gone.

## CHAPTER SIX

IAN GRABBED an oil lantern from the worn table and shoved a match to the wick. The spark had barely caught before he plunged outside into the night. Chill waves of cloud pressed at his face as he listened to the silence, his heart pounding. "Dammit, Jamee, where *are* you?"

Water slapped somewhere to his left. He gripped the lantern, skidding down the muddy slope, then called again.

A tiny, broken sound drifted up the hill.

"Answer me, Jamee."

The sound came again. Ian lurched forward, stumbling in the mud while the lantern swung wildly in his hands.

He glimpsed her through the mist, huddled against a rock. Beads of water gleamed on her pale skin and her eyes were wide, frightened like an animal's.

Ian could almost smell her terror. "Can you hear me, Jamee?"

She whimpered again. Her hands moved restlessly, shoving at invisible walls.

Ian knelt beside her, holding the lantern high, trying to keep the fury from his voice. Jamee would not understand that his rage was not for her, but the men who had left her like this. "It's Ian, Jamee." He kept his voice to a whisper. "Everything will be all right. Let's go in by the fire now." He reached out for her, then stopped. His hands clenched helplessly. How could he reach her, locked as she was in the past?

He remembered the chilling images from Adam Night's videotape. She was back there now, looking through the eyes of a frightened child helpless in the dark. And Ian could only kneel beside her, terrified to do anything that might add to her pain.

He held out the lantern, letting the light filter around her. "You take it, Jamee. Then we'll go home. The fire will feel good."

She moved jerkily, like someone who had been drinking. Her fingers gripped the lantern handle and the broken, keening noise came again. "Light," she said hoarsely.

"There's more light in the cottage. You can lead the way. You remember, don't you?"

She blinked, stiff with cold. Her eyes were dazed and unfocused. Ian yearned to pull her into his arms, but he knew the wrong movement could trigger the terror anew. If she bolted now, he wasn't certain he could catch her in the fog.

Not in time. Not if someone else was waiting for the same chance.

"Ready?"

She rose awkwardly, her arms rigid. How long had she been there, huddled in the mist? Dammit, why hadn't he heard her go out?

She took a step forward and swayed, then caught herself on the rock. Ian had to clench his hands to keep from touching her. Not yet, dammit. Not while she was so afraid. "Up the hill, Jamee. See the fire through the door?"

She frowned, moving awkwardly up the muddy slope. Her body glowed, as pale as the fog in the light cast from the lantern she carried.

At the door, Jamee blinked, then moved jerkily to the fire

and sat before it. Her hands anchored her knees as she swayed from side to side, crooning softly.

In that second Ian understood Adam Night's anguish and fury at a nightmare no amount of love could erase.

She made a low sound as Ian slid a blanket around her shoulders. "What is it, Jamee?"

Her hand rose toward the fire.

"Cold?"

A jerky nod.

Ian reached for another blanket, then paused as he saw her hand rise. Toward him.

His breath twisted in his throat as he gently took her fingers, feeling them grip and tighten, like those of a swimmer finding a lifeline in a storm. He knelt beside her and pulled the blanket closer.

He didn't speak, understanding the silent war she waged every night in dreams that would have made grown men sink to their knees, broken.

Grimly, he held her hand while her tension ebbed. It felt like hours later that he stretched out beside her, while the peat hissed gently beside them.

As Ian watched the fire, rigid and unblinking, he swore that no one would get past him to hurt her again.

JAMEE SAT UP, shoved her hair from her face, then froze. Ian slept behind her, one broad hand curled about her blanket. His muscled thigh had pillowed her cheek as she slept.

Thank God, she was still dressed. Sweater, jeans, everything appeared to be in place. Maybe she hadn't had the Dream after all.

She eased to her feet, careful not to wake Ian. Banks of cloud still paled the windows as thickly as before, but some morning light managed to filter through the fog. She washed her face in rainwater from a copper bowl by the far wall, feeling strangely restless. How had she and Ian come to be sleeping only inches apart? Had he heard a sound in the night? Or had she cried out in her dreams, causing him to comfort her?

She could remember nothing.

But her body was leaden, tense, the way she always felt after her recurring nightmare. And as always, she could remember none of the details.

Drawing a deep breath, she looked at Ian. Asleep, he looked younger, though tension still gripped his shoulders and kept his fingers clenched on the blanket.

Like it or not, his mouth *was* beautiful.

Jamee frowned, wondering why she felt so safe in Ian McCall's company. He exuded confidence and power, both discreet, sensed more than seen. That was part of the reason, but not all.

She decided that Ian McCall looked like what he was—a man who had made hard decisions, maybe once too often. The shadows of those choices haunted Jamee every time she looked into his green eyes.

What would it take to know him deeply, to slide past his defenses and smooth the shadows from that hard face?

Not her right. She was a woman who never stayed, a woman who skated over the surface of her life, wary of the dark currents beneath. Yet for a moment, with this man she had felt a hunger for something deeper. A touch that would join, expose and bind deeply.

*Definitely* not her right.

Jamee studied the blank windows. Honest feelings were usually dangerous; with this man they would be more dangerous than most.

Sighing, Jamee put Ian McCall from her mind. One thing was certain: they wouldn't be going anywhere today. After a last disgusted glance at the fog, Jamee picked up her bag. If she was stuck here, at least she was going to finish some work.

IAN TWITCHED, hugged the pillow then sat bolt upright. "Jamee?"

Her bed was empty. He was on his feet when he heard the clatter of pans across the room. "Where are you?"

"Right here." Her hair was held back by a swatch of indigo satin the same shade as her eyes. She was dressed in jeans and a fluffy sweater, with a tartan tossed around her shoulders like a shawl. Shadows ringed her eyes. "Sleep well?"

Her radiant smile ran through Ian like 50,000 volts of direct current. He cleared his throat. "Fine. What about you?"

"Well enough. I thought I'd let you rest, since you looked exhausted." Her head cocked. "Bad dreams?"

*She doesn't know,* he thought. *She truly doesn't remember anything about last night.* Adam had said forgetting was part of her trauma, but Ian hadn't believed it until now.

He turned away and pulled on his sweater, afraid she would read the shock in his eyes. "I don't know. I never remember my dreams." He took his time pulling down one sleeve. "Do you?" he asked casually.

"Sometimes." She frowned and made a sharp gesture, as if shoving a cobweb from her face. Then her smile slid back, full and utterly real. "Breakfast is served, my lord."

"Excellent. That would be salmon lightly roasted with sage and scones with fresh blueberries." Ian steepled his fingers. "After that I'll have coffee, very strong."

Jamee held out a chipped bowl. "What you'll have, my lord, is oatmeal." She looked rueful. "Very dark."

Ian's lips curved. "*Wheesht,* and how did you know that I was wishing for a bowl of oatmeal, lass?"

"It's burned, I'm afraid. I haven't got the hang of cooking over an open fire yet."

Ian took the bowl and settled back on the floor. The cereal was hot and creamy and he ate with relish. "Only a little scorched. What did you have?"

"The last of the granola bars and my chamomile tea." Jamee rested her chin on her palm, watching him eat. "It made me feel very dangerous to be finishing off the last of my larder."

"Don't worry, I'll find us something." Ian put aside the bowl, stood up and stretched. "What have you got over there?" He nodded at the line of pots ranged over the long pine trestle table.

"Just dye."

Ian's brow rose. "Is that an order?"

"Not die. *Dye*. As in madder. Also logwood, indigo, weld and walnut husks." Jamee lifted a mound of dusky-pink yarn from a pan over the fire. "This is the madder batch. I've nearly run out of mordant."

"Mordant?"

"Chemical to set the dye." Jamee pointed toward a plastic bottle. "I usually use alum or copper sulfate." She moved restlessly from yarn to yarn, touching each color as if compelled. "This one needs to simmer for another half hour or so to reach the fullest shade. These two are nearly done."

So that's what she carried in her bag, Ian thought. Mordants and dyes. Madder and indigo. He suppressed a smile. Most women would have packed lipstick and a curling iron, but not Jamee.

Jamee Night was clearly one of a kind.

But Ian was worried about her. He'd cleaned the mud from her body and dressed her before falling asleep. Now the night was a blur, but her memories were still there. They burned in her eyes and in her restless movements. Talking about the trauma would be painful, but it was the only way she'd ever close the book on her experience.

Ian rubbed his jaw. "Jamee, maybe you should—"

"Hmm?" She stirred a batch of simmering yarn the color of ripe plums. "Do you like this one?"

"It's very nice, but—"

"The landscape is so lovely here, soft and muted. I took this color from the mist on the heather."

She had captured the shade perfectly, Ian thought. But he was far more concerned about what had happened to her last night. "I wanted to ask you about—"

"My materials?" She gestured eagerly, and her wooden spoon struck one of the pans. "All natural. Why wear something dyed with coal tar? Besides, you can't get this kind of subtle color with an aniline dye." She laughed suddenly and ran a hand through her hair. "Sorry. I do tend to rage on about color."

Ian thought she was a study in color herself, with her hair a dozen hues of red, her eyes and skin gilded by the flickering fire. The fine flush to her cheeks made him want to ease close and—

"Ian?"

He realized he was inches from her cheek. He straightened, his breath hot and tight in his throat as he fought the spell she wove around him. Feelings didn't count, he told himself. Not when he was working.

"I think I'd better have a look around. See what the fog is like." He strode to the back door, making the same circuit he'd made a dozen times since they'd arrived. He checked the narrow back scullery and made certain the bolts were sill secure. There was no way he would be caught unprepared again.

Meanwhile, he was neither Jamee's priest, nor her guardian,

Ian reminded himself. He was here to protect her body, not heal her soul.

Somehow he would have to remember that.

WAS IT SOMETHING she had said?

Jamee stirred the plum-colored dye, remembering the wariness that had filled Ian's eyes before he strode outside. Maybe her monologue about dyes had sent him running. She was a fanatic on the subject, and most men developed glazed eyes at the mention of anything remotely connected to color, texture and fabric design.

All except for her brothers. Jamee had Adam, Bennett and William well trained by now. They could tell the difference between a twill and a jacquard at ten paces.

But Ian McCall was different from her brothers and any other man she'd known.

Finished with her dyes, she sat down before the fire and pulled her knitting needles out of her bag. Back on the cliff she had expected to freeze up when Ian had kissed her. At first she *had*. Then something unexpected had happened, something that welled up from her toes and skittered through her chest, leaving her shaken.

Why had Ian McCall sent her pulse racing when she tensed at the touch of any other man? Even Noel had made her anxious when he kissed her. He had been willing to wait for more, offering her a nice civilized pact. Nothing intimate—not now and maybe not ever.

Jamee had been the one to refuse. She wanted a real relationship or nothing. Trust didn't come in fractions, after all.

Ian would never make that kind of pact, she thought. When *he* loved, it would be all or nothing. Lucky would be the woman who shared his passion.

She gnawed on her lip as another row of knitting slid away.

Maybe she felt at ease with him because of his formality. He was more mature than the men she knew, his control never slipping even when he'd fallen in the stream.

The needles dropped from Jamee's fingers as a sudden idea unfolded. A wild idea.

An impossible idea.

## CHAPTER SEVEN

"YOU WANT ME TO DO *WHAT?*" Ian asked as he closed the door.

Jamee had been waiting for him. His first thought had been that something was wrong. His second was that she'd inhaled too much dye.

She asked the question again in one quick breath.

Ian simply stared at her.

Her damp palms skittered over the length of the soft mohair she had just finished knitting.

He propped his hands on his hips. "I don't think I heard you right."

Jamee closed her eyes. When the silence held, she clutched her yarn and spun around. "Forget I asked."

Ian's palm covered her arm. "I don't want to forget it, Jamee. I just want to understand. Explain it to me." He cleared his throat. "You want me to...*touch* you?"

Jamee took a ragged breath. "With you, it's different, don't you see? You kissed me on the cliff."

"I'm sorry."

"No, that's the point. With *you* I didn't get clammy hands. In fact, I didn't feel anything at all."

"I'm delighted to hear it," he said dryly.

"You don't understand." She paced the room. "When you kissed me, it was just that, a kiss. Nothing else. You see, usually

I—I freeze up. Straining body parts and probing tongues make me go absolutely *berserk*."

Ian stared at her. "You're asking me to be part of an experiment to help you stop…going berserk?"

"I suppose no one ever asked you that before?"

"I can't say that they have."

Jamee gnawed at her lower lip. "You won't do it then."

"I didn't say that." Ian shoved a lock of dark hair off his brow. "I need some time to think about it."

"How much time?"

"How about a century or two?" he muttered.

"So it was a crazy idea." Jamee flushed. "Just forget it."

"No, it's not entirely crazy. Unexpected. Unconventional." Ian fingered one of her lengths of drying yarn, the deep green of a Highland loch at dawn. When he looked up, Jamee was watching him, wide-eyed, as if there was no one else in the world. As if there was no other place she'd rather be. It did extraordinary things to Ian's ego.

Maybe her idea wasn't crazy. After all, he knew the effects of hostage trauma inside and out after years of dealing with victims in the field. He knew how to dig up the memories in order to lay the raw past to rest. He was a *professional*.

Maybe he could do what Jamee asked.

Then what? Would he be able to stop when the lesson was finished?

Abruptly he remembered the sight of her as she trembled by the fire. Her waist was slender. He tried to forget the high, full breasts and the gentle sweep of her hips. To his disgust, Ian couldn't drive the hot images from his mind. He had barely been able to keep his hands steady as he'd put her clothes back on. Instead of dressing her, he'd wanted to do the opposite.

Sweet God above, did the woman have any *idea* what she

was asking? What she wanted would strain any man's control, let alone a man who had just been through three months of enforced celibacy during the agonizing day-and-night conclusion of a kidnapping case.

Not that she knew that.

Cursing silently, Ian reached for the teakettle, only to collide with Jamee as she reached for a length of yarn. She gasped, all softness and silk beneath his hand.

Every muscle in Ian's body clenched with male awareness as heat flared in primal response. Touch her? What she wanted was out of the question. There was no way he could allow it. Any distraction could be dangerous now, especially when his own control was in question.

"The answer is no, Jamee. For more reasons than you know."

Jamee didn't breathe. "Did…I offend you?"

"No," he growled. Suddenly the single room was far too small, far too intimate. "I forgot something in the back."

He strode to the narrow scullery. Maybe dunking his head in a basin of frigid water would restore his sanity.

Then again, maybe not.

How could she have been such a fool?

Jamee strode to the fireplace, kicked the wall, then paced back to the door. She was too impulsive, too damned honest. Even so, what in heaven's name had possessed her to blurt out her wild plan to a man she barely knew?

Because for some reason Ian McCall didn't seem like a stranger. She felt comfortable around him and entirely safe. He'd obviously been shocked by her request, yet she hadn't seen revulsion in his expression.

Maybe he had been too shocked to be repulsed.

She remembered how his eyes had narrowed, his hands had

tightened and there had been a momentary intensity in his face that might have been the stirring of desire.

Unless she had imagined it.

As she knelt before the fire, Jamee turned her head and sniffed. Chocolate, here? A hallucination from caffeine withdrawal, she decided glumly. There couldn't be *any* chocolate chips within miles of this place.

When her brother Terence had been alive, their house had been filled with that smell. Whenever something bad happened, Terence insisted on baking cookies by the dozen, which the Nights finished off together before a roaring fire.

Jamee still missed Terence. All of her family felt the gaping hole of his absence. His laughter and joy had lit their lives until he had been run down while sweeping a pregnant woman out of the path of a drunken driver. Yet even in the midst of her sadness, Jamee had felt his spirit among them, laughing in the birch trees that lined the fields at the family compound in northern California, joining in the reckless hilarity of a swim in the stream that bordered the fields of wildflowers he loved. He had cast a long shadow over all of them, but it was his light that they remembered now, not his loss.

Or at least, they tried.

Jamee frowned at the fire. Why was she thinking about Terence all of a sudden?

Outside the wind hummed past the windows and sighed down the chimney. The fire hissed and popped, rising in waves of orange and gold. He would have adored the simplicity of this old stone cottage, Jamee thought, especially its thatched roof and fireplace of weathered stone.

The curtains drifted before the window. Light seemed to flicker over the rough floor. She tensed, sensing something enter the room, creeping into the silence which was broken only by the restless hiss of the fire.

Jamee bit back a strained laugh. More hallucinations. There was no one here but herself, of course.

And the ghosts of her own sad past.

JAMEE CORNERED IAN the moment he returned. "I have something to tell you," she said, then closed her mouth and stared. His hair was soaking wet, molded sleekly to his head. "What happened? Did you fall into the stream again?"

"I decided that a basin of cold water and a wash might clear my head."

"Did they?"

"Not in the slightest."

"Here, use this to dry your hair." Jamee handed him a length of butter-soft wool streaked with mauve, silver and indigo.

Ian stared down at the beautiful weaving and shook his head. "I couldn't possibly. You made this, didn't you?"

Jamee flushed with pleasure. "It's a blend of mohair and cashmere. One of my current experiments."

"It's amazing." Ian slid the fine yarn through his fingers. "The fiber is soft but springy. Almost alive."

Jamee was shocked that he had noticed. Few men would have. A crazy smile climbed to her lips, and she suppressed it with difficulty.

Smiling because of a few words about her work? Was she a complete and utter fool?

Ian went into the adjoining scullery to change. Jamee tried not to hear the hiss of his belt and the rustle of falling clothes. When he reemerged, he wore worn Levi's with frayed knees and a soft gray turtleneck that hugged his muscled chest.

He looked clean and sleek and more than a little dangerous. He also looked good enough to eat.

Jamee felt a warm, sensual haze settle over her.

"What was it you wanted to tell me?" Ian said, tucking his

damp clothes into his bag and then shrugging into his jacket again.

Jamee liked him better without the jacket. He had looked younger, more relaxed. For some reason his face had hardened when he'd pulled on the muted wool, checking each pocket in turn.

*Stop looking for secrets,* she told herself.

She forced her unruly thoughts back under control. "I want you to forget what I said. I had no right to presume that you—that we—" She made a breathless sound and tried again. "We're complete strangers. There is no earthly reason why you should consider doing what I asked."

Ian moved across the floor, making no sound, more sleek and dangerous than ever. "There is only one reason I would consider touching you, Jamee, and that's the same reason I *can't*. You said you felt nothing, but I *did*. A hell of a lot, in fact. Do you understand what I'm saying?"

Jamee nodded. "I understand. Touching me was... distasteful."

Ian shoved his belt into place, cursing harshly. "Dammit to hell, woman, that's *not* what I was trying to say. Just the opposite."

Jamee blinked. "The opposite?" Suddenly her cheeks felt hot and breathing seemed more than she could manage. "But I thought you—"

Ian laughed roughly and plowed his fingers through his damp hair. "Why you should think that is beyond me. You make a man want to run his hands through your hair and catch all those impossible shades of auburn and gold. You make me want to take my time learning the taste of your mouth. And kissing would only be the start," he said hoarsely. "Now do you understand?"

"Oh," she said very softly.

"And there's another problem," Ian continued savagely. "I'm not going to lie to you any longer, Jamee. I *did* see another light in the fog last night. It could mean something or nothing, but I don't like it. There's no reason for people to be wandering up here in this kind of weather."

"Maybe they were lost."

"Damn unlikely. Besides, this is Dunraven land and private property."

Jamee tried to ignore the fear that skittered along her neck. She might always be a target, but she refused to let that possibility ruin her life. "You think someone is following us?" She didn't ask why. Though Ian wouldn't know it, the reason was far too clear.

For the money, of course. For the chance to carve out a luscious wedge of Nightingale Electronics's annual profits courtesy of a ransom payment.

"I'm not sure."

"What do we do now?" she asked, clutching a ball of yarn to her chest.

"Nothing. There's not a damned thing we can do in this fog except stay inside and keep alert," he said angrily.

"Then I guess…you won't be wanting any more distractions."

He cradled her chin with both palms, impossibly gentle as he met her gaze. His dangerous, edgy energy was carefully leashed now. "Want it or no, you will ever be a distraction to a man, lass," he said huskily. Then he released her and straightened his shoulders. "But right now, I'm going to check outside one more time. After that, I think we should talk."

*TALK.*

Talk was the last thing Jamee wanted to do. Talking meant dredging up memories that still oozed blood and probing wounds that had never closed.

She was no closer to being prepared when Ian returned. "I don't want to talk. I—I have to go out," she said tensely. "I need some fresh air, just for a few minutes." She moved to the door. "I can't stand being cooped up. It reminds me of—things I don't want to remember."

Ian closed the door, but did not move away, his arms crossed over his chest. "I don't think you should go out. It's impossible to see anything. You could be hurt."

Jamee studied his face. "Is there something you aren't telling me?"

"No."

Could he be one of Adam's hired guards? He had the necessary look of confidence. The cool competence. But there was none of the arrogance she had come to expect in men who were paid to protect others weaker than they were.

No, it was impossible, Jamee told herself. Lying wouldn't come easy to this man. Besides, he didn't even have a gun, and no self-respecting security officer went *anywhere* without a gun. Even to bed.

She flushed. She was going to go crazy if she stayed in here with him much longer. Staring at those broad shoulders was killing her. Wanting to touch the cool planes of his face was a torment.

She paced to the fire, then braced her back against the wall, praying the warmth of the solid stone would help her relax.

It didn't.

"So," she said evenly. "How is the fog?"

"Exactly the same." Ian clattered around in the cupboards and pulled out a handful of cooking implements.

"What are you doing?"

He poured flour into an old earthenware bowl. "Making scones. Cooking helps me relax."

Jamee's brow arched. "I didn't realize you were nervous."

He met her gaze squarely, and this time, hunger darkened his eyes. "Being cooped up here with you isn't exactly fun for me, either."

Jamee couldn't help glancing lower, where his thighs were lovingly cradled by faded denim. She blinked, then looked away.

"That is the general area of the problem," Ian said dryly.

Jamee crossed her arms nervously, determined to pretend she hadn't heard his remark. She wasn't used to discussing things like this—not with men. "So what do we talk about?"

"Why don't we start with men?"

"Men?" Jamee swallowed. "As in relationships?"

"That's the usual idea." Wrist-deep in a mound of flour, Ian bent over the bowl. He might have been smiling, but she couldn't tell. "When did you first fall in love?"

"I take it you don't mean Will Mazzoli."

"Who's that?"

"Fourth row. My first-grade pottery class."

Ian's lips twitched. "Tell me about Will."

"The class was my mother's idea. Something to put me in touch with my artistic feminine spirit. We ran around and pretended to be butterflies."

Ian opened a tin of evaporated milk and added some to the flour. "Even Will?"

"He pretended to be a net, as I recall. After that came the clay. I made figures that looked like that little dough boy and Will smashed them into pieces. Then I decked him. It was love ever after. We were inseparable."

Ian chuckled. "So Will was love number one. How about number two?"

"Oliver Gardiner," Jamee said promptly. "He put a frog down my back in computer class and I retaliated by throwing his backpack out of the bus. His homework papers were scattered for blocks, after which he was grounded for a month. We became inseparable, too."

"You appear to have a knack for becoming inseparable with men." When Ian looked up, flour dusted his cheek.

Jamee had a sudden urge to lick the white powder off slowly, until he cursed and took her in his arms and—

"What did you say?" she blurted.

"Something about your knack for making men want to be around you."

Jamee toyed with a skein of yarn. "I used to. A good knock in the head always seemed to help things along." Her smile came and then faded.

"What happened to change all that?"

She wound the skein into a ball, smoothing each curve. Suddenly it was very important that each thread lie perfectly flat. One bump or tangle would throw the balance off and cause something terrible to happen.

Jamee took a shallow breath. "What happened? The summer I turned seventeen," she said carefully. "The summer…that I was kidnapped."

Ian put down the dough. "*Dhe,* lass." He dried his hands, then crossed the floor and pulled the yarn from her fingers. "Sit down."

"I think I'd rather walk," Jamee said softly. "Moving makes me feel more…in control."

"If you'd prefer not to discuss this—"

"Maybe it's time I did." Jamee shoved her hands into her pockets. Anything to keep them from sliding up to Ian's powerful shoulders. "Not many people know." She gave a ragged laugh. "It's not the kind of thing that comes up very often, you know. 'Pass the ketchup and by the way I was kidnapped when I was seventeen.'"

"Jamee, you don't have to do this." Anger flared in Ian's

eyes. He started toward her, then frowned and sank into the chair beside the fire. His fingers opened, then locked on the worn wooden arms.

The raw emotion in his face should have made Jamee anxious, but it didn't. His fury was for those who had harmed her. "Maybe I should have talked about this long ago. Talking to a stranger is different from family." She paced idly, lined up several copper pots, then stirred the fire. "Of course, there were the doctors. The trauma experts helped me stop watching for shadows and hyperventilating at the sound of a car backfiring or the squeal of tires." She gave a tight chuckle. "Pretty lame, right?"

Ian's fingers gripped the chair arm. His voice was taut. "Not lame. You had a problem and you dealt with it. I'd call that damn brave of you."

"I still wake up in the night, remembering how it tasted. You wouldn't think memory has a taste, but it does. Like moldy leaves. Dank air. The faint metallic tang of blood, where I bit my lip to keep from screaming," she said flatly. "Oh, yes, I know that Dream well by now. It always starts the same way: the scream of tires and two gunshots. Then shouts and someone pulling me from a car. They shove me into darkness and stifling silence." She didn't look at Ian as she continued. She couldn't bear to see the pity fill his eyes. "They used rope on my hands and feet so I couldn't move. When the door slid shut, I thought I was dead. Maybe I wished I was dead. But I told myself I had to keep busy and I worked at the ropes every second. It kept my mind off…all the rest."

A muscle moved at Ian's jaw. "Do you remember what kind of ropes?"

Jamee shrugged. "Heavy, rough. They were damp with a green kind of smell."

"Mexican hemp," Ian murmured. The chair creaked as he leaned forward. "How thick were they?"

"Maybe an inch or slightly less." She frowned, finally meeting his gaze. There was no pity that she could see, only a focused intensity. "Why?"

"Because remembering the details might help you put the experience behind you, Jamee." Ian nodded at her hands, which were rubbing her wrists. "You obviously remember the feel of the ropes. They're still hurting you, Jamee. Every movement you make shows that pain."

"I didn't realize it was so obvious."

"Only to someone who's looking."

She stared dumbly at her hands. "It took weeks for the rope burns to fade. When they finally came to take me out, all my nails were gone, broken down to the quick."

"You were bloody brave."

"Was I?" Jamee shook her head. "Not then. Not in the darkness. I wanted to scream at them. I wanted to beg them to take Adam or William or Terence or Bennett. *Anyone* instead of me." Her voice broke at the terrible admission, which she'd never revealed to anyone until now. "How can I ever forgive myself for wanting that? My own family," she said brokenly.

Ian's nails scored the wooden chair arms. His hands opened and closed helplessly, fighting an urge to crush her in his arms—an urge that could only bring her more pain. With great effort, he kept his voice level. "It's perfectly normal to wish someone else was there instead of you."

"But not my own *brothers*..."

"They were bigger than you, Jamee. Braver, you thought. I'd say it was a perfectly normal wish for a girl to make during a time of terror."

She looked shocked. "You do?" She took a sudden, gulping breath. "I've never mentioned it. Not to anyone. The guilt has been eating at me all these years." She blinked, shoved away a tear, then picked up the skein of mohair again, her fingers shredding the fine yarn to threads.

"I'm sure that your brothers were waiting at home, sick with guilt and wishing that they could have taken your place, Jamee. So there's nothing to feel guilty about, is there?"

"Are you some kind of psychiatrist?" Jamee demanded. "You ask exactly the right question at the right time. And when you listen, it's frightening—at least it would be if you didn't make me feel so damned comfortable." She jerked to a halt. "Don't tell me you're a *priest!*"

Ian broke into startled laughter. "I'm afraid the church would have thrown me out long ago."

Jamee frowned. "You're not like any man I've known. Most would be fidgeting by now, uncomfortable at what I just told you about the kidnapping and my crazy dreams. They would probably have laughed at my problem with being near men. But you understand, Ian. Why?"

"Because I've been in a few tight spots myself," Ian said coolly. "And I've learned that judging other people makes as much sense as trying to fly over the moon in a basket made of feathers."

Jamee made a low sound that wasn't quite a laugh. "I think with enough time you could probably manage even that."

Ian watched her pace the floor, her bare feet soundless on the old wood. He realized that Jamee Night already had a clear idea of why she behaved as she did. In fact, she was probably the sanest person he knew.

Sane, but desperate.

Ian couldn't deny his jolt of satisfaction that she had never spent the night in bed with another man. That she felt comfortable enough to ask him to touch her intimately. He wanted to be the first man to hold her through the night, to watch her body dappled with firelight while she cried out in passion, her fear forgotten.

Ian propped one elbow against the chair arm and frowned. There was no way around it. He was becoming involved with a client. *Intimately* involved. The growing tension in his lower body told him how completely he had fallen under Jamee Night's artless and irresistible spell.

But involvement was stupid and dangerous. The relationship never lasted. Inevitably, a victim wanted to put the trauma behind her. Sometimes the people didn't even make it out alive, because one second's distraction in the field could mean the difference between life and death.

Right now, watching Jamee pace in stiff, jerky movements, Ian realized that logic didn't seem to carry a whole lot of weight.

"Not that I haven't ever—well, you know," Jamee muttered.

"No, I don't know."

"Been with a man." She jammed her hands into her pockets. "In bed. Intimately."

Intimately. Ian clutched at the chair as every muscle in his body leaped to fierce awareness. He didn't want to hear—and he couldn't bear *not* to hear. "Is that so?" Somehow he managed to give the illusion of sounding calm.

"There were three. The Big Three." She gave him a crooked smile. "I had to get myself very drunk first. Now I don't remember many details. They were all perfect gentlemen about it, but I still have the feeling something was lacking. I mean, I should *remember,* shouldn't I? Probing tongues. Sweaty hands. At least one straining body part."

The confusion and humor that mingled in her eyes brought Ian low, humbled by her ability to find something to laugh at amid the dark nightmare of her past.

She was a very brave woman, he decided. Considering all

she had been through, her honesty was nearly frightening. And when she smiled crookedly, Ian felt something slam into his chest. His breathing seemed loud, hollow in his ears. His body felt weightless, buoyant, giddy.

Terrified.

He had a terrible suspicion that he was falling in love with Jamee Night. The real, old-fashioned way, that made a man think of bridal veils and stable, long-term bonds and the sound of children laughing.

He couldn't let that happen. Jamee deserved more than he could give her. Especially now.

Ian cleared his throat. "You can't remember anything?"

"Not much." She straightened a row of seashells on the mantel above the fire. "I mean, it's supposed to be *earthshaking* and yet I don't remember any of it." She shook her head. "I suppose that says something about me."

"Not you," Ian said harshly. "It says something about them. Any man with half a brain could have made the experience special, something you would always treasure." He broke off, scowling at his locked hands, forcing himself to stay in the chair so he wouldn't pull her into his arms and kiss her until they were both pleading for mercy.

Ian wanted to do all that for Jamee. Right now, he wanted her so badly it was painful, damn his corrupt, degenerate soul. He was savagely jealous of each and every one of the Big Bloody Three. His zipper was straining with the evidence of his need.

He was relieved when she wandered to the window and stared out at the mist.

"I don't like knowing I'll have to get blotto every time I want to—well, you know."

"Kiss a man?" *Stay calm, McCall. She needs that much and no more.*

"And then let him take off my clothes. Feel him crawl into bed beside me. Touch me. And then— Like with the Big Three."

Ian felt sweat streak his brow. The Big Three. How many women would write off their disappointments with such whimsy?

Ian couldn't think of one.

"That's why I thought this time. With you…" Jamee's eyes were huge as she turned, toying with the satin ribbon until it slipped sideways, trapping her lustrous hair on her left shoulder.

When had this fragile, indominable woman come to hold such fatal power over him? Ian wondered. How had she unerringly found the door that led into his heart, a heart he had thought sealed since the day he had learned of his bleak future?

"At least with me you'd remember, *mo cridhe.* You'd damn well recall every sigh and every moan. You'd remember the feel of us, the taste of us."

Color rose and fell in her cheeks, hotter than the firelight that streaked the floor. "Would I?" It was the softest of questions, but it was also a challenge. The kind of faint, sensual challenge no man who was even half alive could ignore.

The challenge sent heat streaming through Ian's body. At that moment, he knew he was about to make the worst decision of his life.

Suddenly he didn't care.

# CHAPTER EIGHT

"JAMEE." HE SAID THE WORD slowly while he pushed to his feet, giving her time to run. To curse. To scream.

She only watched him with those huge indigo eyes. "You'd be number four. Doesn't that bother you?"

"I'd be number one. The first one who counted," Ian said roughly. "The one you will always remember."

*Will, not would.*

By the time Ian realized what he had said, it was already too late. His fingers had memorized the texture of her hair and his lips were nuzzling her cheek, her mouth.

God, her lips were like warm velvet.

"Ian." It was a soft puff of sound.

"Tell me, Jamee. What you want. Where you want it."

"I think," she said very carefully, "that I want everything. All at once."

Ian swallowed and framed her face with his hands. Where were the aliens when you needed them? "You don't know what you're saying."

"I know. I've been waiting a very long time to say that to a man. To *want* it from a man."

Dear God, she was serious. She wanted him, only *him.*

Her fingers smoothed his rigid shoulders. His stomach tensed as her breath feathered his neck. Electricity snapped through him, leaving him acutely aware of every move she made.

*Take her,* a voice urged. *Have her. Love her.*

His hand trembled. His hand, not hers. The tension in his body surged to painful urgency as her fingers traced his mouth.

The mouth she had said was beautiful.

Dammit, this was madness. He couldn't let matters progress any further. She stirred up feelings that were far too powerful and the timing was all wrong.

Ian stared over her shoulder. "Jamee, I don't know if this is a good idea." He ran one hand over his jaw. "Hell, I *know* it's a bad idea."

"You're probably right." Her hand settled over his and she stared at his mouth as if it were a chocolate sundae she wanted to take her time over. Her fingers dug gently at his chest.

Ian felt like wreckage left from a tsunami. How did she manage to shatter his control this way?

He cleared his throat. "I think I'd better check around outside."

She made a soft, breathless sound and tugged at the top button on his shirt. "You just did that."

Ian swallowed. "If I stay, I'm going to do something I'll regret and you will probably hate me for." He couldn't keep the edge from his voice. Jamming his hands deep into his pockets, he pulled away from her. "So I'm going to put what just happened out of my mind. Not because I want to, Jamee. Because it's the only sane thing to do."

IAN MANAGED to put Jamee out of his mind for exactly twelve and one-half seconds. He knew because he was staring at his watch.

God, what a mess.

With fog swirling around him, he circled the cottage, searching for footprints or signs of intrusion. He listened for suspicious noises and checked the locks on all the windows and doors.

Nothing was amiss, but the knowledge didn't make Ian feel the slightest bit better. Only getting away from this enforced confinement with Jamee would help. Meanwhile, he had work to do.

He moved to the back of the cottage and checked the trip wire he had set earlier that morning. Strung seven inches above the ground, the copper wire would be invisible in the fog and a perfect height to send any intruders flying. The tin cans tied on both ends were a bonus in the form of a primitive, but effective alarm system. A second set of wires ran along both sides of the house, extending his defense system. At the front, Ian had been even more inventive, zigzagging half a dozen wires in a random pattern over the sloping hillside.

It wasn't Fort Knox, but it would have to do until he had backup.

Cursing softly, he pulled the cellular phone from his pocket and dialed the number of Dunraven Castle.

Just as when he'd tried earlier, static broke in shrieking waves.

"—Castle…"

"This is Ian McCall calling for Lord Dunraven."

"Dunraven—" Static crackled again. "Hello? Hel—" The voice was swallowed by a metallic whine.

Ian muttered in Gaelic. There was no hope of getting a message to Dunraven or anyone else, not with this static.

Muttering, he pocketed the phone and stared out at the blanketing white mist. No telephone. No car. No radio.

Only Jamee.

He took a deep breath. Took another. Time to go back inside.

He was a man, not a teenager. He could deal with his feelings for her.

When he pushed open the door, the first thing he saw was a pair of slender legs below an incredible silken skirt that stopped at the middle of her thighs. "What is that?" he rasped.

"My new skirt, a blend of silk and mohair. I just finished it." Her voice was breathless. "Do you like it?"

Did he like it? Did he like breathing or whiskey or fishing on a silver loch at dawn?

The skirt was short and silky and clung like a second skin to her softly rounded hips.

Did he *like* it?

"It's…different." Ian managed to sound calm.

"I found the silk noil on my last trip to Asia. I bought all I could find." She spoke in a rush. "I think maybe I can even sell some of these."

If she modeled a skirt like that, short and sleek and gorgeous, knit so that it shimmered and clung, she would have women lining up to purchase one.

And men would be lining up to watch.

Ian scowled.

"You don't think it will sell?"

"I think it will sell. In fact, I think women from Terre Haute to Timbuktu will be clamoring to have one. Maybe two or three."

"You do?" Jamee eyed her legs thoughtfully, then turned, a pan of steaming water balanced in her hands. "Just a minute while I—" As she spoke, the pan struck the edge of the table. The metal edge swayed dangerously, sloshing hot water onto the floor. "Oh, damn."

Ian leaped for the handles just as the pan went flying. Quickly, he swung it up onto the table, ignoring the water that had splashed on his jacket. Rescue complete, he turned to Jamee.

She was bent low, wiping the floor with a towel.

Dear God, the skirt had almost vanished. All Ian registered were long golden legs and bare feet. Even her *feet* were beautiful, he thought blankly. Any minute, he was going to be grinning like a bloody fool, kneeling beside her and tasting that glorious mouth of hers. "No," he rasped.

"No, what?" Jamee looked up. "It's just water."

"No, I— Let me help," Ian muttered as he strode around the table and bent down beside her. As he did, one hand caught the edge of a copper frying pan, which went flying onto his head.

Jamee gasped. "Ian, are you all right?"

He gripped the end of the table while red and blue lights flashed before his eyes.

"Ian?" Jamee was beside him, holding his shoulder. He caught the scent of her subtle perfume and the lights flashed all over again.

"Can you hear me? Can you talk?"

He eased one hand over the knot at his temple. Blood streaked his fingers. "I can talk. I might even live. If I'm lucky." But not if he had to watch her in that skirt much longer.

"Sit down at the table and let me help."

The last thing he wanted was Jamee's fingers brushing his face. That pain would be worse than a dozen pans tossed onto his head. "There's no need for you to—"

"Don't be silly." She pushed him firmly into a chair, then carefully brushed back his hair. Every movement sent heat straight to Ian's groin.

"Jamee, I—"

"I doubt you'll need stitches, though there is some blood. Sit still now. I have some dyeing alcohol in my bag."

"You have everything in that bag." Ian sighed and gave

himself up to the pleasure of her voice and her gentle touch. There was no reason to deny himself. It was strictly a medical necessity.

"I've done this quite a bit, growing up with four brothers. One or the other was always limping inside with a scraped knee or a bleeding elbow." She bent her head and brushed his forehead. "This may hurt."

God, how it hurt—every sweep of her hands, every nudge of her breasts. Her thigh pressed against his back. Ian tried not to think about what would happen if he turned around and explored the warmth hidden beneath that incredible skirt of hers.

"Okay?"

He was sweating. His body was rigid. "Just fine. You have good hands." The understatement of this or any other century.

"Adam tells me that. But he's my brother, so he's biased." She rubbed gently, then bent closer, blowing across his skin. "This should help."

Help? He was dying, swallowed alive by urges he had always been able to control before. Nothing had been the same since Jamee Night had thrown him to the ground, determined to save his life. "What I really need is some whiskey," he rasped.

"There isn't any whiskey in the cottage."

Ian couldn't help himself. He snagged her wrist and brought her palm to his mouth. The slow kiss was edged with the slightest pressure of his teeth. "You're sure you're not an angel?"

"Positive," she said huskily. "Look, no wings."

Ian didn't want to look. It *hurt* to look at something he couldn't touch. "Angels come in all shapes and forms, don't you know? My nanny always said they could appear like the best or the least among us."

"What a lovely thought." Her breast nestled against his ribs.

Ian swallowed a curse. "Are you sure there's no whiskey *anywhere* in that bag of yours?"

"I'm afraid not. I don't drink. Except when—well, the Big Three."

Ian took a slow breath. Her crooked smile played havoc with his pulse, starting guerrilla wars all over his body.

"Even if I had whiskey, I wouldn't drink it with you. With you, I'd want to feel everything, remember everything."

Ian's eyes closed. He tried to fight the hot fantasy her words invoked. Nothing helped.

"Maybe there is one way I can make you more comfortable," Jamee whispered.

Ian sat up rigidly. "As in the Big Three?" Now *he* was talking the same crazy language she did. "You think I'd let you do something that intimate just to distract me?"

"Intimate?" She laughed in shock. "No, I meant something else."

Ian wasn't sure if he was relieved or disappointed. "So a head wound doesn't entitle me to the Ultimate Sacrifice?"

Her laugh filled the corners of the room and worked its way deep into Ian's chest, cutting off his breath. "All you have to do is ask," she said huskily. "Around you, it seems I'm easy, McCall."

Ian closed his eyes and shook his head. This conversation was not happening. This situation was *not* going any further.

Something scraped on the wooden floor. Ian opened his eyes and found Jamee sitting in a chair beside him, her head cocked.

Ian sighed. "Just one glass, that's all I ask. Two inches neat. Perfect single malt, with a smell like pine smoke and peat."

"Forget the whiskey, McCall. Let me try something. Turn a little to the left."

"What are you going to do?" he said suspiciously. "Nothing that involves tuning forks and New Age crystals, I hope."

Jamee chuckled as she pulled him sideways and slid her hands across his shoulders. "I think this may help."

Ian didn't move. She did something to his neck, something slow and unbelievably wonderful.

She had marvelous hands, he thought, as she stroked down his neck and along his tense shoulders, tracing each knotted muscle gently.

But Ian couldn't relax, not with the threat that waited somewhere in the fog. His physical reaction to her presence didn't help, either.

"Why don't you relax and stop fighting me?"

"That's supposed to be my line," he muttered.

"Not this time, Braveheart."

Ian muttered darkly. But his whole body started to relax, beginning at the knot between his shoulder blades. Even the two inches of agony at his right temple began to feel fractionally better. "Where did you learn that?"

"I used to work for a man who was very tense. This was almost the only thing that could make him relax."

Ian sat up straight. "*Almost* the only thing?" he growled. Something soft and firm pressed at his rib. He tried not to think what it was. "What else worked?"

Her fingers dug and feathered, stroked and skimmed. "Oh, this and that. Poetry sometimes. He liked me to play Chopin when nothing else worked."

"God bless Chopin." Ian groaned as her hands hit another pain point. "How did you learn the massage?"

"I picked it up in Japan and Asia. The Swedes have their own style, too. I've done a lot of traveling over the years."

He gasped as she worked the tense muscles in his shoulder.

"Sorry. You're tied up in knots. Is that better?"

"Yes." His breath emerged in little puffs. "It feels—too good—to be legal."

"I'm sorry that you've never had a real massage before. I'll have to remedy your neglect." She moved to the upper corner of his back. "You never told me your occupation, by the way."

Ian thought he might be melting. "Being laird of a decrepit old castle isn't enough?"

Her eyes crinkled. "I know a bit about the costs of repairing old properties. I also know a bit about British inheritance taxes. They're crippling, I'm told. You must have some other moneymaking skill." She tilted her head. "You have the look of a man who makes his living by…knowing people. Detecting how they think and reading their deepest desires. You would be very good at that. *Are* you a psychiatrist?" she asked gravely.

"No."

"A doctor?"

"Definitely not."

Her teeth snagged her lower lip. "You don't look like one of the titled jet set."

"I didn't know that a particular look was required," Ian said, happy to steer the subject away from his profession.

"Oh, absolutely." Jamee pursed her lips. "Perfectly tailored double-breasted jacket. Bespoke at Bond Street, of course. Faded jeans, very well fitting. Very expensive. Probably with a designer label."

Ian chuckled, recognizing a dozen of his London acquaintances in her description. "But of course."

"Perfect bone structure. Arrogant manner and a year-round tan. Artificial, of course." Her eyes narrowed. "I bet you don't own a single piece of designer clothing," she said accusingly.

"You lose." He eased back into the curve of her shoulder while her fingers turned him into a quivering mass of mush.

"What? An Armani suit? For taking tea with the royal family."

"Afraid not. No Armani suits anywhere at Glenlyle."

"Shoes, then. Handmade in Milan by a fifth-generation shoemaker. The family business has a royal warrant from the Queen Mother. Not that the owner would ever be so gauche as to display it in public. The shoes are…" She wrinkled her nose. "Let me see, brown suede. Wing tip, but very subtle. Worth a fortune. You wear them with your Turnbull and Asser ties."

Ian smiled broadly, enjoying the game. Enjoying the smile in her voice.

Especially enjoying the way her breath puffed against his neck and her breasts nudged his shoulder.

It shook him to realize how long it had been since he had been happy or even comfortable in the company of a woman. He had known physical pleasure with many women, had been generous with his own body and his slow, thorough exploration of theirs, but comfort was not a part of those memories.

There had always been a shadow since he was a teenager and his father's ghillie had told him the story of Blind Laird's Rock and the ancient curse that lay on every eldest Glenlyle son.

But it was hard to think of curses when Jamee's fingers worked such exquisite magic. "Wrong again. No suede shoes, wing tip or otherwise. Does a pair of St. Laurent cuff links count?"

Jamee shook her head, sighing dramatically. "McCall, you are destroying all my illusions about the leisured rich. Next you'll tell me that you don't even have a valet."

"You're damn right I don't have a valet," Ian muttered.

"A pastry chef?"

"None at Glenlyle, nor ever has been." He closed his eyes and groaned as her fingers laid furrows of unbelievable pleasure down both sides of his spine. "I think I'll have to call you Joan of Arc Night from now on."

Her laughter ruffled the dark hair at his neck. Again that strange, slow heaviness invaded his chest.

"Joan of Arc Night. It has a kind of ring to it. Never heard of her, though. I thought I knew all the saints."

Her perfume wafted over him and Ian realized she was bending closer. A pillow slid behind his back. "What now? I doubt you can manage to top yourself." Unfortunately, as soon as the words were out, Ian knew how she could do just that.

He cleared his throat. "So what *do* I look like? If not one of the idle rich."

Jamee traced his cheek from nose to ear as if she were trying to read what lay beneath the skin. "Like one of the fierce clansmen who rescued Alasdair MacIan after the massacre of Glencoe. Someone who has seen the darker side of life."

"My ancestors did shelter the MacIans in the days following the Campbell treachery," Ian said gravely.

Jamee touched the other side of his jaw. "Like one of the warriors who stood with Wallace at Stirling and Bannockburn. A man who would never give up, no matter how bleak the odds."

"There was a McCall at both of those battles. Another McCall hung when Wallace died." Ian opened his eyes and saw Jamee staring at him. Just staring, her cheeks bright with color.

Her gaze told him that he looked like a *hero*.

God help them both when she found out the truth.

HIGH ABOVE the darkened wooded hills, Draycott Abbey glistened in the moonlight. A shadowed figure paced the weathered roof, his hands locked behind his back.

"I mean it, Gideon. It's damnably dull here at the abbey. No interesting people come to visit, only those blasted diplomatic types that the viscount has to entertain. Currying favor with the National Trust, he calls it. A blasted nuisance, that's what I call it. These people have no sense of humor. Even a good, solid apparition in the bedroom can't shake a chuckle out of them."

Out of the shadows a great gray cat appeared, his eyes glimmering in the moonlight.

Adrian frowned. "Yes, I know I've been out of sorts."

The cat flicked his tail.

"Oh, very well, I've been utterly irascible, I admit it. It's the season, I'm afraid. Something about Christmas brings all my worst inclinations to life. Life," the guardian ghost of Draycott Abbey repeated mockingly. "There was a bad choice of words. I haven't trod on real soil for almost two centuries." He sighed and the white lace at his cuffs rippled in the wind. "I remember many a Christmas of gaiety, one with that Dickens fellow in particular. One night of determined apparitions was all it took to send him flying back to London."

At his feet the cat meowed softly.

"Of course, I love Christmas. I love the porcelain angels, the silver candlesticks and the holly and the pine draped everywhere. But this year, I have something different in mind," Adrian said slowly.

The cat curled about his booted feet.

"No, I do not mean the apparition of the Great Huntsman charging through the front hall and up the main stairwell," Adrian said irritably. "That was simply a youthful prank."

The cat purred softly.

"I'm glad to hear that you enjoyed it, Gideon. Nicholas's father was not so happy, as I recall." He tapped his jaw thoughtfully, studying the lace at one cuff. "What I had in mind was tracking down a gift that will be perfect for Gray. It is books she loves, Gideon, and I want the rarest book of all for her as my gift this year."

The cat sat back on his powerful haunches, gray tail twitching.

"No, I do not mean that Magna Carta," Adrian said in exasperation. "Nor do I mean a first edition of the Gutenberg Bible. Much fun she would have reading those to me beside a roaring fire. No, I've been thinking about that Dickens fellow. A first edition of his would put the glow back into her cheeks, I know it. And I have a strong suspicion that I can find that specific volume at Dunraven Castle."

The cat sat up abruptly.

"Do stop carrying on so. I know you love the salmon there, you bloodthirsty beast. Not a single fish is safe when you're anywhere north of the Tweed. But there will be no fishing until we've done our work, do you understand? We need to find that gift for Gray."

The cat paced restlessly, his great amber eyes agleam. For a moment, just a moment, it almost seemed as if a ghostly fish flashed through the air, silver scales bright in the moonlight.

"Yes, I know very well what a salmon looks like, Gideon. I'm afraid they don't delight me as they do you, however. But help me finish my search and I'll be more than happy to watch you eat your fill." The abbey ghost stared thoughtfully at the moon glowing above the horizon. "I suspect we might even find our incompetent visitor there, too."

The cat's ears twitched.

"Yes, I do have my ways. He's gone to Scotland, something to do with that mission he mentioned." Adrian smoothed his lace cuffs. "I suppose I must see that he doesn't make an absolute ruination of the job. I shall leave in two days. That will give me ample time to convince the viscount and his wife that they need to take a little trip to the north." He looked down at the granite roof. "Yes, I said *me*. Alone. Because you, my dearest friend, are leaving for Scotland now." Adrian rubbed his jaw. "I'm afraid your friend is going to need some help up there." His soft laughter drifted over the abbey roof and merged with the murmur of the moat. "Ready?"

At Adrian's feet the great cat stretched once, then twitched his tail.

"Remember the method, do you?"

Silver scales flashed in the air, one phantom fish, then two more. The cat sniffed delicately and raised one paw.

As Adrian watched, his old friend simply walked into the shimmer of air and water and vanished.

"Heaven be with you and guard you," the abbey ghost whispered.


WIND WHISTLED around his ears.

A strange wind, full of strange scents.

His gray paws twitched, then struck muddy turf. He listened intently, ears pricked forward. Here was fowl and sheep and salt-sea air.

And man. Several of them.

Gideon moved silently forward into the fog, his eyes ablaze.

## CHAPTER NINE

IAN HUNCHED one shoulder against the weathered stone of the storage shed and fingered his cellular phone, waiting for the hiss of static that had plagued all his earlier calls.

"Dunraven Castle." The words rang out with crystal clarity.

"Can you hear me?" Ian fairly shouted the question. "This is Ian McCall."

Static crackled briefly, then fled. "Ian, it's Kara. Where in heaven's name are you?"

"Caught in the bloody fog, that's where. Tell that lumbering husband of yours we've been holed up in the crofter's cottage above the cliffs since yesterday."

"At least you're safe. We were starting to worry, because there have been any number of accidents on the shore road. Duncan swears it will be clearing first thing tomorrow. His Scottish Sight at work, you know." Kara MacKinnon laughed. "At least that's what he tells me. I suspect he heard the forecast."

"I hope he's right. I'm getting tired of my own cooking."

"But I thought you said 'we.' You aren't alone up there?"

"No." Ian hesitated, reluctant to say more over the phone.

"Here's Duncan now. Take care, won't you? We're saving a seat for you by the fire."

"And a tall glass of whiskey to go with it, I devoutly hope."

"Done," the laird's American wife said with a chuckle. Ian heard the phone change hands.

"Where are you, man? Angus has had fresh scones and goose pâté waiting for two days now."

"In the bloody fog at the crofter's cottage. Not ten kilometers from Dunraven, and it might as well be the moon."

"You did the right thing to keep off the road," Duncan said. "It would be suicide to take those cliffs now. The fog is expected to clear by the early morning."

"So Kara said." Ian frowned. "Listen, Duncan, I'm not sure how long before this line breaks up, but I should tell you that I'm not alone up here. I also suggest we switch to Gaelic."

"I see. I spoke to Nicholas yesterday and he filled me in." Duncan continued in the liquid sounds of the old tongue both men had learned as children. "Have you had any trouble?"

"Nothing overt yet, but it's only a matter of time. Is it possible for you to get a car through to the cottage?"

Duncan sighed. "I'll be on the way myself the instant it's safe. But right now—well, it can't be done. Not in this fog. And there's no one closer than Dunraven, I'm afraid."

Ian rubbed the knot at his neck. "That's what I thought. Can you at least check out any reports of problems in this area? We've seen lights up here in the fog."

"Three French climbers were fogged in on the slope of Fionn and rescue teams have been out tracking them. Damn dangerous—I was out with them all day yesterday. Could that be what you saw?"

"Possibly, but I'm taking no chances."

Duncan read the subtle warning as Ian had meant him to. "I see. In that case, I'll make a few calls and phone you."

"No, don't do that," Ian said sharply. "I'll ring you back in several hours."

"Why the secrecy, man? If I'm going to help, I need more facts."

Ian scowled at the fog. "We'll talk when I get to Dunraven, Duncan. Assuming that this bloody fog *ever* lifts."

"Sit tight, man. The weather is worst right where you are, along the north side of the bay."

After he rang off, Ian stood listening to the muted hiss of the wind down the glen and the soft pipe of a plover. As he slipped the phone back into his pocket, the clouds seethed around him, beautiful and lethal. He hoped that Duncan was right. Perhaps the pale gleam in the fog had been no more than the flash of climbers' lights up on Fionn's snowy slopes.

Right. And he was the queen's nephew.

The prickle at his spine turned sharp, and Ian had learned never to ignore his instincts.

IN THE CHILL HOURS before dawn, while mist layered the hill below the old cottage, the front door latch shuddered. The bolt quivered and the door crept inward, then halted as the bolt caught.

Jamee stirred, one arm outstretched. Before the fire Ian slept on, dreaming of a pink-sand beach and the hot, white burn of the Southern Cross.

Neither noticed the door close softly. Neither noticed the great gray cat that jumped onto the stone windowsill and sat motionless, fierce amber eyes sweeping the night.

IAN AWOKE TO FIND the cottage lined by shadows, lit only by the soft glow of embers. He had no idea what had roused him. Jamee lay asleep on the sofa cushion, one leg emerging from beneath her blanket. Her sweater hung from the back of a chair, and her skirt dangled from the table. Something white and lacy was pooled in the middle of the floor.

More lingerie.

Ian felt as if he'd been kicked in the stomach.

He reached for the soft lacy thing, which turned out to be some kind of a slip that fluttered to midthigh. The soft ruffles poured through his fingers in an erotic whisper that left his senses ajar.

Fists clenched, he turned. Somehow he had to get Jamee dressed before she woke up and realized what had happened. She would cringe in embarrassment.

He studied the scrap of lingerie in his hands and made a desperate compromise: this and nothing else. This, he just might be able to manage without waking her—and driving himself past the edge of sanity.

Jamee rolled to her side, shoved away the tartan, and dropped one arm. She was totally naked, her golden skin draped in warm firelight. Ian's jaw locked as he eased the silk over her head. Teeth clenched, he worked her hands through the straps, trying to force his gaze above her neck. She sighed softly and snuggled against him, the curve of her breast settling against his palm.

Ian stiffened, slammed by a wave of heat. But he ignored the heavy pulse of need and lifted her head, then shoved the silk over her back and slid her blanket over her.

Sweat coated his brow when he finished. His hands were shaking.

*Bloody fool, Glenlyle.*

He bolted out of reach before any other provocative body parts could tempt his touch. Let her think she had stripped down to the lingerie—or whatever the wisp of silk was called.

Scowling, he inched past her, berating himself. As he leaned down to straighten his blanket, he paused. His senses suddenly focused on the window.

A light flashed out in the fog. Out where no one but a fool would wander.

Or someone desperate. Someone with kidnapping on his mind.

Mist licked Ian's face as he crept through the rear scullery door into the uneasy silence of the night. He slipped around the weathered stones to the front of the old cottage, watching for another telltale shimmer. Down the slope toward the road he saw a brief blur that might have been a shielded light—or simply his overtaxed imagination.

Mist pressed around him. Wind hissed over the hill and a sheep bell jingled faintly in the distance.

The light did not return.

Ian crouched beside the cottage wall. Going down to investigate was out of the question. Jamee lay asleep inside the cottage, and her safety was his top priority. The trip wires were in place and all he could do was wait, hoping for some betraying movement or sound from the darkness.

Five minutes.

Ten. Fifteen. Only a curlew called over the lonely glen. Only the fog whispered over the rough stone walls.

But Ian was a very patient man when he had to be. Crouching beside the bracken, he curled one hand around the pistol in his pocket. He would use it if he had to, as he'd used the weapon before.

Thankfully, he'd been able to reach Duncan again at the castle. The fog still made traveling impossible, but now someone was monitoring the situation throughout the night. As soon as the weather changed, Duncan would head for the cottage like a shot. Ian hoped his backup field team from Security International would be equally ready to move from wherever they were waiting out the weather.

Until then, stalemate.

A dark form shot out of the mist.

By instinct, Ian dropped to the ground. Long wings spread above him, carving the clouds in a rush of wind.

Ian relaxed as he recognized the passing kestrel. He pushed forward, started to rise, then froze.

Something rustled by his foot. He sensed a stirring in the mist and then the press of a warm body, purring softly. His hand met clean fur and a healthy, well-fed body. The cat was no stray, that was certain. Ian wondered how the creature had come to wander so far up the glen.

"Well, now, you're a brave fellow, rambling about in the night. Hunting, were you?"

The cat pressed closer, nudging Ian's palm.

"Not too much to catch up here, I'm afraid. All the salmon are over by Dunraven. You might find a trout or two down in the stream though."

The cat purred more loudly.

"Hungry? I know the feeling. A nice fat salmon sounds bloody fine to me, too."

The cat meowed. At the base of the hill the darkness guarded its secrets, giving Ian no reason to stay. He pushed to his feet with a last stroke along the cat's back. "Happy hunting."

The bracken stirred as he made his way back to the cottage. He was getting better at negotiating in the darkness, thanks to this enforced stay in the fog. That particular ability would become very important in the coming months, Ian thought grimly.

After checking that the windows were secure, Ian opened the rear door. The great cat padded past him for all the world as if he belonged inside.

"Make yourself at home," Ian said dryly.

The gray head rose. Amber eyes blinked.

Ian felt an odd pricking at the back of his neck. What was it about those eyes? Why did they seem *too* keen?

Jamee was still asleep, one bare foot peeking from beneath her blanket. Ian eased down onto his makeshift bed while the cat curled regally on the warm hearth.

"I've let in the monarch himself, it appears," Ian muttered as he eased out of his jacket, then propped his hands under his head and stared at the peat glowing in the grate.

A movement of dark fur drew his gaze to the hearth.

Crazy, of course. But Ian could have sworn the cat was watching him.

SOMETHING BRUSHED Ian's cheek. His eyes shot open and he braced himself for attack.

Instead of an intruder he found Jamee sprawled over his chest, one warm thigh atop his. Her hand was open at his waist and her fingers were tracing restless circles over his bare chest.

Ian's body responded instantly. Blast it, what was he supposed to do now?

The cat stretched gracefully by the hearth as Jamee murmured in her sleep. The damnably beautiful silk slip she was wearing hitched upward as she bent her leg around Ian's hip. Then her knee rose, coming to rest at his groin. Threatening the last of his sanity.

He cleared his throat, trying to wake her gently, but she sighed and burrowed closer, her hands tangled in the hair on his chest. His shirt was half unbuttoned and he had a good idea who had done it.

Ian counted to ten, reminding himself that Jamee had no idea what she was doing. That she was a client. That *he* was a professional.

This wasn't what his bloody body was trying to make it seem.

The cat sat up delicately and licked one paw.

No help there.

Ian coughed again, trying to tug down his shirt and cut off the contact. Jamee merely snuggled closer.

Sometimes the hard way was the only way. He slid a strand of her hair over the sensitive skin above her lip. She muttered and batted at her nose, then turned to her other side, still sprawled atop his chest. Her knee moved between his thighs, triggering graphic fantasies.

Ian smothered a curse. If he didn't wake her in a matter of seconds, he was going to die or do something inexcusable.

The cat's ears pricked forward and he licked his other paw with meticulous care.

The inexcusable option was becoming ever more appealing when Jamee suddenly sat bolt upright. Her hands stabbed at his stomach, making Ian grunt.

She gave no sign of noticing. "I sent the order last week," she rasped. Her leg shifted and her elbow dug into his side. "Three mohair for Paris and ten in lace open weave."

She tried to rise. Her knee moved straight toward Ian's groin.

He jerked sideways just in time. "Dammit, Jamee—"

"Of course. All-natural dyes, just as you wanted. Four pink and two gold."

"Jamee, can you hear me?"

Her head cocked. "The line is very bad. I can't hear you."

Ian sighed, realizing she was still asleep. He was trying to ease out from beneath her when she blinked twice and looked around her. "*Comprenez-vous?* Hello?"

Her voice trailed away. She frowned down at her thigh riding atop Ian's leg. At her fingers open on his chest. "What am I doing?"

"Sending textiles to France, as far as I can make out," Ian said hoarsely.

Her elbow dug into his ribs as she tugged down her slip as

far as it would go. The motion brought her hand across Ian's groin.

She froze. Her face turned beet-red.

Obviously she was aware of his physical response. Only someone in a coma could have failed to notice.

"I—I'm terribly sorry. I don't know how I came to do that." She gnawed at her lip. "I *did* do that, didn't I?"

Ian nodded stiffly, trying to find a comfortable position. Knowing it was impossible.

"I was asleep?" she probed tentatively.

Ian nodded, easing sideways.

"I was all over you." She swallowed hard. "I'm terribly sorry."

"Forget it. I enjoy pain," Ian said dryly. "It builds moral fiber."

Fresh color swept her cheeks. "Pain. Oh. You mean, as in…" Her gaze slanted downward, then instantly fled upward.

"As in," Ian said hoarsely, brushing a strand of hair from her face. "At least you're making progress with your problem."

"Currently, my only problem seems to be keeping my hands off you." Jamee looked down at the whispery slide of silk riding up her thighs, her eyes filled with relief. "At least I kept this on. But I think getting dressed would be in order."

"Don't hurry on my account," Ian said lazily. "I'm getting used to the pain."

Again color filled Jamee's face.

"Your shirt's open. Did I do that?"

Ian shrugged.

"Wonderful. I didn't take off my clothes. I tried to take off yours instead."

"Apparently I didn't put up much of a fight," Ian said coolly. "So forget about it."

"I wish I could." She bit her lip and looked at the hearth, where the cat lay curled in a ball. "We have a visitor, I see."

"The great thing followed me in as if he owned the place. A damn odd place to find a stray, too."

"Maybe he's lost." She pushed upright, only to gasp in pain as her hair wrapped around a button on Ian's open shirt.

"Hold still," he said gruffly. "You're caught." His hands molded her waist, then opened, exploring when he should have been freeing.

God, the *last* thing he wanted to do was free her.

"Ian." Her voice was breathless. "I wish— That is, my hair…"

"Is lovely. Full of a dozen shades of red. And it smells like roses."

"Bergamot and tea roses. I blend the scent myself," Jamee said shakily.

"You should sell it. You'd make a fortune." His hands eased over the sheer silk, warm with the heat of her body.

"Your hands," she said raggedly. "They're—"

"Trembling. I know." Ian challenged her to look away as he slid his fingers into her hair. It was only for a moment, he told himself. He could stop when he had to.

His pulse kicked sharply as color filled her cheeks. "God, don't blush again. I'm in serious danger already."

Her eyes widened as she moved against his thighs, where his arousal was unmistakable. "But before, you said that you— that we—"

"To hell with what I said." His hand slid along her hair and gently freed it from the button. Then his fingers splayed open around her slender waist as he pulled her against him. "Does this frighten you?"

"No," Jamee said slowly. "I feel restless. A little dizzy. More than a little dizzy, actually." Her brow furrowed. "Is it supposed to feel like that?"

"It's supposed to feel however it feels, Jamee. Sometimes it's wrong to bring your preconceptions into this."

She smiled. "The idle rich don't use words like *preconception*. I doubt they're this nice, either."

"Pay attention, woman," Ian said huskily. "I'm trying to be serious here."

"So am I. I've always wished…" Her voice broke. "Any second, I expect the fear to kick in. But it hasn't, Ian. Not with you. It's some kind of miracle how I feel around you."

Her honesty stunned him to immobility. "Jamee…you don't have to…"

"I know I don't." She tilted her head. Smiled slowly. Opened her hands on his shirt. "A kiss would probably be in order about now, McCall."

Ian swallowed. Her hips moved. He felt as if he'd been kicked by a horse. "A kiss?"

"You know, that thing two people do with their mouths. Preferably hot and slow."

"I know damned well what a kiss is," he said hoarsely. The kiss wasn't the problem. The problem was that Jamee's lips were the color of ripe plums and if he kissed her, he'd never be able to stop. She'd be naked before the fire, her slip in shreds, and he'd be buried inside her before either of them knew it.

"Just one." Her head tilted. "What could be so dangerous about one little kiss, Lord Glenlyle?"

Ian found out a heartbeat later when he grasped the back of her neck, urged her head down and touched her mouth with his.

The room tilted crazily.

She sat very still. Waiting to panic, he realized. He slid his lips from side to side over hers with gentle pressure. Her mouth softened, her breath coming in faint puffs.

"Frightened?" he murmured.

She leaned closer. Her fingers eased beneath his collar. "Umm."

"Jamee, tell me if you want—"

"I do." Her lips feathered open beneath his. "Very, very much."

The room took another sudden lurch as her tongue brushed his. Ian was glad he was lying down.

"That wasn't so bad," she said gravely. Her hands circled his neck. Gently, she caught his lip between her teeth.

Ian bit back a groan, slammed by heat that gave new meaning to the word *pain*. But he didn't move, didn't strain, capture or take. The moment was hers, the control in her hands.

God knew, he wasn't in control.

She savored her power, savored him, learning the textures of his mouth and what it meant for a man's strength to be held rigidly in check.

Finally she pulled away and drew a hard breath. "You didn't move."

"No." His voice was husky.

Her eyes widened. "You were waiting…for me?"

The test had been for them both. Jamee had passed. It was his own control Ian was worrying about.

She studied his mouth. "You didn't tell me that this kind of thing could be so pleasant, McCall."

Ian struggled for sanity. For the strength to push her away. "Jamee, what you're feeling is hormones, pure and simple. It means nothing. These things often happen during forced confinement."

"Not to me, they don't." Her eyes glistened. "Never to me."

"Never?"

"Not even with my ex-fiancé. Our relationship was pretty much platonic."

"Then he was a bloody fool," Ian said harshly. "A woman like you needs more than stability and normalcy. You deserve adventure and excitement. A little recklessness." He looked at the fire to keep from staring at her face. Her shoulders. Her softly rounded breasts. "Dammit, you've got your whole life in front of you. Go rent a white house on a Greek island. Sail the South Pacific and camp out on a pink sand beach in Thailand. Make love under the Southern Cross."

"I have," she said. "All except for the last part." She shrugged. "But you know all about that. Why I haven't."

She wasn't doing a damned thing to help his control. "What if I couldn't stop? What if I took this farther than you wanted to go?"

"How far *do* I want to go?" she asked, toying with the hair at his neck.

"Dammit, Jamee, you're not helping here."

"No, I don't think I am." Her eyes darkened to azure. Ian saw flecks of firelight reflected in their depths. "Not a bit."

Against all conscious thought, he covered her warm breasts and traced the dark, silken centers that had tormented him for an eternity. Small but perfect, she filled his fingers, her response immediate.

"Ian," she whispered. Her breath caught on a gasp as he eased the sensitive crests beneath his fingers. "That. What you're doing." Another gasp.

"This?" He slipped his hands beneath the sheer silk and met the eager thrust of her naked skin. "God," he whispered hoarsely. She was too beautiful, too responsive. When had she skated and laughed her way past all his barriers?

She arched her back and rasped his name. Hunger exploded through Ian like a caged animal suddenly freed.

Her gasp became a sigh. Became a husky moan as his hands tightened. She blinked, her eyes luminous with passion. "If you happen to think— Well, to want to—"

"I can't *help* wanting to." Ian tried to ignore the small, restless movements she made against his thighs and the way her fingers kneaded his shoulders. Her breasts were heavy in his hands, pebbled and tight.

Yes, he wanted. His blood was screaming to have her. She was life and color and warmth when Ian had resigned himself to shadows.

The thought brought him crashing back to reality. He closed himself to the waves of slashing hunger, shut his eyes to Jamee's firelit beauty. He thought about the thousand reasons this pleasure could never be taken.

Not honorably.

Not with Jamee.

Slowly, he slid away from her and rose to his feet. "We've got to stop," he grated. "This can never happen again."

Jamee gave a throaty laugh. "Never is a long time, McCall. I like the sound of 'tonight' or 'ten minutes' a whole lot better than 'never.'"

Ian clenched his jaw and said nothing.

She hugged her knees to her chest. "What's wrong?" she whispered.

*Everything,* Ian thought, cursing the fact that he had ever accepted this bloody job. Wishing he could have met this woman under different circumstances.

She gave a wobbly smile. "You're not going to tell me you have a social disease, I hope."

He didn't smile back. "No."

Jamee stared at his obviously aroused body. "I…see."

Ian felt the strain at his zipper grow and knew what she

must be seeing, what she must have felt while she was curled against him.

"I hate to tell you this, but the excuse of a tragic war wound just isn't going to carry much weight right now."

Ian cursed silently. No, that lie wouldn't work. If so, he might have tried it.

Other equally weak excuses came to mind, but he knew that lies simply weren't an option. Not now. Jamee Night deserved a whole lot better than that. Lies were degrading to teller and listener and they were generally useless in the end.

Ian frowned, remembering the light he had seen earlier. Even now, someone watched them in the darkness. Jamee deserved to know that, in spite of his promise to her brother. She deserved the rest of the truth, too.

Ian held her gaze. "Not because of that," he said tersely.

"Then why?" Her face was pale, too pale.

Ian forced himself to watch her eyes as he spoke, waiting for her anger and shock. "Because I'm a bodyguard, Jamee. I'm not a casual traveler who was caught in the fog. I was hired two weeks ago by your brother Adam to protect you."

## CHAPTER TEN

"HIRED?" JAMEE BLINKED HARD. "You're a bodyguard?"

"That's one word for it."

She clutched her legs tightly. Something hot filled her throat and made it impossible to breathe. "Adam—my brother *hired* you?"

"I'm afraid so, Jamee."

She couldn't seem to stop shivering. "But you said you were—"

"I know exactly what I said," Ian growled. "Glenlyle is the name of my estate. That much is true. Duncan MacKinnon knows that I've been following you, keeping you in sight to protect you."

Jamee clutched at the arm of the chair, wanting stability. Wanting solidity. Wanting Ian's arms around her.

But not because he was *hired.*

"Go on and yell," he said. "You're entitled."

She wanted to deck him first, then do the same to her interfering brothers. But Jamee saw the pain in his eyes. The tension in his locked shoulders. The betrayal had hurt him almost as much as it hurt her, she realized. He wasn't the sort of man to take lying lightly.

*A man of honor.*

More than decking Ian, she wanted to touch his face and soothe the anger that burned in his eyes. The intensity of that wish shocked her. "If I screamed, would it make you feel better?"

"It would be a start. I *lied* to you, Jamee. Your own brother lied to you. This whole business was a world-class act."

Jamee clenched her fingers to keep from touching the frown cut into Ian's forehead. "You must be very good. Adam only chooses the best."

"Oh, I'm good." The acknowledgment was bitter. "At least I used to be."

"Used to be?"

He shrugged. "Until I met you. Then every sane thought seemed to fly out of my brain."

Jamee reached out a hand, then let it fall. "It's not your fault. The wealth my parents left will always make me a target."

"That's true," he said gravely. "You need to take precautions—real precautions—for your safety. Not just for a day or two, Jamee. This is forever."

Something blurred her vision. "Are you signing on, Lord Glenlyle? Forever?"

"Forever's not an option for me, Jamee."

"The story of my life."

"Jamee, I—"

"Don't bother, Ian." She looked away, frowning as the cat nudged her ankle. "I'm not stupid. I don't take wild risks or court danger. I just want to have some semblance of a life without bars and a cage. But I don't want anyone hurt because of me." Her fingers trembled against the cat's sleek fur. "Especially not you."

"So you're asking me to resign?"

Jamee frowned at her hands. "I think I am."

"Because you don't trust me?"

"No."

Ian caught her trembling hands. "Because I frighten you?"

"No. Not that."

Ian's face grew more grim. "Then why, Jamee?"

"Because…one day I might look up and see you taking a bullet meant for me. If that happened—" She looked down at their cradled fingers, at his hands rigid against her own. Her voice broke. *"No."* She turned away, her knees pulled rigidly to her chest.

With a meow the cat jumped onto her lap. Jamee welcomed the brush of warm fur and the keen, unblinking eyes. Somehow they helped her bear the shock of Ian's revelation and the sudden certainty that he was going to be harmed.

"Nothing's going to happen to me, Jamee." Ian moved behind her, bracing her back, his voice doing breathless, dizzy things to her blood.

Jamee didn't turn. She had her pride, at least. She wouldn't let him see the fear in her face.

His breath touched her hair. "I won't let you be hurt, either. I always keep my promises."

Jamee glanced at him over her shoulder. There was a harsh set to his jaw. "Adam sent you," she whispered. "Something's going to happen, isn't it? There's going to be another…attack."

"Jamee, I can't predict what—"

"How close are they this time?"

The cat watched her intently, ears pricked forward. *Almost as if he understood,* Jamee thought. "Tell me, Ian."

"Dammit, we don't know. There's still not enough information."

"Adam knows," Jamee said quietly. "He can feel things. He always has. Like the night my mother and father…" Memories glittered, cold and swift. Jamee straightened her shoulders. "Adam was the first to know, even before we got the call from the hospital. It was the same when the news came about my brother Terence. Don't ask me how he does it, but he's not wrong. Not ever."

She looked down at the cat curled against her chest and swore she wouldn't fall apart. And she *wouldn't* reach out for Ian. She had to be reasonable, to send him away as soon as this cursed fog lifted. If she gave in, he would never leave.

A man of honor.

All the more reason she couldn't let him be hurt.

Suddenly, Ian wrapped his arms around her and hauled her against his chest, sending the cat to the floor. "They won't get to you, Jamee." His voice was gravelly. "It won't be like before."

Jamee stiffened. "You know about the last time? Adam told you? Even about…my dreams?"

Ian cupped her neck gently. "All of it."

"My brother can be too damned thorough sometimes." Jamee closed her eyes, fighting the warmth of Ian's hands. Just for a moment, she let Ian anchor her against his chest. Then she would send him away. She couldn't let this proud man with the weary eyes be harmed, no matter how much it hurt to make him go. "I'm glad it was you Adam sent."

Ian said something low and hoarse in Gaelic. His arms tightened, bringing her back against him.

Jamee shivered as she felt the unmistakable force of his desire. "Ian?"

"What?"

"No war wounds?" she whispered raggedly.

"It would make things a whole lot easier if I had," he muttered.

Her head rose. "Now, *that* would be an incredible waste."

Ian's jaw clenched. "One of us is going to stay very sane right now, Jamee. I wish I could be certain it was me."

"Don't look at me, Hercules."

"Freckles." He traced the line of her cheek, her lip, her nose. "I never noticed them before. They're small and faint, just the color of a chunk of Russian amber my father always prized."

"Not only on my face," she whispered. "On my arms. And on other…places."

Ian's eyes darkened. "Don't, Jamee."

"Why not? You can't understand how wonderful this feels. All these years I've been blocked, afraid. Wondering how it would feel to want a man's touch. Now I know."

He cupped her face. "What you're feeling has a name and a clinical explanation. It's predictable, explainable and it never lasts."

She stabbed at Ian's chest, chilled by the flat certainty in his voice. "Don't spout medical text at me, Ian McCall. I *know* what I'm feeling and it's real."

He didn't release her. "It feels real, Jamee. And in six months you won't even remember my name."

Jamee shook her head, shoving at his hands. "I won't forget you."

"You have to, Jamee." Ian pulled her palms to his chest. "It's part of the healing. When you forget, that's good, because it means you've gotten on with your life."

"Not for me," she said mutinously. "And how can you be so sure?"

"I'm the expert, remember?" There was an edge of bitterness in Ian's voice. "I'm the one who helped document all the statistics in those medical texts." Suddenly he frowned. "Something's wrong." Ian turned, scanning the room. "Do you smell something?"

Jamee looked down. The cat was bumping at her ankle, meowing shrilly. "What kind of smell?" She pushed to her feet.

"Acrid. Oily." Ian stepped around the cat.

A dark tendril of smoke drifted over the floor. "Fire," Jamee whispered in horror.

"Dammit." A cinder dropped from the thatched roof, singeing Ian's cheek.

"It must be the roof. We've got to get out before everything burns through." Jamee started toward the front door. Even as she spoke, there was a clatter of falling metal from somewhere at the front of the cottage.

Ian stepped in front of her. "Not that way."

"Why?"

His eyes were icy.

"Oh, God, they're outside, aren't they?" Cold terror crawled up Jamee's spine. "They're waiting for me. This—this fire was no accident."

"That sound was one of the trip wires I scattered over the front slope. That leaves one chance for us."

As Jamee watched, he became a different man, all steel and cold deliberation as he yanked on his jacket, checking each pocket with swift efficiency. Gone was the gentleness in his hands. No flecks of humor brightened his emerald eyes now. In a second, he had changed, all fighter, a cold-blooded strategist determined to keep two paces ahead of his opposition.

If anyone could save her, this man could.

Her fingers clenched. "Ian, talk to me. Don't shut me out of this. I need the truth."

"We're going out the back," he said harshly. He grabbed a tartan from the sofa and tossed it over to her, along with her clothes and shoes. "Get dressed as fast as you can."

Somehow she kept her voice steady. "What happens now?"

"In a few minutes, smoke is going to overwhelm this room. We won't have much time, but there's a single high window that leads to a storage shed at the corner of the cottage. We're going to use it."

Fear pressed at Jamee's chest. He had been watching from the start, expecting something like this. If it hadn't been for his planning and thoroughness, she would be trapped her in the smoke while a faceless criminal waited for her to bolt right into his arms.

"We can make it, Jamee." As Ian spoke, flames leaped through the dry thatch and angry cinders plummeted down from the ceiling.

*No, don't think about that. Listen to Ian. Block out all the rest.*

Jamee straightened her shoulders. "Let's go."

"Stay close." Ian gripped her hand and pulled her through the roiling wall of gray. "From now on, no more talking. Our best defense is going to be surprise." His jaw hardened. "We can do this, Jamee. I swear it."

"I'm getting my bag and the cat."

"There's no time—"

But Jamee swept up her bag, then caught the big gray animal and tucked him into the front of her suede jacket. "I'm not leaving him behind," she said fiercely. "Not in this blaze."

When Ian pulled her forward into the smoke, the cat did not struggle, almost as if he were aware of the danger hissing around them. Nor did he move when Ian and Jamee worked their way to the back, crouched low beneath the dark air billowing down from the ceiling.

Jamee's throat burned as they reached the narrow rear scullery. Peat was stacked in one corner beside a dozen fishing poles slanted against a rickety table.

Ian tugged a linen towel from an old ceramic basin and pantomimed wrapping the towel around his face. Then he handed another to Jamee. As she pulled the damp linen up over her nose, Ian unlatched the window, opened his knife and worked three nails out of the sill.

Cold air gushed in, swirling smoke around them. Ian put a finger to his lips and motioned for Jamee to stay low, then climbed onto the table and vanished into the shed.

The air grew thick and heavy with acrid soot. Jamee waited anxiously, counting the seconds. What if the kidnappers came now? What if they found Ian outside?

She bit down hard on the damp linen and refused to give way to panic. Smoke swirled around her as she strained to keep from coughing, aware that any sound could betray her location.

The cat wriggled in her arms and Jamee smoothed the warm gray head. Had she been less concerned with escaping, she might have wondered at the creature's willingness to remain in her arms. But her focus was on the darkness outside. She tried not to think of Ian clubbed from behind. Ian bleeding. Ian captured. Ian shot at point-blank range.

Metal scraped softly. Jamee's heart lurched as a dark figure appeared below the sooty glass of the open window leading to the shed.

"It's me." Ian's voice was low and clipped. "We're clear. Climb through and I'll help you out. Once we get through the shed, we'll head up the glen."

Jamee rose into the oily layer of smoke. Her eyes burned as she searched blindly for the outline of the window. A hand caught her shoulder and tugged her forward into darkness, but before she could cry out, Ian's arms were around her, his lips pressed to her ear.

"They're busy in front," he whispered. "We'll be fine as long as they're watching the fire."

"How many?" Jamee rasped.

"Two."

*Two.* It could be worse, she told herself. It could also be a whole lot better.

"Ready?"

She nodded.

Arm in arm, they inched through the darkened shed, then scrambled up the stony slope. Behind them the fire cast a sulfurous glow over the ground. Gorse and brush tore at Jamee's legs and her lungs burned as she struggled to match Ian's pace. Finally silence closed in around them.

There were no shouts. No slam of feet.

No one seemed to notice their escape.

Through the mist, occasional patches of sky appeared overhead, dotted by stars. Jamee took a deep breath of cool Highland air, sharp with sea salt and pine. She tried not to think about the chaos at the cottage and the unknown men waiting back down the hill.

She was shivering by the time Ian pulled her behind a granite outcropping and tugged the linen from her face.

"In a few minutes they'll realize we're not coming out. Then they'll have to decide whether to go in after us," he explained tightly. "If they're professionals, they'll be prepared for that option and it won't take them long to find out we aren't there. By then I plan to be well hidden."

"Where will we hide out here?" Jamee whispered, her voice hoarse with smoke and fear. "The fog is finally lifting. If they have lights, they'll see us."

"Not where we're going," Ian said, pulling her over the gorse, into the unrelenting gloom of the moors.

THE STONES ROSE like arms of darkness caught in worship of the night sky. Around their massive flanks mist drifted in loose wisps that veiled the damp earth.

The cat stirred at Jamee's chest, suddenly restless. Jamee felt the same tingle of uneasiness. "Here?" she asked. "But this is some kind of ancient circle, a sacred place. We can't just—"

"We can and we will," Ian growled, tugging her past three giant upright stones. "There's a vault behind the capstone. Duncan and I discovered it when we camped here as boys one summer."

"But—"

"Don't worry, no one has used the old chamber for centuries. I only hope the inner stones haven't fallen and blocked the entrance."

Jamee trailed him reluctantly past the ghostly stones, feeling like an intruder in this place of age and tangible power.

Ian stopped before two massive verticals capped by a great horizontal slab of granite. "Here it is. The barrow entrance was just below this." Ian's voice faded as he crouched at the base of the huge stones.

Jamee knelt beside him. "What exactly are we looking for?"

"Any sort of hole. It may be overgrown with bracken by now."

As Jamee searched the cold stones, thorny shrubs dug at her fingers. If they didn't find someplace to hide soon…

"I think I found it. Help me clear away these weeds."

Twigs snapped. Ian cursed. Jamee felt him beside her, tugging at layers of dry vegetation. Abruptly, the dark outline of a hole appeared, cut into the mound beneath the capstone.

"Is this a burial chamber?" Jamee felt a prickle at her neck. Once again she had the odd feeling they were not alone. "Do you feel that, Ian? That…sense of something not quite right?"

"I feel it," he said dryly. "Almost as if a band of bearded savages with stone axes is about to come charging over the hill. This place is probably three thousand years old. When Duncan and I found it, all the grave goods were gone except for a handful of copper beads. We were crushed because we had been hoping to find at least one thing that would make us famous. But no luck." A clump of vegetation went flying over his shoulder. "There, that's the last of the bracken. I'll go first and check that the stones are stable inside."

"I'll be right behind you," Jamee said before he could protest. "Give me a good Neolithic ghost over a modern-day kidnapper anytime." One step behind Ian, she slid into the hole on her bottom and landed against a floor of damp earth.

"Everything seems fine," Ian announced after a careful search. "The outer columns are still intact and the walls are solid. I'll pile the gorse back over the hole before I go."

"*Go?*" Jamee's voice rose unsteadily. "Go where?"

"The mist will cover any trace of the opening. Just sit tight and stay calm."

"Are you nuts? You can't leave." As Jamee spoke, the cat wriggled free of her tartan and jumped down to the ground. "Now you've frightened the cat, blast it."

Ian caught her cheek. "He'll be fine. So will you," he said gently. "I promise I won't be any longer than I have to be."

Jamee stood stiffly, her breath coming in angry spurts. "You *can't* go. They're waiting right down the hill."

"That's exactly where I'm headed," he said. "Even if I can't catch the bastards, I'm going to match up the odds a little."

Jamee's fingers flattened on the cold stone. She expected to feel suffocating panic at the thought of staying alone in the dark. Instead her fear was for Ian. "They'll be waiting for you. By now, they'll know we escaped."

Ian cupped her cheek. "If you need me here, I'll stay, though I'd rather take this chance to nail these men."

Jamee swallowed. He was right. She could endure an hour or two of darkness.

She felt the cat press at her feet and lifted him into her arms.

"Go on then. I'll be fine here with my friend. Just don't get yourself shot down there, understand?"

His hand tightened for a moment. "I promise. Keep my side of the rock warm." Then he vanished through the gorse.

## CHAPTER ELEVEN

THE TWO MEN had moved closer to the cottage in the half hour since Ian had seen them last. One hunched behind the front door. In the light from the burning roof Ian made out a second figure crouched to the side of the rear entrance.

Ian's hands twitched, restless to cup the smooth grip of his well-worn Browning. He had been issued other weapons over the years, including a state-of-the-art 9 mm Glock with hollow-point bullets, but Ian had relied on the Browning in too many dark alleys to feel comfortable with anything else.

He sighted, his pulse racing as he imagined how the first bullet would drop the man at the front door cold.

But anger always lost the game. Emotion was a lapse no professional was allowed, and Ian knew that rule better than anyone. He had negotiated with the demented, the greedy and the idealogue using only the force of his mind. When it came time to act, Ian was the one the victim's family and the police turned to because his plans were always based on cold, hard reason. Never on emotion.

Until now.

He looked down, furious to see that his hands were shaking.

Because it was Jamee they were after, and that changed everything.

Ian drew a ragged breath and inched closer, forcing himself to wait and watch and analyze as he had been trained to do. The man at the front was pushing six feet, dressed in black with a camouflage field jacket and paratrooper boots. Ian could see little of his face beneath a black knit cap. Keeping to the shadows, he worked his way toward the second man, who was huddled by the rear door. His hands tightened on his weapon as he thought about trying to pick them off in turn. But if he were hit, Jamee would be left alone, a certain target should Ian's own bullets fail.

No, it was too risky for Jamee.

Ian inched downhill. A four-wheel drive vehicle was angled behind the three boulders. As he eased open the door, a pile of discarded soda cans shuddered and nearly toppled.

Careless, as well as messy, he thought. But well financed and well supplied, judging by the shortwave radio and headphones lying on the seat next to a state-of-the-art satellite-navigation device.

Ian disabled the navigation device, then tossed it back on the seat. At the least he could slow them down.

A quick search through the glove compartment revealed two packs of Gitaine cigarettes, a screwdriver and a pack of matches. A length of rope jutting from beneath the passenger seat caught his eye. He shoved it in his pocket, along with a nearby scrap of paper, then edged back outside just as the roof of the cottage exploded in an angry orange storm, sending embers hissing down through the smoke.

No more time.

Ian crouched by the back tire and went to work. He was nearly done when a fuzzy pointed face butted his arm. *Sheep.* Two more trailed close by, bleating softly.

Ian's eyes narrowed. He calculated the distance to the cottage, then thumped the first sheep firmly on its hindquarters and watched with a smile as the trio charged wildly up the trail.

No one would notice his own departure now, thanks to his noisy friends.

WHAT WAS TAKING Ian so long? Jamee wondered. She crouched behind the stones at the entrance to the barrow. A half hour had to have passed since he'd left.

Her eyes locked on the trail downhill, where light spilled against the receding fog. The muted crack of an explosion reminded her of Ian's warning about the roof giving way.

Shivering, she tugged the tartan closer around her shoulders. *Nothing to do but wait. Try not to think…*

A cold wind cut over the hillside and gusted through the narrow opening. The temperature was dropping swiftly and she didn't relish the thought of spending the rest of the night here. She glanced at her watch. Where was Ian? What would she do if—

Jamee shook her head sharply, refusing to give in to the fear. But determined or not, as she hunched against the damp earth of the barrow, memories surged up out of the ragged hole of her past.

*Sharp voices.*

*Footfalls in the night.*

The old Dream assailed her, dank with moldy leaves and the metallic taste of her own blood on her lips.

Dimly, Jamee felt the cat press against her arm. Blackness yawned before her. She bit her lip to keep from crying out as memories continued to flood out of the darkness. Every second, the line between past and present grew dimmer.

*Not again.*

Laughter rose around her, cold and mocking. Even the warm fur beneath Jamee's fingers ceased to calm her.

Close. Too close.

A shadow surged out of the night.

Jamee froze. "Stay back. You're not getting me," she rasped, twisting sideways.

A rain of pebbles struck her feet. She tried to scream as hard hands locked over her mouth. The Dream, but more real than ever before…

"Jamee, it's me. You're safe. They won't find you here."

She shoved at the fingers, hearing the words but not understanding them.

"It's Ian, Jamee. You're *safe* here. No one will find you now. Do you understand?"

A long shudder shook her. "Safe." She nodded slowly. "Ian?"

"Right here. I'm going to let go." Ian's hands eased from her mouth. "We'll be fine, I swear it. We have to be very quiet for a bit, that's all."

"Quiet." Jamee swallowed. "It was quiet then, too." She couldn't see Ian's face in the darkness. Suddenly it was crucial that she see him. "It's too dark here. Too quiet. Those men might be—"

"Jamee, the past is not going to be repeated. You won't be taken, do you hear me?" Ian anchored her face. "I won't let it happen. Listen to me. *Believe* me."

"I…wish I could." Her hands trembled, locked against her waist.

"Then start now, because I'm not going away. I'm sticking with you, Jamee, all the way to the end," he said hoarsely. "Now, get that tartan wrapped tighter. You're shivering like a leaf."

Shivering? She hadn't even noticed.

"I've covered the opening and it's completely invisible. Everything will be fine now."

Jamee bit back a ragged laugh. *Fine?* Oh, how she wished.

But *fine* meant no nightmares. *Fine* meant not waking up covered with sweat from terror. *Fine* meant falling asleep and knowing you would be in the same place in the morning instead of halfway across the room with your clothes scattered in a wild tangle while you fought unbearable memories.

Suddenly Jamee felt too tired to pretend. For the first time in years, she needed someone to lean on, someone she could be honest with. "Oh, God, how I wish, Ian. I just want to be normal. To cross a street and not have to look over my shoulder, wondering who's behind me, waiting for their chance."

Ian covered her lips with his finger. "That's what I'm here for—so you don't have to worry. Believe me, I'm damn good at what I do, Jamee."

"I believe that." Smiling sadly, Jamee touched the furrows in his brow. "Maybe that's why I trust you so much. You already feel comfortable here." She pressed at her chest. "Familiar. Like an old part of my life."

"Come here." As Ian pulled her against him, Jamee felt something break inside her. Her knees gave way and she hugged his shoulders while dry sobs shook her.

With a curse he sank to the floor, cradling her in his lap and whispering soft Gaelic words.

Words that comforted and soothed. Words that adored.

Jamee made a broken sound and tangled her hands in his hair. "Talk to me, Ian. Say more of those lovely things. Maybe the old words have the power to keep my memories at bay."

This time when Ian spoke, there was English, too, words that told Jamee how brave she was, how beautiful and stubborn and irritating and downright wonderful. As he spoke, his hands smoothed her cheeks and his lips brushed her eyelids.

Without any warning desire burst through her, immense and wordless. Jamee shivered, her nerves stretched to breaking. She needed Ian. She needed to feel his skin slide against hers and his hands clenched around her in passion.

But what then? Would she become another statistic in someone's medical textbook? Was her desire as he'd said, a simple case of dependence brought on by stress, a delusion that would be forgotten within hours?

Jamee's hands dug into Ian's shoulders.

"You're freezing. Hold me as if you mean it," he said gruffly, slipping the tartan around her shoulders.

Wind whistled past the entrance, rustling dried heather and eddies of dirt. Jamee heard her heartbeat pounding in her head. "You saw them, didn't you? Down at the cottage."

Ian's hands tightened. "I saw them."

"Tell me." Jamee straightened her shoulders, trying to read Ian's face in the darkness. "I need to know, Ian. Faceless is worse, because they become monsters I can't defeat. And I have to win. Somehow," she whispered.

"There were two of them," Ian said flatly. "In their thirties, I'd guess. They were waiting by both doors. Thank God we got out when we did."

Jamee tried to think clearly. His hard body cradled beneath the thick wool. Every touch seduced; every movement of his hands kindled fresh heat.

She closed her eyes and shut away the need. "Something else is bothering you."

He didn't answer.

"Tell me, Ian. I have a right to know."

He muttered a curse and gripped her tightly. "They were well financed and well briefed. They knew we were alone. They were following us from the cliffs. It means, Jamee, that they know more than they should."

*Briefed.* The word slammed through Jamee's head, causing a new kind of cold to grip her. "Then you're saying it's someone close to me. Someone who knew my schedule and my destination."

"I'm saying it's possible. And I don't like the idea," Ian muttered.

Jamee didn't like it, either. She wanted to scream and fight, but there was no one to fight. So she held on to Ian, her only source of stability in a world turned upside down, a world where she could trust no one, not even those closest to her.

"So, Scotsman," she said with a shaky laugh, "don't you ever have any good news?"

Ian rested her face against his chest and slid his hands into her hair. "Don't you ever lose your sense of humor?"

"Only when I'm deprived of my morning coffee."

"I can see I'm going to have to teach you the merits of a good Darjeeling," Ian said. "For the record, here's the good news. The fog is lifting."

"And the bad news?" she asked.

"Tonight you get to sleep with me."

Jamee sighed, burrowing closer against Ian's broad chest. "That's not bad news at all. The bad news is that sleeping is *all* we'll do." She raised her head. "It is, isn't it?"

Ian muttered darkly. "It is."

"I was afraid you'd say that." She eased her head back down on his shoulder and five minutes later, she was asleep, sprawled over his chest. By then, her hands were wedged beneath his sweater, pressed against his naked skin.

Ian knew when she relaxed, knew when she finally slept. Even though every breath brought him fresh pain, he didn't move beneath her. Her soft thighs fit so snugly against his rising erection that he had to concentrate on staying motionless.

But he didn't pull away. The feel of her body was too precious in spite of his fevered reaction.

Carefully, he eased the cellular phone from his pocket and dialed Dunraven Castle.

"MacKinnon here."

"You appear to have had a little accident with the crofter's cottage, my friend."

"Ian? Are you and Jamee—"

"Fine. I can't say the same for the cottage, unfortunately. Any hope of getting a car up here?"

"Within the hour, I hope. The fog is lifting as we speak. Where are you now?"

Ian gave terse directions. "Remember the night we found the barrow?"

"Of course, it's right at the top of the—"

"That's the place," Ian interrupted. "No need to announce it to the whole world, however." Jamee murmured once, and Ian slid a hand over her shoulder, soothing her. "Send some men after us as soon as you can. We might have been followed here," Ian explained grimly. "I can hold them off for a while, but I'd prefer not to."

"Understood. Sit tight," Duncan snapped, than rang off.

Ian sank back. Two hours until dawn. So little time—and yet in some ways, an eternity. He whispered Jamee's name as his hands slid through the warm silk of her hair. He would hold back the past for her until dawn. He would help her fight her dark memories.

For the last hours of the night, Jamee would sleep without shadows.

DAWN FILTERED SLOWLY over the brown hills, shadowing the solitary ring of stones. At the top of the pass a golden plover soared on the high currents, oblivious to the landmarks left by ancient men. The last tendrils of mist ebbed to the high peaks as the sun burst free.

Jamee winced as her knee struck a rim of stone. She sat up stiffly. The tartan was draped over her legs. She was alone in the barrow and the fog was completely gone.

Ian was gone, too.

In the pale daylight, the chamber seemed small and unremarkable, its shadows hiding no terrors. Jamee shoved away the bracken and heather covering the narrow hole, then pushed outside, blinking in the pinkish light. Before her the high hills rolled implacably away toward stone cliffs and the girding sea. The charred roof of the cottage sent plumes of smoke trailing against the sky, but the memory of the dangers of the night faded before the peace of the landscape, where green lay upon green in a dozen shades that Jamee knew would haunt her dreams.

It was a beautiful place. A desolate place, filled with shadows of a restless past. Ghosts might well walk here—if Jamee had believed in them, which she did not.

Did Ian feel these same stirrings? She thought of an old castle somewhere to the north, circled by a river and ancient hills. How could he sell such a part of his heritage?

Something rumbled beneath Jamee's feet. A car, coming fast. Maybe more than one car.

Dear God, where was Ian?

She spun awkwardly at a sudden noise behind her. Ian stood a few feet away smiling in the sunlight, one shoulder propped on the massive capstone. Dirt streaked his face and hands.

"You look terrible," Jamee said, running over the heather and throwing her arms around him.

"Maybe I should look terrible more often," he murmured, smoothing her hair with one hand.

"Don't change the subject, McCall. Where have you *been?* That rumble is the sound of a car, in case you hadn't noticed."

"Oh, I noticed. That should be Duncan MacKinnon, right

on schedule." He checked his watch, then gave a crooked grin. "I phoned him while you were sleeping."

"Phone? How?"

Ian patted his pocket. "Cellular. I never leave home without it." His smiled faded. "Duncan knew where we were, Jamee. The problem was getting to us."

"The fog?"

Ian nodded.

Jamee pulled away, her body stiff. "You could at least have told me about the phone."

"Things happened too fast."

"I don't like deception," she said tightly. Her emotions were in turmoil. She wanted Ian's arms around her, but at the same time, her reliance on him frightened her.

"Neither do I. But I gave your brother my word that I'd keep my participation a secret."

Her eyes widened. The rising sun left shadows over the hard planes of Ian's face. "What made you change your mind?"

"You did."

Jamee swallowed. Feelings engulfed her. It was too much too soon. She wasn't ready to feel so painfully aware of another person. She wasn't ready to trust a man with her vulnerability. She took a step away from Ian. "The men at the cottage are gone?"

"As fast as they could manage with four tires losing air fast."

A smile tugged at her mouth. "You did that?"

"I wasn't going to make it easy for them. From the look of it, their tracks run southeast, back toward the village. The constable's men should be able to trace them. Duncan's already phoned in an alert." Ian shoved his hands into his pockets. "I'm here, Jamee. If you're cold. If you need me."

"I'll be fine."

"That's not what you said last night." A muscle moved at his jaw.

"That was last night." Jamee turned her face to the sun, shivering. "Someone could have killed you down there. I'm not going to lie, Ian. That bothers the hell out of me." She pulled up her jacket collar as wind knifed through her hair. "Maybe things are happening too fast. For *both* of us."

Before she could say more, a trio of Land Rovers bucked over the steep incline, then shuddered to a halt below the stone circle. A tall man with black hair jumped from the lead car and sprinted over the rocky ground, smiling broadly.

"Glad to see that the ghost of the dead Druid prince didn't seize you in the night, Glenlyle."

"No one said anything about a ghost," Jamee said tightly.

"Oh, this old ring is haunted without a doubt. Many are the lights we've seen from Dunraven." Duncan MacKinnon looked at Jamee, his blue eyes crinkling. "You must be Ms. Night." He enveloped her hand in a firm grip and shook it twice. "Length of life and sunny days and a belated welcome to Dunraven land."

"I don't believe in ghosts," Jamee said.

"No? Don't tell that to Ian here. He once throttled a lad who said the Glenlyle legends were naught but poppycock."

"What legends?" Jamee frowned at Ian.

"Forget the legends, MacKinnon," Ian thundered. "Where's that whiskey you promised me? We want a hot bath and a hot meal. On the way you can tell me what took you so long to get here."

## CHAPTER TWELVE

THE LAND ROVER pitched to a halt at the end of a narrow gravel drive. Up the hill, light danced from Dunraven Castle's pink stone walls. A roof of black slate rose in a fantasy of gables and turrets above the rugged landscape.

Jamee pinched herself to be certain she hadn't stepped into a dream.

"Twenty-two kings have slept here in the castle," Duncan explained with pride. "Three wars were planned here and more than a few affairs of the heart."

"It…it's magnificent," Jamee breathed.

Duncan chuckled. "Wait until you see Ian's great wreck up at Glenlyle."

Jamee's eyes widened. "It can't be bigger than this."

"You'll see," Duncan said.

Jamee glanced at Ian, who smiled calmly. "Where's that wife of yours, MacKinnon? I've been wanting to give her a kiss for months now."

"One kiss, laddie, and no more. Otherwise it will be claymores at dawn on the beach."

Ian sighed loudly. "It never fails to amaze me that Kara settled on an oaf like you."

"For one reason and one only. The lady obviously has excellent taste." Duncan opened Jamee's door with a flourish. "Welcome to Dunraven Castle, Ms. Night." With that, he swept Jamee up into his arms and headed toward the massive oak door.

Jamee looked around her with great interest, not at all put out by his dashing gesture. "Is this standard procedure or is the fanfare only for impressionable Americans?"

"Quite standard, I assure you. The custom began several centuries ago when one of my more debonair ancestors insisted on carrying a queen of Scotland over the muddy paths beside the pigsty. The pigsty is gone, but the ritual remains, I'm glad to say."

"You can put her down now, MacKinnon," Ian said with an undercurrent of irritation.

"Not until we reach the front door. Ritual is ritual, you know."

Ian snorted. "Only when it suits you."

Jamee hid a smile, relishing the sunlight on her shoulders and the wind that rose from the sea, fragrant with salt and pine. "I like your kilt, Lord Dunraven."

"Call me Duncan, my dear." Duncan chuckled at the irritation on Ian's face. "And do not be misled. A kilt is the best costume for a fight, you understand. There is nothing to bind or restrict a man's movement. Scratch a Scotsman's customs and you'll generally find something to do with fighting or planning a fight."

"Or drinking," Jamee said helpfully.

"There is that," Duncan conceded. "As I recall, your father did a fair bit of that himself when he and your mother visited at Rose Cottage for their second honeymoon. I can't tell you how sad I was to hear of their accident."

"They did so much love it here," Jamee said wistfully. "I think it was all of Scotland, in fact. They both had family here generations back. In a way, it was like coming home for them."

Jamee swallowed, keeping her voice steady. "Could I see the cottage this morning?"

"Anytime you like." Duncan nodded at a lean man with wiry white hair who pushed open the front door. "Here they are at last, Angus. Bedraggled but no worse, I think. Meet Angus McTavish, Ms. Night. Angus rules us all with an iron hand. The McTavishes have been here at Dunraven almost as long as the MacKinnons, and they'll be the first to tell you we couldn't have managed without them, whether in war or in peace."

"Nor could you," the old servant said smugly. "It is a pleasure to welcome you to Dunraven, Ms. Night. I remember your parents well. You have the look of your mother about you, lass. The same wonderful eyes."

"Thank you," Jamee said, flushing. "They mentioned how kind you all were here. You, too, Mr. McTavish."

"Ach, lass, call me Angus, like the rest do."

Duncan carried Jamee over the threshold and set her down in the Great Hall.

Ian stared over Angus's broad shoulder through the open door. "Good lord, Angus, what have you done to the braw old place?"

The beams were draped with holly and tinsel. Tiny colored lights flashed from the mullioned window and vintage ornaments of satin and glass gleamed on Dunraven's massive mantel.

Jamee caught her breath in awe, feeling like a child set down in a chocolate shop.

"It's prepared for the photo shoot by Lady Dunraven," Angus explained. "Most of the staff of *New Bride* magazine are helping out."

Jamee looked from wall to tabletop, unable to decide which fabric to examine first. Dozens of tartans lined the stairway and covered the magnificent oak chairs. The beauty of the old house reached out, touching Jamee's heart.

"This is the MacKinnon tartan, isn't it? I recognize the red-and-green design." She studied a length of old fabric draping a heavy oak hunt table beside the front door.

"So it is," Duncan said proudly. "At least six generations old, by my father's reckoning. It was said to be woven by an ancestor with magic hands and rare skill."

Jamee felt a curious tension at her neck as she studied the fragile old wool. Some part of her yearned to touch it, while another part of her drew back.

"Her name was Maire MacKinnon," Duncan said. "I believe there's a portrait of her in the attic if you're interested."

Before Jamee could answer, footfalls sounded on the broad stone staircase. A woman with deep auburn hair slid a foot over the bannister and sailed gracefully down, right into her husband's arms.

Duncan tried to look angry and failed miserably. "I thought we agreed there would be no more of that, Kara. Not for the duration."

His wife gave him a cajoling smile. "Of course we agreed. But I didn't want to keep our guests waiting."

"Blast it, Kara, you promised me."

Kara Fitzgerald MacKinnon wriggled out of his arms. Her purple sweater brought out glints of red in her auburn hair as her gaze swept over Ian, then settled on Jamee. "Here you are at last, my dear. What a nasty welcome to Scotland you've had." She shoved a pencil into her auburn curls and shot another measuring look from Ian to Jamee. "I hope you've taken good care of her, Ian." She tucked her arm through Jamee's. "Your boxes arrived yesterday in perfect shape. We'll send someone for your car shortly." Kara smiled apologetically. "I'm afraid it's a little chaotic here. We're finishing the Christmas issue for

*New Bride.* I thought you'd like to rest and change before you meet everyone."

Jamee thought about the bits of bracken and heather caught in her braid. Her face had to be streaked with soot. Cleaning up seemed like a wonderful idea. She wasn't ready to meet the curious stares of a dozen strangers.

Not while she was still trying to sort out her emotions about Ian.

She glanced across the hall, where Ian was caught in quiet conversation with Duncan. Neither man was smiling. Jamee could guess the subject.

So he really was a bodyguard. She could probably live with that.

He might be hurt at any moment taking a bullet if her kidnappers decided to rush her. Jamee felt a knot of dread fill her chest. That she couldn't live with.

Ian had taught her to trust him. He had made her feel safe in his embrace. No, she thought sadly, he had made her feel much more than safe. He had made her feel alive. Wanted.

Beautiful.

Now that she knew the threat in store, how could she wait patiently for Ian to take a blow or deflect a blade aimed at her?

Damn, why couldn't life ever be *simple?*

"Here, give me your bag."

Jamee blinked, realizing Ian was standing in front of her. "What?"

"Your workbag. It has to weigh a ton. Hand it over."

Jamee's shoulders straightened. "I'll manage. I always have. I always will."

His eyes darkened. "But this time you don't have to manage. That's what I'm here for."

"Is it?" Jamee's fingers tightened on the leather handle. She was driven to fight him, to resist the effortless sense of security he spun whenever he was around her. She had worked too hard for her independence and self-reliance to let them slide away now. "No, I'll keep it. I always carry my own weight."

Irritation flashed through his eyes. "I know what you're trying to do, Jamee. In a way, I even applaud it." His voice fell, audible only to her as Duncan and Kara moved toward the main corridor of the house. "You need to keep in control, especially after what you saw at the cottage. Unfortunately, that's not going to be possible. They will be closing in, and I'm here to protect you when they do. You're going to have to use me, like it or not."

Jamee's lips trembled. "I don't like it. Not one damn bit."

"If it helps," Ian said harshly, "I don't like it, either."

"It doesn't help."

Ian muttered a low phrase of Gaelic and tugged the heavy bag from her shoulder. "Trust me a little."

Jamee swallowed. He didn't understand. There was nothing halfway about trust, not for her. How did you trust someone to kiss you, but no more? How did you keep trust from spilling over into everything you did? No, it was all or nothing. "I'll try to remember that. Meanwhile, the trust works two ways. I want to know exactly what's happening, Ian. Every minute. If you have any news, I want to hear it, too."

"If I can."

"Dammit, Ian—"

"Don't fight me, Jamee. It will only make this harder. And that's the last thing I want for you," he said softly.

"I *have* to fight. It's either fight you or—"

Her words were swallowed up by an excited ripple of laughter as people spilled into Dunraven's Great Hall. Like exotic tropical birds, rail-thin models in long velvet dresses huddled around a striking man with almond-shaped eyes and bright purple hair. When he saw Jamee, his face broke into a smile.

He hurried across the room, shoving aside the German camera around his neck, and thrust out a hand. "Hidoshi Sato," he announced. "You must be Miss Night. I've seen your work in *Textile Quarterly*. Great use of color. And you've been doing some fabulous things with alpaca and flax."

Jamee flushed slightly. "You saw those? I thought only about twelve people ever read the magazine. You know, I actually began my fabric work in Japan. I worked with a kimono weaver in Kyoto."

*"So desu ka?"* Hidoshi said in Japanese. "No kidding."

Jamee answered easily.

"You speak Japanese?" Kara looked impressed. "How do you say, 'One more shot of me without makeup and I'll deck you'?"

"Far beyond my language abilities, I'm afraid," Jamee said with a laugh. "I can just about order a bowl of soba noodles and buy tickets for the Bullet Train."

"Where is Rob, by the way?" Kara handed a silver-and-red wreath to Hidoshi. "He said he would be finished shooting the Wise Men twenty minutes ago."

"Beats me," the photographer said. "Probably waiting for the light to be perfect. That's why I like him for an assistant: he takes his time so he'll get things right on the first shot. No wasted film to explain to the suits up in accounting." Hidoshi held up the wreath and frowned. "Way too bland. How about adding two angels and some more candy canes? You can never have too many angels or too much candy at Christmas."

"I don't think you've met Megan O'Hara, my colleague at *New Bride* magazine. Megan is the keeper of the records, the keys and my general sanity." Kara put one arm around a fresh-faced young woman with masses of freckles. "This is Jamee Night, Megan. And since everyone else seems to have come along, why don't you make the introductions, Duncan?" Kara looked uneasily at her husband.

Jamee realized why. Kara was uncertain how much of the truth to reveal to the gathered company, and she was leaving the decision to her husband.

Did one of the smiling faces in the crowd belong to a criminal? Were the friendly eyes even now hiding secret knowledge of all that had happened at the cottage?

Jamee took a sharp breath. *Stop being paranoid,* she told herself as Duncan MacKinnon took a spot on the winding staircase.

"Very well, my love, I'll be happy to do the honors. I want everyone to meet Jamee Night and her friend Ian McCall. They'll be staying here for a few days while Jamee finishes a set of textile designs we've commissioned for the castle. Any questions?"

One of the models tossed back her mane of honey-blond hair and eyed Ian hungrily. "And just what is Mr. McCall going to be doing while Ms. Night is busy working? I wouldn't want him to be lonely."

Duncan raised one brow. "I'm sure Lord Glenlyle will find something to keep him busy."

"Lord, is it?" The model licked her lips with predatory delight. "I'm available, Lord Glenlyle. Just remember that."

After a startled silence, Hidoshi cleared his throat. "You aren't going to have time for any moonlit strolls, Tania. Tonight is the dinner scene and tomorrow is the Victorian wedding. We've got fittings to finish, remember?"

The woman smiled. "Oh, there's always time for a good thing, isn't there, Lord Glenlyle? Especially since you don't look like a man who lets time go to waste."

"Sorry, but I'm going to be fairly busy myself," Ian said easily, slipping one arm around Jamee's waist. "I have to be sure that the woman I love doesn't get lured away by a dashing stranger."

Jamee felt her face fill with heat. His voice was low, tender, filled with emotion. *The woman he loved?*

She stared at Ian, shocked to realize how much she wanted to believe his words. He looked entirely sincere, his eyes those of a man in love.

She took a ragged breath. "Ian, why are you—"

He cut her off neatly. "Shall we tell them now, my love?"

"Tell them *what?*"

Ian took her wrists and slid them around his waist, drawing her against his chest. "About what happened up at the cottage."

"You mean, the cold, the fog and the fire?"

He laughed huskily, as if sharing a private and very intimate joke. "No, I mean, the other part."

Jamee stared back at him in confusion. Her pulse hammered at the press of his body. "*What* other part?"

"The most unexpected gift in the world. There we were, just the two of us. No phones, no faxes and no distractions." He brushed a curl from her cheek. "That's when I realized the depth of my feelings."

"You did?"

"Absolutely. Now there's no way I'm going to be separated from you, even for a second. Not until we're married."

"Married?" Jamee repeated weakly. The same warm security was enfolding her, making it impossible to think clearly.

"Of course that's what I mean. If you'll have me."

Jamee swallowed. "Married. You and me?"

"You know the word," Ian said, with a self-effacing grin. "That thing two people do with a minister and lots of white rice."

Jamee managed a laugh. He couldn't really be saying this

to her, could he? She couldn't allow herself to believe him, not when she wanted to so badly. "To me, lots of white rice means a meal in Chinatown."

Ian cupped her cheek, his eyes suddenly intent. "How unromantic of you. I can see I'm going to have to change all that." He turned to Duncan. "I hope you've left the Blue Bedroom free for us."

"Er…it's all yours," Duncan said, sounding startled.

Jamee blinked. *The depth of his feelings?* Why was Ian talking like this, mentioning a shared bedroom in front of all these strangers?

And then the world narrowed to the span of Ian's shoulders and the hot sweep of his mouth. His hand opened, stroking the small of her back and pulling her closer.

"Kiss me," he whispered hoarsely.

At any other time Jamee would have stiffened. She wasn't used to being on display before so many curious strangers. But desire hummed through her blood, driven by every touch of Ian's mouth. "Now?" she whispered. "Here?" When Jamee saw the hunger in Ian's eyes all her doubts fled. She parted her lips and kissed him, sliding her hands deep into his hair. Dimly she heard him groan as she eased her tongue sleekly over his.

Heat shimmered. Suddenly Jamee didn't care who was watching.

When Ian lifted his head, his breath came heavy and his face was as flushed as hers. "Sorry," he muttered to the fascinated bystanders. "I just can't seem to keep my hands off her."

"So when is the ceremony?" the model named Tania demanded icily. "The sooner the better, by the look of you two."

"Just as soon as Duncan can arrange it," Ian answered calmly.

"Gee, were you two caught in that fire we saw?" another of the models asked.

"I'm afraid so," Ian answered. "We must have generated even more heat than we realized."

Jamee barely heard the ripple of laughter. Ian was too calm, too cool about all this. Suddenly warning lights went off in her head.

"Where will the ceremony be held?" Hidoshi asked eagerly. "Can I take some photos? They'd be great for the magazine. Hey, wait a minute. We've got this amazing Victorian wedding gown and veil upstairs. Maybe Jamee could wear it for *our* shoot."

Jamee stiffened, overwhelmed by the curious stares. The bodies seemed to press closer. Tania's gaze followed her. "I— I don't know."

"Of course you don't," Ian said. "We'll discuss it later."

"How many children are you planning to have, Lord Glenlyle?" Tania called. "An even dozen?"

"A dozen sounds wonderful to me," Ian answered, guiding Jamee to the staircase. He frowned as she stiffened. He bent his head, whispering. "Don't look so worried, Jamee. This will be the shortest engagement in Dunraven's history. I'm sorry it happened like this, but I wouldn't dream of holding you to any promises," he murmured.

*Holding her to any promises?* Jamee's heart lurched. So it was all part of his job, a perfect excuse to stay close and protect her. Nothing more.

She swayed slightly, rocked by disappointment. *Stupid,* she told herself. *But you're not going to fall apart here, not in front of all these people.*

*Especially not in front of that Tania creature.*

With a brittle smile she took Ian's arm and began to walk toward the stairs. The marble steps seemed miles away, separated by a sea of curious faces. But she had her pride if nothing else, Jamee thought. She looked at Ian and smiled seductively.

"More than a dozen children. Definitely more. Do you think you'll be up to it, Lord Glenlyle?"

A muscle flashed at Ian's jaw as Jamee made a great display of planting a slow, hot kiss dead on his lips. "Maybe sooner than you think," he said harshly.

Disappointment filled Jamee. It was all an act, the clever stratagem of a man who was always one step ahead and perfectly in control. She took a slow breath, summoning anger to replace her regret. Anything so Ian wouldn't see how much she had wanted to accept the offer he had so calmly dismissed.

Her hand stayed on his arm as they climbed the stairs, but her smile was now as false as his proposal of marriage.

Appropriate, Jamee thought bitterly.

"I told you I don't like deception, McCall."

"There was no other choice, Jamee. Don't worry, this engagement is in name only. I won't make the mistake of assuming it means anything more," he said gravely.

For a moment, the stairs blurred in front of Jamee. Then her chin rose. "That's right, name only, McCall. Just remember that or I'll show you the left hook Adam taught me when I was fifteen."

Ian's hand tightened on her waist. "Maybe you just did. I didn't know a woman could kiss a man like that."

"Eat your heart out, McCall." Pride kept her walking. Pride kept her brittle smile in place. "There are probably a lot of things you don't know about me."

Footfalls sounded behind them. "I'm sorry about Tania," Kara said, frowning up at Jamee. "We had to take her at the last minute when one of the other girls came down with the flu."

"No problem," Jamee said with a confidence she didn't feel.

"Ian, what you said…" Kara hesitated, looking from one to the other.

"About the wedding?" Jamee gave a calm laugh. "Totally

convincing, weren't we? Not bad considering there wasn't even time for a run-through."

Kara studied her uncertainly. "For a moment I thought—"

"That we were serious?" Jamee gave a trill of laughter. "Sorry, it's all business—right, Ian? It wouldn't do to forget that. Not with…*them* somewhere about."

"Jamee, Duncan told me what happened," Kara said quietly. "If there is anything we can do, you have only to ask."

Jamee nodded, seeing the genuine concern in Kara's eyes. "Thank you, Kara, but I'll be fine." She glanced up at Ian. "After all, I've got a professional to guarantee it, don't I?"

"HE'S CHANGED." Kara looked at the top of the stairs where Ian and Jamee had just disappeared.

Her husband frowned. "He looks worn-out. Camping in that cottage with kidnappers on your back will do that to a person." Duncan steered Kara the rest of the way up the staircase and along the corridor toward their private rooms, wincing as they passed a life-size reindeer wearing a long red stocking hat. "Hidoshi's humor is hard to fathom sometimes."

"Nonsense," Kara said briskly. "Rudolph will look perfect in the front hall. Hidoshi and Rob have done a wonderful job with the decorations."

The halls were draped with popcorn chains and wreaths of pine. A pair of Victorian angels in white damask glittered on a Regency highboy, next to a pair of silver candelabra.

"I'm glad Angus finished the track for the steam train outside on the lawn." Her husband gave a long-suffering sigh, for which Kara immediately punched him. "Angus and Hidoshi did a lovely job and you know it. Hidoshi's assistant has been a godsend, too. We never could have managed all this without Rob."

"My only complaint is that I never get you alone anymore," Duncan said gruffly.

"Don't try to change the subject. I don't mean that Ian looked tired. It's his eyes," Kara said slowly. "They always used to be so hard, so controlled. Now they're softer, more vulnerable. Do you think it's because of Jamee?"

Duncan shook his head. "You always see the best in people, Kara. That's why I love you." He frowned. "But Ian's a hard one to read and always has been. Growing up in that great wreck on the cliffs at Glenlyle would do that to any man. Even without…"

"Without what?"

Duncan rubbed his neck. "Nothing."

Kara's eyebrow rose. "Duncan MacKinnon, do you actually believe you can keep a secret from *me?*"

Duncan backed up and found the door to their suite just in time. "No you don't, my love. No more using that Sight of yours."

His wife gave him a devilish smile and started after him. Three steps later Duncan toppled onto a pile of tartan blankets with his laughing wife right behind him. As her hands circled his waist, he smiled. "You win. I'll talk."

"I always win," Kara said smugly. "Now, tell me the rest."

"Later." Duncan's lips slid over hers. "First, I know a way that we'll both win."

JAMEE SHOVED ASIDE the turquoise velvet curtains and stared down at the endless vista of water stretching below her window. Then she tossed down her jacket, kicked off her shoes and turned to Ian. "One bed? Where will *you* be sleeping?"

Ian slid her bag onto a chair and closed the door. "On the sofa, of course."

"Of course," Jamee repeated.

"Do you want me to go now so you can get some rest?"

She desperately wanted him to go.

She desperately needed him to stay.

"Whatever you want. You must have business to discuss with Duncan, after all."

"Business can wait," Ian said. "You look pale, Jamee."

"Hey, it isn't every day that a girl gets caught in a fire, sleeps in a Neolithic barrow and then gets handed a marriage proposal." Amazingly, her voice was light. Jamee discovered that she could handle this role. Ian didn't have to see the pain his words had caused her. "A little pallor fits the part."

"Does it?"

Jamee looked away from his too-knowing eyes. "Sure. So what's the game plan, Coach?"

"I stay glued to you at the hip."

"Sounds uncomfortable," Jamee murmured, moving to the adjoining bathroom. She turned on both faucets and tossed in a healthy amount of lilac bath salts from a bottle on the windowsill. "By the way, did you see where that gray cat went? He was gone when I woke up."

Ian shook his head. "That animal knows exactly what he's doing. Probably headed home to a nice warm fire. And stop trying to change the subject."

"Who, me?"

"Yes, you. I saw the look in your eyes downstairs, Jamee. I'm sorry I took you by surprise, but I didn't want a lot of questions from people I can't trust."

"You were just doing your job. I understand perfectly." Jamee stirred the fragrant bubbles rising beneath the faucet.

"What happened at the cottage—your feelings toward me—" Ian braced one shoulder against the door. "You're coming to grips with it, aren't you?"

*Not a snowball's chance in hell,* she thought. But she summoned a perfect smile. "Of course I am. You were right, Ian. My attraction to you was just a passing phase. I understand that now."

"That was fast," he muttered. "You play havoc with a man's ego."

"I'm sure you'll survive. Now, if you don't mind, I'd like to clean off what feels like an inch of soot."

"Not quite an inch." Ian brushed her cheek gently. "Somehow it only makes you more beautiful."

Jamee stiffened at his touch. She couldn't fall apart now. "No need for any performance here, McCall. We're all alone, remember?"

"Maybe being alone is the hard part," Ian said. Then he turned. "I'll be right outside. Call me if you need me."

"I think I can scrub my own back," Jamee said tightly.

"Too bad."

ALL BUSINESS, Jamee thought as the door closed behind Ian.

All a perfect performance.

She stepped out of her clothes and sank down into the hot, frothy water, wondering how she was going to keep up her painful charade. Ian was too sharp to miss the hurt in her eyes.

*So keep it buried,* she thought. *Keep the smile in place.*

And then what? She was still a target and that left Ian as point man for any attack. How could she bear to see him hurt?

She stirred a mound of bubbles with one toe. She had seen the flash of heat in his eyes. She had felt his body tense when she'd kissed him. That meant he was telling the truth. He *did* feel some physical attraction for her.

An idea crept into her mind. A wild idea.

Ian was a man of honor. A man of control.

Maybe there was another way to handle this whole business.

She eased back down into the bubbles. "Ian?" she called.

The door jerked open. "Are you okay?"

"Fine. It's just—" Jamee drew a quick breath. "I decided I could use some help with my back after all."

His eyes narrowed. He took in every inch of her, from neck to toe—including the parts hidden under water. "Really."

Jamee nodded, all innocence. "Just between my shoulders. I thought you could help."

Ian didn't move. "Let's get this straight, Jamee. You're my job now, like it or not. I was paid to keep you safe and that's what I'm going to do. I'm sorry I had to lie. I'm sorry I caught you off guard. But I'll lie again if I have to because all that counts now is your safety."

He meant it, Jamee realized. Passion and lust wouldn't sway him. This could be harder than she'd thought.

"I understand, even though I don't like it. I'm in danger and you're going to keep me safe. What's not to understand?" She gave a delicate shrug and pointed to her back, which was hidden in bubbles. "Now that that's settled, how about some help? Right over here."

Ian's jaw flexed. Jamee saw a mask close over his face. "I think you'd better handle it yourself."

"I'm afraid there's one tiny little problem with that," she said, easing her calf from the water and angling it over the edge of the tub.

White foam clung lovingly to the sleek curve of her leg. All the while, Ian's eyes remained locked on her face. "And what's that?"

Jamee reached for the towel draped over a nearby chair. With every movement she dared him to watch. "If I rely on you, I rely on you for everything. Fair is fair, isn't it?" Slowly, she stood up, every inch of her body outlined in bubbles.

Ian swallowed. He averted his gaze as water sloshed gently and bubbles streaked her bare, wet skin.

His mouth tightened. "Don't do this, Jamee. Don't make it harder."

"Oh, there's nothing hard about it. We're glued at the hip, remember? Just business."

"What do you want from me, Jamee?"

The question brought her up short. Want? She wanted not to want him. She wanted not to feel a blinding wave of relief wash over her whenever he was nearby.

She wanted not to care.

Jamee glared at the exquisite damask walls and realized that her hands were shaking. She admitted the truth to herself then. She wanted the laughter and the camaraderie they had shared at the cottage.

She wanted Ian's rakish smile.

His gruff laugh.

His touch that made her pulse quicken with instant yearning. Jamee wanted those things very badly.

But it was business now, and at any second, Ian could be hurt because he was protecting her.

"I want you to quit. I want you replaced. Today."

"Forget it," he said flatly. "I don't back out of a promise, Jamee. Not ever."

BROAD SHOULDERS. Powerful back. Lean hips outlined beneath a towel draped low and sinfully tight.

It was ten minutes later and Ian stood before the mirror, fresh from the shower.

Jamee eased open the door, propped a silk-covered arm against the wall and drank in the sight of him. Water gleamed on his arms, outlining full muscles. He swung around, frowning. "What do you want?"

"To get something straight," she purred. "I'll go along with your masquerade, Ian. I'll follow your leads and I'll take your cues because it's for my safety." She tilted her head and glared at him. "Understood?"

"Understood." Ian's eyes narrowed, full of wariness.

"But only until someone can be sent from London to replace you." Jamee smiled with icy calm.

"I'm not going to request it, Jamee."

"No? I think you will. Because there's one more thing." She stepped closer, caught Ian's face between her hands and pulled him down to her. Her lips opened, warm and searching, while her tongue tantalized his. Jamee put a lifetime of hunger into the kiss, an eternity of dreams. She had to make him back down somehow. He was a professional and a man of honor. He wouldn't allow his personal feelings to compromise his client's safety.

He stiffened, then his damp palms slid over her back. His desire was instant and unmistakable through the towel.

But he didn't hold her, not even then. "It won't work."

Jamee tried to ignore her own racing pulse. "Yes, it will. Your honor won't allow you to stay."

"I might surprise you."

"I don't think so," Jamee murmured. "And don't bother to pretend it's *only* business between us, McCall, because that wet towel tells us both that's a lie." As she pulled the door shut behind her, Jamee heard what sounded like three feet of wet cotton slapping against the tub. Then a brush cracked against the wall.

She waited for the count of five. Unsettling him was her only tactic in this war she had begun. "By the way," she called sweetly, "lunch will be served in twenty minutes. The towel is nice, but you might want to change. I suggest something a little less…revealing."

## CHAPTER THIRTEEN

IAN PACED back and forth across Duncan's study. He dug his fingers through his hair, scowling.

Some operative he made. He couldn't see Jamee's laughing face without wanting her hands on him. He couldn't watch her walk across a room without envisioning her body naked and restless while he made her blood sing.

Ian finally accepted the truth. He'd been in turmoil from the first moment he had set eyes on Jamee Night. Even now, while he fought to remain controlled and detached, he couldn't get the thought of her soft lips and trembling hands out of his mind. She would sheathe him perfectly, all silk and heat beneath his hands.

All woman.

He slammed his fist down against the desk and cursed. *Jamee was not a woman, she was a client.* It was bloody well time for him to follow his *own* rules, which meant head straight and eyes forward.

He loosened his tie and cursed. Just business, that's the way it would be from now on. In his eyes, Jamee Night was no longer a woman.

She was *work.*

He looked up and saw Duncan standing in the doorway.

"At ease, McCall. You can relax now."

"I *am* relaxed," Ian snapped.

"Sure you are," Dunraven said knowingly. "Almost as relaxed as you were two years ago when we were about to go in after the DEA agent's child who was being held by the cartel in lieu of two plutonium devices and a SCUD missile."

Ian drew a harsh breath. "I look that bad, do I?"

"Worse." Duncan sank into the chair before the fire. "What's bothering you this time?"

"Nothing much. I have a pair of kidnappers I can't trace, an informant on the inside who's too damned good and a client who's driving me steadily insane. Add it all up, and I'm having one hell of a week. Why should anything be *bothering* me?"

"Sorry I asked," Duncan muttered. "Still, we're getting close. The constable has put out an alert in the village and that pair from the cottage will turn up soon. They won't get far on foot with their tires nearly flat."

Ian stared out at the dark outline of the hills above the burned-out cottage. "I'm not so sure they'll try."

Duncan frowned. "Do you mean they'll go to ground somewhere in the area?"

"Maybe. Or they could have other transport waiting nearby. They've been bloody well equipped this far, and somehow I think their tricks aren't over." Ian turned from the window. "Any word on that telephone number I found in their car?"

"It's a Glasgow exchange. Your people at Security International tell me it appears to be a popular pub just off Buchanan Street."

"Grand. That narrows the search. Only about ten thousand people could have been in and out during the last month."

Duncan made a flat, hard sound. "Something has to break soon, Ian. Until then, what can we do to help?"

Ian rubbed the knot at the back of his neck. "Just keep your eyes open. I take it your usual security is in place?"

MacKinnon nodded. "Upgraded every three months. Even

that ghostly ancestor of yours isn't going to slip past the gate without setting off an alarm or two."

"I hope you're right," Ian said tightly. "Just see that no one new comes to stay. I've made an initial check on everyone who's here, including the models and the photo crew from the U.S. Everyone seems to pass so far, but I'm still waiting for photo identification on each one."

"You can't really think that—"

"I don't take chances, Duncan. I never have." Ian shrugged. "Something feels…wrong. I just wish I could be certain Jamee was safe here."

Ian ran a hand across his eyes. For a second, light blurred, then exploded in a flash. The colors in the room glowed and then faded slowly.

"What's bothering you?" Duncan growled. "There's something else."

Ian steepled his fingers against his forehead. "I suppose you have a right to know." He swallowed, feeling a hollow pain at his chest. "It appears that…I'm going blind."

Duncan's hands closed tightly on the arm of his chair. "Good God, like your father. You're certain?"

Ian laughed dryly. "It's not the sort of thing a person makes mistakes about. I've been having symptoms for the last year. Blurred vision, headaches, that sort of thing. I told myself it was just the old Glenlyle legends that made me imagine things. But I had a battery of tests last week, and the results were quite conclusive, believe me."

"Damn the tests," Duncan hissed. "Is there *nothing* that can be done?"

Hadn't Ian asked himself the same question a thousand times? "Apparently not, according to three specialists I've seen. It's some sort of long-term degeneration of the optic nerve. Unfortunately, the disease appears to be a genetic feature of the

Glenlyles. You know that my father had it, as did his father. I didn't want to take this job, but Adam Night is a hard person to refuse." Ian's eyes darkened. "So is his sister."

Duncan took a slow breath. "Do you know how long before…"

"Before my vision starts going?" Ian shrugged. "Maybe a year. Maybe ten. The art of prognostication is best left to psychics and card-carrying Theosophists, I'm told." He winced at the bitterness in his voice. "Sorry, Duncan. I'm being a bloody fool and I'm sorry. I only pray I can see this through. I don't want Jamee to be hurt."

"She doesn't know about your eyes?"

"Of course not. And I mean for it to stay that way," Ian said flatly. "She already wants me replaced."

"Why?"

"Because she's afraid I'll be hurt. The woman is trailed by professionals, burned out of a cottage, and she worries about *me*."

"I see," Duncan said slowly. "And what do you plan to do now?"

"The backup team is expected in two hours. I want them fully briefed about the cottage and given what little description I could get of the pair with the four-wheel-drive vehicle." Ian paced the room, his eyes narrowed. "I want to be notified as soon as those verified photos of the people here at the castle start coming in. The more problems we can rule out, the better."

"What you said to Jamee about marriage was just for the sake of the others, I take it."

Ian stopped pacing and shoved one hand into the pocket of his jacket. "Of course it was." He pulled out his Browning and studied it. "She's a client, Duncan. Even if I did have feelings for her, I'd be honor-bound to ignore them."

"If?" Duncan prodded, one brow raised.

"What are you getting at?"

"Just tell me this," Duncan said calmly. "What if Jamee *weren't* a client? What if she was just another beautiful tourist eager to soak up a little Scottish culture?"

"I don't play 'what if,' Duncan."

"Maybe it's time you did," his old friend said slowly. "Otherwise you both could lose something very rare and special." Duncan strode to his desk before Ian could answer. "Now, I think we'd better put through a call to Jamee's brother and fill him in on what's happened."

JAMEE LOOKED over the broad staircase to a towering Christmas tree decorated with shimmering silver bells. Holly covered the oak door and tiny white lights blinked along the Great Hall's massive oak rafters. An air of expectation filled the breathless quiet.

Jamee fingered the box holding the design Duncan and Kara had commissioned for Dunraven's stately halls. She had been overjoyed to receive the request, but now that she was finally here, she wasn't certain her weaving could live up to the magic of this ancient home. It was clear to her now why her parents had loved Dunraven Castle.

She found Kara and another woman stringing holly in the foyer. Angus McTavish was beside them, very dashing in a bright tartan kilt and a black turtleneck.

"I don't think I've ever seen so many men in kilts before," Jamee said.

"Get used to it," Kara answered. "After a while, their scrawny legs actually begin to look rather attractive."

Jamee tried not to laugh as Angus scowled. She took a deep breath and turned to Kara. "This is for you and Duncan. I hope you like it." She held out her box.

"So soon? We only spoke to you three months ago. Nicholas Draycott told us that it took ages for you to finish a design."

"This time an idea came almost immediately. Of course, if you don't like this piece, I can try something else. I'm already working on another weaving, something far more colorful. I have it upstairs if you'd like to—"

Kara's gasp cut through Jamee's anxious explanations. "Jamee, it's—it's—"

Jamee's heart sank. "You don't like it."

"Not like it? It's incredible," Kara said in a rush, cradling the heavy midnight-blue weaving Jamee had finished only a week earlier. "I see a dozen shades and textures of blue here, a blend of alpaca, mohair, even raw silk. But what are these?"

Jamee fingered the tiny knots of gold that glimmered through layers of blue fiber. "Silk stars. This is the moon peeking through the clouds. For every star, you have one wish, to be made at midnight with an open heart. That's the custom in the village I visited in Bali. Since I've always thought of Dunraven towering beneath a midnight sky while magic walked abroad, the night sky and stars seemed appropriate."

"Where magic walks—you're right in that. I've felt the enchantment in this castle since the first moment I saw it," Kara whispered. "Duncan will be beyond words. I don't know how you managed to capture such magic."

Jamee shifted restlessly. "If you'd like me to change the layout, I can. Even the colors."

"There's no way that Duncan or I will let you have this back, my dear. This goes in the place of honor at the foot of the stairs. There's a single light that will pick up the gold flecks of the stars. And we'll be very careful how we use our wishes, I promise."

"What wishes?" Duncan appeared at the foot of the stairs, then halted at the sight of Jamee's weaving. He studied the layered tones of blue dotted with tiny spots of gold and inhaled slowly. "I don't know what to say, Jamee. It's enchanted. Is that actually how you see Dunraven?"

Jamee nodded. "Ever since my parents described it to me. I can see why they loved staying here. But I was afraid you'd want something more...realistic."

Duncan touched the textile reverently. "I don't know when a piece of art has moved me more." He looked at Kara. "Shall we hang it now?"

"Yes, let's."

Dozens of tiny fiber stars gleamed beneath the single hall sconce as Duncan hung the weaving at the foot of the stairs. Fabric met stone in a primal complement of textures as old as woman against man, the result as natural as if the blue fabric had grown against the wall rather than been shaped by Jamee's hands.

"I can't thank you enough," Duncan said. "Your gift of vision changes this whole space."

"My other piece is very different," Jamee said, pleased with how the muted blues blended with the weathered granite wall. "The colors are extraordinary, all yellows and reds and peach. But I need to be more familiar with the castle before I can decide the bottom half of the design."

"Take your time. Every room is open to you, and I'll be delighted to show you through anytime. On the other hand," Duncan added with a gleam in his eyes, "Ian knows his way around Dunraven almost as well as I do."

"I wouldn't want to bother Ian," Jamee said stiffly. As she spoke a current of air brushed her neck.

"But I insist that you bother me." Ian moved behind Jamee. "And I'd like nothing better than to give you the grand tour. But first, your brother wants to talk to you. He's on the phone."

He took Jamee's arm, guiding her to Duncan's study. As they

neared the door, Ian added, "I told him about what happened at the cottage. I suspect he wants you to go home."

Jamee stared at Ian, unable to read the expression in his eyes. "What about you? Do *you* want me to go?"

"It might be safer, Jamee. So far we haven't come up with much."

"That's not what I asked, Ian. I asked what you *wanted.*"

"What I want doesn't matter," Ian answered. "If you'd feel safer back in the States, you should go."

She was torn by the thought. If she left, Ian would no longer be a target and she could begin the hard work of reclaiming her independence. But if she left now, there would be no resolution, and Jamee was no quitter.

He was making it too easy, she thought. Out that door and vanish, then their paths would never cross again. Someone else would escort her home; someone else would guard her until the kidnappers were finally cornered.

So easy.

"No," Jamee said tensely. "I'm not running away now." She caught the phone from the desk. "Adam?"

"Jamee, are you okay over there?" Adam Night's voice was edged with worry. "Duncan told me about what happened at the cottage. I'm not certain this man McCall can be counted on to keep you safe."

"Ian saved my life. Without him I would either be a captive now or I'd be dead in that fire."

"He told you exactly what's happening?"

"He told me."

Adam muttered harshly. "Come home, Jamee. I'll have someone travel with you, and I'll meet you myself in London. There are too many risks this way."

"There are always risks, Adam. Even in crossing the street. Terence could tell you that." For a moment Jamee's eyes blurred as she thought of her brother's carefree grin and the off-key tunes he always whistled. "No, I'm staying here. Ian has a few ideas."

Adam cleared this throat. "Jamee, there's one more thing. Something you don't know about Ian."

She turned, studying the man standing in the doorway. "What about him?"

She saw Ian's eyes narrow at her words. He strode across the room and pulled the receiver from her hand.

"I'll talk to him now." He lifted the phone. "Night, this is Ian. Your sister seems to have made her choice. It's up to me to back it up."

"Dammit, McCall, they nearly got her at the cottage. How many chances are they going to have?"

"No more. She won't be out of my sight again. Now it's your job to get some answers. Who made those inquiries? Where are they now?"

"Still no luck. We're trying everything, but—"

"Then try harder," Ian snapped. "I'll expect your call tonight, and I'll expect some answers." He shoved the phone down.

"What did he mean?" Jamee said slowly. "What aren't you telling me, Ian?"

"Nothing that matters." He crossed his arms. "Let's get some rules straight. From now on I know where you are every second. And you don't leave the house unless Duncan or I go with you. Understood?"

"You can't—"

Ian ignored her interruption. "If you make any change in schedule, I'll expect you to check in immediately. Otherwise, I'll come after you and I'll be assuming the worst." His hand eased into his pocket and Jamee saw the glint of metal.

*A gun.*

Fear feathered across her neck. This was real. Handling

guns and worrying about being jumped from behind had put the hard lines in Ian's face and the shadows in his eyes.

Jamee didn't want to hear any more. "I'll do it. Whatever you say is necessary, Ian. But it makes me mad as hell."

Even worse, it made her afraid.

"Don't be mad. Leave the anger to me." A smile twisted his lips. "I'm a lot better at it than you'll ever be. Where are you going now?"

"I think I'll do some work in my room. Angus brought my car up and carried in my bags. I've got a small loom set up."

"Get some rest. The weaving will wait."

"Is that an order?"

"No, it's a suggestion." Ian's hand rose toward her, then abruptly fell. "You look tired."

"So do you."

"I'll sleep when I know you're safe."


THERE WAS A TRICK to coming and going in physical form. Unfortunately, Terence Night still hadn't mastered it.

He took shape in the middle of the front hall, as clumsy here as he was everywhere else.

White lights winked on the great tree as he sank to the floor and braced his chin on his palms. "I've made a mess of everything. I thought they would be perfect for each other, but all they do is fight."

Something rustled at his feet. Terence looked up to see a gray cat stalking across the marble floor. "What do you think, Gideon? I'm open to any and all suggestions about now. I don't want to ruin things."

The cat coiled about his feet.

"Do you really think that would work?"

The cat gave a soft meow.

Terence looked doubtful. "I don't know, my sister is very independent."

The gray figure meowed again.

"Yes, I'm aware that other people would call her willful. It's just that she's out of her element. She needs to feel in control. And I can feel the danger all around us. If only I could do *more*."

The cat brushed against his foot.

"You can do that? Even finding the portrait?"

The cat's eyes gleamed, very large and very keen.

Terence held up a hand. "No, I don't think I want to know how." He frowned at the winking lights on the tree. "So you're leaving it up to me. The choice has to be mine." Light filled the room as Terence paced back and forth, a shimmer of gold and a dozen other pastels. He stopped before the Christmas tree and touched the wings of a satin angel. "It's for her own good. Jamee needs someone with a heart, someone who will take care of her. She's been alone far too long. Oh, she's got Adam, William and Bennett, but it's not the same. And I can see what Ian McCall feels for her. The man is a positive volcano of color when he's around her. Too bad she can't see it." Terence sighed. "It all used to be so simple: wake up in the morning, worry about what you're going to do that day, worry about what you would eat and worry about where you would go after you died." He laughed. "No one told me that dying would be like this. Where are the little cherubs with harps? Where are the clouds of white cotton and the gates of solid pearl?"

At his feet Gideon blinked.

"I know. I've no reason for self-pity. And I'll stumble through this somehow. I just wish I could talk to Jamee, if only for a second or two."

The cat went still, his head tilted.

"I know it's not allowed. She doesn't believe in ghosts or

angels anyway. And yes, your help would be most appreciated. I am grateful to Lord Draycott for letting you come along to help me." His form shimmered, picking up a silver glow as his spirits rose. "When do we get started?"

The cat pranced forward, his head proudly erect.

"You're certain the portrait is still there?"

Gideon's gray tail flicked back and forth.

"Maybe that will make them remember." Terence smiled and whistled the first off-key notes of his favorite Neil Diamond song. It was an odd choice for an angel, but Gideon didn't seem to mind.

Then both figures vanished into the thick stone walls of the castle.

## CHAPTER FOURTEEN

"A Christmas tableau?"

Ian scowled at his reflection in the bathroom's full-length gilt mirror two hours later. Next door he heard the hiss of Jamee's loom, just as he had for the last fifteen minutes.

He couldn't think of a more difficult time for Kara's dinner to take place. He needed to focus on the threat to Jamee, not prance about in a Victorian costume.

He bit off an oath as he fumbled with the ornate silk closing at the front of his smoking jacket, assigned to him personally by Kara. Ian only wished he'd had the heart to turn her down.

The loom went still.

When the door opened, Ian swung around, scowling. "Jamee, I don't suppose you could help me with—"

"Ian, I can't get this blasted thing closed."

Jamee spoke at the same moment, a similar irritation on her face as she tugged at a row of tiny satin buttons that ran down the back of her lavender Victorian tea gown of lace and satin, also courtesy of Kara.

The dress might have been made solely for her, Ian thought. The lace spilled over her shoulders and hugged her slender wrists. She would be a natural for the photo.

And at least Jamee's frown reassured him that he wasn't alone in his frustration.

"I don't know how people wore these clothes," she muttered, plucking vainly at her back.

"Turn around," Ian ordered. "They managed only because they had an army of servants who did nothing but get them in and out of the bloody things."

Jamee stood rigidly while he worked the tiny buttons into their closings. Ian didn't tell her that he had seen his mother wear elaborate lace gowns similar to this one, her hair caught high and not a single strand out of place, even on a sweltering July afternoon. She had loved dressing up for ornate tea parties in Glenlyle's gardens.

He had also seen his fragile mother turn pale and hopeless as she waited for the Glenlyle curse to take its toll.

"You're sure that people actually *wore* these things? I thought maybe it was a huge hoax, something to put fear into little tomboys in torn pants." Jamee lifted one arm, waving a voluminous leg-of-mutton chop sleeve of silk and lace. "Ridiculous."

Ian swatted her hand. "Cooperate here."

She shot him an irritated look over her shoulder. "I'm not very good at *that,* either."

Ian heard her mutter, but she made no more protests as he worked at forcing two dozen exasperating silken buttons through a row of minuscule holes. All the while, he tried to ignore how her hair fell warm and thick over his wrists. Her perfume, a spicy blend of citrus and roses, intrigued him.

He cleared his throat. "Another perfume that you blend yourself?"

"Adam came up with this one. I helped him a little, but it was mostly his creation." Jamee gave a low chuckle. "I was all of eight and he was barely fifteen. We were going to run away from home and start our own cosmetics company."

Ian felt a smile tug at his lips. "What was the great injustice?"

"I wanted a set of rockets that I could launch from the backyard with a remote detonator."

"May God preserve us," Ian said faintly.

"Nonsense. I was superb at calculating trajectories. Of course, there was that minor accident with our neighbor's clothesline, but the lawsuit never came to anything."

Ian felt his smile growing larger. "What was your brother's complaint?"

"Oh, Adam wanted a red motorcycle. Something grand and expensive with chrome and real leather. My father absolutely forbade it in spite of weeks of arguing. So we packed ham sandwiches and a change of clothing in a hobo bag and ran away from home."

"How far did you get?"

Jamee's brow wrinkled. "I believe we got as far as the public library. The librarian happened to be an old friend of my mother's. She was a very clever woman. As I recall, she never once commented on our being absent from school at eleven o'clock in the morning. She didn't even ask about the bags we were carrying over our shoulders. She just ushered us into her private office as if it were the most normal thing in the world and gave us milk and cookies, then entertained us with the new editions of *Boys' Life* which had come in."

"Sounds like heaven," Ian said.

"When my father came to get us, he managed to seem surprised to find us there." Jamee chuckled. "What a pair of idiots we were."

As the last button closed, Ian caught her shoulders and turned her slowly. "On the contrary, you both sound perfectly wonderful. I think you must have been almost as enchanting as you are today." He couldn't keep his hands from running slowly down her arms, savoring the fragile lace beneath his fingers.

"Is that so? And what were *you* doing up at that drafty castle when you were eight years old?"

"Boring things." His voice hardened. "Lonely things."

"Like what?"

Like worrying about his bitter father and his silent mother, Ian thought. "It doesn't matter."

"It does to me," Jamee said.

"Why?" Ian didn't want to ask but he couldn't help himself.

She stood very still, her eyes huge and luminous. "I suppose the fact that you have a beautiful mouth wouldn't be reason enough?"

Ian smiled crookedly. "I *don't* have a beautiful mouth. Lairds of Glenlyle—"

Jamee rose onto her toes and kissed him before he could say more. Her hands circled his neck and she made a small, lost sound as their lips met hungrily. Her tongue eased against his, heat to heat, until Ian's heart felt in serious danger of slamming out of his chest. When he pulled away, he was glad to see that Jamee was almost as breathless as he was.

"Don't expect me to apologize," Jamee said defiantly. "I liked that and so did you."

Ian didn't try to deny it. The woman never did what he expected. "Now what?"

"We go down for this dinner Hidoshi is going to shoot."

Just like that, Ian thought. Over and done with. If only his unruly body could agree.

Turning away, Jamee shoved at the door, frowning. "It's locked."

"What do you mean it's locked?"

"Just what I said. The blasted door is *locked.*"

"That's not possible. The lock is on this side." Ian gripped the doorknob and twisted hard.

Nothing moved. He put his shoulder to the door frame and heaved again, without the slightest effect.

Ian crouched on the floor in front of the door.

"What are you doing?"

"I'm trying to see if the key dropped on the other side." He pressed his face to the floor and peered under the narrow crack at the bottom of the door.

"Well?"

"I can't see a damn thing."

"Then why don't you yell?"

Ian's brow rose. "Why don't *you* yell?"

Jamee smiled sweetly at him. "Because delicate ladies in enchanting Victorian gowns don't bellow for help."

"And Victorian gentlemen in expensive smoking jackets do?"

"I expect they did a great deal of bellowing," Jamee said. "Most of the time they were convinced that the servants were cheating them. The rest of the time they were probably afraid that their *wives* were cheating on them. Yes, I guarantee that Victorian gentlemen had a great deal of practice at bellowing."

Ian stood up and glared at the door.

"Your jacket is all dusty," Jamee said helpfully. "And two of your frogs have come undone."

"I don't give a damn about my frogs," he snapped.

Jamee clicked her tongue and reached up to straighten the thick braided silk at his chest. There was a wicked gleam in her eyes as Ian looked down at her. A moment later, he realized she was not closing, but opening.

"Blast it, Jamee, what are you doing?" He felt her fingers slide under the thick velvet and open over his chest.

"So Victorian gentlemen wore nothing beneath their jackets,

did they? It makes the velvet sinfully warm from your body." Her fingers parted the heavy velvet and she planted kisses down his chest. "I can feel every muscle."

"Is this retaliation for this afternoon?" Ian said hoarsely. "Because I gave you orders?"

"I think it might be."

It was effective retaliation. Ian was certain he was going to explode at any second. Then he decided his own retaliation was in order.

He caught Jamee's wrists and kissed the pulse that hammered beneath her delicate skin. His mouth found hers hungrily. "You taste like cinnamon," he muttered.

"You taste like tea and apples. I could get to like the taste." Her tongue teased the sensitive corner of his mouth.

Damn Kara's dinner party, Ian thought blindly. He wanted Jamee now while desire hazed her eyes. He wanted her laughing, pliant and happy, beneath his fingers.

When Ian looked down, Jamee was staring at him, a smile on her lips. "We'll be late for the dinner photos," she said raggedly. "Not that I didn't like every second."

Ian's fingers tightened. He wanted to nip her bottom lip, to plunge his hands into her hair and bury himself in her sweetness. A part of him long closed away sprang growling to life. Looking at Jamee, he wanted things he couldn't need, things she couldn't give. But logic meant nothing to the hungry creature staring out of Ian's eyes now. "You look like an angel in that dress."

"I'm not an angel. I'm a woman, Ian. I won't shatter or run away." She took a slow, uncertain breath. "And I won't quit."

"You won't quit what?"

Her smile was crooked. "That's the question, isn't it?"

God give him strength, Ian thought.

"I didn't want to want you," she said softly. "I didn't want to look at you and need you until I hurt with it. You tell me the rules, Ian. Right now my body just doesn't seem to listen."

Pain came in many different forms, Ian discovered at that moment, and his own body wasn't exactly answering to any rules. He took a long breath and wished she wasn't so vibrant, so honest.

So beautiful.

"The first rule is, we open that door," he said.

The door rattled once. Abruptly the bolt turned and the lock slid free.

"Did you see that?" Jamee asked breathlessly.

Ian wished he hadn't, because it made no sense. He shoved open the door, his face hard. If this was one of the models' idea of a joke…

But there was no one in the corridor.

"Maybe it was the wind?" Jamee whispered. "After all, in a castle this size there must be gaps in the stone. Holes for a draft…" Her voice trailed away.

"No holes could let in a wind strong enough to throw an iron bolt," Ian said grimly. He pointed to the solid piece of lead pulled back from the lock.

"Then what do you think it was?"

Ian hadn't the slightest idea. Scowling, he fumbled with the silk closings on his jacket, then took Jamee's arm. Until he did know, he was going to assign one of the backup team to the corridor outside their bedroom.

Just in case.

But first, they had a Victorian dinner to attend.

As JAMEE AND IAN walked down to dinner, lights gleamed from the walls, outlining rows of portraits and old tapestries. The tapestries were in good shape, considering that they were over three hundred years old. In fact, everything about Dunraven Castle was in excellent condition, Jamee decided.

She was careful not to look at Ian, who was walking beside her, though she wanted to do nothing else. Instead she focused on Dunraven Castle, where every room was filled with memories and Highland history. The great house was bright with the love of generations of men and women who had made the castle their home.

Jamee tried to ignore a heaviness in her chest. She wanted that same kind of love, a bright net of joy that would fill the four walls of her home, whether that home was a boat moored by an obscure Pacific island or a shack in the hill country of Thailand. All that mattered was being with the man she loved.

Jamee wanted the intensity of sharing that came body to body in the night with a man who wanted the same from her. She wanted fingers twined and hearts slamming while desire became a storm in the blood. And after that, she wanted dogs and cats and the laughter of noisy children, along with the quiet pleasure of seeing family traditions passed down to another generation.

What she wanted, Jamee decided, was *Ian*.

But Ian was a stranger now, a man with a mission, all humor submerged as he focused ruthlessly on his job.

And she was the job. A job that might at any moment cost him his life.

Maybe Adam was right. Maybe she should go back to the States. At least that would put Ian out of danger.

She looked up and realized they were on the far side of the castle. Deep oak beams were sunk into walls of four-foot stone. "Where are we going?"

"To find a portrait Duncan mentioned. Since you're a weaver, I thought you might like to see Maire MacKinnon."

A gust of cold air feathered over Jamee's cheek. The name seemed to echo in her head. "Who is she?"

"One of Duncan's ancestors. She had a rare skill with the loom, it's said. She designed the original MacKinnon hunting plaid, according to family legend."

Jamee should have looked forward to seeing the face of such a woman. She should have been eager to make her way through the shadows cast by sconces high on the thick walls.

But something held her back, making her breath come fast.

Ian took a sharp curve and pushed open a door nearly hidden against a wall of wooden paneling. "I think it's in here."

Jamee didn't move, her hand on the cold wood.

"What is it?"

Jamee tried to shake her sense of dread. "I must be tired. Maybe we'd better go back."

Ian frowned and switched on a switch, bathing the narrow alcove beyond the door in golden light. "The portrait is right here. I'd forgotten all about it until Duncan mentioned it."

As if in a dream, Jamee moved in front of the tall painting. She saw a mane of red-gold hair and eyes of smoky green. She saw a woman of pride and grace smiling gravely while one hand rested on a length of brightly patterned wool.

The image blurred before Jamee's eyes and then seemed to move. In the portrait one slender hand rose, outstretched as if in a plea.

Or a warning.

Suddenly Jamee couldn't breathe. The stone walls closed in on her, dark and threatening. She heard the stamp of horses' hooves and felt the bite of windblown snow as a line of angry men set off to war.

She closed her eyes, gripped by a blinding sense of loss. In her head the portrait seemed to gleam, haunting in its beauty, a puzzle she should have been able to solve, but couldn't.

She panted, fighting the heavy shadows of the past that clung to this deserted corner of the castle.

Then Ian's hands were in her hair and she was caught against his chest. The words he said were low and almost familiar though Jamee realized they had to be Gaelic.

She made a soft, broken sound as she felt the heat of his hands, the hard, reassuring outline of his shoulders.

"Don't go," she whispered wildly. "You won't come back this time. I'll wait, but you won't return. I can hear it in the wind."

"I'm not going anywhere, Jamee. I'm sorry I brought you to see that bloody portrait."

Jamee turned her face against his chest, unable to forget the sight of Maire MacKinnon's haunted eyes. When Ian lifted her into his arms, Jamee made no protest. The shadows were too close, too painful. She couldn't understand their power.

Or she didn't want to understand.

Ian carried her back to their bedroom. "You're staying here and resting. I'll bring your dinner up on a tray," Ian said in a tone that allowed no argument as he laid her on the big bed.

Jamee felt the lace gown ease from her shoulders. A damask coverlet slid over her. "Don't go," she whispered, suddenly feeling unwelcome, an intruder within Dunraven's cold, beautiful halls.

"I'll be here," Ian said, his head bent close. "Don't worry. And I'll have Angus come up to watch outside our door."

But when darkness pooled round Jamee, fear pounded in her veins like the beat of angry drums and horses on a lonely winter hillside. As her head sank back, Jamee gripped Ian's hands and felt the sad eyes of Maire MacKinnon follow her down into restless dreams.

# CHAPTER FIFTEEN

"WHAT DO YOU MEAN they got away again?" Ian glared at Duncan over the cluttered desk of solid marble. "You told me the constable had traced the motorcycles to a cottage up the coast."

Duncan sighed and rubbed his neck. "He tried. Fergus Montgomerie knows these hills as well as any man."

"Then what went wrong?" Ian demanded.

"The tracks simply vanished. They stopped at a cove not six kilometers from here."

"So they had a boat moored." Ian muttered a curse. "They could be anywhere by now."

"I'm afraid so."

Ian looked across the glen toward the stone circle. "Bad. Very bad."

"You're safe here," Duncan said firmly. "No strangers will get in or out."

"There are other concerns," Ian said after a moment.

"Your vision?"

Ian's fingers tightened on the windowsill. A tiny silver angel with lacy white wings trembled at the movement of his hand. Ian stared at the porcelain features while the room filled with silence. "I knew this time would come, Duncan. My concern now is how long I have left."

Duncan sank into the worn leather chair at his desk. "What do the doctors say?"

"The progress is unpredictable. They call it slow atrophy of the optical nerve and they can't give any timetable, I'm afraid." He stood motionless, staring at the lacy wings of white.

Duncan's hands slammed down against the desk. "I don't see how you can be so bloody calm about this."

Ian smiled bitterly. "I'm not calm. I've just had thirty years to get used to the idea. Don't forget, I've watched two relatives succumb to the Glenlyle curse already."

Duncan made a flat, angry sound. "I don't believe in curses carried down over time, dammit. Neither should you."

Ian turned slowly. Light filtered over his strong features, pitching half his face into shadow. "Yet you believe in the story of the piper and the legends about Rose Cottage. I'd say you have superstitions enough of your own here at Dunraven, my friend."

Duncan sighed. "That's different."

"Is it?" Ian stared out at the leaden waves of the sea. "History is all around us, Duncan. Like it or not, we walk with shadows. Those shadows touch us every day, in mind and in body. It's not weakness to acknowledge that."

"But—" The phone on the desk rang shrilly, cutting off Duncan in midsentence. He swept up the phone. "Dunraven here."

He listened for several seconds and nodded. "I see. Yes, of course. He's right here." Duncan handed over the phone. "It's Adam Night. He wants to talk with you."

Adam spoke first. "How is my sister, Mr. McCall?"

"She's safe."

Adam breathed in relief. "Have the men been traced yet?"

"I'm afraid they were lost. Apparently, they were very well informed about Jamee's itinerary. The whole operation was carefully planned. They even had alternate transport waiting to get them off the island."

Silence stretched out as Ian's words sank in. "If you're implying that someone close to Jamee is involved, you're crazy. Only Bennett, William and I knew her itinerary."

"Is that so? And I suppose you also made her travel arrangements. You even purchased her tickets and arranged for her rental car. I suppose you saw that her passport was up-to-date and her immunizations in order, too," Ian continued.

"No, of course not. Nightingale Electronics has an in-house travel agency to handle all those arrangements." Adam cursed softly. "And any one of them could have slipped the information to an accomplice, is that it? That means, dozens of people could be implicated."

"Exactly," Ian said harshly. "I want you to make a list of everyone who had access to Jamee's schedule. Friends, family and business associates, I want them all. I don't care how casual or how innocent, each one is to be checked out. And you're going to have to be discreet. Until we have more information, we have to assume that any one of them might be involved."

"There's one other possibility. We've been checking it out from our end as soon as we heard." There was a rustle of papers and Adam cleared his throat. "One of the men involved in Jamee's kidnapping seven years ago had a brother. He was only a boy at the time, but the two were very close. He was recently in jail for passing forged checks, but he was released for good behavior. After that, he vanished. We only found his location because he was wanted for back alimony payments. According to his ex-wife, he was headed for Scotland."

"Then go get him," Ian said curtly.

"We tried. The people at your end haven't exactly been helpful. Apparently two pieces of paperwork were missing, and they refused to order a trace until every document was received."

"I'll put all the resources of Security International on it," Ian said. "Our government contacts are good, but our police connections are even better," he said with a grim smile. "We'll have the man within three days." He touched the knotted length of rope in his pocket. "I have a feeling we'll find out that he or one of his compatriots has a Navy background."

"What makes you say that?" Adam asked.

Ian pulled the knotted rope from his pocket, studying it silently. He tested the cut end with one finger. "Because I found a knotted length of rope in the front seat of their car and I doubt it was a coincidence. Have your people check to see if the kidnapper's brother served in the Navy."

"I'll get right on it. Any fingerprints on the rope?"

"Rope is a notoriously bad medium for oil impressions."

Three thousand miles away Adam Night cursed graphically. "Should I send you some backup, Glenlyle? Maybe even come myself? I've done some tracking in my day," he said tightly. "The moors can't be any rougher than the high desert."

"That won't be necessary. Your presence would only add to Jamee's anxiety."

Adam made a sound of disbelief. "She obviously trusts you. You must be amazingly persuasive, Glenlyle. The last man assigned to her security lasted about two hours, as I recall."

"Jamee's no fool. She knows this is the real thing, not some vague possibility. Besides, we have an understanding. I do whatever is necessary to keep her safe."

"And what does Jamee do?" Adam asked curiously.

"Jamee…gets irritated, acts stubborn and becomes thoroughly aggravating," Ian said. But there was a smile in his voice he didn't bother to hide.

"I see," Adam Night said slowly. There was a pause. "Keep me posted. My brothers and I are at your disposal. If you feel it's advisable, we can leave at a moment's notice."

"I appreciate that," Ian said, "but to be blunt, right now your participation here would only complicate things."

"You're certain?"

"I'm paid to be certain," Ian said. "Besides, I have a few surprises of my own planned."

"Such as?"

"I'd rather not go into detail," Ian said calmly. "The fewer people who know, the better."

"Dammit, Glenlyle, you're not suggesting that one of *us* is involved?"

"I'm not suggesting anything, Night. I'm simply doing my job the best way I know how. And if you need to get in touch with Jamee or me, you can arrange it through Duncan." His face was hard as he put down the phone.

"We won't be down for dinner," Ian said to Duncan. "Make our apologies, will you?"

"Of course. You both could use some rest."

"Jamee sleeps even more fitfully than I do," Ian muttered. "Duncan, what can you tell me about the portrait of Maire MacKinnon in the north wing?"

"Not much. It was commissioned by her father just before he announced her betrothal to one of the Forbes clan. But she vanished a fortnight before the wedding was to take place. She was never seen again. Her father believed..." Duncan looked uncomfortable.

"Believed what?"

"You know there was no love lost between MacKinnon and McCall in those days. Her father claimed her death was your clan's doing. I'm sure it was just the ravings of a grief-stricken man. The legends about the curse laid on your family could have begun from that tragedy."

Ian shook his head. "Something about the portrait bothered

Jamee. Hell, it did a lot more than bother her. She acted like she'd seen a ghost."

"The result of stress?" Duncan suggested. "This has to be bloody hard on her."

"Maybe." Ian strode to the door. "I've left Angus outside our room. Until this is over, I want one of us with her at all times. The backup team could handle the daily protection, but I don't want her to feel anxious around a stranger."

"Very thoughtful of you," Duncan said slowly. "Does this mean, you might actually be ready to admit your feelings for Jamee?"

Ian's hand closed hard over the oak door frame. "Right now any feelings I have are a liability. They could throw off my timing and cloud my judgment. Either thing would put Jamee further at risk." His hand fell to his side. "I can't, Duncan."

"Can't or won't?"

Ian made a bitter sound and found himself cursing that he hadn't met Jamee Night five years earlier. "Sometimes the two are the same."

THE HILLS ROLLED AWAY to the north, brown merging into a deeper blue beneath gray, racing clouds. As he stood at the high-arched window in the Blue Bedroom, Ian saw the remnants of an ancient barrow built centuries ago by the first MacKinnon inhabitants of Dunraven. Somewhere beyond that, in the curve of the highest hill, lay the old stone circle where he and Jamee had hidden from their pursuers. Everywhere the hand of time lay heavy. Here, as at Glenlyle, history walked among them with all its shadows and the hint of old voices.

For a moment, colors flashed before Ian's eyes. He watched the clouds blur for a split second while pain raced across his forehead.

*The curse.*

For ten generations the legend had dogged the McCalls. There was always the awareness in the eyes of the villagers at Glenlyle, although they worked hard to hide it whenever Ian was present. Every man and woman knew the story and the curse laid down so long ago.

Again the pain tore at his eyes, setting off streaks of color while the words of the curse echoed in his mind.

*On the first night of the first moon of the new year, the laird of Glenlyle shall see no more. The pain he has dealt shall return full force until his eyes are hollows of darkness.*

There was no shaking or evading the old curse. Ian had seen too many of his ancestors stricken in their prime by the illness that had no cure.

His turn would come soon.

Clouds billowed over the northern hills, and Ian felt a wisp of cold that always struck when he thought of the ancient curse. For generations, the blindness had come to every eldest son, penance for some ancient betrayal of a local woman.

Ian ran a hand over his eyes, wondering when the next wave of pain would strike. Twice in the last week his vision had blurred, and each episode was more severe than the last.

The reason was lost in the mists that veiled the glen. Some said that generations before, a laird of Glenlyle had lain with his lover inside a circle of stones, pledging his faith to her for eternity. But the world had intruded and the laird had cast his eyes higher in marriage. The lover was betrayed. One moonlit midnight, she had climbed to the cliffs above the sea where the water churned against the rocky beach. There, within sight of Glenlyle's dark walls, she had thrown herself from the highest ridge, laying her curse on the eldest Glenlyle son for eternity.

There were many such stories in the Highlands, where every tor and broch seemed to hold a tragic past. But the facts could not be denied. Three specialists had examined Ian's eyes in London and each had confirmed the diagnosis: idiopathic degeneration of the optic nerve. In layman's terms, a disease of unexplained origin and unknown cure, leading irrevocably to blindness.

In other words, the Glenlyle curse had claimed its next son.

Ian had nothing solid to give to Jamee, no future or stability. He had planned for the day his vision failed, refusing to dwindle into a useless relic. If he could not be a positive asset to the castle, contributing to its upkeep, then he meant to sell Glenlyle.

Lightning crackled far out over the sea, stabbing the heavy gray sky. Ian made his only Christmas wish then, praying that he would not lose his sight until Jamee's pursuers were behind bars.

Across the room Jamee moved restlessly. Ian watched her tuck one hand beneath her pillow and sigh. For now, her dreams were calm, without pain or dark memories. Tonight, she would not walk, for he would stay close to protect her. Vibrant, unpredictable, she would set a man on his ear and shake up every second of his life. Was Ian brave enough to ask her to consider sharing his future and the uncertainties it would bring?

He ran his fingers over his eyes and frowned. There would be time enough to worry about the future once he had made certain Jamee was safe.

After checking the door and nodding to the backup-protection officer on duty in the corridor, Ian went back to the window. Rain struck the pane as he wondered what Jamee had seen in the portrait that had left her so frightened. Was it the regret in Maire MacKinnon's eyes?

*FROST CLUNG to the hard soil. A pair of crows screamed as they darted over the dark hills. Smoke rose in puffs from the roof of the cottage at the top of the glen, where light shone golden from two windows.*

*Inside Maire MacKinnon sang beneath her breath, her hands plunged deep into a cauldron of pungent dye. The rich brown skin of walnuts and the dry husks of onions topped her long oak table, piled next to elderberries and madder. The red yarns were finished, bright as roses where they hung to dry before the fire. Nearby lay skeins of tan and gold that shimmered like a dawn in mist.*

*Only the green tasked her, and the green would be the most important in the cloth she was soon to weave. Green required indigo, rare and precious, the dye of kings. Maire had tried every other source, plant and berry, but none carried the deep tones of indigo. The rare blue powder came from far to the east, in lands of heat and jungle, and after months of searching, Maire had finally found a merchant returned from the Crusades who could sell her one precious handful of the rare ingredient.*

*It had cost her dearly, she thought, studying the dark dye held in a tiny box of ivory. But indigo would stain her wool as nothing else could, and when mixed with ochre would provide the perfect green for her plaid.*

*She hesitated a moment. The wind changed and smoke filtered back down the chimney. A storm was coming, she sensed. The wind had gusted all morning and now the air held the smell of snow.*

*She wondered if Coll would find his way free and gallop across the glen to her tonight. She hid a smile as she returned to her work. She must be done well before he came, for her weaving was a surprise not to be revealed until the dawn of Christmas day.*

*The dried strands of wool slid through her fingers. She*

*savored each texture, knowing the thick, oiled wool would keep
Coll warm in his wandering. He would be the finest figure of
all his clan when he rode out from the gates of Glenlyle Castle,
his great sword in hand.*

*Maire shivered, feeling a sudden premonition of dread. The
MacKinnons and the MacColls had been at war for years.
Should Coll's father learn where his son found haven on cold
winter nights, he would take steps to end the affair by any
means.*

*Maire frowned, watching sparks shoot from a wedge of
burning peat. Her own father would feel the same fury, she
knew. But her heart had driven her out of Dunraven's walls,
away to this cottage where she could ply her shuttle in solitude.
Or so she told her kin.*

*It was also because the deserted hills would bear no tales
of the man who pulled her laughing into his arms.*

*Smoke gusted down the chimney. The door rattled, as if
ghostly fingers sought their way inside. Maire murmured a
prayer of protection and crossed herself quickly as the door was
flung open and broad shoulders filled the frame.*

*"So shocked to see me, are you?" Coll's voice boomed out
as he caught her up in his arms. "Expecting another braw warrior, were you?"*

*"'Tis only one man I wait for, and well you know it, Coll of
Glenlyle."*

*"So I do, my sweet Maire." He buried his hands in her hair,
his lips to her white brow. "Thoughts of nothing else have tormented me every second since I left you. You are a MacKinnon, daughter of my clan foe, and we are forever forbidden to
touch. But my blood burns for you, fierce beyond denying.
What shame could there be in a pleasure so fine as this?"*

*His hands tightened. Already he was working the bright
sash from her waist.*

"Coll, stop," she rasped. "You must be hungry, and we have yet to talk—"

"'Tis hungry I am, but only for your sweetness, Maire." He released the cords from her mantle of patterned wool and freed her brooch of beaten silver.

Her eyes darkened. "How is it I can never say you nay?"

"Because we are meant for this joining, fated to be bound in our two souls," Coll said fiercely. He caught her in his arms, and there before the peat fire, he laid her down on a bed of bright wool and dried heather. As he flung aside his own long mantle, he heard the clatter of a pan on the table. "What business is this?" he muttered. "You've found indigo?"

"'Tis a surprise, Coll. Close your eyes, for I'll not have it spoiled before Christmas."

He threw back his head and laughed. "Secrets, is it? The lairds of Glenlyle have ways to work answers from their enemies, woman." His hands were warm and unerring as they found her lush sweetness. "I'll have your secrets and your moans while your body shudders beneath me. I care not for clan superstition and the gossip of old women. You are my heart, Maire. All the best of my life comes in the minutes I spend here with you." His eyes were hot and sharp as he studied her, white curves gilded by the firelight. He thought of the pulse that throbbed at her throat, the desire that hazed her eyes.

His joy, she was. His most precious gift.

His mortal life.

Madness filled him. He knew her body intimately now, secure in all its secrets. He teased her to ragged moans with lip and tongue until she arched beneath him.

But even then, regret lay bitter upon the eldest son of the laird of Glenlyle. "I would give you my name, Maire of Dunraven. I would pledge my heart to you before our clans, assembled to witness our marriage."

*"It matters not,"* she whispered, her fingers stroking his jaw. *"Our love is pledged now, here before the firelight and God who watches all."*

Coll wished he could believe it. He wished he could shake the dark fears that woke him blind and sweating in the night, shuddering from a sense of loss so keen that darkness blocked his eyes.

*"It matters,"* he said harshly. *"I will turn my father to share my view, I swear it. All I need is time."*

Something whispered to him that time was one thing they did not have.

Maire smiled up at him with sadness in her face. *"No one told me that a MacColl talked so much,"* she whispered. *"'Tis actions I demand now."* Her hands found him, bold in their searching. As she traced his hot, hard length, Coll threw back his head, shuddering as pleasure spiraled through him.

Her perfume rose, a mix of heather and roses and rare spices from her dyeing herbs. Blinded by need, Coll pushed to his knees above her. *"I am your enemy, Maire. I am a man you were trained to hate and fear since birth, a man who can bring you nothing but pain. Why do you welcome me and give such joy to my life?"*

She slid away the brooch that glittered on his shoulder and sighed as his naked skin met hers. *"Only because I love you, Coll of Glenlyle. For now,"* she whispered, *"for tomorrow. For all eternity. These are my three wishes."*

Fear blinded Coll at her words. They did not have eternity, nor even tomorrow. Their meetings could not be kept secret much longer, in spite of all his care.

Which left only now.

He stiffened. In one fierce stroke he parted her sweetness, sheathing himself deeper with each powerful thrust. Wildly, he drove her over the rich wool until she cried out and arched be-

*neath him, whispering his name. Her body tensed, white and beautiful in the firelight. Passion sheened her brow and tremors drew her rigid against him.*

*Coll watched, savoring her soft moans as her body closed in velvet tremors against him.*

*All they needed was time, and time they would not have.*

*When her eyes opened, he gripped her hands and moved within her, desperate to drown the fear, desperate to feel her passion yet again.*

*Desperate to stay with her forever.*

*He groaned and found the pounding pace of release within her while their hands linked. But even as fire swept through Coll, the north wind screamed over the glen and a pair of ravens laughed mockingly from the old stone circle.*

*Somewhere a noose was closing around them.*

TWO HOURS LATER, the moon floated behind a veil of clouds and something tapped at Ian's window.

He flinched and began to sweat. A man in a black jumpsuit leveled a gun on Jamee as she ran through the fog. She was terrified, close to exhaustion, and Ian could do nothing to help her.

Gasping, he sat up, gripping the sheets. Only a dream, he told himself, waiting for the terror to fade.

Sweat streaked his forehead. *Only a dream.*

Then he heard a sharp cry of panic from the far side of the room.

Dear God, it was Jamee.

## CHAPTER SIXTEEN

JAMEE STOOD BESIDE the door, shaking the doorknob. The blankets were shoved in one corner and a long ribbon lay draped around her shoulders.

She looked like a Christmas gift, Ian thought, satin over gold skin and silken curves.

"Jamee?" he whispered, afraid to move. Afraid his touch might spiral her deeper into nightmares.

She turned slowly. Her face was sheet-white. Her hands clutched her gown against her chest, where she had scooped it from the floor.

"I woke up," she whispered. "Just now. In spite of the dream I woke up, and this time I almost remembered." Her dark eyes were enormous in the pale oval of her face. "You were there, too. At least, it *felt* like you. What does it mean, Ian?"

"It means you're beginning to control the memories. When you stop fighting them, they lose their power, Jamee."

"Do you really believe that?"

"Yes," Ian said, pulling his jacket around her shoulders. Wanting to pull her against his chest instead.

"I'm not running," she said. "There's a reason I've come here and a reason I've found you. I've got to find out what it is."

Ian didn't answer.

"Do you believe in fate, Ian?"

His eyes narrowed. "Sometimes fate is just an excuse for our own mistakes."

"And the other times?"

"We make our own fate, fashioned out of our fear and our hopes." He smoothed the sheets and spread the coverlet over the bed, then turned down one corner. "Now, forget about fate and get some rest."

Jamee didn't move. "Only if you're beside me. Otherwise the dreams...they're so close tonight."

Pain, Ian thought. But he nodded and moved to the far side of the bed. If he was very, very careful, he might be able to keep from touching her.

AN HOUR BEFORE dawn Ian lay asleep with one leg sprawling off the end of the bed. As he dreamed about pink sand beaches and the hot, white burn of the Southern Cross, something warm and soft poured over his chest.

He opened his eyes and saw Jamee's hands, Jamee's warm silky hair and slumberous body. She was draped over him like tinsel on a Christmas tree.

A cold shower, he told himself tightly. No, a dozen cold showers, he decided as her hand slid under the covers and nudged the hot skin that hardened at her touch. In spite of his discomfort, Ian felt a grin curve his lips. She had turned to him in the night, drawn because she trusted him—even in her sleep. That fact made his grin grow huge.

Another part of his anatomy grew huge, too.

With a drowsy sigh Jamee laid her head against his arm. Her leg slid beneath his while her hand opened over his naked chest.

Ian swallowed hard and felt all his careful rules go soaring out the window.

JAMEE OPENED her eyes and looked around her as sunlight spilled through the curtains. A briefcase was shoved against the corner of the desk and a man's comb and brush occupied the dresser.

Ian's comb.

Ian's brush.

She remembered the feel of warm muscles flexing beneath her fingers and the dense springy hair that covered his chest. Which meant she had poured herself over him.

Again.

Her face flamed. Why did she have no willpower where Ian McCall was concerned?

A sound came from the bathroom. Ian emerged wearing a pair of black jeans unbuttoned at the waist. His hair was slicked back and beads of moisture skittered down his chest.

Jamee couldn't take her eyes off him. Her throat felt dry and her heart began to hammer. "I—I'm sorry."

"For what?"

She forced her gaze away from that glorious expanse of wet skin. "Bunking with me wasn't part of your job description," she said tightly. She tugged the sheet close, wrapped it twice around her body and pushed swiftly to her feet.

"Jamee, stop." Ian caught her wrist and pulled her to a halt. "We need to talk."

"I'm *not* falling apart, if that's what you're worried about."

"I didn't say you were."

"But you thought it. I can read it right now in your face. And don't try to tell me that waking you up in the middle of the night without a stitch on is standard procedure for your clients."

"You know it isn't."

Jamee took a hard breath. "You asked me once what I wanted from you, Ian." She watched a drop of water inch down his neck. She could barely keep from brushing it off with her fingertip. Or maybe with her lips, while her tongue did slow, carnal things to his skin. Then maybe he'd stop frowning and the light would fill his eyes again as it had in the cottage.

Maybe not.

"All I want is for the waiting to be over. I want to be in control of my life again." She ran a hand awkwardly through her hair. "How close are you to having answers?"

Ian pulled on a black turtleneck. "Every lead is being checked. It's only a matter of time until we find the clue we need."

Jamee gave a ragged laugh. "In other words, you still haven't got anything solid. The kidnappers could even be one of the people here at Dunraven."

Ian's jaw moved, but he didn't answer.

"Tell me, Ian. The truth. Please, no more lies."

After a moment, he shrugged on his jacket. As before, his hand moved unconsciously, checking each pocket. "All right, no lies, Jamee. They could be anyone, anywhere. I can vouch for Duncan, Kara and Angus, but beyond that…" He didn't finish.

He didn't have to.

Jamee swayed as his meaning hit. *Anyone. Anywhere.*

She straightened her shoulders. "Thank you for being honest at least." She ran one hand over a cone of silk bouclé thread. "You wanted my schedule?"

Ian nodded.

"I'll be here working for two hours. I want to finish my last design for Duncan and Kara. After that, I don't know. I thought maybe I'd walk down to Rose Cottage. My parents were very happy there…"

"Don't go alone. Duncan or I will go with you."

He was right, of course. He was doing everything necessary to keep her safe, and she couldn't make his job any harder.

"I understand." At the same time Jamee felt as if she were suffocating, held captive in the shadows of this beautiful old castle while every choice was inexorably taken from her control.

KARA PUSHED ASIDE a curtain and looked out at the dark curve of the sea. "Something's not right, Duncan."

Her husband moved behind her. "What do you mean? You've got a house full of Christmas decorations, twelve dozen racks of vintage clothing and a steam train on the back lawn. What could possibly be wrong?"

"I'm serious, Duncan." Kara shivered. "Something's out there. Watching. Waiting."

Duncan made a sharp sound and pulled her around to face him. "Did you see something, Kara? Something that might affect Jamee?"

Her eyes widened, staring over his shoulders. Her body went very still. Seconds passed before Kara took a sharp breath and shook her head. "No, I didn't *see* anything. Not the way you mean. It's just a feeling, like an itch at the back of my neck that won't go away."

"Then forget about it. Jamee's in the best of hands. Between Ian, myself and the rest of the men from Security International, she's as safe as the queen."

Kara rested her hand against his cheek. "Are you always so confident?"

"I wasn't once. You saved my life then, and I'll never forget it. I know what you can do, Kara. What you can *feel*. If you're feeling something specific like that now—"

"No." She sighed and sank back against his chest. "Not like before, with your brother Kyle. I guess I'm just tired from the pregnancy and finishing up this shoot. Tell me to shut up, why don't you?"

Duncan's eyes darkened. His hand slid into hers. "Actually, I had something else in mind for you to do, my love."

TWO HOURS OF WORKING warp textures of green and smoke and rose into a huge bouclé landscape left Jamee with a stiff neck and a raging appetite. She smoothed the six-foot tapestry, pleased with the curve of Dunraven's dark hills above a darker coast. She rubbed her aching neck and thought of the scones she'd been smelling for an hour. Her hair flowed unbound around her shoulders, as she pulled on a sweater and slipped on her shoes.

She almost bumped into Hidoshi at the kitchen door.

"In search of food?"

Jamee nodded conspiratorially. "Those scones that Angus makes would be just the thing."

Hidoshi smiled. "Especially smothered with butter and fresh honey."

"You get the butter, and I'll get the tea going." As Jamee moved around the kitchen, she frowned. "Are you nearly done with your shoot?"

"Two more days. Maybe three. Having us here has been the devil of a nuisance for Kara and her husband, but Dunraven's been very good about it. I think he's worrying that Kara will overwork. Now especially."

Jamee set three blueberry scones on a Wedgwood plate and went searching for honey. "Now?"

"She's expecting a child." Hidoshi's face creased in a grin. "She doesn't think that anyone else knows, but Duncan's so delirious he's been telling everyone he's a father-to-be. Then he remembers and he swears us all to secrecy." Hidoshi shook his head. "She'll be spitting nails if she finds out, not that it matters. She forgives him for anything when he gives her one of those hot Highland looks."

Jamee didn't laugh. She'd seen those looks from Ian and knew how absolutely lethal they could be. She frowned down at the honey and licked a drop from her hand.

"I hope you won't mind if I take some photographs of your weaving. It's got incredible texture, just the sort of thing I like to shoot."

"Be my guest. I'm sure Kara and Duncan wouldn't mind."

Hidoshi slid his lanky body into a chair across from Jamee. "Actually, Kara suggested it. I think she wants the pictures as a gift for Duncan."

The door creaked open. A young man in a baseball hat with a smiling Mickey Mouse face on it grinned at Hidoshi. "I wondered where you'd gone. I should have known food was involved."

Hidoshi held up a half-eaten scone. "Come and join us in gluttony, my friend. There's honey and Jamee's made tea." The photographer turned to Jamee. "This is Rob Day, my assistant. Be careful you don't play poker with him, because he never loses. I think he cheats, but I've never been able to catch him at it."

"Because I'm too good, boss." Hidoshi's assistant grinned and held out a hand. The baseball cap inched back on his head. "Nice to meet you, Ms. Night. The weaving is cool."

"Thank you." Jamee handed over a scone and another teacup. "Have you been working outside all morning?"

The young man rubbed his neck and nodded. "Setting up for a series of shots from the cliffs. Damn tiring work in this wind." He pulled up a chair, wolfed down one scone, and grabbed another off Hidoshi's plate.

"Hey, get your own grub," Hidoshi barked.

"Try to make me!"

In a moment, the two were scuffling like teenagers. Jamee

watched them in silence, feeling about a hundred years old. Maybe having a price on your head did that to you.

*No self-pity,* she told herself curtly. Self-pity was stupid, as well as useless.

"Have you seen Rose Cottage?" Hidoshi asked after landing a final punch on Rob's shoulder that nearly sent his teacup flying.

"Not yet."

"You should go right now. The sun's out and the hills are beautiful in the light. According to Dunraven legend, whoever spends the first night of their honeymoon at Rose Cottage will never part." His brow rose in a wicked slant. "I for one hope so, since Duncan and Kara were nice enough to let Megan and me stay there on our honeymoon. The place really is magic, you know."

"So was the magnum of champagne I heard Duncan sent down to you." Rob grinned. "You two were probably drunk for a week. Talk about *magic.*"

Another scuffle seemed imminent, but Hidoshi abruptly looked at his watch and jumped to his feet. "Kara will be going nuts in the ballroom. We're setting up a period shoot of a Victorian Christmas and the lighting is a killer. By the way, I'm sorry you missed the dinner scene last night. Hope you're feeling better."

"Like a new woman," Jamee said lightly.

Hidoshi tapped his jaw, then looked at Rob. "Maybe you could take Jamee down and show her the cottage. I still need a few shots of the exterior, and I suppose I could trust you to manage them without ruining all my film," he said, breaking into a smile.

"Righto." His lanky assistant finished off his fourth scone and looked at Jamee. "If you still want to go, that is."

"Fine with me." Jamee finished her tea and pushed to her

feet, then remembered Ian's warnings. "Have either of you seen Ian this morning?"

"Wasn't he with you?" Hidoshi asked. The calm assumption of their intimacy made Jamee flush.

"He left several hours ago."

Hidoshi worked a hand through his purple-streaked hair. "I haven't seen him. Have you, Rob?"

His assistant pulled off his cap and scratched his forehead. "I think he was talking with Angus and one of the workmen down by the orchard."

"Perfect. That's right on your way to the cottage," Hidoshi said decisively. "What are you waiting for?"

"You're sure he was there?" Jamee hesitated.

"No doubt about it. Not unless there's another man around here who's wearing solid black and watching everyone who comes in and out like they might be alien cyborgs sent to take over earth. What did you say his job was, anyway?"

Jamee looked out at the hills, golden in the morning sunlight. "He analyzes things."

"Like the stock market?"

"No, not that kind of thing. Things that are far more important than blue-chip stocks or municipal bonds." She walked to the door, suddenly anxious to see Ian again. "Down the hill to the right, isn't that the way?"

ROSE COTTAGE was just as magical as Jamee had expected from her parents' description. The low, thatched roof was bare of roses now, but pine trees and holly clustered by the front door and slanting sunlight left squares of gold in the narrow windows. In spring, the cottage would be smothered in colors, awash in the fragrance of roses.

Inside, wooden beams crossed the painted ceiling above a vast stone hearth streaked with sunlight. "I had no idea the

cottage was so old," Jamee said. "There's some kind of stillness about it. Almost like an air of expectation. It makes the
hairs prickle on my neck."

"Weird, isn't it? I noticed that right away." Beside her, Rob
crouched low, busily clicking pictures of the roof. "One of my
shots was full of shadows that shouldn't have been there.
Hidoshi claims it's because I held my camera toward the sun,
but who knows? After visiting Dunraven, I'd believe in
anything—even a few ghosts." He was quiet for a moment, then
gave an uncertain chuckle. "Why don't you go inside and look
around?"

As Jamee pushed open the door, something rustled in the
bushes beside her.

"There he is again," the photographer whispered.

"Who?"

"That big gray cat. He's curled up in the sun at the edge of
the walk."

Jamee looked back, stunned to see a long gray form resting
languidly in a bar of sunlight between two hedges. How had
the animal gotten all the way up here?

The gray head tilted and his amber eyes flickered. Once
again, Jamee had the disturbing sense that the cat was looking
deep into her mind, reading images that even she was not aware
of.

Ridiculous, of course. The cat no doubt lived here at Dunraven and had simply strayed over the glen in the fog.

"So you've come home, have you?" The keen amber eyes
closed with pleasure as Jamee bent and stroked the cat's warm
fur. He stretched, purring loudly.

Rob slung his camera over his neck. "An old friend of
yours?"

"You could say that." Jamee frowned, remembering the last
time she had held the cat, while she ran from the roiling smoke.

The cat stirred, stiffening beneath her hand, almost as if sharing the memory.

Rob framed the roof in his camera. "I need to take some pictures out here, but if you're cold, you can go inside. Maybe you'll hear the phantom piper."

"Don't tell me there's a ghost."

"Several of them, actually. Kara says that the piper of Dunraven plays whenever a maiden of virtue enters the castle grounds."

That would leave her out, Jamee thought. She was no maiden. Given her feelings about Ian, she was a total flop in the virtue department. She thought of his hard chest streaked with water after a shower. His hands, callused and searching.

"So," Rob said, his camera clicking without a pause, "what do you want for Christmas? There must be something special on your list."

Christmas. Jamee had hardly thought about it. There had been too many other things to worry about. "One wish."

"For a friend, I'll bet." The young photographer's hat slipped and he shoved it back down on his forehead. "You look like the type who wants things for other people."

"Maybe the right wish would touch all of us," Jamee said softly, remembering the way Ian's eyes crinkled when he laughed. She sighed at her foolish hopes. She didn't know what she wanted right now.

The cat looked up. Once again Jamee felt the amber eyes were far too keen. "What about you, Rob?"

The photographer was looking toward the hills, his eyes narrowed. He was lost in a world of angles and F-stops as he disappeared around the side of the cottage, camera clicking.

Opening the door, Jamee stepped into the shadowed hallway of Rose Cottage.

IAN FROWNED at Angus McTavish, who was stringing rows of tiny colored lights above the back courtyard. "Is Jamee out here?"

"I'm afraid I haven't seen the young lady," the Scotsman said, scratching his head. "Not since last night."

Ian frowned. Where could she have gone? It was ten o'clock precisely, but she wasn't working. He had just come from the bedroom, which had been empty.

His next stop was Kara's office. He found her surrounded by a dozen models in various states of undress.

"Did you want something, Ian?" Kara called.

"Have you seen Jamee?"

"Not since last night. Maybe you should ask Angus."

"I did. He hasn't seen her, either."

Kara looked at Ian's face, then dropped the ornate Victorian hat and followed him out into the hall. She put a hand on his arm. "Do you think something is wrong?"

Ian frowned out at the ragged cliffs. "I don't know. She could be anywhere, Kara. I told her *not* to go out without me."

"Have you tried Rose Cottage? She might have gone down for a look. It was her parents' favorite place."

Rose Cottage. Ian muttered a curse and ran for the door.

His heart was pounding as he sprinted down the path from the castle. Holly and yew boughs slapped at his legs beneath a sky of blinding blue and the sea churned up white ridges of foam at the foot of the cliff. Ian barely noticed. "Jamee? Are you there?"

Over the hill a curlew cried sadly. Ian felt the cold touch of terror.

The kidnappers could be anywhere, even hidden somewhere on Dunraven's grounds. He should never have let Jamee out of his sight.

There was no way to tell where or when they would strike next. And if something happened to Jamee…

Ian shoved past a towering yew hedge. Rose Cottage stood haloed in sunlight thirty yards down the hill. His breath caught when he saw a slender figure standing beneath the towering oak tree.

*"Jamee."*

Before the word left his mouth, a man bolted around the corner, headed straight for her. Ian pushed himself harder, pounding over the hill, but knew he couldn't make it in time. Meanwhile, Jamee didn't even see her assailant. She was standing on a ladder, stretching toward an overhead branch when the man appeared beneath her, pulling her down.

"No," Ian bellowed as Jamee toppled backward with a cry of surprise. His lungs were screaming for air when he pounded into the quiet glade where Jamee twisted with the man's arms clamped around her shoulders.

Ian didn't stop for questions.

With one powerful movement, he wrestled Jamee free, then slammed the man to the ground with a savage right uppercut. "Run," he ordered, panting as he shoved her attacker facedown into the grass.

She didn't move. "Ian, don't. You can't—"

*"Go,"* he growled.

The man groaned and tried to raise his head. He was young, fresh-faced and frightened. Almost too young to be a kidnapper, Ian thought. But looks meant nothing. Years of experience had taught Ian that the most angelic face could hide a deranged mind.

Ian's eyes narrowed. There was something about that brown hair and the red baseball hat that seemed faintly familiar.

"You don't understand, Ian," Jamee rasped. "That's Rob, Hidoshi's assistant. I was looking through the cottage while he took some photographs for Hidoshi. Then the cat got caught up in the tree."

Ian barely heard her. Fear and fury still hammered through his veins.

"Ian, you've got to *listen*. Rob was simply taking some photographs. Then I called him to help me get down."

Photographs.

Ian's jaw clenched. *Rob. Hidoshi's assistant.*

Jamee was right. It had been the most innocent of adventures. There had been no threat to her at all.

Silently, Ian lifted the befuddled photographer to his feet and straightened his jacket. "Sorry," he said gruffly. "It appears I've made a mistake."

Rob blinked uncertainly and brushed off the back of his pants. "No problem." He glanced from Ian's scowling face to Jamee's pale one. "I guess I'd better get back. You two probably want to talk. Or whatever…"

As the bewildered photographer disappeared up the hill, Jamee whirled to face Ian. "Why didn't you listen? He was just trying to keep me from falling off the stepladder."

"I act first and listen later," Ian said harshly. "I told you *not* to leave without me."

"Hidoshi and Rob said you were down by the orchard. I couldn't find you inside, so I thought…"

"Next time have someone track me down. Don't leave the house alone, understand?"

"But I wasn't alone. Rob was…" She stopped, seeing the coldness in Ian's eyes. "You don't trust him, do you?"

"I don't trust anyone I don't know personally, Jamee. You're my job. Keeping you safe is all that matters. If I make a mistake while I'm doing that, it's too bloody bad."

Jamee stiffened. "There's something else, isn't there?"

"I don't know what you mean."

"Something's upset you. I can see it in your eyes."

Dammit, the woman saw too much. He didn't mean to tell her that the kidnappers had vanished and he was back where he had started. He didn't want to add to her anxiety.

He shrugged. "You're wrong."

"If there's something else, I have the right to know, Ian. It's *me* they're following, not you."

"When I have solid facts, you'll be the first to know."

"Will I?" Jamee snapped. "Or will you just go on cutting me out, blocking your feelings while you try to make yourself into some kind of perfect protection machine."

"You need a machine to protect you," Ian said.

"What I *need* is emotion and honesty. You need them, too, Ian. Just as much as I do."

"Emotions cause mistakes. Emotions are dangerous."

"Maybe I need the kind of danger that comes with being honest emotionally. After all, you were the one who told me I shouldn't settle for anything less."

"Jamee, listen."

"No, *you* listen. I want to touch you, Ian. Otherwise I'll think about running, and if I run now I'll always hate myself."

His eyes darkened. "You're not a quitter, Jamee. There would be nothing wrong with leaving now and going back to the States."

"There you go, making it easy for me," she muttered.

"I want to make things easy for you, dammit."

"Why? That's not part of your job any more than letting me wrap myself around you in the night is."

His lips curved faintly. "It's a dirty job, but someone's got to do it."

"Don't joke about this, Ian."

"Why not?" His smile slowly faded. "If I don't joke, I'm going to do something unbelievably stupid."

# CHAPTER SEVENTEEN

"RIGHT NOW, YOU MEAN?" There was a ripple of joy in her voice. The sound made Ian want to groan.

"Right here."

"That's fine with me."

Two security officers were patrolling the lower edge of the orchard, Ian knew. A third was watching from his post in one of the castle's turrets. Ian made a hard sound and gave up to the angry singing in his blood. At the first taste of her mouth, desire flared through him. She shivered in the instant flush of heat and her body leaned into his.

Ian forgot about being stoic. He pulled her against him with a low groan.

The wind sang over the glen. The sky shimmered in a haze of light. Need exploded to the flashpoint.

With exquisite care she kissed his eyelids while she murmured his name.

"Why didn't you run when you had a chance?" Ian whispered. "Why didn't you leave me the way I was, dammit? Now touching like this will never be enough. I want all of you, Jamee. And after I've touched you all those ways, I'll only want you more, God help me."

Jamee shivered, hearing the pain in his voice. Hearing the loneliness of a man who had wandered in far lands for too many lonely nights.

She wouldn't let him be lonely, not at Christmas.

Easing her fingers around his neck and leaning close, she met him kiss for hungry kiss. Her body molded to his, thigh to thigh.

Ian pulled free, his breath labored. "Have I frightened you yet?" he growled.

"No way." It was true. Instead of fear, Ian had given her passion. At the same time, Jamee sensed his own control was weakening. She smiled gently and touched his face, yearning to see him smile.

Passion would be her gift back to him, and joy would be their shared reward. Jamee sensed the hand of fate just as she had before Maire MacKinnon's portrait.

His hands relaxed as he captured a lock of her hair. "You've taken down your braid," he whispered, pulling the sun-warmed strands to his lips. "I didn't think you could be more beautiful, but you are."

Then Ian took a step back and shoved his hands into his pockets. "We'd better go. Kara and Duncan will send out a search party after that young photographer tells them how I nearly killed him."

Jamee brought her arms around his neck, feeling the sudden tension that gripped his muscles. "I'm not running, Ian. Not from the danger. Not from you."

"Maybe you should," he said grimly. "You don't know what you're getting into."

Jamee rested her forehead against his chest. "I'm getting a man of honor. A man I want to share my life with, in hard times, as well as good. I can't lie about this, Ian. I won't close myself off to any part of you. Consider it my personal Christmas gift."

A shudder ran through him. "Jamee, you don't understand. There are reasons why—"

She raised one finger to his mouth. "*No,* Ian. I don't want to hear why loving you is impossible or unsafe or illogical. We Nights have never been very good at conditions or negatives. Especially when it concerns the heart," she said with a crooked smile. "Besides, Christmas is a time to believe, not to deliberate."

"You could deliberate with Einstein and rip him to shreds," Ian said hoarsely. "If you were any sharper, you'd terrify me." He cupped her cheeks, his eyes bleak. "I don't want to lose you, Jamee."

"I'll be around, McCall. In fact, I intend to stick to you like one of my brother William's alien droids attacking the mother ship. You'll like William, by the way."

Ian's hands tightened. "I already do. We met three weeks ago."

Jamee frowned. "You did? I see, he came with Adam to talk you into taking this job. You never had a chance."

"They were very persuasive, I'll admit. But it wasn't anything they said or did that convinced me."

"No?"

"It was the sound of your voice when you called from Bali."

"You were there, listening?"

"Every word. How did the boar taste, by the way?"

She chuckled. "Don't ask."

"It was your laughter. It lit the room," Ian said gravely. "After hearing you, I couldn't turn away. I think maybe I fell in love with you then."

Her eyes widened. "But—"

Ian made a curt sound and ran a hand through his hair. "Don't push me, Jamee. No more questions. Not now." His gaze moved over the orchard, then uphill to the house. "I'm a fool to keep you out here. The only good thing is that everyone will know I've been out here kissing you senseless. Anyone watching will realize that they'll have to get through *me* to get to you."

Jamee gave a crooked smile. "I thought I was kissing *you* senseless, McCall."

He didn't return her smile. "Let's call it a draw."


IAN WALKED her back to the house, aware of several sidelong looks. No doubt Rob's story had already begun to circulate.

Ian didn't care. He was supposed to be a man besotted, head over heels in love. The performance would be amazingly easy.

At the hall stairs he caught Jamee's hand and pulled her to a halt. "Wait."

"Why are we stopping here?"

"I didn't finish before." Ian slid a hand beneath her chin and raised her head. "Look." A sprig of mistletoe hung from a braid of holly and dried lavender.

"You Scotsmen seem to be up on all the legends."

"Oh, we observe all the ones that count." Ian drew her closer.

"Ian, I—" Jamee felt her pulse quicken. She tried to think straight, struggling to use some of her God-given logic, but it always seemed to desert her when she was around Ian. "Is this another part of your masquerade?" she murmured.

His hands tightened over her waist. "Tell me if this feels like a masquerade."

The kiss was slow and searching. Tiny lights on the Christmas tree winked off and on, casting a glow over their faces. Jamee inhaled the tang of pine needles and the citrus scent of Ian's skin. Just as always, she lost all sense of the outside world, all sense of reason when she was anchored in his arms.

Behind them three of the models giggled. Someone cleared his throat. "I'm delighted to see that the mistletoe isn't going to waste."

Jamee stiffened and turned to see Duncan smiling benignly from the staircase, flanked by Kara's curious models.

"Just testing it out," Ian murmured. "It seems quite satisfactory."

"I'm delighted you approve," Duncan said. "Now, if Jamee would like the full tour of Rose Cottage, I'd be happy to oblige. Rob is understandably too frightened to take anyone anywhere after the mishap."

"My fault," Ian murmured. "I'll talk to him later." As he spoke, his hand curved protectively on Jamee's shoulder.

"If you're up to it, lunch will be served in fifteen minutes."

ALL THROUGH LUNCHEON Jamee smiled and chatted but she felt the suffocating lack of control overwhelm her. She was too vulnerable, too much on display, and Ian's unshakable control of his own emotions only made her more irritated.

Despite Jamee's discreet tugging, he did not release her hand as the other guests gathered to join them for lunch in a sunny room with green damask walls.

"You can let go of my hand now," she whispered. "There's no need to pretend. No one is watching under the table."

"I like holding your hand," Ian murmured. His eyes darkened as he slid her palm against his thigh, then turned to answer a question of Duncan's.

Jamee fumed. How could he be so calm and stoic while *she* sat in a daze, bewildered by a thousand conflicting emotions?

It wasn't *fair.* Why should Ian McCall show total control when *she* was turning into mush?

Beneath the table, her leg brushed against Ian's. For a moment, their thighs touched. Jamee saw Ian go very still, his jaw clenched.

Maybe he *wasn't* in total control after all.

"And what do you do, Lord Glenlyle?" the model named Tania asked, her eyes narrowed.

"I have a castle north of here."

"What kind of castle? Is it bigger than Dunraven?"

"It's big enough," Ian said calmly.

"I'm sure it is." Tania batted her eyelashes at Ian. "Tell me more," she purred.

So he was going to be calm and civilized, was he? Beneath the table, Jamee's fingers moved to Ian's thigh.

Ian didn't move. His voice didn't change by a shade as he answered the model's questions. "Something old and drafty, I'm afraid. We have no Victorian angels hanging from the rafters and no steam trains traveling around the Three Wise Men."

"You do have bears," Duncan interposed.

"Bears?" The model laughed seductively. "I'll bet they wear kilts, too. I'd love to see *you* in a kilt," she gushed.

Ian's cool smile didn't waver.

Blast the man and blast the giggling female who couldn't stop staring at him. Jamee explored higher, her fingers gently nuzzling suddenly rigid muscle.

Then she froze. The full male power of him pressed against her palm, barely restrained by wool flannel. Her pulse hammered as she felt his heat beneath her fingers.

Ian's head turned. His eyes gleamed, hard and smoky, promising sweet, sweet revenge.

"By the way, what *do* you Scotsmen wear beneath your kilts?" Tania asked throatily.

"Nothing, of course."

Jamee blinked, mesmerized by the heat in Ian's eyes. The tumid muscle grew harder beneath her hand. She moistened her dry lips and flushed, suddenly aware that she was playing with fire.

Silently, Ian caught her wrist beneath the table, then moved her hand onto her own thigh. His fingers opened, tracing the soft skin through her skirt. Jamee sat frozen, unable to move. Her left hand tightened on her water glass as Ian dipped beneath her skirt and found the curve of her inner thigh. Slowly, he traced the sensitive skin above her stockings.

With every movement, heat poured through her in delicious waves.

"Enough of this talk about kilts," Duncan said tensely. "What about you, Miss Night? You've traveled all over the world, I understand. Perhaps you'll share some of your wilder tales. Nicholas Draycott assures me you have quite a few."

Jamee swallowed hard. Her wildest experience was taking place right now. She shivered as Ian's relentless fingers moved up her inner thigh. She wanted him to stop, even as she prayed he would continue. *She* was in control, after all. That was what she had to prove to both of them. "Er, that must have been Bali. In the jungle. It was—hot. Very hot." Ian's hand eased slowly upward. "They were burning silkworm cocoons in the fields. An absolute waste. I said I would take everything they could give me."

"Everything?" Ian murmured silkily. As he spoke, his hand glided higher.

Jamee nodded, feeling electricity hum where Ian's fingers continued their hot, stroking climb.

"I understand that the chief was interested in marrying you," Duncan said.

Ian's fingers tensed.

"Actually, it was the chief's son," Jamee couldn't keep the breathlessness from her voice. "I would have been wife number fourteen. Das offered to pay six knives and a cow for me."

"Das?" Ian muttered.

"We—got to be fairly close. His offer was some kind of record, I was told."

Ian brushed her sensitive flesh, his eyes narrowed. "And what did you say to the chief's proposal?" As he spoke, his fingers splayed open, only inches from the warm delta at the juncture of her thighs.

Her sanity shredding fast, Jamee raised her chin and smiled sweetly. "I told the chief I never mix business with pleasure, of course." If her laugh sounded shaky, no one seemed to notice in the general laughter that followed.

Only Ian sat unmoving without the hint of a smile. His focus was savage in its intensity. "No?" he murmured.

And then his hand curved, palming the sleek folds covered by the sheerest barrier of silk.

Jamee drew a ragged breath. Desire rippled through her, spurred by each knowing movement of Ian's fingers. His exploration was slow and sweet, and Jamee felt her traitorous body yield to his touch even as her mind struggled to remain aloof.

The conversation ebbed and flowed around them, but Ian's dark eyes never left her. It was obvious that he felt every detail of Jamee's response. "Never?" he murmured, finding the lacy edge of silk and inching past.

Jamee cleared her throat. "N-never."

The conversation shifted again. Somebody laughed at one of Hidoshi's jokes and then chairs scraped against marble.

Jamee barely noticed, trapped by the hunger in Ian's eyes. His face was hard, his jaw tense as he eased deeper, parting her silken skin. He made a low sound, then sheathed himself inside her.

Jamee sat frozen. She couldn't wriggle free. Moving was impossible. The table was empty except for the two of them now and she was drowning in his eyes, feeling everything unravel inside her. With each slow brush of his callused fingers, pleasure surged through her body and her heart slammed in aching anticipation.

She bit her lip, unable to stop thinking about what he was doing.

Unable to stop wanting him to do more.

Her hand tightened around her wineglass. Beneath the table, her dewy skin parted layer by layer beneath his fingers. She felt desire shimmer through her, pulsing and hot like a mirage that faded endlessly into the horizon.

"Ian, I—"

"They're gone, Jamee. We're alone here. At last, dammit. God, how I've wanted to feel you." His voice was thick, smoky with desire. "Let me touch you now."

"I can't— I don't—"

Colors Jamee had only experienced in dreams teased her eyes. A low sound caught on her lips and she barely managed to bite it down as a rush of blinding pleasure slammed through her.

The world blurred. Sound faded. She shuddered, falling deep, delight like a summer wind that kissed her very soul. Tremors seized her legs, her arms, and she tightened her hands as he slid a fraction deeper, a fraction faster. A shudder tore through her as she felt Ian's lips brush her face, her eyelids. Patterns of joy danced through her being, driving her toward a peak that had no end. Then she was over, gasping. Flying. Lost in blind sensation.

Ian whispered her name hoarsely as his hand stilled. His forehead was dotted with sweat and his jaw was clenched. "Sweet God," he said raggedly, easing away from her slick heat. "I must be mad."

Too late. Waves crested. Color flashed anew, worked in the magic of his retreating touch. She shattered, dizzy and lost, entranced by the only man who had unlocked the secrets of her heart.

Ian cursed softly and bent closer. "Dammit, Jamee, I want you." He took a hard breath. "It's the last thing I should be thinking about, and yet I want you now."

Hunger blazed in his eyes. His hand lay on the table, rigid. His face was pale.

No, he wasn't immune, Jamee realized. He wanted her just as much as she wanted him.

Her body shivered in the aftermath of his knowing touch.

"Say the word, Jamee," he whispered. "Say the word and to hell with everything else. Maybe it's time we made this masquerade real."

Her hand settled over his cheek and she felt the rigid line of the muscle beneath.

He was a man of honor. If they went upstairs now, he would hate himself for betraying his duty. He would always believe he had endangered her by a lapse of control he could never forgive.

"You don't really mean that," Jamee said softly. "Besides, I don't want your mind wandering when I finally get you into bed, Lord Glenlyle. I'm picky that way." She gave a crooked smile. "You see, I want all the time in the world."

Ian's eyes closed. "I'll give you what I have when this is over. Then we can both think clearly."

"I mean to hold you to that promise, Scotsman. Otherwise I'll send my brothers after you, fearsome in all their wrath."

"They've never fought a Scotsman before," Ian said gruffly.

"True, but you've never fought a Night before, either."

THE WALLS OF Dunraven Castle were quiet. No voices drifted from the ballroom. No giggling strangers huddled around the great smoke-stained fireplace. In the Great Hall, the Christmas tree glittered beneath layers of tinsel and silver bows.

As the silence lengthened, light seemed to gather and spin along the tree's highest branches. Flecks of gold and pink clung to the polished face of a ceramic angel with silver wings outspread. Brightness shimmered over the figure's damask skirts and haloed the nearby branches, where three white bells hung from a bright tartan ribbon.

As the light clung, spiraling out in sparks of silver and gold, a faint chiming rose like fairy bells and drifted through Dunraven's silent corridors.

There was no one in the Great Hall to hear the high, crystal peals. No one felt the giant tree sway slightly, sighing as if touched by a phantom wind.

And no one saw the proud gray cat ghost through the shadows and curl up at the tree's foot.

HE DIDN'T LIKE IT. In fact, his phantom blood was boiling.

Adrian Draycott stalked across the abbey's darkened roof, kicking at bits of gravel and scowling. Nothing had gone right since Gideon had left. Not one wretched thing.

"I miss him, dammit. There's the beginning and end to it." He propped his arms on the edge of the parapet, surveying the patchwork of forest and fields. The long years of comradeship with Gideon had left their imprint on him. Nothing felt *right,* suddenly.

"Adrian?" Light shimmered over the roof, touching the granite stones. "We both miss him, my love." A woman with luminous eyes took form beside him, draped in a dress of gold.

Adrian felt his heart leap as it always did when he saw the woman he loved. He gave her a crooked smile and tried to hide his restlessness. "I'm sure Gideon is perfectly happy at Dunraven. Probably a dozen people are fawning over him, feeding him salmon in a little silver bowl. In fact," Adrian said darkly, "the spoiled creature has probably forgotten all about us. No doubt he finds those damned misty glens far more interesting than my drab abbey grounds. I expect I'll have trouble fetching him home for Christmas." There was a hint of pain in his voice as he spoke.

The woman linked her fingers with his. "Gideon, forget you? You name the impossible, my lord. Besides, 'twas you who sent him to Dunraven, as I recall."

"Don't remind me," Adrian growled. At his words wind hissed over the roof and dead leaves skittered across his boots.

"He is needed at Dunraven, is he not?"

"I fear so. The danger is real and grows as Christmas draws near."

"The woman named Jamesina?"

"I fear so."

"Then you were right to send him. We will blunder along here in our fashion."

Adrian gave a long sigh. "But there's so much to do. The old year has to be rung out with proper ritual and all our spells cleared. After that, there's a tree to be selected from the high woods."

"I suppose Nicholas and his family may be trusted to do *some* things right," his lady said with the faintest touch of irony.

"Bah! Left to his mortal devices, he will surely bungle everything."

"In that case," the woman in gold said quietly, "you and I had better get to work, had we not? As it happens, I have had my eyes on a particular fir tree at the top of the clearing near Lyon's Leap." Her beautiful eyes glittered. "It happens to be the same tree where we spent quite a few happy hours together in the spring."

Adrian's lips curved. "*That* fir?"

"None other."

"You mean, the one where we—"

"Exactly." Her voice was purest silk.

Adrian cleared his throat. "It was a most remarkable afternoon, as I recall. That tree provided a most delicious shade while we…" He cleared his throat a second time, chuckling. "Very well, the choice is made. We shall bumble along without Gideon somehow." He studied the figure shimmering beside him. "I'm afraid I, too, have a business matter up north that I must tend to. I shan't be away long. But the most enjoyable of my tasks begins here."

"Here?"

Adrian's hands eased over her creamy shoulders and circled her waist. "There is joy to be spun, beauty that will encircle all of my abbey's walls." He moved closer. Though it was the dead of winter, the scent of roses suddenly filled the air, mixed with lavender and honeysuckle. The old granite stones shone with light as the fragrance grew.

*Petite Lisette, Gloire Des Mousseux,* and *Fantin Latour.* The flower names were as rich as the rose fragrance they bore. Each was Adrian's pride and joy.

As the two figures met, light swirled to dancing sparks and cascaded over the weathered walls. Love flowed through casement and capstone, past mortar and oaken beam. Faint yet tenacious, their fragile molecules trembled, then melded in a longing beyond time, beyond mortal limits.

Perhaps even beyond understanding.

And in that moment, a faint high peal of bells rang out over the dark, barren fields. Twelve times and then once more.

FAR AWAY TO THE NORTH where a proud Scottish domain rose above raging seas, a great cat raised his head at the sound of phantom bells. There was sorrow in his eyes for a moment, longing in his tensed gray body. He gave a low meow.

Then he sank back beneath the great pine tree.

There he stayed, eyes alert, waiting for the danger that was to come.

## CHAPTER EIGHTEEN

THE EVENING that followed was a time of pure magic talked about for years afterward at Dunraven. Soon after dinner, it began to snow, great soft flakes that dusted the cheeks and the eyes. Kara scrambled to the window, giggling like a girl of ten and Jamee was nearly as excited. When the models ran outside and made snowballs, Hidoshi followed and crouched in the snow, his shutter clicking.

"Let's take the little train and see the Wise Men," Duncan said to his wife as he led her outside.

Standing by the window, Ian hid a smile. He hadn't seen his friend look so happy in ages. Jamee was bouncing from foot to foot in her eagerness.

"Come on, McCall," she challenged. "I've got a snowball that has your name on it."

Ian wanted to say yes and join her in the lighthearted frolic, but it was out of the question. In the dark, with visibility further reduced by the snow, she would be a perfect target.

He shook his head.

"Chicken, are you?" She raised her fist and lightly tapped his chest, dancing like a boxer. "I didn't grow up with four brothers without tucking a few tricks under my belt."

Kara pulled Duncan down into the snow, both reveling in the general giddiness as the first snowfall of the year swirled around them.

"No, Jamee." Ian moved closer. "I'm afraid we can't."

"But why—" Realization filled her eyes. In a heartbeat she went from joy to sadness. "Oh. You think they might be…" She didn't finish.

"I'm sorry, Jamee. Genuinely sorry."

She turned and looked wistfully out at the lawn, where Kara was rubbing snow all over her husband's face while Hidoshi pelted his assistant with snowballs. Ian ached to change the situation.

And he knew it was impossible.

A golden bell moved in the wind where it hung from the hand of a marble Cupid, brought back from the Grand Tour by some MacKinnon ancestor. One of Kara's snowballs hissed through the air and set the bell chiming madly. With each high peal Ian felt the light, electric brush of movement along his spine.

What Jamee asked for was so little, surely. "Oh, hell, come on," he muttered, grabbing her hand.

"Are you sure?"

"Maybe I've got a snowball that has *your* name on it."

Snow dusted their faces as they charged outside. Jamee instantly scooped up a handful of snow and hurled it at Ian, striking him in the chest.

"Not fair! I wasn't ready," he growled.

"Lame, McCall. Very lame. My brother could have found a better excuse when he was five." As Jamee spoke, she hurled another well-packed missile.

This time Ian ducked, and the snowball struck the gold bell.

Jamee halted midlaugh as a pure ringing filled the air. "Do you feel that, Ian? It's like a kiss. Like all the Christmas wishes wrapped up into one."

Ian wanted to bundle her into his arms and kiss her. Standing in the snow and watching her smile, he felt the magic and wild enchantment that he had put away so long ago as a lonely child. He hadn't realized until that moment how much he had lost in the process.

The bell chimed again.

Light shimmered off Jamee's hair, flecked with snowflakes. Ian grabbed her braid and held her still, while he sprinkled snow down the back of her blouse.

She shrieked and whipped around, pummeling his neck. "*Cheat!* Hair-holding is a foul."

"No rules, lass: We play snowball the hard way here in the Highlands."

"Is that so, Braveheart?" Jamee scooped up a handful of powder and reached beneath his jacket and his shirt, then spread the cold flakes all over his naked chest. "And that's what *we* do to big bullies like you." Before Ian could move, she caught his foot and sent him flying facedown into the snow.

Duncan exploded with laughter. "Aye, a McCall is a hard man to topple, but when he falls, he falls hard."

Ian pushed to his feet, fire in his eyes. He stalked toward Jamee, who immediately sent a volley of snow at his face and shoulders.

But Ian was not about to be distracted.

Jamee held her ground. This was a game she seldom lost, even against four rowdy brothers. Her aim was perfect and her pacing even better.

Down the hill the little steam engine began to chug. Someone blew a whistle, but neither Ian nor Jamee paid any attention. "Fight to the death," Ian muttered, shaping a huge ball of white between his hands.

"Fight to the death," Jamee agreed, her eyes riveted on the hard-packed mass.

"Winner takes all," Ian said, his eyes unreadable.

"Agreed," Jamee said cockily.

She ducked as the giant ball sailed past and struck a pine tree. Powder dusted her face. While Ian bent to scoop up another handful of snow, Jamee attacked and struck him squarely on the forehead.

He never wavered. He just kept coming, his eyes unrelenting.

"Give up, McCall. You're outclassed. Face it, that snowball you're making will never touch me." She took a dancing step back with each word.

He just kept coming.

Jamee hurled off another handful of snow, striking his neck. Snow trickled beneath his collar and soaked the front of his shirt. "You can't possibly hope to win. I've been beating my brothers at this game for twenty years."

He still kept coming.

She stopped, put her hands on her hips. "Is this some kind of man thing?"

"I'd say it's some kind of man and woman thing." Ian's voice was as smoky as the peat fire that had danced in the cottage. It sent fine textures of heat playing up Jamee's spine. He wasn't the sort of man who would be deterred from a goal. She saw it in the set of his shoulders and in the narrowing of his eyes.

Another snowball hissed free and exploded over his shoulders. His head barely bent.

Jamee felt her first inkling of uneasiness. She danced behind a holly bush and caught up a huge handful of snow, wet and heavy. When Ian came left, she darted right and dumped the white mass down over his head.

She could read the glint in his eyes, primal now, an elemental challenge that made her pulse race.

Time for a new strategy.

Three pine trees up the hill. Jamee estimated her distance and bolted.

Ian was right behind her. He watched the snow dust her face, flushed and vibrant with color. The stillness of the night settled upon him and with it a fine, heady magic. Snowflakes feathered down and one landed on her eyelash. There it hung, torn like a tear from the eye of heaven.

Something swelled inside Ian. Heat and more, magic and more.

It was not a game, nor had it ever been. His need for her was too real. Too strong. Too physical.

And yet far more.

She turned, laughing as she ran up the snowy hill. The wind cast her long hair up around her, dusted by little eddies of snow.

*How can I leave her?* Ian wondered bleakly. *How can I see her once, touch her once, and not want her for a lifetime?*

She was at the top of the hill now, her high laughter drifting down to him as she scooped up a huge wad of snow, then sent it against him with unerring aim. He was too enchanted to duck and took the brunt of it on one shoulder.

"Ready to quit, McCall?"

Even the rain of snow did nothing to diminish the heat he was feeling. But as Ian watched Jamee dance toward him, her foot slipped in the snow and she swayed sideways. One shoe went flying, the other skidded over the snow, and she landed hard, the breath whooshing out of her.

Ian crouched beside her as the snow drifted down around them. "Jamee," he said urgently, pulling her against him. "Dammit, are you hurt?"

She blinked, unable to speak.

He felt her head carefully. "Did you land on a rock?" He

touched her neck, her cheeks, her face, afraid he would find traces of blood. "Dammit, Jamee, *talk* to me."

She shuddered. There was something in her eyes, something that spoke without any words at all while the snow whispered down around them, soft and silent as the night.

Ian pulled her into his arms and stood up.

"Where are we going?"

"To Rose Cottage." His jaw clenched. "If you'll go with me."

Jamee heard the question in his voice and the conflict. Emotions she didn't understand rocketed through her. Her only fear was disappointing him. But if she moved fast... Attacked boldly...

She traced his jaw and slid her fingers past the open collar of his denim shirt. She saw his eyes narrow and darken. She snagged his belt and waited, hunger in every surge of her blood.

Their eyes locked. Ian's lips burned over her forehead, eyelids, and finally met her hungry, trembling lips.

"Jamee," he said hoarsely, stopping at the cottage threshold and setting her on her feet.

Her mind was a haze of need. She popped two buttons from his shirt and yanked the tails free, then played her fingers over all that warm, muscled chest. "Do you mind if I do this?" she breathed.

"I'd seriously consider suicide if you stopped," Ian said raggedly. "But—"

She pulled his face down, eased her lips against his. His mouth was flavored with tea and strawberries and Jamee decided it was the most delicious combination in the world. "Ian," she whispered, loving the sound of his name on her lips.

He was too busy unbraiding her hair to answer. He brushed her neck, the flawless curve of her cheek. He hadn't wanted like this since he was a boy of fifteen with adolescent hormones run amok.

But Jamee Night seemed to do that to people.

He remembered where his hands had been at lunch. How could he be honorable and wait when every second was so precious, their future so unsure?

Her eyes darkened. "Ian, take me inside. I want to touch you. Everywhere."

He swallowed, trying to retain his last shred of sanity.

Her fingers traced his jaw. When she raised her head, her eyes were hazed with tears.

"Jamee?"

"I'm sure, Ian."

It was too late for talking. Some voice of honesty whispered that he'd always meant to have her this way, ever since she'd enchanted him by trying to save his life on the cliff. "We can't. It's a bloody bad time." Even as he spoke, Ian's fingers worked her blouse from her skirt, sublimely indifferent to what he had just said. It was crazy. It was reckless. It was—

The only thing Ian McCall had wanted in years. Maybe in centuries.

The thought made icy fingers play over his spine. He thought of the stone circle and the wind that moaned over the glen like a woman's cry of loss and pain.

He wouldn't lose Jamee. He wouldn't deny what they both wanted so badly.

Images pressed at his eyes, shadows that melted when he caught her in his arms and carried her over the cottage's threshold. Firelight spilled over old wood and freshly cut flowers. Even a hardened cynic could feel the emotions captured in each room. "If you believe in magic, you've come to the right place."

"I believe. So do you, Ian. I can see it in your eyes. My parents did, too. They were so happy here," Jamee whispered. She looked around her, awed by the dark crossbeams, the fine old prints, and the roses in every window. "I've wanted to come here ever since I was twelve and my mother told me how beautiful it was."

Ian kicked the door shut with his foot and set Jamee on the ground. He touched her hair, frowning. "It feels like I've wanted you for a lifetime." His hand slid over her neck and found the taut peak of her nipple. He pushed aside cotton and lace and covered her with his mouth until her skin flamed.

Suddenly she understood the dark songs and all the sad movies from her youth. Love was feeling naked, being turned inside out. It was terrifying, without rules. Nothing could have prepared her for this aching need and total vulnerability.

And yet Jamee couldn't think of anything she wanted more.

She finished unbuttoning Ian's shirt and shoved it from his shoulders, then took an unsteady breath. His skin was golden in the firelight, ridged with muscles.

Panic shook her. The Big Three were something else. None of them had mattered. After all, she could barely even remember them.

She wanted to remember this. She wanted to be perfect for Ian.

She bit her lip.

*Don't think,* a voice said. *Get him deep, so far lost that he doesn't have time to think, either.*

She worked tensely at the button on his waistband. She tried to ignore his mouth, his fingers stroking the curve of her breast.

His jeans came free. She worked them down his muscled body, smiling faintly when she heard him curse. She experienced a heady sense of control, of being wanted.

Fast and hot, she thought, praying he wouldn't be disappointed. She couldn't bear that.

He shoved off her blouse and sent it flying.

"Ian," she whispered, tonguing the warm planes of his chest, reaching for his heat.

"Hold on, Jamee," he said tightly. "This isn't exactly a race." When she didn't answer, he forced her to look at him. "Why do I get the feeling you're rushing through this?"

"Who, me?" she asked throatily.

"Talk to me, Jamee."

She swallowed. She didn't want to talk. She didn't want to give him time to see how poorly she was managing this. "We can talk later."

"Now." His hands circled her wrists. "No secrets, re-member?"

"I'm a little afraid," she whispered. "Okay, I'm a lot afraid. I'm not beautiful, I'm not experienced and I'm—"

"You're gorgeous, you're smart and you make me feel like I've been hit by a runaway train. Dear God, woman, would I be here if I weren't crazy with lust?"

"Truly?"

He gave a strained laugh. "Beyond hope of recovery."

Lust. She liked the sound of the word.

Her skirt flew up. His trousers skidded to the floor.

Jamee looked down and caught an audible breath. His thighs were burnished in the dancing light, muscles tense. "You're beautiful," she whispered.

Ian's eyes glinted. "I'm not beautiful. Lairds of Glenlyle are *not* beautiful." He pulled her close and kissed her eyelids. "We're stubborn, foolhardy and generally impossible. But we're not beautiful."

But he was. Her hands brushed the warm muscles at his shoulders, the lean expanse of his waist. He was as beautiful as a man could be.

Then Jamee looked into Ian's eyes and knew he would be

the only man who mattered in her life. She wanted to savor every second of what was happening between them.

"No more rushing?" he said.

"No more." She eased her hands beneath the soft white cotton that was his last piece of clothing.

He was huge and hard already. Jamee closed her eyes, loving the feel of him against her hands.

"You might have to revise that statement," Ian whispered, gathering the silk of her hair and pressing it to his lips.

Jamee looked at the hard lines of his face and knew there would be no turning back. "Does this mean I'm going to get my Christmas gift a little early this year?" she asked breathlessly.

Ian made a ragged sound and slid the fragile lace camisole over her head.

Then he took a breath. Another one, long and shuddering. "Santa Claus must have worked a lot of overtime this year," he said.

Jamee had never known that her skin could sing and her heart could fly.

Ian taught her. Generous, careful, infinitely patient, he made her long for sensations she had never dreamed existed. He showed her how to wait and trust while his slow, thorough kisses raised her to heights unimagined. As he moved down her body inch by inch, she gasped, mindless in his arms, surrendering to his tender mastery.

"Ian, stop. I want you to—"

"Soon." He found her hip and moved, finding the dewy heart of her.

Jamee caught a ragged breath at the stab of tiny claws of pleasure. "But you haven't…"

"I can wait. Hell, I've fantasized about this long enough."

His fingers pushed deeper. "God, you're tight. I'm going to enjoy every second of touching you like this."

Jamee flushed, wriggling slightly, which was a mistake considering that she was locked against his thighs. "I'm trembling, Ian. So are you."

His eyes hardened. "Trembling is good," he said thickly. "Wriggling is even better. Number one and number two, right at the top of my Christmas list." His fingers moved, fully sheathed in her heat, and need raced into heady madness. "Tremble for me now, princess. There's no one here but us."

She caught his shoulders and arched her back. Colors that had no names flashed before her eyes and unimaginable textures kissed her skin. Ian muttered hard words in Gaelic as the desire built between them.

Then Jamee cried out, the ends of reason unraveling. He drove her high, toppling her into a storm of color with his touch. "Merry Christmas," he whispered.

Her choked cry set Ian's blood aflame. He wanted to fill his hands with her. He wanted to take all day and all night, learning the taste of her passion.

Even when pain nudged at his eyes, he paid no attention. She clenched against his hand, hot and incredibly tight.

Pressure drummed through his head. The room blurred for a moment.

Bits of silver flecked Jamee's hair. He felt pieces of holly dotting his forehead. Merry Christmas, he thought bitterly. He had to tell her. She had a right to know about his future.

Muttering, Ian shoved Jamee's skirt down over her knees as there was a light tap at the door.

Ian pulled on his trousers while Jamee tugged on her camisole and blouse. Then Ian went to open the door.

Snow fell softly over the threshold. Angus looked from one

to the other, his expression unreadable. "Duncan sent me down. He said you two should come back to the house right away."

Ian felt the muscles tighten at his neck. "Did he say why?"

"There was a telephone call from London. He seemed to be doing more listening than talking, but he stopped long enough to send me down here after you."

"Thank you, Angus," Ian said. "We'll be right up."

The door closed. The tiny bell hanging above the mantel chimed softly in the wind. Jamee's hands trembled and she locked them at her waist. "Is it something to do with those men?"

"It's possible," Ian muttered.

Her eyes were huge. Passion was changing to fear, and the sight clutched at Ian's heart.

"You would tell me the truth, wouldn't you, Ian? If they were very close and something was about to happen..."

Once again Ian noticed a subtle shifting of colors, blue that blurred into purple and black. He managed a tight smile. "I'll tell you the truth as soon as Duncan tells me."

"And what about the rest?" Jamee caught his hand and held it tightly. "Tell me what's wrong."

He spent an eternity lost in her eyes. Somewhere he heard the slow, relentless tick of a clock.

His decision did not come easy. He had lied to people before, in the line of duty. Sometimes they had been women with lost children, and Ian had said the words they needed to hear, even when they weren't true.

But this was Jamee. Jamee, whose eyes lit with laughter when she ground snow over his neck. Jamee, who heard the chime of a bell and found magic like a child.

Jamee, who was being hunted down by men who had no souls.

He took a deep breath. "The truth, then." He squinted,

watching colors shift, the restless discharge of dying nerves. "Very well, the truth is that I'm…going blind."

He heard her gasp. He was extraordinarily still, at peace now that the words were said. And in that fragile, aching moment of peace Ian felt every sense work with extraordinary clarity.

Her body was rigid. Her breath came in husky little breaths. "Blind?"

"I'm afraid so. It seems to run in the family." He did not tell her the whole story of the Glenlyle curse. For someone who was not born in the Highlands, it would sound like madness. "Color change is one of the symptoms, along with the pain."

She straightened, moved awkwardly like someone waking from sleep. Her hand circled his arm. "Ian, I don't believe you. Your eyes—this is truly happening?"

"For two months now," he said, looking out over pale fields dusted with snow. Strangely, he felt no hint of bitterness, only regret. He had had thirty years to grow used to the idea and his fury was that he should find this woman only now. "It was one of the reasons that I refused the job when your brother offered it. I wasn't certain how long I had. I still don't know, Jamee." He turned, his face hard. "From now on, we'll take this hour by hour. The color has begun to change, and my vision could deteriorate quickly. I have backups, precautions, but if my sight goes, someone else will take over. No arguments. Can you accept that?"

He looked down at her face gleaming in the moonlight. Slick with tears. "Don't, Jamee. Don't cry for me. I've thought about this for a very long time and I suppose I'm as ready as any man can be for such thing."

She made a rough sound and slid against him, her chin to his chest. "But *I'm* not ready," she rasped. "I don't want *you* to be ready, either. There must be things that can be done."

"Don't." Ian ran a hand over his forehead, where an ache

was beginning to build. "It's a solid diagnosis, Jamee. There's no cause and no known cure. Anything else is delusion and I won't grab at phantom hopes."

Her hands trembled, twisted in the folds of his shirt. "You knew. All this time, you knew and you thought only about me. Ian, I don't want your last days of sight to be spent like this, full of work." She drew a ragged breath and pushed away, rising to her full height. "You told me once that I should never settle for anything but the best. That I should sleep on a pink sand beach and make love beneath the Southern Cross. Dammit, if what you said is true—"

"It is true," Ian said, without emotion or anger.

"Then go. Find that curving beach. Make love all night to a woman who isn't being followed. I won't let you stay here with me and become a target for a madman." With a little broken cry, she stumbled backward over the floor. "I meant it, Ian. It's over. I'm calling Adam and having him send someone else."

"No, you're not, Jamee." Ian walked slowly past a tiny mahogany chest covered with Christmas ornaments. "I don't quit until I can't keep you safe anymore."

"Adam doesn't know. He couldn't know. He would never have chosen you for this job if he did." Her hands clenched to fists as she stared at him with stiff dignity. "I'll tell him and then he'll fire you."

Ian kept coming. "Adam knows. The last time I spoke with him he insisted that I tell you."

She swayed, blinded by tears. Ian caught her by the door.

"Don't, Jamee." His voice was a hoarse caress. "I would rather spend every day of vision with you. Forget about some calculating beauty on a pink sand beach."

She shoved at his chest. "It can't happen, Ian. I won't let it."

She gave him a stricken look. "If you can fight for me, you can fight for yourself."

Ian gathered her carefully in his arms, overwhelming her rigid body with gentle strength.

A strength he was only now beginning to discover, as snow drifted softly past the windows and he realized that Jamee was the future he'd never expected to find.

She studied his face. "It's true? You're absolutely certain…"

"It's true." He tucked her head in the warm hollow beneath his chin. There were no other words to add.

So all he did was hold her while snow veiled the glen in an unspoiled blanket of white.

# CHAPTER NINETEEN

JAMEE WAS PALE and tense as they walked over the snow to the castle. At the door Ian stopped to pick a piece of silver tinsel from her hair while the bells in the gazebo chimed softly.

Sadly, Ian thought.

He touched her cheek. "I'll be up as soon as I talk with Duncan."

"But—"

"No arguments, remember? I'll tell you everything Duncan tells me, I promise."

They looked up to see their host standing in the hall, framed in a halo of tiny flashing lights. He cleared his throat. "Sorry to interrupt."

Ian watched Jamee slowly mount the stairs. At the top she turned, looked at him once. Her smile was shaky.

"Damn," he rasped as he fell into step beside Duncan.

"You're in love with her." It was a statement, not a question.

"What I feel for Jamee is irrelevant." A muscle flashed at Ian's jaw. "All that matters is keeping her safe. Tell me what you've found."

Duncan opened the door to his study and pulled a file from the paperwork on his desk. "Adam Night just faxed me these papers. They're photos of the brother of the man who planned Jamee's kidnapping seven years ago."

Ian studied the grainy photograph of a bearded teenager

staring brashly at the camera from behind mirrored sunglasses. His head was lowered, like a bull ready to charge, and shadows hid his features.

Ian stiffened as he looked closer.

There appeared to be a length of knotted rope sticking out of the boy's back pocket.

"Something wrong?" Duncan asked.

"That rope reminds me of the one I found in the kidnappers' all-terrain vehicle. Did Night find out if there was any Navy connection?"

"Apparently not. But Night had his people try the merchant marines. The brother was in for six months, then was asked to leave."

"Why?"

"Unstable personality. Paranoia alternating with periods of rage."

"So the motive may be more than simple profit."

Duncan rubbed his neck. "I'm afraid there's something else," he said. "Hidoshi's assistant, Rob…"

"What about him?"

Duncan jammed a hand through his hair. "He looked genuinely upset."

"Upset at what?" Ian growled.

"He said he met an American at a pub in Edinburgh. The man told Rob he was a friend of Jamee's and wanted to surprise her for her birthday. Rob's been phoning a number and leaving messages on a machine, giving him updates of where she is and the best times he can meet her by surprise. It was the same number that you found in the kidnappers' vehicle."

Ian's hands opened and closed. "When did Rob tell you this?"

"Just a few minutes ago. He said he realized that you and Jamee were—involved. That's when he began to suspect something was wrong with this American's story. Obviously, Jamee's not the sort of woman to have lovers all over the countryside."

"All so simple and innocent," Ian said grimly.

"That's what I've been thinking," Duncan said grimly.

"It's a very tidy explanation, you must admit. If Rob is involved, he would certainly have been prepared with a good story."

"Shall I have the constable hold him for questioning?"

"Not yet." Ian squinted, watching the outline of the fire.

Duncan laid a hand on his shoulder. "It's getting worse?"

Ian simply nodded.

"What can I do to help? Name it, and it's yours."

"I've got to keep Jamee safe and catch these lunatics fast. I want Rob watched at all times. Meanwhile, he might turn out to be very useful." He pulled a map from his pocket and unrolled it on the desk. "Here's what I think we should do."

THE NEXT MORNING Kara came down Dunraven's front steps holding her husband's hand while Jamee walked next to Ian. Rob came running out at the last minute. His face was flushed as he piled into Duncan's Land Rover after the others.

Snow fell around them, silent and pure as Duncan maneuvered over the glen toward the village.

The night had been long and busy, and the five faces were grim as they drove over the hill and down toward the quiet cove. When the peaks of the houses grew closer, Duncan looked back at Ian. "Almost there."

Ian took Jamee's hand. "Smile. You look as if the world's ending, *mo cridhe*."

Jamee straightened her shoulders and gave a tentative smile.

"Bigger," Ian said.

She forced the smile wider.

The narrow streets of the village opened before them, hemmed in by three dozen slate cottages. Beyond lay the ocean.

"It looks as if we have an audience," Duncan called from the front seat. He looked at Kara. "All set?"

She nodded. Her face was pale, but determined.

"Duncan, I can't thank you enough," Ian began. "You don't have to—"

His friend said something low and hard in Gaelic and then the car bucked to a halt.

Noisy and very visible, they made their way through Dunraven Village. Their laughter spilled between the narrow whitewashed cottages and drifted down to the single dock beside the sea. They passed the bright-red village telephone booth and continued toward the tiny pub, where a weathered shop sign creaked back and forth in the wind.

After ten minutes, everyone in the village was aware that Lord Dunraven and his guests had come to visit. After careful instructions, Rob had placed his calls.

Which was exactly what Ian had planned.

The others moved ahead and Ian turned to Jamee, frowning at her pallor. He tucked her scarf into her collar and pulled out her hair, which drifted about her shoulders in a silken cloud.

"So they will be absolutely certain it's me?"

A muscle played at Ian's jaw. He nodded. "It's the only way, Jamee."

"I know it is and I'm so frightened I'm about to heave up my breakfast."

Their fingers locked. "It's not far to the dock. Beyond that is the beach. Can you still manage this?"

After a moment, Jamee nodded. "I have to, don't I? Otherwise it will go on and on."

Duncan and Kara walked in front of them, shoulders brushing as they spoke quietly. The wind tossed bits of dried heather and gravel over the cobblestones like the hiss of angry voices. Jamee watched a line of breakers explode into foam, then spill away to nothing on the deserted beach. "How much farther?"

Ian's face was hard. "Less than a mile, I expect." High up in the glen a row of clouds dappled the purple hills.

"Ian, what if—"

Ian gripped Jamee's hand. "No what-ifs. That's *my* job, remember. Do you still trust me?"

Jamee smiled crookedly. "I've trusted you since I first wrestled you to the ground on the cliff. There was never a question of trusting you, Ian." Her fingers tightened on his. She faced the beach, almost as if afraid for him to read her face. "If something should happen—if this goes wrong, I want you to know that I…" She swallowed. "I've seen things differently, been touched and changed by knowing you. No matter what you say, I'll never lose those memories and I'll never want to." She spoke defiantly, her face to the cold sea.

Ian wished they were alone so that he could kiss the pulse that raced at her throat and let his fingers spill through her long hair.

A line of color shifted through his eyes and made his temples throb.

*So little time.*

"Nothing is going to happen, Jamee. It all ends here." His eyes hardened as they moved to the door of the pub. Duncan stood, knob in hand, waiting for Ian, his face tense with expectation.

Ian nodded faintly.

It had begun.

THE VILLAGERS watched with avid curiosity as the Laird of Dunraven and his vibrant American wife finished some last-minute holiday shopping with their friends. It was late in the morning now, and the sun slanted golden over the glen as Lady Dunraven's red-haired visitor excused herself from the hubbub and made her way alone to the pub's side door that led out to the beach.

She stood for a moment, shivering in the wind that gusted up off the sea. Tugging her scarf closer about her head, she started down the beach.

It was said she was a weaver from America. It was said she was a millionaire.

It was said she was a strange, free-spirited creature who liked to be alone.

Gossip traveled fast in an isolated Highland village, especially when the well-loved laird was concerned. Not a few eyes watched Jamee move over the hard-packed sand, though all were too polite to be obvious about it.

She moved on toward the headland that jutted like a brown arm out into the sea, and as she moved out of sight, interest faded. Conversation turned to the latest scandal in Edinburgh and what would happen when the North Sea oil finally ran out.

Only one pair of eyes watched Jamee then.

He darted from the pine trees, his footfalls muffled by the sand. The hard wind carried away his victim's cry as he bore down upon her. She turned and ran in a swirl of skirts, her scarf awry.

Her pursuer seized her roughly and jerked the heavy wool from her face. As he looked down, his eyes hardened in shock.

He pushed free, cursing. His boat was moored just beyond the headland and it would be only a few minutes' work to escape.

In a whine of wheels a battered green Land Rover stormed over the hill. Duncan wrenched at the wheel, plowing straight for the beach, cutting off the fleeing figure in black. The car was still moving when Ian shoved open his door and tackled Jamee's pursuer at a run.

The fight was savage and silent. Ian lunged and sent the man reeling, but he quickly recovered. They circled in silence, each waiting for the other to strike. Ian closed in.

Dropping back, the man dug at his outer pocket. He was raising a revolver when Ian's savage kick knocked him sideways. His arm spun upward and three bullets whined past, zinging harmlessly into the sand.

Two savage uppercuts laid the man unconscious, crumpled beneath Ian's panting form. Slowly, Ian rose to his knees.

Behind them, Duncan reached down to the figure in sandy skirts. "I hope you're all right."

Hidoshi Sato gave a crooked grin and pulled off his red wig. "Most fun I've had in months," he panted, pushing to his feet and wiping the sand off his hands. "I must have been fairly convincing."

"It was an amazing likeness. The bastard didn't realize until he had you in his grip."

The pair started down the beach, where Ian stood scowling over the prone figure of Jamee's would-be kidnapper. There was a loud honk, followed by the whine of a siren. A police car charged toward them.

Five minutes later, it was done. The man was handcuffed and turned over to the constable and the Security International backup team for interrogation.

"I'm nearly positive he was one of the men I saw at the cottage," Ian said. "That means, one down and at least one more to catch."

"He'll talk in custody, don't worry." Duncan watched the car pull away, sirens droning.

Ian frowned. "If not, I'll have a private visit with him. You can be sure I'll have names by the time I'm done."

"Right now, there's nothing more you can do, Ian. Meanwhile, that woman of yours must be terrified where she's hiding in the inn."

Ian turned slowly. He shook his head as if trying to rid himself of unpleasant thoughts. "You're right."

But there were still too many loose threads warning Ian that the danger wasn't over yet.

"YOU BE CAREFUL with those oak barrels, hear? That's eight-year-aged malt whiskey you've got before you." Angus McTavish stood with his hands on his hips, overseeing the movement of a dozen huge barrels of whiskey to the van that would carry them from the Dunraven distillery across the bay and then overland to Edinburgh. The workmen sweated and strained under the approving eyes of the villagers, who knew there would be an extra bonus this year for a magnificent product.

When all the barrels were loaded, Angus shut the doors carefully and locked them, then nodded at Duncan. "I'll see them safely where they're bound, never fear."

"I know you will, McTavish." Duncan turned as Kara appeared, closely followed by Ian and Jamee.

Or what *looked* like Ian and Jamee. It was hard to see beneath the new tartan hats they both wore.

Duncan swung open the door of his Land Rover and climbed inside. "Come on, you two." He joined his wife in the car. They watched Angus climb slowly over the hill, the van heavy beneath the cargo it carried. Only when he disappeared on the road that led east did Duncan start home to Dunraven.

ANGUS PULLED TO THE SIDE of the road on the mainland. There were no watchful eyes on the bare moor stretching around them. "You two can come out now."

As he spoke, wood grated on metal. One of the oak lids popped open and Jamee's head appeared. "I thought you'd never give the signal," she said, her face flushed.

"Never mind then, lass. The bounder's off in custody now. You did your job beautifully. So did Hidoshi."

The adjoining lid pulled free. Ian appeared, his shoulders covered with sawdust. "Everything quiet here?"

Angus nodded. "Perfectly as planned."

They settled into the front seat of the van and then the motor rose as Angus threw the vehicle back into gear.

The old man laughed softly and thumped the steering wheel. "Next stop, Glenlyle Castle."

## CHAPTER TWENTY

BROWN AND GOLD, the hills lay dappled beneath frothy banks of clouds. The grass was low, sheared by generations of sheep who roamed these lonely moors. In summer, wildflowers exploded over the glen and the air was bright with birdsong. But now in the far side of December, life moved more slowly, with an air of age and solemnity that befitted the close of the year.

Jamee stared from one side of the van to the other as they drove north, fascinated by every detail of the landscape, from the high, tree-covered cliffs to the narrow silver streams that spilled through dark crags.

Not quite two hours had passed when an arch of stone jutted above the horizon. Then another and another. Jamee sat forward, her breath catching as Glenlyle Castle soared into view, parapets and portcullis climbing across the rugged hillside.

"Those will be the north towers," Angus said. "Remember the time when you and Duncan hung out a sheet and tried to climb down?"

Jamee looked at Ian. He sat very still, his hands clenched. His eyes held something like regret—or terrible anticipation.

Jamee understood a small part of his torment, aware that he was going home to a place he loved, to people he loved, but unsure how much longer he would be seeing any of it.

She touched his hand. "It's still home, Ian," she whispered. "Nothing can change that."

There was a movement at his jaw. "No," he said softly. "Home. You're probably right."

As they rounded a bend, a massive square tower rose before them. Warm golden stone stretched between four higher towers, each capped with black slate roofs in graceful curves. The setting itself was part of Glenlyle's beauty, vast acres of dark green hills covered with hardwood and pines that ran down to the very foot of the castle.

"Amazing, isn't it?" Ian spoke softly. Emotion hardened his voice.

"Very, very beautiful," Jamee agreed.

A flag snapped at a high mast on the castle's roof. "They're welcoming you home." Angus raised one hand to point. "Duncan must have called ahead and told them you were coming."

Something dark swept through Ian's eyes. "The fewer people who know we're here, the better."

Angus frowned. "That brute is in custody and has already begun to talk. Between his information and the fingerprints that were finally lifted from the kidnappers' vehicle, his cohorts should be rounded up before long."

Ian said something low in Gaelic.

After a moment, Angus nodded.

"What?" Jamee said tightly. "What are you two talking about?"

Ian swung an arm behind her and planted a noisy kiss on her mouth. "Only about what the people at Glenlyle are going to say when they see the beautiful woman who will be on my arm."

Before Jamee had a chance to be nervous at the thought of a welcoming committee, she was distracted by the raised outline of a circular wall only a few feet from the castle gate. She sat forward, her blood hammering. "Stop here, Angus."

Before either man could speak, she opened her door and scrambled up the tangled, overgrown path to the rim of the hill.

Angus frowned. "My lord, isn't that—"

"Yes, it is," Ian said grimly. He started out after Jamee, slipping over the damp stones that had not known the print of human feet for months. As he scuffled up the hill behind her, a nest of birds broke from cover and exploded through the azure sky.

Ian tried to tell himself it meant nothing, but the lurch in his pulse told him differently. So did the pain that spiraled through his forehead as light shifted before his eyes.

*Blind Laird's Rock.*

He found Jamee bent over the broken wall of stone. She stared beyond, to the edge of the rocky cliffs and the sea raging far below.

Ian hadn't been here in fifteen years. Or was it twenty? He tried to stop the pressing images at the edges of his mind, an oppressive weight centuries old. "Let's go back to the car."

She didn't move, staring out to the sea. "What is this place? It pulls me, draws me. I can't say why."

Ian remembered the last time he had been here. Leaden sheets of rain had lashed the water beneath prongs of lightning. The next day, his father had lost his sight.

"It's called Blind Laird's Rock," he said tensely. "Legend says that a local woman laid a curse on the eldest Glenlyle son, then threw herself off the cliffs down there."

Jamee's gaze fell to the sharp rocks below. A shudder went through her. "You don't really believe that, do you? Your eyes weren't affected by some half-forgotten superstition."

"I'd be careful what you say about superstitions," Ian said softly. "We live with superstition every day here in the Highlands. Every tor has its tales, and the glens are filled with ghosts." There was a hammering behind his eyes. His whole body tightened in rebellion at being in this cursed spot. "Let's go, Jamee," he ordered.

Her hand trailed along the weathered stone. "There's something here, Ian. Something I should understand…" She moved slowly around the ruined wall. She was near the edge when her foot struck a loose stone and she staggered.

Ian lunged, pulling her back from the cliff edge. "Leave this alone, Jamee. Imagined or not, the curse is part of Glenlyle and part of me. I didn't come here to do bout with my past."

"Then what *did* you come here for, Ian?"

His fingers tangled in her hair. "To keep you safe. To make you happy…for as long as I can." He turned her back toward the narrow trail. "Now, will you stop asking questions and get into the car? After all," he added, linking his arm through hers, "it appears that there are a lot of people waiting to meet you."

THEY WERE LINED UP in two rows, men with calm, keen eyes and women with bright cheeks. None of them was smiling, Jamee noticed.

She breathed heavily as if she was preparing to run a gauntlet. "Who exactly did you tell them I was, Ian?"

"A textile designer I met in Edinburgh. We discussed the statues at the Royal Museum and I invited you out for tea."

Jamee smiled slightly. "Did I like you?"

"You adored me," Ian said. "Tea stretched into dinner and dinner stretched into dancing until dawn."

"And was I a good dancer?"

"The very best."

"What did we do after we danced?" Jamee murmured.

"My dear, a gentleman never tells."

Jamee bit back a laugh, but her smile faded as she faced the expressionless Glenlyle retainers.

Ian stared down the long line at the weathered faces of those who had served his family for decades. "It is a pleasure to be back on Glenlyle land," he said formally. "I'm pleased to bring a visitor with me this time. I am sure you will make Ms. Night welcome here at the castle." And then he turned. Looking down at Jamee, he pulled her into his arms. "*Very* welcome."

Rooks chattered in the nearby yew trees and from the end of the row a man's voice called out in Gaelic. Muted laughter filled the great courtyard.

Ian answered in Gaelic, never taking his eyes from Jamee's face.

A woman's voice rose, tentative, again in the ancient tongue. This time Ian's answer was gentler, and the courtyard filled with the ring of clapping.

Ian looked neither right, nor left, only into Jamee's eyes.

"What did you say to them?" she whispered, her face aflame.

"I'll tell you someday."

A dignified lady with crimson cheeks made her way over the flagstones, her cane tapping with every step. She stopped in front of Jamee and studied the two for what seemed like centuries, her hands tight on her cane. Then she nodded, speaking a phrase in the fluid, soft tones of the Isles.

Ian stiffened.

"What did she say?" When Ian did not speak, Jamee caught his shoulder. "Ian?"

"She said welcome home. To you, Jamee. Only she called you…Maire MacKinnon."

The white-haired lady held something out to Jamee. "She says this belongs to you," Ian translated tensely.

Jamee looked down at the fragile square of woven wool, its red-and-green pattern faded from centuries of wear. When she touched the fabric, a shudder ran through her. She smelled the tang of peat smoke and heard the drone of pipes, far away over the lonely glen.

The fragment of old tartan twisted beneath her fingers. Dimly, she heard Ian beside her, speaking urgently.

Jamee couldn't make out the words. The castle, too, had changed, surrounded by wild forests that ran all the way to the foot of its huge gate. And now there were horses, the sound of their shoes hollow on the cold stone.

Fear pulled at Jamee's chest. She couldn't be seen, not *here*. They were marching to war and would think her a spy.

No MacKinnon could scale Glenlyle's rough slopes in safety. She would be hung if she were found.

She tried to turn, to run.

But the vision grew, holding her, suffocating her…

*SHE CLUTCHED her shawl tighter about her shoulders, staring anxiously into the gathering dusk. A black cloud of birds scattered over the horizon and she whispered a prayer of protection.*

*No one saw her. No clansman walked the moors this night after the drums of war had been sounded..*

*Only the moon, chill and silver, marked her steps up the dangerous cliffs. Only her heart led her, guiding the precious gift for the man she loved.*

*She felt the thick, pounded wool, safe beneath her arm. Her dyes had set true, red and green, fierce in their fire. Maire thought of the hours she had taken over the dyeing and weaving of her cloth, breathing words of protection with every move of her shuttle. The rows were straight and true, but slightly changed. Maire's border now held a double edging of red surrounding the bold black stripe that dominated the center of the design.*

*She had chosen her pattern carefully. Intuition whispered*

*that the bright new border would provide protection to her be-
loved when he marched into battle. For Maire, as with all the
women of her line, the wool was woven not simply for warmth
and decoration but to strengthen and protect its wearer, by
God's grace.*

*A fine sprinkling of snow lashed her face as the wind
growled down from the north. One savage gust nearly yanked
the dense wool from her grip.*

*An omen?*

*She was close to the castle now. Perhaps too close. To walk
on MacColl soil was a fearsome risk, Maire knew. But some
instinct had whispered to her for weeks that Coll would be in
grave danger when the first snows fell.*

*She clutched her gift tighter as the snow grew deeper. She
saw the outline of the old stone well at the edge of the castle
wall, dim and gray behind a veil of white. There would be
sentries posted nearby, Maire knew. But Coll's young nephew,
Angus, was to wait for her in the shadow of the cliffs.*

*Shivering, she drew back into the lea of the wind, hidden by
a crevice on the stone face. She heard the skitter of small stones
and then Angus's smiling face appeared out of the slanting
snow.*

*"Here I am, Lady Maire. Coll was fashing that he could not
come himself, but the old laird watches his every move now.
Someone has whispered about your meetings, I fear."*

*Maire's hands trembled as she held out the precious length
of wool. "I must be gone then, Angus. Give this to Coll, will
you? And be certain he wears it when he marches away with
his kinsmen." She felt her fear rise, choking and bleak. "Promise me this, Angus."*

*"My promise is given," the boy said solemnly, making the
sign of the cross at his chest.*

*Only then did Maire's tension ebb. The boy would do just*

*as he promised. No vow made in the sign of the cross would be taken lightly.*

"Hurry then." *Maire looked up and heard the great oak gates creaking free. A line of riders clattered over the flagstones out of the castle's courtyard.* "Quick, before he's gone," *she whispered desperately.* "Remember your promise."

*She stood in the slanting snow, watching the small figure clamber up the hill. Through the damp white flakes she saw Angus dart to the second horse and call out.*

*The rider pulled out of the line, then bent down to speak to his young kinsman.*

Coll. *Maire felt the fire of his touch and the burn of his love, even though she could not see his face.*

*But it would be enough. Now she knew he would be safe, wearing her plaid to keep him warm and protected until he rode safely home to her.*

*She turned and made her way back down through the trees. The snow bit at her face, growing ever thicker.*

*So it was that she did not see Angus's small form lifted bodily onto the last rider's horse. Nor did she see the scowl of fury that settled over the face of Coll's cousin as he fingered the finely woven bolt of wool, which was to have been a gift to his hated rival.*

*It was a gift which would never be delivered. He would see to that.*

*Then even the boy's high, thin cry was blotted out, swallowed by the hiss of the gusting snow.*

HARD HANDS.

Biting wind. Voices raised in cold fury like forged steel blades.

Fear twisted in her chest.

An old fear. A wound that would not heal.

"Jamee."

The word was distant, foreign, without meaning. Even the fingers that dug into her shoulder had no impact or familiarity. She had to get home to the cottage, away from the spying eyes of those who would whisper their evil tales to the old laird.

"Dammit, Jamee, talk to me."

Dimly, she heard. That voice she knew. Those fingers, tense and hard, were familiar.

She blinked.

No snow. Only golden sun in an azure sky. Glenlyle Castle loomed before her, gray and proud, walls that she had not gazed upon for years. Perhaps for lifetimes.

Ian's fingers tightened on her shoulder.

*Ian.*

The name took shape; the face took on meaning. Slowly. Slowly.

"What is it, Jamee?"

Her muscles clenched. Danger wrapped around her even now. "I don't…know." Not exactly true. Images crowded at the edge of her vision, cold and heavy like sleeting snow. "I was here. At least it felt like here." Her voice broke. She looked down at the piece of old tartan in her fingers.

The gift. One of her weavings made so long ago.

A voice spoke out of the mist around her, soft, fragile words in an ancient tongue. This time their meaning was somehow clear to Jamee.

"'Tis home you've come to the glens, Maire MacKinnon." Blue eyes twinkled keenly in an ancient face and old fingers brushed Jamee's hand. "Aye, 'tis the weaver's mark you wear here in your palm." A thin, brittle nail traced the tiny scar at the middle of Jamee's palm, a birthmark and no more.

She shook her head. "No, I'm not Maire. I'm Jamee."

The blue eyes narrowed, keener still. "You have her skill,

lass. You have her fire in your blood. And the danger in the mist…" The old voice wavered, then fell away.

Jamee looked down. The fragile scrap of cloth was locked in her fingers. She moved to hand it back, but the old woman pressed her hand closed. "Yours, it is. Yours, the hands which made it. May it bring you rest and a welcome after your long wandering. With a great joy to you and your laird," she added softly.

Her cane tapped away over the flagstones. Jamee stood unmoving, half-expecting to see a line of horses bolt from the castle and a small boy dart through the falling snow.

More delusions? If so, how to explain this scrap of old plaid which dug deep into her memories, far back into the mists of time?

Perhaps she was simply going mad.

Ian's hands tightened over hers. "So now you speak the Gaelic, do you?" The question was teasing, but he looked just as shaken as Jamee.

"Gaelic?"

"That's what you were using just now with Widow Campbell. And *she* speaks not a word of English."

"But I don't speak Gaelic. Nor do I understand it." She looked down, dropping the scrap of plaid as if it burned her fingers.

Which it did.

The shadow of the castle fell over her like hands stretching out from a distant past. Jamee heard the tinkle of sheep bells far away in the glen and the sad whine of the wind.

"Put it from your head," Ian murmured. "I'm sure there's some explanation. Let's go inside now. I have something to show you."

Jamee was certain there was an explanation, too. She just couldn't think what it was.

# CHAPTER TWENTY-ONE

"So, WHAT DO YOU THINK?" Ian raised his arms and gestured to the colorful confusion around him.

Jamee stared at the long row of rooms at the north side of the castle, where the stables had once been housed. Instead of horses, the floor now held scraps of chenille, silk bouclé and bolts of bright velvet. Gold metallic braid was piled beside faceted eyes and tiny knitted caps. And in the middle of the cheerful chaos lay bears of every size and shape, bears of every color and price, spilling from boxes, crowded tables and floor-to-ceiling shelves.

Jamee swallowed hard. "You make bears?" She spun around and gripped Ian's shoulders, shaking him lightly. "You make *teddy bears* here at Glenlyle?"

"For four generations," Ian said without a hint of embarrassment. "My great-great-great-grandmother supplied several to King George IV when he visited Scotland. Back then, she specialized in sheep, as befitting a true Scotswoman. Today we also make rabbits and cats, but the bears are most popular."

As he spoke, a brawny man with jet-black hair strode through the clutter with a fluffy white toy sheep cradled in his arms. "We've had a wee bit of a problem with the eyes, sir. Perhaps you'd care to take a look."

Ian examined the animal carefully. One of the faceted eyes dangled precariously. Ian pulled a needle from the thick chenille. "You'll have to tack the eye securely, Geordie. Use heavier thread, I think. A shorter stitch would also do no harm."

To Jamee's amazement, Ian demonstrated precisely, his needle moving in swift, confident stitches.

"You can *sew?*"

"Sew?" The man named Geordie raised one brow. "The laird can set a better stitch than any man in the Highlands. And there's many a man in Glenlyle Village who has won awards for his skill."

Jamee was speechless. She moved to a row of desks, each with a letter and photograph pinned above the work area. "What are these?"

"Letters from the children who will receive each gift. All the toys made here at Glenlyle are individually planned for a particular child," Ian explained. "Each Christmas over a thousand Glenlyle bears are sent out from Windsor Palace as gifts to children's hospitals, orphanages and to the families of police and soldiers killed in action. Each bear has its own name and individual costume, depending on the particular wish of the child who has written. No two children will ever receive identical bears."

Jamee swept up a delicate silver bear with creamy fur, a velvet jacket and tiny spectacles. "Who is this one for?"

Ian glanced at the letter hanging above the desk. "A six-year-old girl in Liverpool. She lost her father last month in a lorry crash. Her mother wrote us, describing exactly what her daughter wanted, and we're going to see that she has it there waiting under the tree."

Jamee felt a lump build in her throat. She looked down the long row of worktables, each topped by a handwritten letter with a photograph of a different child. Each of those children would be touched with delight when they opened a box on

Christmas morning and found a toy that was specially designed as the answer to a secret wish.

Tears welled up in Jamee's eyes. Ian cradled two bears under his arms, fluffing the lace jabot on a very dignified bear wearing an exquisite miniature kilt.

Not bears, she thought. Ian McCall ought to be cradling children in his strong, gentle arms.

He ought to be holding *their* children.

Wanting swept through her, fierce and wordless. She yearned to see Ian's hands enfold the soft skin of a baby's cheek. She yearned to hear his laughter mingle with the soft chuckle of an infant. What was happening to his eyes mattered nothing to her. Blind or sighted, Ian McCall would be an extraordinary father.

And since he was already an ineradicable part of her heart, it was Jamee's duty to make him see that.

Ian took her arm and guided her back along the stone corridors that led to the main courtyard. "I'll give you the whole tour, if you'd like. Then I'm afraid I need to come back here and work." He rubbed his neck. "It's the busiest season now and I've been away for too long a time."

"Because of me," Jamee guessed.

After a moment, Ian nodded. He looked out at the courtyard, a furrow between his brows. Jamee saw that his jaw was tense. Was he in pain? Was it because of his eyes?

There was no point in asking, of course. He would never tell her.

"I want to see your favorite places, every one of them, beginning with that tower you and Duncan climbed out of. Then I'll let you go, McCall, and not before."

"I take it you don't want to see the dungeon?"

Jamee shivered. She thought of cold stone walls and the

small, scuffling sounds of unseen animals. "I think I'll pass on the dungeon tour."

"I suppose you're not interested in our collection of old tartans, either," Ian said innocently.

"Tartans? Genuinely old?" Jamee's face lit with excitement. "Made with the old vegetable dyes and not these horrible chemical colors?"

Ian nodded.

Jamee realized he was teasing her. She crossed her arms at her chest and tried to look nonchalant. "What would I be interested in old cloth for? Don't you have anything more exciting?"

Ian's lips curved. "I might be able to come up with something."

IT FELT DAMNED GOOD to be home, Ian decided.

He had forgotten how the sun poured golden over the courtyard flagstones and how the old clan flag snapped crisply in the wind. He had forgotten how pleasant it was to hear the rustle of fabric and the soft laughter of villagers making museum-quality toys in rooms that had once housed blood stallions.

Most of all, Ian had forgotten the joy of showing this old castle to someone who could appreciate it as much as he did.

He would call Duncan shortly and alert him to their safe arrival at Glenlyle. After that, he wanted to check the evaluation of the fingerprints taken from the kidnappers' vehicle. At least one and probably several more men were still at large, and Ian wanted them traced as soon as possible.

The danger was not over, not by far, but it still felt good to be home.

He hid a smile as Jamee gasped at yet another stone tower filled with old swords and priceless muskets. The Great Hall had impressed her, but the trip up the stone staircase had nearly been her undoing. There, flanked by rows of tapestries and old clan plaids, she had danced from side to side, while questions spilled rapid-fire from her lips.

And Ian had found an unexpected pleasure in giving every answer, explaining the stories of the old hunting McCall pattern and why its colors were so soft.

Now there was one last place to show her.

Ian rubbed his forehead surreptitiously, trying to ignore the pain behind his eyes.

"Those people in the workrooms," Jamee said softly, "they looked at me—at us—as if we were married. Or as if we were lovers."

"I've never brought another woman here, Jamee," he said flatly.

"I wasn't asking, Ian."

"I know you weren't. I just thought you should know."

The curve of her lips was beautiful in the last rays of the setting sun. Ian had never seen anything so fragile, yet so full of power. An image swept into his mind, and a second later, it emerged on his lips. "Would you?"

"Would I what?"

*Marry me.* Ian wanted her on his arm, laughing at him across the dinner table, smiling at him from his pillow. He wanted her socks in his sock drawer and her towel next to his. The force of that wish left him aching.

It was out of the question, of course.

"Would I do *what?*" Jamee repeated.

*Stay here with me forever.* He cleared his throat. "Pretend something for me. From now until Christmas," he said hoarsely.

Her eyes met his. "I'll pretend whatever you'd like, Ian. I'll be whatever you want."

As always, her honesty and generosity left him reeling. He looked down as her fingers gripped his.

"Shall I be a reckless American who falls in love with a

Scotsman on holiday? Or are you thinking of some sort of captive scenario?" She paused thoughtfully. "I'm not very good at following orders, but for you I'll try. Maybe we can take turns following orders. Although, if you had something with leather and ropes planned, I'm not sure I—"

He pulled her the width of the stone steps, buried his fingers in her hair and kissed her into silence while his heart threatened to hammer its way out of his chest. Even this she would offer, to be his erotic plaything in some dark sexual fantasy.

And Ian knew that she would be superb at her role, the way she was superb at anything she attempted. He decided that *his* heart was not up to the strain. "No, not that. Something gentler, yet far more dangerous." He kissed her eyelids softly, his breath playing over her cheeks. "Be my wife, Jamee. Just until I take you back to San Francisco for that Christmas Eve reunion with your brothers."

Jamee's breath caught as he kissed her nose. "Of course, if we *both* wore leather, that might be better. And instead of ropes we could—" She stiffened. "What did you say?"

"Wife." God help him, it was what Ian wanted. It was unreasonable, unfair to Jamee considering the bleak future before him, but Ian's yearning wouldn't be denied. "Until Christmas Eve when we have to leave. After that…we'll see."

"Ian, I—" Jamee caught a ragged breath. "Yes."

"Yes, what?"

"Yes, I will."

"But—"

Her smile was lopsided, breathtaking. "Don't try to wriggle out of your offer already, McCall." Jamee eased closer and rose onto her toes. Her body brushed his, seduced his. "I've said yes, and I *mean* yes." A dimple showed at her cheek. "Leather and ropes included. Maybe even harem pants and perfume oils and—"

"No more." Ian closed his eyes and groaned. Suddenly the ache in his eyes seemed distant and very unimportant. He reached out with his arms and with his heart, wishing for forever.

But willing to settle for now.

When he opened his eyes, he saw desire sheening Jamee's eyes.

Ian bit back a curse. He didn't need ropes or leather. The touch of Jamee's hands and the look in her eyes were almost more than he could bear.

And there was one place yet to show her.

MIST CURLED OVER the gray stones and lapped against high glass walls.

"Here?" Jamee pressed her nose to a glass door covered with elaborate ironwork, trying to see inside. "Why would you have a greenhouse here in the middle of the castle?"

Ian pulled out an ancient key and unlocked the door. The iron frame grated softly as the door slid open. "I'm going to have to have that door oiled."

Jamee frowned. "Stop avoiding my questions. What is this place?"

"This is the heart of the castle, the reason the stones were raised here centuries ago."

"Don't tell me it's some kind of dungeon."

He shook his head. "Water." He stepped inside. The scent of bergamot and narcissus rushed from the warm, damp conservatory.

"Water? I seem to recall seeing more than a few drops of that up there on the cliffs. Why would you need more?"

"That's the wrong kind. This is fresh water. Drinking water. The priceless element in any siege."

Potted oranges in white tubs scented the air with fragrance.

Against the glass wall cyclamen and daffodils rose in riotous colors. Jamee touched a branch of flowering jasmine heavy with white blossoms. "Siege? You mean, that nasty thing armies did with battering rams and boiling oil?"

"That's the one. Most castles had plenty of provisions stored for such an attack. Freshwater was the one thing no one could do without."

"So Glenlyle has its own spring. Very clever."

"My father sealed it in just before…his eyes gave out."

Dusk gathered against the lilac sky. High over head, Jamee could just make out the first faint sprinkling of stars. "Very nice," she said, stroking the tiny petals of a rare orchid. One brow rose. "My brother raises them. I happen to know these beauties are hell to grow. So who—"

"I take care of them. At least I did. Orchids used to be my hobby. Lately…I haven't very much time for hobbies." Ian cradled the petals tenderly.

Jamee swallowed, thinking about how he had touched her with the same tenderness.

Longing rose within her. "Ian, I want. That is, I wish—"

Their eyes met. This time Jamee was taking no chances on his chivalry.

She wore a peach and purple dress of crepe. She knew exactly how it molded her hips and clung to the soft lines of her breasts.

Ian knew, too, judging by the darkness growing in his eyes.

Steam curled around Jamee as her hands slid to the top button, freed it, moved to the next. "I was thinking…" She shifted her shoulders carefully and a hint of creamy lace appeared above her breasts.

Ian made a low, strangled sound. "You were?"

She nodded, managing to expose another inch of lace. "About something you said."

"I'm afraid to ask."

"It was something about being reckless and making love all night on a pink sand beach." She turned, in the process managing to brush one hip against his thigh.

His very rigid thigh.

"This looks as close to a pink sand beach as I'm going to find in Scotland. What do you think, McCall?"

He didn't move. Her face wavered before his eyes. It might have been the steam that veiled his vision. It might have been his eyesight failing.

Or it might have been the storm of emotions that her words unleashed.

"Jamee—"

A long Victorian daybed of rattan with chintz cushions stretched along one glass wall, guarded by a polished marble Cupid. Beyond that a natural hot spring bubbled up from a cavern in the solid stone. The gurgle and hiss of water seemed very loud in the sudden silence.

Jamee dipped a hand in the warm water, then rested one foot on the soft chintz. With careful grace she drew her skirt over her knee, revealing a silken thigh and a fragile lace stocking.

Garters. Dear God, she was wearing *garters*.

Ian felt sweat cover his brow. He was losing, and losing faster than he should have. "We might as well leave now. There's more to see," he said unsteadily.

Her head tilted. "I'm very sure of that." The white stocking loosened and began a slow descent down her thigh.

"Jamee—"

White silk spilled over Jamee's ankle. "What are you waiting for, McCall? I'm not a patient woman."

Ian swallowed. Raw desire slid into fierce protectiveness. He knew at that moment there would be no other woman for him after this, no other mouth that would provoke him to fine madness.

Jamee raised her other knee. Mist clung to her hair, dampening the auburn strands about her face while moisture clung to the damnably sheer wedge of lace at her chest.

Her dress shifted, its silk cupping her gently rounded breasts.

Ian swallowed. Her nipples were peaked, sweetly distended. He couldn't look away, suddenly sorry he had given her that third glass of champagne at lunch. But he realized the champagne made no difference. Jamee had changed in the last week. She was confident now, sure in what she wanted and willing to reach out for it. At any other time, Ian would have delighted in her confidence.

But not now.

Her fingers slid beneath the second stocking. She made a low, breathy sound. "I'm afraid I'm caught, Ian."

*He* was caught. Skewered. Burning at the sight of her. Electricity was doing somersaults through his body. "I'm sorry to hear it."

She lifted her skirt and turned slightly. "Maybe you could help?"

He wouldn't help. He could uncover, arouse, possess. But never help.

She looked at him, her eyes vulnerable and luminous as twilight gathered into darkness. "Please?" she whispered.

And with that word Ian was lost, lost so deep he didn't remember what he had been fighting. His hands opened, settling carefully over the warm skin above her knee. "Here?" he rasped.

Jamee's head tilted back as she sighed. "And there." She moved her leg against his hand. He felt her shiver when he inched beneath the edge of her stocking. "There's nothing caught, Jamee," he said gruffly.

"I'm so glad to hear it." She turned, her back braced against his chest. "Now you can take it off."

She was like his priceless orchids, velvet petals slick with dew. She trembled when Ian's hands went up instead of down. Her stocking slid on its own to the floor.

Beneath her skirt she wore a tiny, improbable scrap of lace that looked too delicate to have any purpose except to inflame him.

Which it was doing admirably.

Her hip eased back with apparent innocence against his thigh. Heat curled from the pit of his stomach, then plunged to his gut.

"So hot. All this lovely steam." She raised her arms. The silk dress parted, inched over her shoulders, then slid to the floor.

Ian stared, frozen, his heart slamming.

Gold skin spilled from a silk camisole topped with sheer lace. Every curve and shadow was visible beneath.

Jamee turned, her breasts peaked and dark against the silk. The narrow strap trembled and slid down her shoulder. "Ian, if I'm not—" she began unsteadily. "If this isn't what you want—"

*Lost.*

Ian made a flat, hard sound and brought his mouth to all that golden, glowing skin. In a second, the camisole was gone and one delicate crest trembled against his mouth.

Her heart raced. He felt it slamming beneath his fingers as he made his way downward with slow, maddening thoroughness. When she swayed, he guided her back against the marble Cupid while his sensual foray continued.

He wanted to see every soft inch while it was still possible. Then the final wedge of lace was before him, tantalizing.

He looked up and saw the uncertainty in her eyes. "Ian, I—"

The lace disappeared. He cupped her gently like the orchids she reminded him of, fragrant petals glistening with dew. She was fire beneath his hands as he traced the soft shadow of her ribs, then the damp auburn curls that clustered lower.

With lips and gentle tongue.

"Please, Ian, I can't—"

"Yes, you can. Now, *mo cridhe*."

She arched against him, her fingers digging into his hair. She balanced on the fine edge of passion, and then he catapulted her off into worlds that had no name.

The colors in the room faded with the gloom of twilight. But other senses took the place of Ian's vision. He heard the soft, husky rasp of her breath and smelled the sweet, floral scent of her skin.

He wanted more. In a second, he found it.

His mouth settled over her heat with no more barriers. Like a trembling flower, she moved beneath him, sleek with the sweetness of her need. Ian did every carnal thing he'd dreamed of for too many sleepless nights, perversely driven to take forever as he teased her to madness, stretching out the pleasure until they both knew torment.

And Jamee was better than any fantasy, honest and generous in his arms, crying out his name as the stones dissolved beneath her and she fell.

Or she flew. Into forever. Into seas of silver where wishes were tiny fish that nibbled at her hands.

Ian catapulted her off into worlds that had no name. Into colors she had yet to experience. He felt the desire surge through her, lift her high and leave her shuddering, breathing his name.

So beautiful.

His hands tensed and slid deep, his mouth a counterpoint to his hands. "I love you, Jamee," he whispered over the tangled silk that cast back his own heat.

Where she would sheathe him.

Ian channeled all his senses into touch. Slow. Deeply. Until he watched her turn inside out and come apart against him again.

Once.

Twice.

Impossible to want her more or need this less.

His belt hissed free. It was a race now, hunger against hunger. Cursing himself for the pride that had made him wait, Ian fumbled with the last of his clothes.

Her breath caught. Definitely caught. "God, Ian, you're a sight."

"Is that good or bad?" he rasped.

"Magnificent, I'd say." She eased her hands down his chest. Each touch was madness and infinite need. She took her time showing him just how much she wanted him.

The stars were lost high above when her hands cupped his heated male length, sweetly goading. "You said you didn't come to do bout with your past. So prove it, McCall." Her lips curved. "Now."

With a groan, Ian closed his eyes. He caught her hips and impaled her slowly. He could barely see her face, little more than a dim outline against the gloom of twilight. But Ian felt her, felt her hands clench at his shoulders and her hips move in sudden urgency.

With a low groan he tensed. One stroke brought him inside her. He moved with savage focus, inch by inch, pleasing them both even as they perched on the jagged edge of passion.

One more thrust. Her breath caught in shocked delight, while her hands strained against him. Another, while his heart tried to slam free of his chest. Heat was a madness in his blood as she rocked against him, opening, welcoming each hot thrust, as frantic as he was.

"Sweet heaven, Ian, this is— You are—" She gave a soft groan. "Why did you make us wait so long for something so wonderful?"

Ian feasted on the color in Jamee's body, the vibrant textures of her voice.

Every second brought him deeper. He wanted to be the first and the last for her, but he would settle for being the very best, the one she would always remember.

"There are no rules here, Jamee. No conditions. Only what you want."

"You. Just like this." She tensed, her eyes dim. "Ian, I can feel you. You're so deep that we…"

Her nails dug into his back. With a startled cry, she arched against him, skin tight to slick skin.

Desire slammed through him as she spun away, velvet skin clenched around him. And this time, Ian followed, finding light and color hidden in her laughter, joy shimmering from her skin and captured in her hair. She turned him inside out. She made him reckless. She forced him to close his eyes and open his soul instead.

And then she taught him how very much he loved her.

BREATHING WAS a painful effort. Moving was beyond imagining. But smiling Ian could just about manage.

So he smiled. Liking the little sounds she made when he eased her down against the couch. Loving the way his touch made her shudder while aftershocks rippled through her.

"You were…" She raised one hand, then let it fall limply. "That was…"

"Not bad." The feel of her skin had him hardening again. "But it gets better."

She shook her head slowly, more than a little drunk from the power of the emotions flooding through her. "No way. Impossible. Negatory, McCall."

His fingers slid between their heated bodies. His lips nuzzled one rosy nipple.

Her eyes snapped open. "But you just—" She swallowed. Her head fell back as he did slow, forbidden, wonderful things that sent new flames of sensation racing inside her.

"That's right, I did," Ian said harshly. "And now I'm going to do it all over again."

Her hands twisted in his hair, pulling him closer. "I don't suppose arguing would do any good."

"Not a bit."

She settled over him perfectly, her body already knowing just how to touch him, how to cradle and arouse him.

"Good," she whispered raggedly as he moved deep inside her.

JAMEE OPENED HER EYES a century or two later. Every inch of her body felt hot and sensitized, and she seemed to have lost her bones somewhere.

Ian was bent over the spring. She savored the sight of his muscled back, the long tapering legs. He studied the water, then scooped up a handful.

"I'm glad I didn't argue," she said huskily.

"So am I." He sank down beside her and brought the water to her mouth. "Drink this. It's magic. The oldest kind," he said gravely.

Jamee felt her throat tighten at the fierce tenderness in his eyes. "Some kind of love potion that you McCalls have been hiding for generations?"

His lips curved. "Something like that. Go on, drink." His hands moved to her mouth.

Jamee closed her eyes and drained every warm drop, her lips nuzzling his palm. She swallowed, tasting the faint metallic bite of iron and salt and probably a dozen other minerals. Heat teased her mouth, then plummeted, filling all the hidden corners of her heart as Glenlyle's spell was cast irrevocably around her.

Ian's damp hands settled over her breasts and cradled her with infinite tenderness. "Are you seduced yet, lass?"

"Almost. Maybe with some more encouragement…"

He raised her in powerful hands and carried her to the spring. "Legend says that this spring arises from deep within the earth, its waters purer than anything found above ground today. And this is the heart of the castle, Jamee. We keep this locked for safety, since whoever controls this spring controls Glenlyle."

She realized what he was saying, just how much he was offering her then.

Control over this place and himself, as Glenlyle's lord.

"What I'm trying to say," Ian whispered raggedly, "is that I adore you. Admire you. Respect you. Like you." His mouth settled on hers. "*Love* you."

Words failed her. Her vision grew blurred. "That's some love potion, McCall," she said unsteadily.

"Now you have to answer."

"Do I get to answer now? Any way I want?"

"Anyway and anything. All except for no," he muttered.

She pulled him into the water. Slowly, she slid down along his rigid frame while the soft waves bubbled up around them. Her hands moved up his arms and closed over his shoulders while she wrapped her long legs around his waist and brought him all the way home inside her.

"What I'm trying to say here, McCall," she said breathily, "is that I adore you. Want you wildly. Desire you madly." Her back arched as he began to move inside her, slow, shuddering strokes that left them both breathless. "Couldn't even *think* about living without you."

"I might hold you to that."

The current played around them, a silken counterpoint to the deep, pounding rhythm of his body inside her.

Jamee's hands closed. Desire spun a silver path within her. "Hold me to it," she ordered. "Forever, McCall." Her blood sang. Her skin burned.

And the fit of him was smooth, aching perfection.

"No matter *what,*" she whispered as need broke free and drove her high, then swept them both down into oblivion.

# *CHAPTER TWENTY-TWO*

"THERE'S NO *ANSWER*." Duncan slammed down the telephone and sank back in his chair.

Kara drummed worriedly on his desk.

"I've been trying since midnight. Dammit, this isn't like Ian."

"Have they found the other man yet?"

Duncan shook his head. "My contact in Edinburgh says they're close, but still no definite confirmation. It's just not *like* Ian to be out of touch, especially at a time like this." Duncan looked out the window, where snowflakes swirled over the lawn. "I'm going to take the helicopter up there," he said.

Kara stood up promptly. "In that case, I'm going with you."

"But—"

His wife's face turned mutinous. "And don't even *think* about arguing with me, Duncan MacKinnon."

SMOLDERING PEAT.

Wind gushing up through the glen.

Two lovers who slept before the hushed breath of dawn.

Jamee turned and snuggled into the pillow. A muscled thigh pressed against her hip and familiar hands stroked down her back. From somewhere in the distance she seemed to hear a crow call shrilly from the glen.

*For now. For tomorrow. For all eternity.*

Time twisted and turned in on itself, bent by ancient dreams that felt no older than yesterday. She sat up, blinking.

No thatch roof.

No smoking fire. Only a lover whose warm body lay pressed against hers.

Jamee took a slow, ragged breath as her dreams scattered. For a moment, the past was so close that it smothered her. Longing swelled within her like a scream as she remembered the regret in Maire MacKinnon's eyes.

So near. So familiar.

Jamee looked down and saw her hands shaking. Images of a man's face danced before her. Even now, she felt the mark of his lips and the cry of his voice in the furious climax of love.

Delusions brought on by stress? Or was there truly some message she was meant to read in the old portrait she'd seen at Dunraven?

Jamee felt the rise and fall of Ian's chest in sleep. The gentle sound of his breath was barely audible over the soft murmur of bubbling water near the cushions where they lay.

She turned silently, careful not to wake him. Stretching, she caught a handful of spring water. Her reflection stared back at her, broken by tiny ripples. As she stared at the fragmented image, Jamee heard the drum of hoofbeats and the cry of anguished voices.

She closed her eyes, feeling the loss of a woman who had walked these stone corridors centuries before. Like the restless water, memories stirred from deep in her consciousness. Moved by an instinct she could not name, she envisioned the weaving that she had finished only that afternoon. Since her arrival at Glenlyle, the colors had called to her, great streaks of fuchsia and purple laid over squares of plum, teal and gold. Some compulsion had drawn her to her loom, where her restless shuttle had spilled out row after row of vibrant cloth. Now Jamee realized why.

The weaving she had recently finished was *not* meant for Dunraven at all, but for Glenlyle. Only after she had seen Glenlyle for herself could the design be completed.

Her hands shook. She thought of another dawn, another woman whose gift had been in vain.

This time Jamee must *not* fail.

*THE DAYS STRETCHED BY, as cold and cheerless as the wind that growled down from the north. Maire stayed at her loom, driven to create while she fought the despair that came to her every night in dreams. Heather-green and wild crimson ran in slashes beneath her shuttle, but even the bright colors could not touch the shadows that woke her gasping from sleep.*

*Each day, she waited for news of the MacColl men who had marched out to war. And every night, no word came in answer.*

*Her last weaving was finished late one afternoon when she heard voices outside her cottage. The doors were flung open and snow drifted inside on the wind.*

*She had hoped for Angus. Instead it was one of her brothers, bold and confident with a smile that had won him more than one night in the arms of a willing Highland beauty.*

*"I've come to take you back to Dunraven, lass."*

*Maire crossed her arms at her chest. "Nay, not yet. I've still more weaving to finish." It was a lie. Her work was nearly done, but she would not tell her brother that. Meeting Coll at Dunraven would be impossible.*

*She stood up and rubbed her throbbing back, then tossed another wedge of peat onto the fire.*

*Her brother's face hardened. "Who is the man, Maire?"*

*She stiffened. Had the gossip finally reached the halls of*

*Dunraven?* "'Tis no man. I've work to finish, as you well know."

He ran one hand over the fine plaids strung completed at her loom. "'Tis a lie, Maire. Only a man could have put such a light in your eyes. Only a lover could have left such a burn on your cheeks." He turned away and paced silently, stopping at the door. "It's Coll, isn't it?"

Her pale face was answer enough.

"Then you should know that they've come back," he said harshly. "Only two hours ago, they made their way up the glen. The few that were left, at least."

Few.

The room spun. Maire reached out, anchoring one hand against the solid beam of her loom. She did not ask how her brother knew.

Coll.

She swept up her shawl and turned wildly toward the door. Her brother stopped her, one hand clenched at her wrist. "Will he marry you, lass? Or is your love only for shadows, a thing of shame to him?"

She bit back a ragged sob. "He will marry me." She shoved his arm aside and plunged outside. "And I'll have him even if he does not."

"Maire, come back. You can't go up there. No MacKinnon has ever gone to Glenlyle Castle."

"Then maybe it's time one did," she said hoarsely.

DARKNESS LAY HEAVY over the deep forest. The moon was gone, the stars twinkling coldly behind a thin veil of clouds as Jamee made her way along the path toward the cliffs. She had left Ian sleeping in the vast bedroom beneath the stone arches of the highest tower and crept past Angus, who was drinking a cup of black coffee in the quiet kitchen. One of Ian's security men watched the front gate, but she had slipped past while he made his rounds down the hillside. It had been easier than she'd feared, for his worry was for strangers trying to enter, rather than for visitors trying to leave.

She moved by instinct, driven by a vast, wordless sense of dread. It was danger, and yet not danger. It was fear, yet something worse—something that trembled just beyond the edge of her knowing.

At the cliffs she would find her answers.

Beneath her arm, she carried her tapestry, a blaze of colors meant as a benediction. Or a healing.

Bony claws of gorse slapped her ankles as she stumbled through the darkness. The ancient stones were slippery with frost and she kept drifting from the narrow path.

But Jamee straightened her shoulders. She would offer her wish for Ian, here among the shadows of his past. And she must do it now, by darkness, before it was too late. Her mind screamed that the danger lay before him now, not her.

The wind moaned through the pine trees, bending the branches low before her. Jamee thought of clutching hands that reached out from the past.

So close now…

*THE GREAT HALL was shrouded in shadows, veiled with smoke. Bowls lay overturned on the long wooden table and dogs lay sleeping beside the dying fire. Maire clutched her shawl tighter about her face as she searched the great room.*

*An old man sat hunched before the fire, a goblet caught in his gnarled fingers.*

*The laird of MacColl.*

*Maire plunged forward. At the hearth, the dogs growled softly and raised their heads.*

*"Where is he?" she rasped. "Where is Coll?"*

*The old man looked up. His eyes were broken chips of darkness. "Who are you to ask?"*

*"One who cares," Maire whispered. "One who loves him."*

*The old man made a drunken, despairing movement with his hand and the wine goblet toppled to the table. He poured another with shaking fingers. "Many are those who have loved my son. And none more than I." His voice hardened and he emptied the goblet in a single movement, then straightened, staring at his visitor. "Your name—give it to me now."*

*Maire drew herself to her full height. "My name matters not. What matters is Coll. Let me see him, I pray you."*

*The laird of MacColl made a low, furious sound. "Too late. Too late for words or seeing. What's done is done."*

*Fear pressed at Maire's chest. "No," she whispered.*

*The man sat staring into the fire. Maire had the sense that he had forgotten her existence. "Broken, all of them. Our enemies were warned. Well-prepared, they cut us down one by one. Dear Lord, the noise. The slaughter." His voice broke and he threw the goblet into the fire. Light spilled off the jeweled rim as the last of the wine hissed onto the embers.*

*"No!" Maire watched blindly, her nails digging into the wool of her shawl. "My cloth, it was to protect him. It should have kept him safe."*

*Her words seemed to rouse Coll's father. "Yours? What croft are you from that I do not know your voice? I should have seen you here at the castle before. Are you from Angus's people across the glen?"*

*"Where is Coll?" She hurled the question like the great claymore Coll wielded in battle.*

*He sank forward, his eyes mad with loss. "Gone. Just like all the proud MacColls who marched away from the glen."*

Dead. Coll was dead.

*The hall blurred. The fire bled to cruel orange and black.*

*He was gone, slain without her feeling it. Somehow that knowledge was the bitterest of all.*

*She threw up her hands. "No," she moaned.*

*"The laird is right. Coll is gone." Leather shoes moved softly behind her and Maire caught the scent of musk and roses. "Dead. Because of you," a woman's voice said hoarsely, "you cursed MacKinnon."*

*Maire shrank back before that fury. "There was nothing of darkness in my work."*

*"You lie! The cloth you made was evil, loomed for our clan's destruction. This cloth." The woman threw a length of wool at Maire, who caught it, frowning.*

*"No," she whispered. "This is not my work." The pattern was weaker, crooked. The colors were faded and pale. There was no joy to the sett and no life.*

*Maire ran her hands over the fabric, shaking her head. All the prayers she had bound into warp and weft, whispered night after night as she worked, were missing from this indifferent counterfeit. "What have you done with the cloth I made for Coll?"*

*"We took this from his body. He wore it when he fell."*

*Maire dropped the wool, chilled. The edges were crooked, slashed by knife strokes.*

*An oppressive sense of evil settled over her. "What foul trick have you played on Coll?"*

*The laird rose and shoved away his chair. "So you are a MacKinnon. My son lay with a MacKinnon whore and now he is dead." He pulled a jeweled dagger from his cloak, the blade gleaming in the shadows of the hall. "For this you shall die, witch."*

*Maire barely heard, looking down at the cloth on the floor which was dark with Coll's dried blood.*

*"Your sorcery with the loom has brought this death upon*

*us," the laird thundered. He swayed drunkenly, then braced one hand on the long table. At his feet the dogs moved nervously.*

*Then his voice rose in a furious command.*

*Men strode from the stairwell and the arched side doors that led to the kitchen. In a matter of seconds, three dozen clansmen stood with weapons in hand, awaiting orders.*

*"Take her out," the laird cried. "Take the witch to the cliffs. Her evil will stain Glenlyle no more."*

*Maire barely felt the cruel fingers closing around her arms. She barely sensed her body lifted, dragged from the smoky hall.*

*There was no point in feeling or in fighting.*

*With Coll dead, there was no point in anything at all.*

JAMEE HEARD THE SEA somewhere far below her, a low, steady drumming. The stars were gone now, veiled by clouds.

The night was still. The wind was still.

Fragments of memory burned through her head and she knew with blinding certainty that an old tragedy was about to be repeated.

Blackness stretched before her. Jamee felt the rugged outline of the stone well and eased to the crown of the hill. No one would bother her. The security team was assigned to guard the front gate, which was the only place the castle could be penetrated.

She looked east, watching for the first faint specks of pink that would hail the dawn. Her gift would be given then. With it the past would be laid to rest, she prayed.

It was her only wish, offered up in the still of the night with a heart of fierce and focused intensity.

Something moved behind her. Darkness parted and resolved into a hard, angry body. Cold laughter spilled over the hillside.

## CHAPTER TWENTY-THREE

SOMETHING WOKE IAN from odd, fragmented dreams filled with peat smoke and the stamp of horses. He remembered the agonized cry of a woman.

He sat up sharply, his breath coming fast. "Jamee?"

Something brushed against his foot.

"Where are you, Jamee?"

The moon was gone. No light filtered through the glass windows of the master bedroom high beneath the north tower.

Again came the brush of warmth against his leg. Definitely fur. A pair of amber eyes blinked, glowing from the darkness. Cat's eyes.

"What are *you* doing here?" Ian snapped, feeling like a fool for talking to a cat.

The eyes moved. A moment later, something clattered to the floor beside the bed.

Frowning, he turned on the bedside lamp, then reached down for the hard plastic outline of his beeper. Even as he touched it, he felt the vibration of an incoming message.

Cursing, Ian fingered the dial and read the luminous number. *Duncan.*

The phone was just where it had fallen, wedged between his shirt and two damask pillows. Jamee's clothes were gone. Ian stabbed out a number.

No response. The phone was completely dead. A cut line?

He pushed to his feet. Instantly waves of pain dug at his forehead. Dreams tangled his logic, playing at the corners of his vision. From somewhere deep within the castle's heart he seemed to hear a woman's voice, raised in grief.

The sound shook him, phantom and yet truer than the stones beneath his running feet. He had a sudden memory of pain burning through his chest, dealt by an enemy's blade. He thought of a man who had lain in fever, caught on the very edge of death. He had failed her then. And he had lost the woman known as Maire MacKinnon.

Ian's hands shook as he found his way to the Great Hall and pounded up the stairs to his office. The phone line was dead there, too. Cursing, he shouted for Angus and the security officer in the castle courtyard.

"Jamee's gone," he snapped. "Take two men and search the castle. Send the rest out over the grounds. Have one of them use a cell phone to find out why Duncan MacKinnon paged me." He didn't stop for further explanations. The cold stab of fear at his chest told Ian that only perfect logic would save Jamee now.

THE CAT'S FOOTING was sure and certain even on the sharp rocks. He inched through the darkness, eyes burning as he relied on the ancient senses of a hunter.

Light danced beside him. "You are certain this is the way, Gideon?"

The cat meowed once.

There were strange sounds from the shadows, a dozen unfamiliar scents that called to him. But Gideon held to the desperate task before him.

"I should have known. I should have *realized*." Terence Night's lanky frame took shape in the darkness, and the turmoil in his eyes seemed at odds with the color that shimmered around him. "I had a sense about that young man. He was too interested, too quick to be helpful. At the time, I thought he was simply being nice." He made a ragged sound. "When will I learn that most people aren't nice?"

The cat was outlined against the sky as he made a twisting flick of his tail.

"Yes, I know that trusting is in my nature. But if I hadn't been so trusting, Jamee wouldn't be in danger now. She wouldn't be trembling, her fear about to choke her." His light dimmed for a minute. "Gideon, how much *longer?*"

The cat gave a low cry and then disappeared behind a row of rocks.

"BLAST IT, DUNCAN, how much *longer?*"

Adam Night sat tensely, his fingers clenched on the window of the helicopter chattering noisily over the darkened glen. He had arrived at Dunraven just in time to claim a seat as Duncan left for Glenlyle.

"Five minutes. Maybe less, Adam. We're above Glenlyle land now. In a few minutes, we should be able to see the castle."

"What I want to know is why?" Adam said harshly. "Why would he target Jamee after all these years?" His hands opened and closed. "But it doesn't really matter. All that matters is getting her back safely." His voice wavered. "This man, McCall. He's good. The best, you said?"

"He's good," Duncan said grimly.

"He damned well better be." Adam stared down into the darkness, then stiffened. "Isn't someone down there running along the cliff?"

PAIN BURNED THROUGH Jamee's forehead as she tried to push to her feet from the sharp stones. "Who are you? What do you want?"

A match hissed and light flared around her. "I want everything. Everything that's yours. Everything that should have been ours." A face took shape from the darkness. Long hair. Sulky eyes.

Jamee blinked. "Rob? What are *you* doing here?"

His laughter was sharp and very cold. "Not Rob, Thomas. Thomas Starkey. Don't you recognize the name?"

Jamee eased backward, fighting a wave of panic. A corner of the stone well was behind her, digging into her back. Beyond that lay emptiness and two hundred feet of cliff straight down to the beach. "Starkey. Oh, God, not the man in the car. The man who shoved me into the closet." Her voice shook.

"That's the one. You remember my brother even now, don't you? Your brother Adam was in the same foster home that we were in. It was *us* your parents were going to take, *us* instead of him."

Rob's lips twisted with anger. "Then they saw Adam. Adam with his Indian face and his quiet arrogance. How soon they forgot about me and my brother."

Jamee's fingers slid from the rock. "You knew Adam back then?"

"He was cunning. Always so cool. He knew just how to use his power over other people, especially adults. He took away what should have been ours, but my brother and I waited. We survived. And we swore that one day we would have everything he had stolen from us."

His eyes glittered, sharp as glass. "You had velvet dresses and little lace dolls. Your brothers had new shoes, warm coats and laughter, while we had nothing, only each other. He drove trucks so I could enter the merchant marine, but even that was ruined. And one day my brother was taken away, thrown into prison." His boots tore across the heather as he lunged for Jamee. "Now your Adam will die, but first you're going to bleed—to pay for what your parents did, Jamee Night. I promised my brother I would see to that."

Jamee felt his hands scrape at the stone wall, only inches from her neck. She threw herself backward with a gasp. She fell sideways, then plunged down the sharp, rocky incline. Little stones hurtled after her, digging into her cheeks and drawing blood.

The figure in the shadows loomed over the edge of the hill. "Where are you, Jamee? Talk to me. You can't get away this time."

His voice fell. Changed. "Come out, little girl. You're the meal ticket, remember?"

Gray light stole across the horizon where the sun struggled to break free of the hills. Jamee clawed her way over the gorse and heather, trying to find a place to hide before dawn broke.

"There's no escaping. Why even try?"

She heard the snap of metal and then a beam of light tunneled through the darkness.

"I'm right here, right behind you. We'll squeeze all the money we want out of your brother. Then we'll dispose of you—just the way we're going to dispose of Adam." He spoke in a strange singsong, and Jamee realized he was no longer reachable by logic.

She bit back a moan as light crisscrossed the ground before her, capturing her hand in its glowing beam before she pulled away.

"I see you," her stalker hissed. His feet scraped on the rocky incline, already far too close.

And then the earth fell away. A row of ragged stones rose before her, and beyond that lay the chill darkness with the wind snarling off the sea.

Jamee stumbled to her right until the way was cut off by a solid overhang of impassable granite. There was no going forward and no going backward. She would die here, caught on this cliff, just as another woman had died here centuries before.

Dry undergrowth rustled behind her. "They won't find me. I took another photographer's place at the last minute. I've been watching you for months with a little help from a woman in your brother's office. It didn't take much to get her to fill me in on every one of your destinations. It must be because of my kind face," he said, the words grotesque and mocking. "Now I know everything there is to know about you, Jamee Night," he whispered. "It was so easy to pass as one of Hidoshi's staff. All I had to do was pretend to be waiting to shoot—always waiting for the weather to clear or the light to be better. Fools, all of them."

From the far side of the hill came the shudder of motors. Jamee stood at the edge of the cliff while wind gusted up around her, straight up from the sea. Dear God, they would be too late.

"No one can help you. Either come with me now or you'll take a pleasant dive off the edge of this cliff." His laughter grew sharp as rocks rattled hollowly in the darkness. "Do you hear me, little girl?"

Motors coughed and lights exploded over the hillside. Jamee blinked, blinded. A second later, she realized that her pursuer would have the same response. She lurched toward the ruined well, her feet slipping on the bare stone. Her shoulder struck bone and muscle, then she plunged sharply down the hill.

"Dammit, you're *mine!* You're not getting away now. I've waited too long for this."

Jamee slid desperately down the hill. Jagged fingers of scree dug into her legs as light flooded the stone ridge. A helicopter screamed over the top of the castle, then dived toward her.

Jamee could have sworn she saw a dark shape outlined against one of the rocks, tail erect and ears arched forward.

She heard a panting breath behind her and ran, biting back a cry of pain as a boulder grazed her ankles.

A blade hissed through the air, striking her shoulder.

Wincing, she stumbled as the whirling blades rushed down above her.

"Get down, Jamee!" Ian roared. A shot screamed over the heather.

Twisting, she leaped a row of boulders and fell in their lea as another shot rent the air. Gravel and dry heather dug at her face, caught in the updraft of the helicopter while Rob worked his way down behind her, cursing.

He clambered over the rocks, inches away. "You're mine." His knife burned in the cold light cast from the sky. "No one's taking that away from me," he hissed.

A blur of gray plunged over the hillside as he spoke. Cursing, he toppled backward, his knife clattering onto the well. Jamee heard the high, shrill cry of a cat and then Ian hurled himself from the helicopter.

There was another burst of gunfire, and Jamee saw her brother plunging over the hill. Then Ian's arms were around her, his hands locked against her waist.

"Thank God, you're safe."

The faint, sweet smell of bruised heather filled her lungs as Adam cursed at the top of the hill.

"Go, Ian," she rasped. "It was Adam he was after, Adam all along. He—he's mad."

Ian's hands left her. He stumbled toward the two bodies silhouetted against the beam of the helicopter while Jamee's heart raced in sickening fear.

Adam twisted, driven back toward the edge. It might have been her imagination, but years later Jamee would still wonder at what she heard next. The sound was low, almost other-worldly, the furious growl of an animal from the wild. There was a blur of movement from the gorse and her kidnapper twisted sideways, his hands raised protectively over his eyes.

He screamed in pain or terror, then lurched backward, only to find a greater terror. His hands rose, flapping at emptiness while his eyes filled with the unspeakable certainty of the death that waited below, in the sharp rocks at the base of the cliff.

He fell.

Jamee turned away, her eyes squeezed shut.

His scream seemed to go on forever.

# CHAPTER TWENTY-FOUR

DAWN HAD NOT COME, only its faint precursor, when Ian crouched beside Jamee and pulled her against him. "Did he touch you?" His hands were trembling. "If the bastard did, I'll—"

"No, but he was close, so close all this time. He hated us, Ian. He said it should have been *him* instead of Adam who was adopted." She gave a broken sob and turned her face to Ian's chest as the memory of her pursuer's mad eyes flashed before her.

"It's done, *mo cridhe*. He'll never bother you again," Ian whispered. His hands clenched on her shoulder. "You'll not escape me again, either. Blind or not, I'll tie you up. I'll use ropes of silk and leather if I have to." His breath was as ragged as hers was. "You're going to marry me, Jamee Night. If you say no, I'll hold you here, captive in my keep. Day by day and night after night I'll hold you until you're an old woman whose beautiful white hair slides through my fingers while I kiss you senseless."

"Is that a promise?" Jamee said breathlessly.

"Senseless. I'll seduce you with no remorse. I'll see that you're pleading for release before I'm done."

"I should imagine that will take about five seconds, you execrable man," Jamee said. "Just like you did at dinner…"

Ian turned, his fingers trapping her face. "I never meant

that, love. I never expected you would respond so…generously. You've been a fire in my blood since I first saw you. I don't know which of us has been crazier. When I woke and thought I'd lost you— Thank God, Duncan and Adam arrived when they did." He kissed her then, hungry and desperate while his hands slid onto her shoulders.

A low, male voice coughed behind them.

"Go away, Night," Ian growled. He pulled Jamee closer, fingers buried in her hair.

Another cough followed.

"Dammit, Adam—"

A chuckle came out of the darkness behind them. The helicopter motors had shut down and darkness returned. Only the faint gold fingers of dawn touched the eastern sky.

"Go away. We can talk later. Then you can curse at me for falling in love with my client. Right now I'm going to sit here and kiss your sister until she loses every fragment of logic and agrees to become my wife, even if it means living six months of the year in this old wreck of a castle."

"Yes," Jamee said softly.

"And what if she says no?" Adam Night asked.

"I'll reorganize the Glenlyle weaving cooperative and let her take charge of the hand-loomed tartans produced by ten villages."

"Yes," Jamee repeated.

"What if that doesn't work?" Adam continued.

"Then I'll have to threaten something truly terrible, like selling this castle which has stayed in McCall hands for seven centuries."

*"Yes!"* Jamee threw her body against him, bringing them both down onto the soft heather.

Ian blinked. "Yes? You're agreeing, my lass?"

"Three times already, you great, stubborn Scotsman."

Ian closed his eyes as a shudder ran through him. "You're certain?"

Jamee proved to him just how certain she was, pinning him to the damp earth beneath her determined body. "If you think you're getting rid of me, you're wrong. In fact, if you think you have even a *hope* of getting rid of me—"

He twisted, catching her beneath him as ragged laughter burst from his mouth. "No, not even a shred of hope. I've had none since I first saw you, *mo cridhe,* with your face more beautiful than a dream and your hair like a copper halo. I was afraid to hope." His eyes closed. "The truth is, I'd given up, Jamee. Your laughter brought me back my light."

High over the hills the first fingers of dawn touched the sky.

Jamee made a breathless sound and pushed to her feet. "I have to go. There's one thing left to do." She caught up the bright length of wool hanging at the edge of the stone well. "I'll be back in a moment."

Only at the edge of the cliff did she stop, wool in hand. Across the loch to the east, where the hills rose in steep waves, she saw the faint glow of dawn and offered up her gift. With it came the hope that had slumbered in her soul for centuries since her death on this very rock.

As Maire MacKinnon.

Jamee gave her words to the dawn and tossed the bright colors out before her. They spilled through the air, tumbling end over end in a blur of color. Fuchsia burned into orange and glowing purple until a network of light pulsed against the darkness, flaming outward until the whole horizon lay streaked with the colors that could almost have been stolen from her cloth.

Watching the sun rise, Jamee felt the rush of beating wings, the taste of joy and the presence of all the people she had loved and lost. Mother. Father. Her wonderful, eccentric brother Terence.

So close, suddenly.

The hillside seemed to stir and the air filled with birdsong. Jamee turned to Ian, who stood motionless, watching her in mute shock.

"Can you see it?"

He nodded, unable to speak.

Her hands trembled. "The colors, too?"

"Red. Orange. Gold and purple. Oh, God, Jamee, the colors—" His voice broke. He reached out, gripping her hand. "The colors are beautiful. I can see them so clearly."

She closed her eyes. Tears burned down her cheeks as dawn swept over the serried hills before them.

"How?" Ian whispered.

Jamee watched light fill the heather and thought of a woman who had lost her heart to her enemy's son. Love like that could do many things—maybe even miracles. "Only because I love you, Ian McCall of Glenlyle. For now," she said, repeating the words of a vow that could not be forgotten. "For tomorrow. For all eternity. These are my three wishes."

# EPILOGUE

SNOW HISSED over the glen and brushed the deep, leaded windows of Glenlyle's library. Inside the thick stone walls a fire snapped in the granite fireplace, splashing color over the vibrant tapestries on the wall nearby. Tiny bears decorated a huge blue spruce beside the full-length windows that overlooked the hills circling the loch.

"I'm certain I saw the book in here last night after dinner." The heavy oak door opened and the bears dipped and spun gently on their Christmas boughs. William Night charged into the room, frowning. His shirtsleeves were folded unevenly above his wrists and a dusting of powdered sugar touched one cheek, a remnant of the particularly fine tea he had just finished. "It was a first edition of *A Christmas Carol,* I tell you."

"You're imagining things again, William." Adam Night moved toward the fire and braced one arm on the warm stone. He smiled as the door opened again. "What did I tell you, Ian?"

"That I'd be regretting my marriage into your family inside of a week." Ian looked very dashing in a vintage kilt and a formal short black fitted jacket. His brow arched faintly as he looked down at his wife, lovely in green velvet with a scarf of creamy antique lace. "I think it may take a little longer than that to exhaust my patience, Adam. After all, without you and William I never would have met the charming, irritating and unforgettable master weaver who is now Lady Glenlyle, Countess of Lenox and Kincaid."

Jamee tucked a finger under his lapel. "How do you manage to say all that in one breath?"

"Practice, my dear. One has to do something to pass the time on these dark Highland nights."

Jamee leaned close, her long hair brushing his dress jacket. "I've got a better suggestion."

Ian's head bowed.

Her face rose.

Their lips met gently.

"Sweet heaven, no more of *that*," William protested.

His brother's eyes gleamed. "It's a thing newly married people do rather a lot of, William. Better get used to it."

"At least the food is good here. That nice Widow Campbell sent over a tin of smoked salmon that passes description, and those thin fudge things your cook makes are lethal, McCall." He sank into a deep leather chair and pulled a paper napkin full of fudge from his pocket, grinning shamelessly. "Nice bears," he muttered, raising a fudge-streaked finger toward the Christmas tree. "I never knew they could have so many different faces and expressions." He tapped his jaw thoughtfully. "Say, McCall, have you ever thought of animating these bears of yours? I've been working on a prototype titanium skeleton worked by animatronics. State-of-the-art stuff. It could be a very hot item next Christmas."

Ian brushed the tiny furred nose of a bear in a kilt and sporran. "I think the little fellows are fine just as they are, William. But I *have* been meaning to ask you about upgrading the wiring in my workshops. I'd like your opinion, too, Adam."

"I warned you not to let them get started on wiring. Now they'll never finish," Jamee murmured.

The four were deep in conversation when the door opened

again. The fire hissed and popped cheerfully as Duncan Mac-Kinnon shrugged out of a snow-dusted parka and then took his wife's snug sheepskin coat. "Wiring?" he announced. "What kind of talk is that for a freezing winter day?"

Ian chuckled and went to greet his friends. "I take it you'd prefer to discuss fine aged whiskey?"

"Do I really need to answer that?"

"Don't listen to him," Kara said. "It's lovely outside and not a bit unpleasant. Ours were the first tracks leading up here through the snow, and I almost felt as if we were heading back through time."

Jamee kissed Kara, then Duncan. "I know what you mean." She shot a look at Ian. "This place is almost frighteningly inspiring. If I finish any *more* weavings, Ian won't have any place to hang them."

Her husband smiled slowly. "Actually, that won't be a problem. I found out earlier today that four have already been ordered for Balmoral."

"Balmoral?" Jamee blinked. "As in—"

"As in the royal residence. Unless you'd prefer not to sell, of course." His eyes twinkled. "You would have one very disappointed lady in that case."

"Of course I'll sell them. Balmoral?" she repeated. "This isn't a joke?"

"No more than this." Ian looked at the gathered company. He had walked head-on into a full-blown family, noisy and contentious, and he was enjoying every second of the experience. Never in his lifetime had the castle rung with such laughter and genial quarreling.

Glenlyle's ghosts seemed very far away as he held out a gaily wrapped box to Jamee. "I wanted to give this to you while everyone was here, since they were all involved in bringing about our happy ending." His eyes gleamed. "For you, my love."

"Ian, you shouldn't have. I'm spoiled already."

"You'll have one gift for all the twelve days of Christmas. It's a new ritual here, I warn you."

Jamee pulled off the foil paper, then went very still. "Ian, do you realize what this is?"

"I believe so. Go ahead, take it out," he urged.

Very carefully Jamee removed a carved piece of wood hollowed in the center and pointed at one end. The shuttle was beautifully made, shaped to fit a woman's hand. "Look at the detail," she said. "Whoever used this must have had tiny fingers." She cupped the smooth wood lovingly. "This looks as if it could be two hundred years old."

"Rather more than that, I suspect. I found it up in the attic last week."

Jamee held up the hand-carved tool. The fine grain of the wood was polished smooth by centuries of pressure against threads of rough wool. Just below the pointed end, three interlinking lines had been carved into the shuttle. Jamee touched them thoughtfully. "What are these?"

"Some kind of identifying marks of the weaver," Ian suggested.

"Or something else," Kara said softly. "May I?" When Jamee passed her the old tool, Kara's fingers moved slowly over the surface. She stared at the tapestry on the far wall. "She made that very weaving with this." Her voice was low, jerky. "I can feel her sitting in a cottage. There are pots of boiling dye and peat smoke in the air. She sang as she worked."

"Kara, I'm not sure you should be doing this," Duncan said. "I don't want you taking any chances right now."

She went on as if he had not spoken. "The three marks represent the three prayers she worked into every cloth. Three unbroken lines that crossed over themselves, always connect-.

ing in the end. They were vows. Three vows." Her eyes dimmed
and she swayed slightly. "For now. For tomorrow."

"And for all eternity," Jamee finished softly. "You saw her.
It was Maire MacKinnon, wasn't it? This was *her* shuttle."

Kara took a sudden, sharp breath and leaned against her husband. "Don't fret, Duncan, I'm fine. And yes, this did belong
to Maire. She was very much in love. Her small cottage held
a lifetime of laughter and joy." She shook her head, pulling
away from a world of shadowy visions, and then handed the
shuttle back to Jamee. "Use it well. Her skill and joy go with
it to you."

Silence filled the room, and with it came the sense of others
pressing close. Unseen, unheard, their love still slid around the
corners and tugged at the hearts of the friends and family
gathered in Glenlyle's warm library. It seemed that at any
moment, the door might open again to admit a pair of lovers
who had died centuries before.

When a log collapsed in the grate with an explosion of
sparks, the mood was broken. Ian refilled Duncan's glass, then
sat down before the fire with Jamee close beside him. "Did you
ever find that first edition of Dickens you were looking for,
Duncan?"

"Afraid not. We've turned the library at Dunraven upside
down. I can't imagine what's happened to it." He savored his
drink, frowning. "I was hoping I might have brought it up here
with that bunch of naval engravings I gave you last year for
your birthday."

"It might be there," Ian said. "I haven't yet framed them. The
box was right behind my desk, I believe."

"Will you two forget about books and maps for once?" Kara
said sternly. "It's Christmas, remember? I want to see the kilt
Jamee wove for the newest Glenlyle bear."

"It's hanging there near the top of the tree." Ian pointed to

a bear with dark-brown fur, formal jacket and a vibrant kilt of
McCall plaid, deep blue and red set off by faint lines of white.
"She's going to make one just like it for me." He turned and
looked at his new wife proudly.

"Did you hear that? It sounded almost like whistling or
someone singing off-key," Kara said.

Jamee stiffened. "Off-key?"

"Some popular song from the sixties. I can't remember the
artist."

Adam's eyes narrowed as he stood by the far window. "It
wasn't Neil Diamond by any chance?"

Kara sat very still, eyes narrowed as she focused on the
elusive thread of sound. "It could be. Sorry, but I can't recognize the tune."

Adam walked slowly to the back of the room where shadows
clung to the thick stone walls. His face was unreadable as he,
too, stood listening for confirmation of a strange feeling he had
had for weeks now.

It was almost as if his dead brother, Terence, were nearby,
watching over them, whistling his off-key songs as he always
had.

"Do you hear it, Adam?" Jamee asked tensely. "Is it…
Terence?"

Adam studied the shifting shadows, reaching out for a sign
of his brother's presence. The fire left patterns on the wall, rippling like a river of light, ever restless—ever beyond contain-
ing.

Despite Adam's concentration, there was nothing in the
dark corners but hopes that would not die and dreams that
were just beginning to flower. He was too honest to describe
things he didn't see.

So he turned, straightening his shoulders. "I don't hear anything. But it doesn't matter. Some things live in our minds

even when we can't see or hear them." He moved back into the warmth of the fire and the softly gleaming lights, near the people he loved. "Bennett will be arriving tomorrow. He apologized that his physical therapy has taken so long and he asked me to make a toast for him." Adam raised his glass, watching light bounce off the etched crystal. "A merry Christmas and good health. May all your dreams have wings."

Jamee discreetly brushed away a tear as she clinked her glass with Ian's. Light seemed to fill the room as the fire burst high, crackling cheerfully. The wordless warmth of Christmas found a home in each person's heart in that moment. Like glowing embers, the feeling would stay, burning softly, warming the cold days until Christmas came to them once again.

"VERY NICE. Very nice indeed." Resplendent in his finest black satin, Adrian Draycott surveyed the group ranged around the fire. "It almost makes my exhausting labors here worthwhile." He smoothed the lace at one cuff and studied the room critically. "The rug is adequate, I suppose, though an eighteenth-century Peking would have been nicer. The tree is also passable, though I fail to see the attraction of all these bears. They are quite appallingly maudlin."

Gold satin shimmered at his side as Gray Mackenzie materialized to stroke his cheek. "Perhaps they are meant to be maudlin, my love. It can be very pleasant to feel sentimental and weepy this time of year."

"Hmm." Adrian sniffed. "What I feel is tired. Do you know how hard I've worked in the last few hours keeping an eye over the festivities at Draycott Abbey, then tearing myself away to come up here?"

"Why *did* you come?" the woman he loved asked curiously. "I know you don't like Scotland above half."

Adrian cleared his throat. "Gideon and I had a minor point

of business to finish. It's nothing important. You might as well make your way back to Draycott Abbey while we complete our little odds and ends."

A frown worked between her brows. "What is it that you aren't telling me?"

"Nothing. Nothing at all." Adrian decided that attack was sometimes the best defense. "And don't think I haven't noticed how much time *you've* been spending in the conservatory these last few days. What have you got hidden out there?"

"Nothing important," she answered, repeating his own evasion. She would not tell him of the three antique rose plants that awaited him in the abbey's conservatory. Their petals were peach touched with tiny streaks of red, and their fragrance blended notes of cinnamon and oranges. But Gray had no intention of revealing her present to Adrian until she was entirely ready.

And that meant when Adrian finished his own mission, whatever it was. "It seemed to be the time of year for both of us to keep secrets." She smiled faintly. "I imagine I could work them out of you."

Adrian threw up one hand in surrender. "Without any earthly doubt you could. But don't, my love. It would spoil everything." At his feet a gray shape materialized, long tail flicking back and forth. "Don't you agree, Gideon?"

The cat meowed softly.

"You see? Even Gideon suggests you take yourself back to Draycott and wait for us there. The noisy visitors have all gone now, and you can enjoy the tree in silence for once."

Gray tilted her head. "Only since things are done here. Yes, I think they will be very happy now that their three wishes have finally been granted." Her golden gown began to shimmer, then inch by inch faded away until only a handful of light sparkled in the still air.

"Godspeed, my love," Adrian whispered.

At his feet Gideon meowed softly.

"Thank you, my friend. Now then, let's find that book of Dunraven's and be off." He strode toward the great desk and searched for the box that Duncan had described. After a moment, his boot met a heavy object. "I think I've found it, Gideon. Help me with these, will you?"

None of the people by the fire saw a dozen naval engravings rise silently into the air, carried by invisible fingers. One by one the old designs tilted, then drifted down to the carpet.

"Nothing yet. Blast, I hope they didn't move the book."

Gideon brushed against Adrian's boot, then put one paw gingerly into the deep box. A length of heavy silk slowly unrolled into the air, danced in unseen currents, then cascaded in a flow of color onto the floor.

"Well done, Gideon. You've found something beneath?"

As the cat stared unblinking into the box, a heavy volume of brown leather floated into the air. Firelight glinted off deeply embossed letters highlighted in gold. Suspended above the desk, the cover opened, yellowed pages riffled by invisible fingers.

"By heaven, you've done it. It's a first edition, all right. That fellow Dickens even signed the thing. Gray will be delirious."

Gideon's ears pricked forward.

"Stealing? I don't believe I would use that word. Not entirely." Adrian rubbed his jaw, staring through the window where snow danced in the bright, clear air. "Let's just say it will be a loan in exchange for services rendered." He looked down at Gideon and smiled. "For how long? Several centuries should do, I imagine."

The book closed with a snap and then floated up under his arm. "Now, I believe we should go. I don't want to keep Gray waiting."

He turned to find a tall man seated on the desk. Flecks of color glinted around his head and hands as he clicked his tongue at Adrian.

"I suppose I should try to stop you from stealing that thing," Terence Night said.

"Not stealing, *borrowing*."

"Oh, is that what you call it?"

"Of course. I'll return it." Adrian smoothed his lace jabot. "Eventually."

"I won't try to stop you. I owe you too much for sending Gideon along to help me. We make a good team, don't we, my friend?" As Terence eased a hand over the cat's warm fur, he smiled. "At least this is one project I didn't bumble. I have to thank you both for that." He looked off at his sister, whose head rested against Ian's shoulder. "They look very happy, don't they?"

"And why shouldn't they look happy? We've just saved them from a very nasty fate. Matchmaking can be quite enjoyable, I've discovered." As Gideon meowed, Adrian cleared his throat. "Well, I did do *my* share, blast it. I'm the one who sent you up here, after all. The whole business was damnably fatiguing, too."

Terence smiled, and the movement sent light rippling over the desk. "You were key to our success. I'm sure your beautiful Gray will love the Dickens. As a loan," he emphasized.

"Of course, of course." Adrian waved one hand. "Whatever you say." He moved toward the wall, then turned back to look at Terence. "Where are you off to now? I suppose if you have nothing better to do, you might come back to Draycott with us."

"It is very kind of you, but no. I think I have finally gotten the hang of this guardian thing, and I'd better keep in practice." Terence studied the tall man standing beside the fire. "Adam works too hard. I'm going to have to do something about that.

And William needs something new in his life. Or someone," he said thoughtfully.

Adrian nodded. "You'll do very well at the job, I think. But remember my offer should you ever need a little company."

"I won't forget. It will be a pleasure to visit the abbey again one day when my work is finished." He watched Adrian's hand rise in farewell, then slowly fade as his form retreated into the heavy stone wall, with Gideon at his side.

Terence Night sat back on the desk, tapping his toe as he whistled an off-key tune. Jamee was rising, her hand in Ian's. A smile softened Terence's face as he picked the thoughts from his sister's mind.

Yes, it would be a very, very fine Christmas at Glenlyle.

"YOU'LL EXCUSE US for a little while, won't you? I have a gift to give my dashing husband." Jamee took Ian's hand and pulled him to his feet. "I have to try to top that beautiful shuttle he gave me."

"Jamee, there is no reason for you to—"

"Come on, McCall," she ordered, laughing as she tugged Ian toward the door. "Why is it so hard to get you to accept a present?"

"I said you would be henpecked," William called helpfully as he finished off the last of his fudge. "We've had to deal with her for years. Now it's your turn."

Ian's eyes darkened as he caught Jamee's waist. "A punishment I think I will savor for seventy or eighty years."

"Romance," William said in disgust. "Give me a good set of electrical circuits any day."

Ian followed Jamee outside into the hall and up the granite steps. "Where are you taking me?"

"To the master bedroom." Her lips curved. "Of course."

"In the middle of the afternoon?"

"I've got everything set up. I think the Widow Campbell has finished her part by now."

Ian's brow rose. "What did she have to do with this project of yours?"

"Just wait and see." Jamee tugged him down the hall and threw open the door to their bedroom.

Candles gleamed on the rosewood dresser and on the windowsills, their glow refracted in the long mirror opposite the door. Bears in kilts and capes and cowboy hats lay scattered over the bed and seated in every chair.

"Widow Campbell helped me," she explained. "We found all the old bears in the village and collected one of each kind. You need to begin some sort of a museum here, Ian, something that will document the designs over the years. And I thought you might like to have them all around you while I…"

"While you what?" Ian sat on the bed, moved aside three bears in full fighting regalia and drew Jamee down onto his lap.

"Thank you for the miracle I've been given," she said fiercely.

"What miracle?"

"You. The way you make me feel. All the things you inspire me to do. Even if I live a century, I don't think I'll finish half the projects I have in mind." Tears streaked her face, but Jamee continued, oblivious. "And in case you haven't noticed, there are a whole lot of people here who feel just the same way about you, Lord Glenlyle. You are brave and stubborn and very much a hero to them."

"I'm no hero."

"Most of the people in Glenlyle would argue about that. I know that I would." Jamee slid her hands over his shoulders. "By the way, did I mention that you tear my breath away every time I look at you?"

"Every time?"

"Afraid so."

Slowly, Ian eased her against him. "Like this?"

Their bodies met. Jamee felt his growing arousal. "You bet."

"Funny, you do the same thing to me."

"Oh, yeah?" Her fingers caught his sporran and sent it flying. In one jerky movement, she freed the buckle of his kilt. "Maybe you'd better prove that." She caught his lips with hers, nuzzled slowly. "After all, we don't have a lot of time."

"Umm. Why is that?"

"My disgraceful brothers will come looking for us." Her fingers found his rigid heat and circled him slowly. "And here we would be." She smiled wickedly as the velvet gown slid from her shoulders. "How very incriminating."

Ian's pulse slammed hard. As always, she tore him into tiny pieces. One smile, one touch was all it took. He shoved off his kilt and went to work on her lingerie. "Then we'll have to be certain they don't find us. Actually, I was thinking of somewhere besides the bed. The kitchen, perhaps. Or maybe the back stairs."

Jamee's hair spilled back in a wild flow of amber as she fitted herself to him. "We tried the floor last time, and I think I still have a splinter in my hip. I know I found two in your thigh."

"I liked the way you removed them." His hands cupped her hips. "You have a lovely mouth." Silken muscles rippled, making his pulse slam dangerously. Ian made a harsh sound somewhere between pain and ecstasy. "Among other things."

Jamee arched, seating him deeper, inch by sleek inch. Her fingers slid through the warm hair at his chest, then meandered lower, where their bodies met. "I could say the same for you, Scotsman."

Ian closed his eyes as she traced his heat. When she tightened around him, desire leaped to the flashpoint. "God, Jamee. Do any more of that and I'm either going to die or explode."

"Exploding sounds good," she breathed. "You do that very nicely, as I recall. At least you did that night in the car when we drove back from visiting Duncan and Kara. Maybe next time I should wear something in black. All lace and transparent, revealing more than it conceals. And satin garters—"

Her breath whooshed free as he twisted and caught her beneath him, pinning her to the white sheets. "Garters would probably kill me," he growled. "They did last time." He tensed his body, easing his hard length nearly free.

"Ian, what did the doctor say? I know he called just before Adam and William arrived. Tell me about the tests."

"Later," he growled.

Her hips rose, seeking his heat.

"Now I just want to watch you and feel you lose control."

It was impossible to say who moved first. Desire darkened Jamee's eyes as Ian pressed within her. When she tightened, fighting to hold him, Ian decided explosion was a very real possibility. "I have those measurements for the new looms. They arrived this morning."

"Later," she whispered, sliding her hands into his hair as she drew him deeper. "I'm too busy making love to a mad Scotsman who keeps managing to sneak into my bedroom."

Sweat dotted Ian's brow as the hot, heavy pulse of release drove closer. He claimed her mouth, all his control lost, desperate to lose himself in the feel and scent of her as he palmed the skin where their bodies joined.

Damp skin parted. He traced the tight bud. Retreated, teased slowly.

Her breath caught in a gasp. As pleasure spiraled through her, Jamee rose against him, her fingers digging into his shoulders.

"I love you, Glenlyle. Love you—love you—love you. Don't ever forget it."

HE WATCHED HER SLEEP. Around her the guttering candles outlined the furry faces of the bears piled over the chairs, tables and bed. Her rest was calm, untouched by nightmare fears. There was no sign of the tremors or haunted walking Ian had seen that first day at Draycott Abbey in Adam Night's harrowing video.

The wind whispered against the deep windows while the fire crackled beneath mantels green with yew. Ian sank into a wing chair beside the bed and rested his chin on his palm.

Watching Jamee sleep.

A silver ball hanging above the fire turned slowly in the currents. Snow hit the window like the brush of soft fingers.

As Ian watched, her hand cupped a threadbare toy, the same battered bear he had slept with every night until he was eight. So she could feel what he had felt going to sleep, she had explained.

Ian slid his fingers over his jacket pocket and felt the outlines of the embossed leather box he had brought from the bank vault in London. A family heirloom, the beaten silver band was crowned with three winking sapphires the same shade as Jamee's eyes when she was furious.

Or when she spun away into passion beneath him.

Beside him on the side table lay the thick file that had arrived that morning. The pages were crammed with scientific terms like *idiopathic* and *indeterminate progression* and *acute phase completion.*

The meaning was far simpler.

His vision was stable, color perception fixed at eighty percent of normal.

No explanation why.

The miracle that had begun on Blind Laird's Rock had not wavered. Ian had no doubt that he had been cured by Jamee's love that chill dawn.

Faint images teased his mind. Falling snow and angry men. Warhorses that clattered through Glenlyle's courtyard. Ian wondered if there might not be other sources of the miracle he had experienced—sources that dated to a far earlier age, when love had been betrayed and loss had left a man's heart closed to light. Perhaps love truly did abide, reaching out from beyond the veil of time. Sometimes in dreams Ian could almost remember the pain of that loss and the look of a woman's face lit by firelight. At such times, he felt with utter certainty that the legend of the doomed lovers was untrue. They had been betrayed not by each other but the hatreds of a primitive clan system that declared two people eternal enemies, no matter the yearning of their hearts.

Color flashed at the corner of his eye. He studied the ancient McCall tartan hanging proudly above Jamee's head, its colors faintly softened by age and handling. The heirloom wool had been passed down among the McCalls for generations, said to be the work of a local weaver of extraordinary skill, and its design had been preserved on all later family setts.

The creation of one Maire MacKinnon.

Ian still remembered how Jamee's eyes had softened when she had touched the plaid. Perhaps the source of her skill lay earlier than either of them had guessed, deep in Glenlyle's sad past.

No matter. Her nightmares were banished, along with his own. Now her chest rose and fell slowly and her breathing was relaxed.

No more walking in her sleep. No more cold memories.

Ian smiled crookedly. The only thing that hadn't changed was her habit of draping herself over him in the night like a soft, pliant blanket. More than once he had awakened to find her breath warm at the hollow of his neck and her thighs nestled between his.

Her trust had been absolute.

His desire had been instant and painfully evident.

Ian smiled at some of the more unusual ideas she had come up with for resolving that pain.

Abruptly the covers stirred. Jamee blinked sleepily. "What are you doing over there?"

"Watching you sleep."

"I never did like spectator sports." She sat up slowly. "Come back to bed. We'll try for a team effort."

As the cover slid from her shoulders, Ian saw the curve of one full breast gilded in the firelight. "After what just went on in front of the fire, I might not have anything left."

Her grin was swift. "If you're fishing for a compliment, you've got one, McCall. You've been voted the player most likely to succeed." Her eyes slanted downward. "Definitely."

He loved how she smiled. He loved her cheeky laugh and unshakable generosity. Most of all, he loved the confidence that now shone in her eyes. "No more nightmares?" he asked softly.

She shook her head, rising to hold out her arms. "Must be because of my bodyguard." Her eyes narrowed as she saw the file beside him on the table. "What are those papers? Ian, is it the new reports? Did the doctor—" She was across the room in a second, her body draped over his.

Ian wrapped a vast tartan around her as he settled her in his lap. "It's the reports."

"What do they *say?* Blast it, why didn't you tell me right away?"

"Because, my lovely Jamee, I had more important things on my mind."

She glared. With every slide of her warm hips, fire began to uncoil through him anew. "More important than the results of your eye exam?" She gave him a shake. "What do they say?"

He gave her the full medical jargon.

She frowned. "What does that mean?"

"That I'm cured. Color will remain at my current level."

With a ragged breath Jamee sank down against his chest. "You're not making this up to humor me?"

"I wouldn't dare. You'd send those bloodthirsty brothers of yours after me."

"You bet I would, if I thought it would help. But it wouldn't. You're too stubborn, too independent and far too generous." She moved against his legs. "And I wouldn't change you for a million pounds."

Ian filled his lungs with her scent, a haunting mix of bergamot and roses, feeling desire pool thickly at his groin.

Her voice fell. "I can't help but think about him sometimes. Rob. I mean, Thomas Starkey."

"He was a lonely, mixed-up boy, Jamee. He and his brother found someone to hate, someone to take the darkness out of their life. They only wanted you because hurting you would hurt Adam most."

She shivered slightly, and Ian's hands tightened.

"I wish things might have been different."

He didn't answer, knowing that evil was sometimes as certain as good. But Jamee didn't need to know that. In fact, Ian meant to spend the rest of his life seeing that she had no opportunity to learn.

She shook her head and frowned. "I might have to change a few things about the workrooms. You need better lighting and central heating. It's too hard to sew in the cold weather. And Angus and I have been working on those new blueprints for the looms. By widening the work bed, you could double the markets you sell to. I know designers in Paris who would *kill* to have fabric of Glenlyle's quality. Tartans are all the rage, you know. Just last month, Armand told me how hard it was to find good wool with a soft drape. When he heard I was coming to

Scotland, he asked me to scout some out. Unofficially, of course."

"He did, did he?" Ian settled his hand against her back and drew her forward. "Maybe you could convince a hidebound Scotsman to change. Unofficially, of course."

Her eyes darkened as she eased her legs around him. "It would be my definite pleasure to try. Do you think we could start…right now?"

Ian closed his eyes as she moved against him. "There should be something in it for you, I hope."

Her laugh was low and husky. "Oh, there's plenty in it for me. And every inch is absolutely unforgettable." Her sleek muscles closed around him, sheathing him perfectly. "Unofficially, of course." She closed her eyes, shivering as Ian buried his fingers in her hair. "You see, miracles really do happen, Ian. Sometimes wishes really can come true. Terence told me all it took was the right dream. Sometimes I almost think I feel him taking care of all of us. I only wish he could see how happy I am now…" She smiled crookedly. "Now *that* sounds certifiable."

"Not a bit," Ian said. "And why shouldn't he be here? Glenlyle had seven ghosts at last count."

"Ghosts? But you said—"

"By the way, someone wants to meet you."

"Who?"

Ian said three words.

Jamee's eyes widened in shock. "No."

"Yes. In fact, it amounts to something of a royal command. She was very taken with those weavings for Balmoral."

She froze. "But when—how?" She swallowed hard. "What should I wear to meet her?"

"What you're wearing now would be nice," he said huskily. "But she is advanced in years and might be a little shocked."

Jamee looked down, blushing. The only thing she was wearing was a diamond solitaire necklace glinting on a fine silver chain. "All I seem to be wearing is *you,* my lord. And very pleasantly, I might add."

Ian groaned as Jamee's arms closed around him. Desire speared through him, and he forgot all about three nosy brothers named Night and an impending royal visit.

Time shimmered, drawing them both deep. Pleasure roared in his ears as the lingering shadows of loss and betrayal were swept away. For a moment, a woman's laugh seemed to echo up Glenlyle's dark stone stairs and through the empty halls.

Above the bed the ancient tartan glimmered in a light that was not from fire or any manmade source. The hum of low, ancient voices rose against the crackle of the flames.

Jamee did not notice, her body locked to Ian's.

Her laird didn't see, too finely tuned to her soft cries and the satin thread of pleasure that was already unraveling through his own body.

His fingers tightened. His back arched as he rasped a low phrase of Gaelic.

Somewhere an off-key tune drifted down the quiet halls and up the stairwell. And if a cat cried far in the snow-swept distance, out beyond the ruined stones of the old well, no one heard but the wind.

# REQUEST YOUR
# FREE BOOKS!

## 2 FREE NOVELS
## FROM THE ROMANCE/SUSPENSE
## COLLECTION PLUS 2 FREE GIFTS!

**YES!** Please send me 2 FREE novels from the Romance/Suspense Collection and my 2 FREE gifts (gifts are worth about $10). After receiving them, if I don't wish to receive any more books, I can return the shipping statement marked "cancel." If I don't cancel, I will receive 4 brand-new novels every month and be billed just $5.49 per book in the U.S. or $5.99 per book in Canada, plus 25¢ shipping and handling per book plus applicable taxes, if any*. That's a savings of at least 20% off the cover price! I understand that accepting the 2 free books and gifts places me under no obligation to buy anything. I can always return a shipment and cancel at any time. Even if I never buy another book from the Reader Service, the two free books and gifts are mine to keep forever.

185 MDN EF5Y   385 MDN EF6C

Name _____ (PLEASE PRINT) _____

Address _____ Apt. # _____

City _____ State/Prov. _____ Zip/Postal Code _____

Signature (if under 18, a parent or guardian must sign)

### Mail to **The Reader Service:**
### IN U.S.A.: P.O. Box 1867, Buffalo, NY 14240-1867
### IN CANADA: P.O. Box 609, Fort Erie, Ontario L2A 5X3

Not valid to current subscribers to the Romance Collection,
the Suspense Collection or the Romance/Suspense Collection.

**Want to try two free books from another line?**
**Call 1-800-873-8635 or visit www.morefreebooks.com.**

* Terms and prices subject to change without notice. N.Y. residents add applicable sales tax. Canadian residents will be charged applicable provinãal taxes and GST. This offer is limited to one order per household. All orders subject to approval. Credit or debit balances in a customer's account(s) may be offset by any other outstanding balance owed by or to the customer. Please allow 4 to 6 weeks for delivery. Offer available while quantities last.

**Your Privacy:** Harlequin is committed to protecting your privacy. Our Privacy Policy is available online at www.eHarlequin.com or upon request from the Reader Service. From time to time we make our lists of customers available to reputable third parties who may have a product or service of interest to you. If you would prefer we not share your name and address, please check here. ☐

HARLEQUIN

*More Than Words*

# "Changing lives stride by stride— I did it my way!"

—**Jeanne Greenberg,** real-life heroine

*Jeanne Greenberg is a Harlequin More Than Words award winner and the founder of **SARI Therapeutic Riding**.*

**Discover your inner heroine!**

MTW07JG1

"Jeanne proves that one woman can change the world, with vision, compassion and hard work."

—**Linda Lael Miller,** author

*Linda wrote "Queen of the Rodeo," inspired by Jeanne Greenberg, founder of **SARI Therapeutic Riding.** Since 1978 Jeanne has devoted her life to enriching the lives of disabled children and their families through innovative and exciting therapies on horseback.*

Look for "*Queen of the Rodeo*" in
**More Than Words, Vol. 4,**
available in April 2008 at eHarlequin.com
or wherever books are sold.

MTW07JG2

# CHRISTINA SKYE

| | | | | |
|---|---|---|---|---|
| 77262 | ENCHANTMENT & BRIDGE OF DREAMS | ___ $6.99 U.S. | ___ | $8.50 CAN. |
| 77209 | CODE NAME: BIKINI | ___ $6.99 U.S. | ___ | $8.50 CAN. |
| 77123 | CODE NAME: BLONDIE | ___ $6.99 U.S. | ___ | $8.50 CAN. |
| 77069 | CODE NAME: BABY | ___ $6.99 U.S. | ___ | $8.50 CAN. |

*(limited quantities available)*

| | |
|---|---|
| TOTAL AMOUNT · | $ _____ |
| POSTAGE & HANDLING | $ _____ |
| ($1.00 FOR 1 BOOK, 50¢ for each additional) | |
| APPLICABLE TAXES* | $ _____ |
| TOTAL PAYABLE | $ _____ |

*(check or money order—please do not send cash)*

To order, complete this form and send it, along with a check or money order for the total above, payable to HQN Books, to: **In the U.S.:** 3010 Walden Avenue, P.O. Box 9077, Buffalo, NY 14269-9077; **In Canada:** P.O. Box 636, Fort Erie, Ontario, L2A 5X3.

Name: _____

Address: _____ City: _____

State/Prov.: _____ Zip/Postal Code: _____

Account Number (if applicable): _____

075 CSAS

\*New York residents remit applicable sales taxes.
\*Canadian residents remit applicable GST and provincial taxes.

# HQN™

## We *are* romance™

**www.HQNBooks.com**

PHCS0408BL